Dedalus Europe
General Editor:

MW01200072

THE RELIC

Eça de Queiroz

THE RELIC

translated and with an introduction
by Margaret Jull Costa

Dedalus

Supported using public funding by
ARTS COUNCIL
ENGLAND

Published in the UK by Dedalus Ltd
24-26, St Judith's Lane, Sawtry, Cambs PE28 5XE
email: info@dedalusbooks.com
www.dedalusbooks.com

ISBN printed book: 978 1 912868 40 7
ISBN ebook: 978 1 907650 91 8

Dedalus is distributed in the USA & Canada by SCB Distributors
15608 South New Century Drive, Gardena, CA 90248
email: info@scbdistributors.com   www.scbdistributors.com

Dedalus is distributed in Australia by Peribo Pty Ltd
58, Beaumont Road, Mount Kuring-gai, N. S. W. 2080
email: info@peribo.com.au

Publishing History
First published in Portugal in 1887
First published by Dedalus in 1994, reprinted in 2003
New Dedalus edition in 2021

Translation copyright © Margaret Jull Costa 1994

The right of Margaret Jull Costa to be identified as the translator of this work has been asserted by her in accordance with the Copyright, Designs and Patents Act, 1988.

Printed and bound in the UK by Clays Ltd, Ecograf S.p.A
Typeset by RefineCatch Ltd

A C. I. P. listing for this book is available on request.

The Translator

Margaret Jull Costa has translated the works of many Spanish and Portuguese writers, among them novelists: Javier Marías, Benito Pérez Galdós, José Saramago, and Eça de Queiroz, and poets: Sophia de Mello Breyner Andresen, Mário de Sá-Carneiro and Ana Luísa Amaral. She won the Portuguese Translation Prize for *The Book of Disquiet* by Fernando Pessoa in 1992 and for *The Word Tree* by Teolinda Gersão in 2012. With Javier Marías, she won the 1997 International IMPAC Dublin Literary Award for *A Heart So White*, and, in 2000 and 2011, she won the Weidenfeld Translation Prize for, respectively, *All the Names* and *The Elephant's Journey*, both by José Saramago. In 2008, she won the Pen Book-of-the Month-Club Translation Prize and the Oxford Weidenfeld Translation Prize for *The Maias* by Eça de Queiroz. In 2015, she won the Marsh Children's Fiction in Translation Award for *The Adventures of Shola* by Bernardo Atxaga, and in 2017, with her co-translator Robin Patterson, she won the Best Translated Book Award for *Chronicle of the Murdered House* by Lúcio Cardoso. Most recently, she won the 2018 Premio Valle-Inclán for *On the Edge* by Rafael Chirbes.

In 2013, she was appointed a Fellow of the Royal Society of Literature; in 2014, she was awarded an OBE for services to literature; and in 2015, she was given an Honorary Doctorate by the University of Leeds. In 2018, she was awarded the Ordem Infante D. Henrique by the Portuguese government and a Lifetime Award for Excellence in Translation by the Queen Sofia Spanish Institute, New York.

Over the sturdy nakedness of truth
the diaphanous cloak of fantasy.

INTRODUCTION

Eça de Queiroz was born in 1845, the illegitimate son of a magistrate. His parents did not marry until Eça was four years old and his father only acknowledged him as his legal heir shortly before Eça's own marriage in 1886. His parents' marriage was not a love match and his mother and father were always cold and distant figures in Eça's life.

Whilst at university in Coimbra, Eça participated in the student struggles and debates of the time and, along with his contemporaries, was influenced by writers such as Hegel, Proudhon and Darwin and, in particular, by the great Portuguese writer and thinker Antero de Quental. After a brief period working as a lawyer in Lisbon, Eça became the youthful editor of a provincial newspaper in Évora and completed his move from Romanticism to Realism. Although he wrote articles in praise of traditional skills and customs, the reality of provincial life proved rather too real for him and he soon escaped Portugal altogether on a trip to the Near East with his best friend and future brother-in-law, Manuel de Resende, taking in Egypt (a country that had an enormous impact on him) and Palestine. From 1870 onwards, after his return from his travels, Eça worked abroad in various diplomatic posts in Havana, Bristol, Newcastle and, finally, Paris.

In 1876 he published *O crime do Padre Amaro* (*The Sin of Father Amaro*) and, in 1878, *O primo Basílio* (*Cousin Bazílio*). The Brazilian novelist, Machado de Assis, accused him of plagiarising Zola and of being incapable of creating anything but cardboard characters. Eça was wounded by this criticism but it only echoed his own doubts about his abilities as a novelist. He was in fact suffering something of a crisis in his work. He was concerned that living so far from Lisbon and the subject matter of his novels might be having an adverse effect on his writing. It was possibly as an escape from the problem that Eça ventured into fantastic literature with *O Mandarim* (*The Mandarin*) (1880) and *A Relíquia* (*The Relic*) (1887). The former was a reworking of a tale already told by Henri Monnier but *The Relic* was very much his own – giving him the chance not only to draw on his experiences as a traveller in the Near East (he wrote a detailed diary which was published posthumously as *O Egipto*), to attack the religious and social hypocrisy of his age and to debunk what he considered to be the Christian myth, but also to use fantasy and the imagination to discuss real moral dilemmas.

Although subsequently Eça only returned to fantasy in short stories, writing these two novels seems to have had a liberating effect as regards both style and subject matter. *The Relic* also coincided with his marriage to Emilia de Resende (a marriage not dissimilar to that between Teodorico and Jesuína in *The Relic* – not a love match exactly, but based on a mixture of mutual respect and convenience) and a posting to Paris, where he lived until his death in 1900. He soon grew disillusioned with Paris and with French culture in general, taking almost no part in the literary life there. But, curiously enough, that disillusion also finally freed him from his subjugation to French culture and ideas. His greatest novel *Os Maias* (*The Maias*), the portrait of a family and a class in decline, was also written at this time. In it he returns to his attack on the hypocrisy and sterility of Portuguese life but his writing is enriched by the stylistic freedoms he found in *The Relic*.

His last book, *A cidade e as serras* (*The City and the Mountains*), published the year after his death, was written in praise of the simple rustic life as opposed to the falseness of the city. Although a delightful book, it is a million miles from the acerbic wit and vision of his other novels.

The Relic was first published in serial form in the *Gazeta das Notícias* of Rio de Janeiro in 1887 and in book form that same year. He entered it for a competition held by the Academy in Lisbon knowing that he stood not a ghost of a chance of winning, but eagerly looking forward to the

2

jury's reaction to his anti-hero Teodorico Raposo. He was not disappointed. The book received not a single vote from the jury, whose spokesman, Pinheiro Chagas - a Romantic author and a devout Catholic – explained their decision in trenchant terms. He said that a vulgar hypocrite like Teodorico, the book's hero, could never have dreamed the dream that forms the central part of the novel; the person who goes to sleep is Teodorico, but the person who has the dream is Eça. To some extent Eça agreed with this verdict, but felt that fantastic fiction granted the author full poetic licence 'to place in the heart of a concierge all the idealism of an Ophelia and to have a peasant speak with the majesty of a Bossuet'. Subsequent critics decried it as lacking both good sense and good taste whilst others described it as the book with everything: farce/epic, belly-laughs/tears, picaresque/the sublime, parody/history. Generally though, it tends to have been considered one of Eça's less successful works: a rather slight, flawed sally into fantastic literature, a view conditioned perhaps by the reader's expectations of a typical Eça novel.

Both *The Mandarin* and *The Relic* are very different from his realist novels of social comment and satire. Both books, notably the latter, are really the first examples of the picaresque in Portugal. The *pícaro*, an amoral rogue living on his rather limited wits, is not so far from Eça's description of his ideal character: a man without an ounce of character or intelligence. Both novels also accord with M.H. Abrams' definition of the picaresque as being 'realistic in manner, episodic in structure and usually satiric in aim'. By venturing into the picaresque Eça gave himself licence to be as stereotypical as he pleased, while the use of the first-person narrator freed him from the constraints of being the all-seeing author. The *pícaro* is very often an orphan (as Teodorico is) with no real moral centre or integrated sense of self. He becomes what the world wants him to be, status in society being gained only by his own astuteness. Duplicity and dissimulation are second nature to him. Thus, Teodorico falls easily into the double life

3

required of him if he is to inherit his aunt's millions without giving up any worldly pleasures.

One of the main criticisms levelled at the novel is that it lacks coherence, mainly because the central panel of the triptych - the journey via dream into ancient Jerusalem – uses a language and evinces an aesthetic wonderment which a Philistine like Teodorico could never aspire to; whilst the central panel is written in the style of Flaubertian exoticism, the flanking panels are in the naturalist/realist mould of social observation and satire. This hardly seems a problem: Teodorico is still Teodorico. Though filled with wonderment at the beauties of the Temple, he remains utterly at the mercy of his own libido and manifests a very modern disgust for some of the customs he witnesses and a certain amount of unthinking anti-Semitism. He continues, in short, to be a man of his time and to play Wooster to Topsius' learned Jeeves.

There is also a satisfying duplicity, or rather doubleness, in the novel. There are two Jerusalems: the late nineteenth-century one, which was as profound a disappointment to Eça when he visited it as it is to Teodorico (Eça described it as a 'dark, low, miserable place') and the Jerusalem of Jesus' time with all the dazzling beauty of the Temple. There are also two sets of two Teodoricos: the supine pietist and the frustrated sensualist; and the Teodorico of the prologue – now a valued member of society, full of windy rhetoric – and the Teodorico hustling his way through the novel, skidding along the edges of social acceptability. There are also two Passions – Christ's and Teodorico's – and two relics – Mary's nightdress (profane) and the crown of thorns (bogus sacred). Although the nightdress should have led to ruin and the crown of thorns to great wealth, in fact it is the profane relic that leads indirectly to Teodorico's eventual re-encounter with Crispim, his fortunate marriage to Jesuína and acceptance into the bourgeois fold.

Like *The Mandarin*, the novel eschews any neat moral. Although Teodorico initially continues his life of lies

4

through the sale of fake relics and only achieves the wealth and social status he craves through honesty and the rejection of hypocrisy, when pondering the reasons for his failure to inherit his aunt's fortune, his conclusion is a surprising one. He realises that, at the critical moment, he lacked both the quickness of wit and the imagination to lie, the very qualities which Teodorico perceives as being the basis of all human knowledge and religion, the same qualities, for example, shown by Joseph of Arimathea (in Eça's version of events) when deciding what to do with Jesus' body and thereby creating the myth that provided the foundation of Christianity.

It was precisely the combination of this rejection of any conventional moral focus and his rewriting of Christianity as a myth based on a well-intentioned lie that brought Eça and *The Relic* into disfavour with the more Catholic writers of the time. Quite apart from placing Christ's divinity in doubt, it was considered heretical to have an immoral ne'er-do-well like Teodorico witnessing and describing the Passion.

In his attack on suffocating provincialism, Eça shows himself to be in the tradition that began with Flaubert's *Madame Bovary* in 1857 and reached a high point with Joyce's *A Portrait of the Artist as a Young Man* in 1914. What is special about Eça's assault on the hypocrisies of his day, however, is his style, which blends sprightly good humour with lyrical description, and, above all, his enduring ability to make us laugh.

Margaret Jull Costa

During the summer holidays I spent at my villa, the Quinta do Mosteiro (the former country seat of the Counts of Lindoso), I decided to write a memoir of my life which contains – or at least so I and my brother-in-law Crispim believe – a clear and potent lesson for this century so overly preoccupied with the ambiguities of Intelligence and so troubled by concerns about Money.

In 1875, on the eve of St Anthony, my whole being was shaken by the bitterest of disappointments: around that time my aunt, Dona Patrocínio das Neves, bade me leave our home in Campo de Santana to go on a pilgrimage to Jerusalem. Within those holy city walls, on a blazing hot day in the month of Nisan, when Pontius Pilate was still the procurator of Judaea, Aelius Lamma the imperial legate in Syria and J. Kaiapha the supreme pontiff in Rome, I was witness, by some miracle, to scandalous events. When I returned to Portugal a great change took place in my life both materially and morally.

These events – as rare and lofty in the life of a mere university graduate as tall, leafy cork oaks full of sun and murmurous shade might be in a field of scythed grass – are what I wish to recount here, soberly and sincerely, while swallows fly about my roof and clumps of red carnations perfume my orchard.

This journey to the lands of Egypt and Palestine will always constitute the supreme glory of my career and I would very much like to leave a solid yet elegant monument to it in the world of Letters, for Posterity. However, writing, as I am today, out of peculiarly spiritual motives, I would not want these personal jottings to resemble some *Picturesque Guide to the Orient*. That is why (despite the promptings of vanity) I have omitted from this manuscript any succulent, glowing accounts of ruins and local customs.

Furthermore, the land of the Gospels that so fascinates

7

the more sensitive among us is far less interesting than my own arid homeland, the Alentejo. Nor indeed do I think that lands favoured by a Messianic presence necessarily gain thereby in grace or splendour. I have not had the opportunity to visit the holy places of India where the Buddha lived – the groves of Migadaia, the hills of Velluvani, or that sweet valley of Rajagaha upon which the loving eyes of the perfect Master were gazing when a fire broke out amongst the reeds and He taught, in a simple parable, how ignorance is a fire that devours man, a fire fed by the deceptive sensations of Life which are fed in turn by the deceptive appearances of the World. Nor have I visited the cave of Hira or the holy sands between Mecca and Medina so often crossed by Mohammed, the Excellent Prophet, slow and thoughtful on his dromedary. However, from the figtrees of Bethany to the silent waters of Galilee, I am well acquainted with all the places wherein dwelled that other divine Intermediary, full of tenderness and dreams, whom we call Jesus Our Lord, and there I found only brutality, aridity, squalor, desolation and rubble.

Jerusalem is an Arab town crouched behind city walls the colour of mud, full of filthy alleyways stinking to high heaven and filled by the constant pealing of sad bells.

The Jordan, a thread of feeble, muddy water dawdling along through desert lands, hardly bears comparison with that clear, sweet river Lima that runs past the villa here, bathing the roots of my alder trees. And yet, these sweet Portuguese waters never flowed about the knees of a Messiah, were never brushed by the wings of armed and glittering angels bearing warnings from the All High from Heaven to Earth!

However, since there are certain insatiable spirits who, reading of a journey through the land of the Scriptures, long to know everything about it from the size of the stones to the price of beer, I recommend the vast and illuminating work written by my companion on the pilgrimage, Topsius, a German doctor from the University of Bonn and a member of the Imperial Institute of Historical

8

Research. It consists of seven dense volumes *in quarto*, printed in Leipzig, and bears the elegant and profound title: *An Annotated Walk Around Jerusalem.*

On every page of this comprehensive guide, the learned Topsius speaks of me with a mixture of admiration and regret. He always refers to me as 'the illustrious Lusitanian nobleman' and the nobility of his travelling companion, whom he traces back to the Barcas family, clearly fills the erudite plebeian with delicious pride. Indeed, in these weighty tomes, the enlightened Topsius goes a step further and places utterly fictitious words on my lips and in my head – sayings and opinions that positively brim with pious credulity – purely so that he may rebut and demolish them with due wisdom and fluency. He says, for example: 'Standing before such and such a ruin, dating from the time of the Crusade of Godfrey, the illustrious Lusitanian nobleman claimed that Our Lord, when out walking one day with St Veronica … ' and then unfolds the solemn and ponderous arguments he employed to enlighten me. Since, however, the harangues he attributes to me are in no way inferior in their wise profligacy and theological arrogance to those of Bossuet, I refrained from commenting in the note I wrote to the *Cologne Gazette* on the tortuous artifice employed by sharp German wit in order to garland itself with triumph at the expense of the doltish faith of the South.

There is, however, one point in his book which I cannot allow to pass without a robust reply. And that is the learned Topsius' allusion to the two brown paper packages which accompanied and greatly preoccupied me throughout my pilgrimage from the backstreets of Alexandria to the slopes of Mount Carmel. In the verbose style that characterises his academic eloquence, Dr Topsius says: 'The illustrious Lusitanian nobleman carried in them the remains of his ancestors which he himself had gathered together before leaving the sacred soil of his fatherland and his ancient, turreted family home.' This is a downright lie and deserves to be condemned as such. Why should he wish erudite Germany to believe that I travelled the land of the Gospels carrying with me the bones of my ancestors wrapped up in a brown paper parcel?

No other imputation could displease or discomfit me more. Not because he reveals me to the Church as a frivolous profaner of domestic graves (the fulminations of the Church weigh less on me – as a knight commander and a landowner – than the dry leaves that occasionally fall upon my parasol from some dead branch above me); nor because the Church, once it has pocketed its fee for burying a bundle of bones, cares whether they lie forever beneath the rigid peace of an eternal marble slab or go rattling about inside the soft folds of a brown paper parcel; but because Topsius' statement discredits me in the eyes of the Liberal Bourgeoisie. For in these times of Semitism and capitalism, the good things in life – everything from jobs in banks to ecclesiastical benefices – are entirely in the gift of the omnipresent and omnipotent Liberal Bourgeoisie. I have children, I have ambitions. Now, the Liberal Bourgeoisie is happy to welcome and, indeed, assimilate with alacrity a gentleman with ancestors and a family seat – he is the precious, old wine that will purify the coarse, new wine – but, quite rightly, it has nothing but contempt for the graduate, one of the genteel poor, who strolls past it, proud and intrepid, with his hands weighed down with the bones of ancestors, like some silent rebuke to the ancestors and bones that the Bourgeoisie itself lacks.

That is why I would suggest to the learned Topsius (who, with his penetrating spectacles, actually saw the parcels being wrapped, the first in Egypt, the second in Canaan) that in any subsequent edition of his book he should free himself from chaste, academic scruples and narrow-minded, philosophical concerns and reveal to scientific and sentimental Germany alike the true contents of those two brown paper parcels as frankly as I do to my fellow countrymen in these pages written at leisure on my holidays, pages in which Reality reigns supreme, sometimes halting and hampered by the heavy vestments of History, sometimes skipping free beneath the colourful mask of Farce!

I

My grandfather was Father Rufino da Conceição, graduate
in Theology, author of a devout *Life of St Filomena* and
prior at Amendoeirinha. My father, a protégé of Our Lady
of the Assumption, was called Rufino da Assunção Raposo
and he lived in Évora with my grandmother, Filomena
Raposo, nicknamed 'the Dumpling', a confectioner who
lived in Rua do Lagar dos Dízimos. Papa had a job in the
post office and amused himself writing articles for *O Farol
do Alentejo*, the local newspaper. In 1853, a famous cleric,
Dom Gaspar de Lorena, Bishop of Khorazin (which is in
Galilee) came to Évora to celebrate the feast of St John. He
stayed at Canon Pita's house, where Papa often used to go
in the evenings and play his guitar. Out of courtesy to the
two priests, Papa published a report in *O Farol*, laboriously
gleaned from *The Clergyman's Treasury*, congratulating
Évora on 'its great good fortune to be sheltering within its
walls that eminent prelate, Dom Gaspar, shining light of
the Church and a renowned pillar of sanctity'. The Bishop
of Khorazin cut out this article from *O Farol* and placed it
between the pages of his breviary. And he began to find
everything about Papa pleasing, from his spotlessly clean
linen to the melancholy grace with which he sang the
'Ballad of Count Ordonho', accompanying himself on the
guitar. But when he found out that this same Rufino da
Assunção Raposo, with his dark good looks and pleasant
manner, was the godson of old Rufino da Conceição with
whom he had studied at the São José seminary and moved
in the same theological circles at university, his affection
for Papa knew no bounds. Before leaving Évora, the
bishop gave him a silver watch and it was through the
bishop's influence, after a few slothful months' apprentice-
ship at the customs house in Oporto, that Papa was named
director of the customs house in Viana, an appointment
that caused considerable scandal.

When Papa reached the soft, fertile plains of Entre Minho e Lima the apple trees were just coming into blossom and that same July he met a gentleman from Lisbon, Knight Commander G. Godinho, who was spending the summer with his two nieces in a riverside villa called Quinta do Mosteiro, the former home of the Counts of Lindoso. The elder of these two ladies, Dona Maria do Patrocínio, wore dark glasses at all times and, every morning, accompanied by a liveried servant, would ride down to the city on a donkey in order to hear mass at the church in Santana. The other lady, Dona Rosa, was a plump brunette, who played the harp, knew by heart the words of 'Love and Melancholy' and would spend hours by the water's edge, her white dress sweeping the grass, making nosegays of wild flowers beneath the shade of the alder trees.

Papa became a frequent visitor to Quinta do Mosteiro. An officer from the customs house would carry his guitar for him and, whilst the Knight Commander and another friend of the house, Dr Margaride, a magistrate, sat absorbed in a game of backgammon and Dona Maria do Patrocínio was bent in prayer over her rosary, Papa would sit on the verandah by Dona Rosa's side, gazing at the moon, round and white above the river, and in the silence, he would gently pluck the strings of his guitar and sing of the sorrows of Count Ordonho. At other times he too would play backgammon and Dona Rosa, a flower in her hair, a book lying neglected in her lap, would sit at her sister's feet and Papa, shaking the dice, would feel the promising caress of her long-lashed eyes.

They got married. I was born one Good Friday evening but Mama died even as the rockets were exploding in the joyous Easter morn. She lies in the cemetery in Viana do Castelo, in a grave overgrown with gillyflowers, by a path near the wall, in the damp shade of the weeping willows, where she liked to walk on summer evenings, all dressed in white, with the shaggy little puppy she called Traviata.

The Knight Commander and Dona Maria never returned to Quinta do Mosteiro. I grew up and caught all the usual childhood illnesses. Papa grew fatter and his guitar slept, forgotten, in a corner of the living room, inside its green baize case. One very hot July day, my maid Gervásia dressed me in my heavy black cotton suit and Papa put a black crepe band around his straw hat. We were in mourning for Knight Commander G. Godinho, whom Papa often used to refer to under his breath as 'that old rogue'.

Later, one night during Carnival, Papa died suddenly of a stroke, as he was coming down the stone steps of our house dressed in a bear costume ready to go to a dance being held by the Macedo sisters.

I was seven at the time and I remember seeing in our courtyard the next day a tall, stout lady, wearing an ornate mantilla of black lace, sobbing over the bloodstains left by Papa, which no one had washed away and which had dried on the stones. An old woman was waiting at the gate, hunched inside her woollen cape, praying.

The windows at the front of the house were shut. On a bench in the dark corridor stood a flickering candle in a brass holder, giving off the guttering, smoky light of a candle in a chapel. The wind was blowing hard and it was raining. Through the kitchen window, while Mariana snivelled and fanned the fire, I saw a man crossing the Largo da Senhora da Agonia bearing Papa's coffin on his shoulder. In the high, cold hills, the little chapel of Our Lady, with its black cross, looked sadder than ever, white and naked amongst the pines, almost lost in the mist, and beyond, amongst the rocks, a heavy winter sea endlessly rolled and moaned.

That night, in the room where she did the ironing, my maid Gervásia wrapped me in a woollen petticoat and sat me on the floor. From time to time, outside in the corridor, I would hear the creaking boots of João, the customs officer, who was fumigating the house with lavender. The cook brought me a slice of sponge cake. I fell asleep and dreamed I was walking along the banks of a clear river, whose ancient poplars seemed possessed of souls that sighed and with me walked a naked man with two wounds in his feet and two wounds in his hands, Jesus Christ Our Lord.

After some days had passed, I was woken up one morning by the sun shining full on my bedroom windows so that they glittered prodigiously, as if presaging some holy event. Beside my bed stood a plump, smiling figure, who was gently tickling my feet and calling me 'little rascal'. Gervásia told me the man's name was Senhor Matias and that he was going to take me a long way away to Aunt Patrocínio's house. And Senhor Matias, a pinch of snuff halfway between snuffbox and nose, looked shocked at the holes in the socks Gervásia was putting on my feet. They wrapped me in Papa's grey cloak. João, the customs officer, picked me up and carried me in his arms as far as the street door where a litter was waiting; it had curtains made out of oilcloth and was drawn by two mules.

We then set off down long roads. Even when I slept, I was aware of the slow ringing of the bells round the mules' necks and, every now and then, Senhor Matias, sitting opposite me, would stroke my face and say: 'There now.' One evening, as it was growing dark, we came to a sudden halt in a deserted place where there was a bog. The muledriver was furious and swore loudly, brandishing a flaming torch. We were in the middle of a pinewood, black and doleful, that murmured all about us. Senhor Matias grew pale, took his watch out of his pocket and hid it in the top of one of his boots.

One night, we crossed a city where streetlamps in the form of open tulips gave off a cheery light, strange and brilliant, unlike anything I had ever seen. Gonçalves, the waiter at the inn where we stopped knew Senhor Matias and after bringing us our steaks, he stayed with us, leaning casually on the table, a napkin over his shoulder, retailing gossip about the Baron and the Baron's English ladyfriend. When we went up to our room, our way lit by Gonçalves, a tall, white-skinned woman pushed past us in the corridor with a loud rustle of pale silk and a rush of musky

14

perfume. It was the Englishwoman. Lying in the iron bedstead, kept awake by the noise of the coaches, I thought about her as I said my prayers. I had never before been in close contact with such a beautiful body, with such a potent perfume. She was full of grace, the Lord was with her and she passed, blessed amongst women, in a rustle of pale silk. The next day we left in a large carriage that bore the King's coat of arms and set off along a smooth road to the rhythmic trot, heavy and ponderous, of four sturdy horses. Now and then Senhor Matias, his slippers on his feet and taking a pinch of snuff, would tell me the name of some hamlet we passed, which was huddled around an old church in the cool of a valley. Sometimes, as evening fell, the windows of a quiet house on a hillside would glitter with the brilliance of new gold. The coach would pass by, leaving the house asleep amongst the trees; I would see Venus shining through the steamed-up windows of our coach. In the depths of the night, a bugle would sound and we would ride into a sleeping town, thundering along its paved streets. At the door of the inn, dim lanterns would be swaying silently. Above, in a cosy room, the table would be set with knives and forks and steaming soup tureens; unkempt, yawning travellers would pull off their thick woollen gloves. In a daze, not even hungry, I would drink my chicken soup beside Senhor Matias who always seemed to know at least one of the waiters who would ask him how he was and how things in government were going.

At last, one drizzly Sunday morning, we reached a large house standing in a muddy square. Senhor Matias told me this was Lisbon and, wrapping me in my cloak once more, he sat me down on a bench at the back of a damp room full of luggage and massive iron scales. A bell was slowly tolling for mass. A group of soldiers passed by the door, their guns beneath their oilskin capes. A man took charge of our trunks and we got into a carriage where I fell asleep on Senhor Matias' shoulder. When he set me down on the ground again, we were in a gloomy courtyard, strewn

15

with gravel, with black-painted benches. On the steps sat a fat girl whispering to a man wearing a scarlet surplice who was clutching a poor-box in his arms.

The girl was Vicência, Aunt Patrocínio's maid. Senhor Matias chatted to her as he went up the steps, leading me tenderly by the hand. In a room lined with dark wallpaper, we met a very tall, thin lady, dressed in black, with a heavy gold chain around her neck. A purple scarf tied beneath her chin formed a lugubrious hood about her head and, in the depths of the shadow it cast, I caught the black glint of a pair of dark glasses. Behind her, on the wall, an image of Our Lady of Sorrows was watching me, her breast pierced by swords.

'This is your Auntie,' Senhor Matias said to me. 'You must love her and always do as she tells you.'

Slowly, reluctantly, she lowered her greenish, sunken-cheeked face to mine. I felt the vague brush of a kiss, cold as stone. My aunt recoiled at once, furious.

'Good gracious, Vicência! How dreadful! I think someone's put oil on his hair!'

Frightened, my lower lip already trembling, I looked up at her and mumbled:

'Yes, they did, Auntie.'

Then Senhor Matias praised my character, my courage on the journey and how cleanly I had eaten my soup at table in the inns we had stopped at.

'Just as well,' my aunt grunted. 'Considering what I'm doing for him, any bad behaviour on his part really would be the last straw. Go on, Vicência, take him inside. Wash the sleep out of his eyes and see if he knows how to make the sign of the cross.'

Senhor Matias gave me two resounding kisses and Vicência led me into the kitchen.

That night they dressed me in my velvet suit and Vicência, wearing a clean apron and looking very serious, led me by the hand into a room hung with curtains made from scarlet damask, where the table legs were golden like the pillars of an altar. My aunt was sitting in the middle of the sofa, wearing a black silk dress and black lace covering her hair; her fingers glittered with rings. By her side, on golden chairs, two clerics sat talking. One of them, plump and smiling, with prematurely white curly hair, opened his arms to me in a fatherly manner. The other, dark and sad-looking, merely mumbled: 'Good evening'. And from the table, where he was leafing through a large book of prints, a small man with a clean-shaven face and a huge collar gave an embarrassed bow that sent his pince-nez sliding down his nose.

Each of them gave me a tentative kiss. The sad priest asked me my name, which I pronounced 'Tedrico'. The affectionate one, revealing a set of perfect teeth, said I should separate the syllables and say Te-o-do-ri-co. Then they commented on my resemblance to Mama, especially round the eyes. My aunt sighed and gave thanks to our Lord that I looked nothing like my father. And the fellow with the huge collar shut the book he was reading, put away his pince-nez, and enquired timidly whether I missed Viana do Castelo. Terrified, I murmured:

'Yes, Auntie.'

Then the older, plumper priest took me on his knee and told me I must fear God, be very quiet around the house, and always obey my Auntie.

'You haven't got anyone else but your Auntie now. You must always do what your Auntie tells you.'

Shyly I repeated:

'Yes, Auntie.'

My aunt ordered me brusquely to remove my finger from my mouth. Then she told me to go straight down the corridor back to the kitchen, to Vicência . . .

'And when you pass the chapel, where you see a light and a green curtain, kneel down and make the sign of the cross.'

I didn't make the sign of the cross, but I did peer behind the curtain. I found my aunt's chapel truly dazzling. The walls were all lined with purple silk, with painted panels set in flowery frames, touchingly depicting the works of our Lord. The lace on the altar cloth brushed the carpeted floor; the saints carved in ivory and wood, with gleaming haloes, inhabited a little wood of violets and red camellias. Two fine silver salvers, leaning against the walls like holy shields, glinted in the light from the wax candles, and raised up on his blackwood cross, beneath a canopy, was our Lord Jesus Christ, burnished and golden.

I went slowly over to the green velvet cushion placed before the altar and still bearing the imprint of my aunt's pious knees. I raised my sweet, dark eyes up to the figure of the crucified Jesus. And I thought that Heaven must be like that, that all the angels and saints, Our Lady and Our Father, must be made out of gold, studded perhaps with precious stones, and that it was their brilliance that gave us the light of day and the stars were the light that glanced off the precious metals, glinting through the black veils in which the holy love of men wrapped them at night when it was time to sleep.

After tea, Vicência put me to bed in a small room next to hers. She made me kneel down in my nightshirt, put my hands together and raise my face to Heaven. Then she dictated the prayers that I should say for my aunt's health, my Mama's peace and tranquillity and for the soul of a certain Knight Commander, who was very good, very holy and very rich and whose name was Godinho.

I was barely nine years old when my aunt had shirts and a black suit made for me and placed me, as a boarder, at the Colégio dos Isidoros, which at the time was in Santa Isabel.

Within the first few weeks I had embarked on a warm, affectionate friendship with a boy called Crispim, who was older than me, and was the son of Teles, the owner of Crispim & Co., the textile mill in Pampulha. Crispim assisted at mass on Sundays and, with his long, golden hair, looked as gentle as an angel when he knelt at the altar. Sometimes he would grab hold of me in the corridor and plant voracious kisses all over my face, which at the time was soft and girlish. At night, in the study room, at the table where we would sit leafing through the sleepy pages of dictionaries, he would scribble notes to me in pencil, calling me 'his idol' and promising me presents of boxes of steel-nibbed pens.

Thursday was the day set aside for the unpleasant task of washing our feet. And three times a week grubby Father Soares would come, toothpick in mouth, to question us about doctrine and to tell us about the life of our Lord.

'Then they took him and dragged him to the house of Caiaphas . . . Hey, you, the one on the end of the bench, who was Caiaphas? Wrong. Wrong again! No, that's not right either! You dimwits. He was a Jew, one of the very worst. Now, they say that in a certain very barren place in Judaea there grows a tree covered in thorns, so ugly it would make your flesh creep . . .'

The bell for the break would ring and we would all simultaneously slam shut our books on Christian doctrine.

Due to its proximity to the latrines, an unpleasant smell pervaded the gloomy, gravelled playground and the older boys' chief delight was to sit passing round a cigarette in a room on the ground floor where, on Sundays, we were taught mazurkas by the old dancing master, Cavinetti, who wore pumps and curled his hair.

Each month, Vicência, in cloak and scarf, would come to meet me after mass to carry me off to spend a Sunday with my aunt. Before I left, Isidoro Junior would always examine my ears and fingernails. Often he would give me a furious soaping in his own basin, muttering under his breath: 'filthy little swine'. Then he would take me to the door, pat me on the head, call me 'his dear little friend' and ask Vicência to send his respects to Senhora Dona Patrocínio das Neves.

We lived in Campo de Santana. When I walked down the Chiado, I would stop outside a shop selling prints and gaze upon a picture of a young woman, blonde and languid, with bare breasts, reclining on a tigerskin and holding in the tips of her fingers, finer even than Crispim's, a heavy pearl necklace. The paleness of her naked skin

19

made me think of the Baron's English ladyfriend and I would smell once more the perfume that had so troubled me in the corridor at the inn, scattered now along the sunny street amongst the silk dresses of the grave, elegant ladies heading for mass at Rua do Loreto.

At home, my aunt would hold out her hand for me to kiss and I would spend the morning leafing through volumes of *A Panorama of the Universe* in her sitting room where there was a striped sofa, a fine blackwood wardrobe and coloured lithographs of affecting scenes from the purer than pure life of her favourite saint, the patriarch St Joseph. With her purple scarf pulled well down over her forehead, my aunt would sit at the window poring over a large accounts book, a blanket tucked round her feet.

At three o'clock she would close the book, peer out at me from the shadows cast by her headscarf and start questioning me about doctrine. Eyes lowered, I would say the creed and list the Ten Commandments, all the time aware of the smell she gave off, the bittersweet odour of snuff and formic acid.

On Sundays the two clerics came to dine with us. The one with curly hair was Father Casimiro, my aunt's proctor. He would smile and hug me, invite me to decline *arbor, arboris, currus, curri* and affectionately declare me to be 'a boy of great talent'. The other ecclesiastical gentleman would praise the Colégio dos Isidoros as being a splendid educational establishment whose peer was not to be found even in Belgium. His name was Father Pinheiro. He seemed to me to grow ever darker, ever sadder. Every time he passed a mirror, he would stick out his tongue and stand there studying it, a look of suspicion and terror on his face.

At dinner, Father Casimiro would always congratulate me on my healthy appetite.

'Go on, have another mouthful of this veal stew. Boys should be well-fed and contented!'

And Father Pinheiro would pat his stomach and say:

'Ah, happy days, when one wasn't afraid to risk a second helping of veal!'

He and my aunt would then discuss their various ailments. Father Casimiro, his face slightly flushed, his napkin tied about his neck, with plate piled high and glass brimming, would smile at me beatifically.

When the gaslamps amongst the trees in the square began to glow, Vicência would put on her old plaid shawl and take me back to school. At that hour, on Sundays, the fellow with the clean-shaven face and huge collar would arrive. He was Senhor José Justino, secretary to the Brotherhood of St Joseph and my aunt's notary, with an office in the Praça de São Paulo. In the courtyard, where he would already be taking off his coat, he would chuck me under the chin and ask Vicência about Senhora Dona Patrocínio's health. Then he would go up the steps and we would close the heavy door behind us. And I would breathe a sigh of relief, for that big house with its red damasks, innumerable saints and its churchy smell depressed me.

Along the way, Vicência would talk to me about my aunt, who, six years before, had plucked her from the poorhouse. Thus I learned that my aunt had problems with her liver, that she always kept large quantities of gold coins in a green silk bag and that Knight Commander Godinho, her and my own mother's uncle, had left her two hundred *contos* in the form of property, investments, the Quinta do Mosteiro near Viana, as well as silver and porcelain from India . . . Auntie was very rich! I must always be good and always please her!

At the school door Vicência would say 'Goodbye, my love' and give me a big kiss. Often at night, clutching my pillow to me, I would think of Vicência and of her arms, plump and white as milk, which I had seen when she rolled up her sleeves. And thus there grew up in my heart a chaste passion for Vicência. One day in the playground, a boy, who already sported an incipient beard, called me 'a sissy'. I invited him to meet me in the latrines and, with one fearful blow, I bloodied his whole face. I became an object of fear. I smoked cigarettes. Crispim had since left the school and my sole ambition then was to learn how to fence. One day, my noble love for Vicência suddenly disappeared, almost without my noticing, like a flower one drops in the street.

And so the years passed: towards Christmas the stove would be lit in the refectory and I would put on my wool-lined greatcoat with its astrakhan collar; the swallows would arrive in the eaves and, in my aunt's chapel, perfuming Christ's golden feet, instead of camellias, there would be armfuls of the first red carnations of the season; then it would be the time for seabathing and Father Casimiro would send my aunt a basket of grapes from his farm in Torres . . . I began studying Rhetoric.

One day, our good proctor told me that I would not be going back to school, but would instead complete my secondary education in Coimbra, in the house of a Dr Roxo, teacher of theology. New linen was prepared for me. Written on a piece of paper, my aunt gave me a prayer to St Luís Gonzaga, patron saint of all studious youths, to whom I was to pray every day, asking him to preserve in my body a shining chastity and in my soul the fear of the Lord. Father Casimiro accompanied me to that gracious city, where Minerva, the goddess of wisdom, slumbers.

I took an instant dislike to Dr Roxo. I led a harsh and cloistered life in his house and it was a cause of ineffable joy to me, when, in my first year of studying Law, that unpleasant cleric died a miserable death from anthrax. I moved into far more congenial lodgings with the Pimenta family. And, immediately and quite immoderately, I discovered all of life's freedoms and potent pleasures. I never again mumbled that presumptuous prayer to St Luís Gonzaga or bent my manly knee before a holy image wearing a halo on its head. I got roaring drunk at Camelas and proved my strength by bloodily defeating a bruiser from the Trony. I sated my carnal desires with delicious love affairs at Terreiro da Erva; I wandered in the moonlight, wailing out *fados*; I used a cane; and when my beard grew dense and black I proudly accepted the nickname

'Raposão' – the Big Fox. Nevertheless, every fortnight, in my best handwriting, I would write my aunt a humble, pious letter, in which I would tell her how difficult my studies were, how modest my habits, about my copious prayers and stringent fasts, the sermons with which I sustained myself, the sweet unburdenings of my soul to the Heart of Jesus in the evenings in the cathedral and the novenas with which I salved my soul in Santa Cruz during the quiet hours of my free days.

Consequently the summer months spent in Lisbon proved excruciating. I could not go out, not even to get my hair trimmed, without having slavishly to beg permission from my aunt. I didn't dare smoke a cigarette after coffee. I had to return virginally home as soon as night fell and, before going to bed, had to spend a long time in the chapel praying with my aunt. I had condemned myself to this detestable life of devotion!

'Do you say your rosary when you're studying?' my aunt would ask me coldly.

And I would smile abjectly and say:

'Of course I do! I can't get to sleep if I haven't!'

The Sunday gatherings continued. Father Pinheiro, sadder than ever, was complaining now not only about his heart but also about his bladder. And there was another regular guest, an old friend of Knight Commander Godinho, a faithful visitor to the Neves household, Dr Margaride, the one who was the public prosecutor in Viana and later the judge in Mangualde. Made wealthy by the death of his brother, Abel, who had been the secretary of the Patriarchal Council, the doctor, weary of lawsuits, had retired and now lived a life of leisure, reading the newspapers, in a house he owned in Praça da Figueira. Since he had known my father and had often visited him at the Quinta do Mosteiro, he treated me from the start with a mixture of authority and informality.

He was a stout, rather solemn man, already completely bald, with a large, pale face in which the most striking feature were his thick, coal-black eyebrows. The moment he entered my aunt's living room, and no sooner was he through the door, than he would impart to us news of some great catastrophe: 'Haven't you heard? There's been a terrible fire in the Baixa!' In fact, it would turn out to have been nothing more serious than a chimney on fire. But, as a young man, Dr Margaride, in an access of sombre imagination, had written two tragedies, which had left him ever after with a morbid taste for exaggeration and a desire to shock. 'I'm the only one,' he would say, 'who has a true appreciation of the grandiose.'

And, as he terrified my aunt and the two priests with some new tale, he would always take a large pinch of snuff.

I liked Dr Margaride. He had known my father in Viana do Castelo and so had often heard him play his guitar and sing the 'Ballad of Count Ordonho'. They had spent whole evenings together wandering poetically by the water's edge at the Quinta do Mosteiro whilst Mama sat in the shade of the alder trees making nosegays of wild flowers. And he it was who sent me the traditional gift of almonds as soon as I was born as night fell on Good Friday. More than that, he would speak openly to my aunt — even in my presence — in praise of my intellect and my discreet manners.

'Our Teodorico, Dona Patrocínio, is a young man any aunt could be proud of. In him, dear lady, you have found another Telemachus!'

And I would blush modestly.

Now one day in August, as I was walking with him in the Rossio, I first made the acquaintance of a relative of ours, a distant relative, a cousin of Knight Commander G. Godinho. Dr Margaride introduced us, saying only: 'This is Xavier, your cousin, a young man of great gifts.' He was a grubby fellow with a blonde moustache, who had once been an elegant gentleman, but had wildly squandered the thirty *contos* inherited from his father, the owner of a rope factory in Alcântara. Just months before he died of pneumonia, Knight Commander G. Godinho had, out of charity, given him a job at the Secretaria da Justiça with a salary of twenty *milréis* a month. Xavier was now living in a tenement in Rua da Fé with a Spanish woman called Carmen and her three children.

I went there one Sunday. It was almost bare of furniture. The one and only washbasin was fixed in the broken wicker seat of a chair. Xavier spat blood all morning. And Carmen, dishevelled and in slippers, her wine-stained cotton dressing gown dragging along the floor, was sullenly walking up and down the room rocking a child swathed in rags, its head badly cut.

Xavier, who right from the start addressed me as 'tu', lost no time in broaching the subject of Aunt Patrocínio. She was his one hope in the midst of all that gloomy poverty. As a servant of Jesus and the owner of so much property, she could not allow a relative, a Godinho, to waste away in that hovel, with no sheets, no cigarettes, with ragged children all around crying for a bit of bread. What would it cost Aunt Patrocínio to set him up, as the State already had done, with a little allowance of twenty *milréis*?

'You're the one who should talk to her, Teodorico! You're the one who should tell her ... Look at those children. They haven't even got any socks. Come here, Rodrigo, and talk to your Uncle Teodorico. Tell him what you had for lunch today? A mouthful of stale bread! With no butter or anything! That's what our life is like, Teodorico. You've no idea how hard it is!'

Touched, I promised to speak to my aunt.

Speak to her! I did not even dare tell my aunt that I knew Xavier and had gone to that filthy hovel inhabited by a scrawny Spanish woman steeped in sin.

And so, in order that they should not witness my ignoble terror of my aunt, I did not return to Rua da Fé.

Towards the middle of September, on the day of the Birth of Our Lady, I learned through Dr Barroso that my cousin Xavier was near death and wanted to speak to me in private.

25

Somewhat irritated, I went there that same evening. You could smell the fever on the stairs. Carmen was sobbing in the kitchen, talking to another very thin Spanish woman, who was wearing a black mantilla and a sad, skimpy camisole in cherry-red satin. On the floor, the children were scraping out a casserole dish. And in the bedroom Xavier lay coughing his lungs out, a blanket wound about him, a bowl at his head full of gobbets of blood.

'You came then.'

'What's happened, Xavier?'

Using an expletive, he told me that he was ruined. And lying back, his dry eyes glittering, he spoke to me about my aunt. He had written her a beautiful, heartrending letter; the cruel creature had not even replied. So now he intended putting an advertisement in the *Jornal de Notícias*, a plea for alms, which he would sign: 'Xavier Godinho, cousin of the wealthy Knight Commander G. Godinho'. He wanted to see if Dona Patrocínio das Neves would allow a relative, a Godinho, to beg publicly like that in a newspaper.

'But I need your help to soften her heart! When she reads the advertisement, describe to her the poverty we live in. Appeal to her generous side. Tell her it's shameful to allow a relative, a Godinho, to die in penury. Tell her that tongues are already wagging! I've had some soup today, but that's only thanks to Lolita, one of Benta Bexigosa's girls, who gave us four *coroas*. You see how low I've sunk!'

Deeply affected, I rose to my feet.

'You can count on me, Xavier.'

'Look, if you've got five *tostões* to spare, give them to Carmen.'

I gave them to her and left, swearing solemnly, in the name of the Godinhos and in the name of Jesus, that I *would* speak to my aunt!

After lunch the next day, toothpick in mouth, my aunt was languidly unfolding the *Jornal de Notícias*. Xavier's advertisement was obviously the first thing she saw, for she stared for a long time at the corner of page three where it gleamed blackly: distressing, shaming, terrifying.

At that moment, I seemed to see turned towards me, set against the stark backdrop of the hovel they lived in, Xavier's sad eyes, Carmen's sallow face bathed in tears, the children's thin little hands held out in expectation of a crust of bread. And each of those poor, unfortunate beings anxiously awaited the words I was about to address to my aunt – forthright, moving words that would surely save them and give them their first taste of meat in that whole wretched summer. I opened my mouth. However, my aunt was already muttering something, leaning back in her chair, smiling a fierce little smile as she did so:

'They'll just have to put up with it. That's what happens to people who lose their fear of God and get themselves involved with drunken sluts. He shouldn't have frittered all his money away on loose living. Frankly, any man who ruins himself over a woman, any man who's a skirt-chaser, is a lost cause in my opinion. He forfeits both God's forgiveness and mine. Let him suffer, let him suffer just as our Lord Jesus Christ suffered.'

I lowered my head and murmured:

'Nor have we yet suffered enough. You're quite right, Auntie. He should never have got himself involved with that woman!'

She stood up and gave thanks to the Lord. I went to my room and locked myself in, trembling, my aunt's words, chilling and threatening, still echoing in my head, my aunt, for whom any man who got himself entangled with women was a lost cause. I had got involved with women in Coimbra, at the Terreiro da Erva. I had documentary evidence of my sins in my trunk, a photograph of Teresa dos Quinze, a silk ribbon and a letter, the sweetest of them all, in which she called me 'her soul's one true love' and asked if I could lend her eighteen *tostões*! I had sewn these relics into the lining of a woollen waistcoat, fearing my aunt's incessant rummagings amongst my underwear. But there they were, in the trunk to which she had the key, a cardboard-hard lump inside the waistcoat on which, any day now, her suspicious fingers might well alight. And then, in the eyes of my aunt, I would be as good as dead.

Very slowly I opened the trunk, unstitched the lining of the waistcoat, took out Teresa's delicious letter, the ribbon still impregnated with the smell of her skin, and the photograph of her wearing a mantilla. Out on the balcony, I mercilessly burned it all, the sweet words, the sweet face, and desperately swept the ashes of my love out into the courtyard.

I didn't dare go back to Rua da Fé that week. Then, one drizzly day, I did return, hunched beneath my umbrella, as it was growing dark. Seeing me staring up at the dead, black windows of the hovel, a neighbour told me that Senhor Godinho, the poor man, had been carried away to hospital on a stretcher.

Sadly, I went down the Passeio steps. And in the damp evening, I collided with another umbrella and heard someone gaily call out my Coimbra nickname:

'Raposão!'

It was Silvério, known as Rinchão (or Woodpecker), my fellow student and lodger in the Pimenta household. He had been spending that month in the Alentejo with his uncle, the famously wealthy Baron de Alconchel. And now that he was back, he was on his way to see a certain Ernestina, a little blonde girl who lived in Salitre in a pink house with roses growing over the verandah.

'Do you want to come along, Raposão? There's another pretty young thing there too, Adélia. What, you don't know Adélia? Well, come and meet her then. She's quite a girl!'

It was a Sunday, the night my aunt's friends came to supper; I had to be home at eight o'clock on the dot. I scratched my beard indecisively. Rinchão launched into a description of Adélia's white arms and I fell into step beside him, pulling on my black gloves.

Armed with a packet of cakes and a bottle of Madeira,

we found Ernestina sewing elastic into a pair of serge gaiters. And, languidly smoking a cigarette, stretched out on a sofa, was Adélia, wearing only a dressing gown and a white underskirt, her slippers lying where they had fallen on the carpet. I sat down next to her, dumb with desire, my umbrella clasped between my knees. Only when Silve-'rio and Ernestina ran off into the kitchen, their arms about each other, to fetch some glasses for the Madeira wine, could I bring myself to ask Adélia blushingly:

'And where are you from?'

She was from Lamego, she said. Engulfed once more by shyness, I could only stammer out some remark about how depressing this rainy weather was. She politely asked me for another cigarette, addressing me as 'sir'. I appreciated her good manners. The long sleeves of her dressing gown fell back to reveal arms so white and soft that were one to die whilst in their embrace, death itself would seem delicious.

I held out to her the plate on which Ernestina had arranged the cakes. She asked my name and told me she had a nephew called Teodorico and that one remark was like a strong, subtle thread which she unwound from her own heart and wound about my own.

'Why don't you put your umbrella over there in the corner, sir?' she said, laughing.

The piquant gleam of her small teeth caused a compliment to bloom inside me.

'Because I can't bear to leave your side, not even for an instant.'

She stroked my neck very slowly. Dazed with pleasure, I finished off the Madeira wine she had left in her glass.

Ernestina was in poetic mood and lay nestled on Rin-chão's lap singing a *fado*. Then Adélia turned languidly towards me and drew my face close to hers; our lips met in the most serious, most passionate, most profound kiss that had ever stirred my being.

At that sweetest of moments, a hideous clock with a moon face, which seemed to be spying on me from the marble top of a mahogany table, from between two vases bereft of flowers, began to strike ten o'clock in nasal, ironic, phlegmatic tones.

Good grief! That was the time we took tea at my aunt's house! Terrified, not even bothering to open my umbrella, I trudged panting along the dark, unending streets that led back to Campo da Santana! When I reached the house, I did not even stop to remove my muddy boots, but slipped into the living room, where, at the far end, waiting for me on the damask sofa, I saw my aunt's glasses, even blacker than ever, blazing anger. I stammered out:

'Auntie . . .'

But she was already shouting and shaking her fists, her face almost green with rage:

'I will not permit such laxity in my house! Anyone who lives here must keep the hours that I choose! There'll be no debauchery or goings-on here whilst I'm alive! And if you don't like it, you can leave!'

Father Pinheiro and Justino the notary meekly bent their heads beneath the strident storm of Senhora Dona Patrocínio's indignation. In order to gauge the full measure of my guilt, Dr Margaride consulted his heavy gold watch. And it was left to good Father Casimiro, as priest and proctor, to intervene on my behalf in a tone of gentle persuasion.

'You're absolutely right, Dona Patrocínio, to want order in your household, but perhaps our Teodorico dallied a little longer than usual in the Café Martinho in order to discuss his studies or some coursebook . . .'

Bitterly I exclaimed:

'No, Father Casimiro, I wasn't there. I wasn't at the Martinho! Do you want to know where I was? I was at the Convento da Encarnação! It's true, I did meet a fellow student there, he'd gone to pick up his sister. It was a holiday today and his sister had gone there to spend the day with an aunt, a commander of the order . . . We waited for her in the courtyard. His sister is about to be married and he was telling me about her fiancé, about her trousseau and how in love she is . . . I was dying to get away but I didn't want to offend the young man, who happens to be the nephew of Baron de Alconchel. And he just kept going on and on about his sister and her fiancé and about the letters they write to each other . . .'

Aunt Patrocínio let out a furious roar.

'What kind of conversation is that! I've never heard anything so disgusting! What kind of indecent talk is that for the courtyard of a house of religion! Be silent, you lost soul, you should be ashamed of yourself! And make no mistake, the next time you come home this late, I won't let you in. You can stay out in the street, like a dog . . .'

Then Dr Margaride held out a solemn, pacifying hand:

'Now I see what happened. Teodorico was perhaps imprudent but he was at least in a respectable place. And I know Baron de Alconchel. He's a most discreet gentleman and one of the wealthiest men in the Alentejo, possibly one of the richest landowners in the whole of Portugal . . . I'd even go so far as to say *the* richest. Even abroad there can't be many who own more land than he does. There's no comparison! Why, in pigs and cork trees alone he's worth hundreds of *contos*, millions!'

He had stood up, his great, bombastic voice rolling over those mountains of gold. And good Father Casimiro murmured gently at my side:

'Drink your tea, Teodorico, drink your tea. Your aunt only wants what's best for you.'

With trembling hand, I picked up my teacup and, stirring feebly at the sugar in the bottom, I considered how I might escape for ever from the house of that terrifying old woman who had so shamed me before the Magistrature and before the Church, showing no respect whatsoever for my incipient beard.

But on Sundays, tea was served in Knight Commander G. Godinho's china. I observed its heavy splendour: the big teapot, its spout in the form of a duck's beak; the sugarbowl with a handle in the shape of an angry snake; and the elegant toothpick holder, a mule trotting along beneath the

31

weight of its saddlebags. It all belonged to my aunt. She was so rich. I must always be good and I must always be grateful to Auntie!

That's why, later on, when she came into the chapel to say her rosary, I was already there on my knees, moaning and beating my chest and begging the golden figure of Christ to forgive me for having offended my aunt.

One day I arrived back in Lisbon with my degree certificate rolled up in a metal tube. My aunt examined it reverently, finding an ecclesiastical flavour in the Latin words, the ornamental red ribbons and the seal inside its reliquary.

'Good,' she said, 'now you're a graduate. And you owe it all to our Lord God, so just make sure you don't let him down.'

Degree in hand, I went straight to the chapel to thank the golden figure of Christ for my glorious new status of graduate.

The following morning, I was standing at the mirror trimming my now thick, black beard, when Father Casimiro came into my room, smiling and rubbing his hands together.

'I've got some good news for you, *Dr* Teodorico!'

And, according to his affectionate custom, the good proctor patted me several times in the small of my back before telling me that my aunt was so pleased with me that she had decided to buy me a horse so that I could go out for healthy rides and amuse myself around Lisbon.

'A horse! Oh, Father Casimiro!'

Yes, a horse. More than that, anxious that her now bearded, graduate nephew should not suffer the embarrassment of finding himself without any small change to leave in the salver of Our Lady of the Rosary, my aunt had set me up with a monthly allowance.

I embraced Father Casimiro warmly and asked if it was my aunt's fond intention that I should have no occupation other than riding around Lisbon, occasionally dropping a few coins into the salver of Our Lady.

'It seems to me, Teodorico, that your aunt wants you to

have no other employment than that of fearing God. All I can say is that you're going to have a very pleasant time of it. Now go in and thank her, and say something nice.'

In the sitting room, its walls glittering with the pious deeds of the patriarch St Joseph, my aunt was sitting at one end of the striped sofa, a shawl about her shoulders, knitting.

'Auntie,' I murmured timidly, 'I've just come to thank you . . .'

'There's no need, I ask only that God goes with you.'

I devoutly kissed the fringe of her shawl. My aunt liked that. God was most certainly with me.

Thus began the opulent, pleasurable life I was to enjoy as nephew of Senhora Dona Patrocínio das Neves. At eight o'clock precisely, dressed all in black, I would accompany my aunt to the church in Santana, to hear Father Pinheiro say mass. After lunch, having first asked my aunt's permission and visited the chapel to say three Gloria Patri against temptation, I would don my light-coloured riding trousers and off I would go. My aunt almost always set me some saintly duty, for example, dropping in at São Domingos to say a prayer for the three saints martyred in Japan or going into Conceição Velha and performing the act of atonement before the Sacred Heart of Jesus.

And so great was my fear of displeasing her that I never once failed to deliver the tender messages she sent to the Lord's house.

But that was the worst part of my day, for, sometimes, as I sneaked out of the church door, I would bump into some former fellow student and republican who, in Coimbra, on afternoons when there was a procession, used to join me in poking fun at the figure of Our Lord of the Green Reed.

'What's this Raposão? Surely you're not . . .'

I would deny it, irritated.

'Of course not! The very idea! Me, here out of piety? No! I only went in there after some girl. Anyway, I can't stop, I've got my horse here . . .'

Then I would mount up and prance, idly and ostentatiously, over to Largo do Loreto – my knees gripping the saddle, my hands sheathed in black gloves, a discreet camellia flower in my lapel. On other occasions, I would leave the horse at the Arco do Bandeira and enjoy a pleasant morning in the Montanha billiard hall.

I would go into my aunt's chapel before supper, in my slippers, to say a brief prayer for indulgence to St Joseph, Jesus' guardian, Mary's protector and most beloved patriarch. At the supper table, which would be set only with compote dishes placed around a dish of vermicelli, I would tell my aunt about my day, what churches had best pleased me and which ones had had candles on the altar. Vicência would listen devoutly, sitting in her usual place between the two windows where a portrait of our Holy Father Pius IX filled the strip of bare green wall; below him, hanging from a rope, was an old telescope, a relic of Knight Commander G. Godinho. After coffee, my aunt would fold her arms, her head would begin to nod and her large, ugly face would sink back heavily into the shadowy depths of the purple scarf.

Then, I would put on my boots and, since I now had her permission to amuse myself outside the house until half past nine, I would race off to Rua da Madalena, near Largo dos Caldas. Once there, in great stealth, with my coat collar turned well up and keeping close to the wall, as if the gaslamp hanging there were my aunt's inexorable eye, I would eagerly climb the stairs to Adélia's rooms.

Yes, Adélia! For ever since that first night when Rinchão took me to Salitre, I had never forgotten the kiss she gave me as she reclined, pale and languid, on the sofa. Whilst in Coimbra, I had even attempted to write her a poem and, in my last year at university, the year of Ecclesiastical Law, the love I bore her lay in my breast like a marvellous lily unseen by others but perfuming my whole life. The moment my aunt gave me my allowance, I ran to Salitre in triumph; the roses were still there at the window but Adélia was gone. Again it was that excellent fellow Rinchão who showed me the first-floor apartment, next to Largo dos Caldas, where she was now living under the protection of Eleutério Serra of Serra, Brito and Co. who owned a shop in Conceição Velha selling fabrics and fashions. I sent her a letter, at once ardent and serious, which began reverently: 'Dear Madam'. She replied with dignity: Sir, you will be welcome to visit any day at noon.' I took her a little box of chocolates tied with a blue silk ribbon. My heart pounding, I crossed the new rug in the living room and saw a promise of cool skirts in the starched whiteness of the curtains and a symbol of the rectitude of her feelings in the rigid neatness of the furniture. She was suffering from a slight cold and was wearing a red shawl about her shoulders. She recognised me at once as Rinchão's friend and spoke harshly of Ernestina, calling her a 'pig'. The sound of her hoarse voice, her stuffed-up nose, filled me with a desire to restore her to health by enfolding her in my arms and spending a long day in the soft penumbra of her bedroom tucked sleepily up in bed beneath the weight of blankets. Then she asked whether I was an employee or had my own business. I told her proudly of my aunt's wealth, of her many properties and her silver. Clasping her large hands in mine, I said:

'If my aunt were to die now, my first act would be to set you up in a really chic house!'

Bathing me in the black sweetness of her gaze, she murmured:

'Come now, if you ever came into money, you'd have nothing more to do with me!'

Trembling, I knelt down on the rug and pressed my chest against her knees, offering myself up to her like a mere beast. She opened wide her shawl and mercifully took me in.

Now, every evening at dusk (while Eleutério was playing cards at his club in Rua Nova do Carmo), I would be in Adélia's bedroom having the most glorious time of my life. I even kept a pair of my slippers there: I was her chosen one. At half past nine, she would hurriedly throw on a flannel dressing gown and accompany me to the back stairs, her hair all dishevelled, her feet bare, and on every step she would pause to place on my lips a slow, passionate kiss.

'Goodbye, Adélia!'

'Wrap up warm, my love!'

And I would walk slowly back to Campo de Santana, pondering my good fortune.

The summer passed languidly. The first winds of autumn bore away the swallows and the leaves from Campo de Santana, and that October my life suddenly became easier, more expansive. My aunt had a dress coat made for me and I wore it for the first time, with her permission, to the Teatro São Carlos for a performance of *Polyeucte*, an opera Dr Margaride had recommended as being 'steeped in religious sentiment and bursting with lofty ideas'. I accompanied him, wearing my new white gloves and with my hair curled. The next day at lunch, I told my aunt the whole devout plot, about the overthrow of the idols, the canticles, the noblewomen in the boxes and the beautiful velvet gown worn by the queen.

'And do you know who came to speak to me, Auntie? Baron de Alconchel, that very wealthy man, the uncle of that boy who was my classmate. He came over and shook me by the hand and stayed chatting to me in the salon for quite a while. He was really terribly kind to me.'

My aunt liked that.

Then, sadly, in the tones of a wounded moralist, I complained of the outrageous décolletage of some particularly immodest woman, exposing her arms and her chest, making a display of all that splendid, irreligious flesh, a cause of grief to all righteous men and a great sorrow to the Church.

'It was *so* offensive. Do you know, Auntie, it actually made me feel physically sick.'

My aunt liked that too.

And a few days later, after coffee, when I was already in my slippers on my way to the chapel to address a brief prayer to the wounds of our golden Christ, my aunt, her arms already folded, her head nodding, said to me from the shadows of her shawl:

'Very well, you can go to the theatre again tonight if you like. In fact, you can go whenever you please. Don't be shy, you have my permission, you can go and enjoy the music. Now that you're a man and seem to have your head screwed on, I don't mind if you stay out until eleven or even half past eleven at night. But no later than that. I want the door shut by then and be ready to say the rosary.'

She did not see the triumphant gleam in my eyes. Drooling with devout pleasure I murmured primly:

'I wouldn't miss saying the rosary, my beloved rosary, for all the fun in the world – not even if the King himself invited me for tea at the palace!'

In a state of delirious joy, I ran to put on my dress coat. And that was the beginning of the longed-for freedom I had so laboriously won by bending my back before my aunt and beating my breast before Jesus! A most welcome freedom now that Eleutério Serra had gone off to Paris to buy new stock, leaving Adélia alone, unattached, beautiful and merrier and more passionate than ever!

Yes, I had won the confidence of my aunt with my punctuality, my good sense, my servility and my devout ways, but (as she had confided to Father Casimiro) what had led her to allow such a generous extension of my hours of honest recreation was her conviction that 'I was behaving myself in a properly religious manner and not chasing after women.'

As far as Aunt Patrocínio was concerned, all human actions that took place beyond the church door consisted of but two things: 'chasing after men' or 'chasing after women' and she found both those sweet, natural impulses equally repellent.

She was an old maid and as shrivelled as a vine branch, and the only touch her pasty flesh had known was that of Knight Commander G. Godinho's grizzled, fatherly moustaches. Incessant mutterings before the naked figure of Christ, prayers for indulgence said at the Hours of Piety, all the while aching with divine love, had gradually filled my aunt with a bitter, envious rancour regarding human love in all its many forms.

Not satisfied with dismissing love as a profanity, Senhora Dona Patrocínio das Neves would scowl and brush it away as if it were a piece of dirt. For her, a grave young man, serious in his intentions towards his beloved, was 'a piece of filth'! When she heard that some lady had just given birth, she would spit on the ground and grunt: 'Disgusting!' She almost found Nature itself obscene for having created two sexes.

Though she was rich and appreciated comfort, she had always refused to have a male servant in the house to avoid what she termed any 'brushing of skirts against trousers' in the kitchen or in the corridors. And despite the fact that Vicência's hair was now turning white, that the cook was now decrepit and senile, and the other maid, Eusébia, had lost all her teeth, my aunt nevertheless still rummaged desperately in their trunks, even in the straw in their mattresses, in case she should find a photograph of a man, a letter from a man, or the slightest trace or scent of a man.

Any youthful pursuits such as taking a sedate donkey ride with the ladies, proffering someone a dewy rosebud on the tips of one's fingers, dancing a decorous quadrille on a joyous Easter morning, and other even more innocent pleasures, were deemed by my aunt to be perverse and vile, what she termed 'lax behaviour'. The friends who visited the house were prudent enough to avoid any mention of the kind of affecting stories you read in the newspapers, in which love always plays a large part, knowing that she would be as scandalised by them as she would have been by shameless nudity.

One day she had shouted out angrily: 'Please, Father Pinheiro!', her dark glasses glinting at the unfortunate cleric, when she heard him recounting how a maid in France had thrown her child into the latrine.

'Father Pinheiro! Have a little respect. It's not the mention of the latrine that offends, but that other filthy business!'

Yet she herself made constant references to wild behaviour and the sins of the flesh, in order to heap vituperation and hatred on them. She would throw her ball of wool down on the table and plunge her knitting needles furiously into it, as if she were stabbing the vast, unquiet heart of mankind, rendering it for ever cold. And scarcely a day passed by without her reiterating through clenched teeth (addressing herself to me) that if anyone of her blood, anyone who had eaten of her bread, started chasing after women or indulging in lax behaviour, they would be out on the street, driven out with a broom handle like a dog.

That was why I began to take even greater precautions and, in order to avoid any trace of Adélia's delicious smell clinging to my clothes, I took to carrying small bits of incense in my pockets. Before bounding up the sad steps into the house, I would slip into the empty stables at the back of the courtyard, burn a bit of the holy resin in the lid of an empty barrel and linger there, exposing my coattails and my manly beard to its purifying odour. Then I would go upstairs and have the immediate satisfaction of seeing my aunt delightedly sniffing the air:

'Heavens, what a delicious smell of churches!'

I would sigh and murmur modestly:

'It's only me, Auntie . . .'

I went to still greater lengths to persuade her of 'my indifference to women'. One day I placed a sealed letter on the floor of the corridor as if I had dropped it by accident, sure that that most devout of women, my aunt, would pounce on it at once and rip it open. She did and she liked what she read. It was a letter from me to a fellow student in Arraiolos, written in a noble hand, and containing the following edifying statements: 'You will doubtless have learned that I have fallen out with Simões from the philosophy department because he invited me to go with him to a house of ill repute. I will not tolerate such offensive behaviour. You remember how I always hated such laxness when we were in Coimbra. I believe that only a fool would risk burning for all eternity in the fires of Satan for the sake of some here-today-gone-tomorrow pleasure. *I* would certainly never fall into such gross errors. Yours, Raposo.'

My aunt read the letter and liked it. And so I would put on my dress coat, tell her that I was off to hear *Norma*, unctuously kiss her bony fingers and race off to Largo dos Caldas, to Adélia's boudoir, to plunge headlong into the bliss of sin. In the half-light that filtered through the glass-paned door from the oil lamp in the living room, the cambric curtains round the bed and the petticoats draped about us took on a celestial, cloud-like whiteness; the smell of rice powder seemed sweeter than any mystical joss sticks. I was in Heaven, I was St Teodorico and my beloved's black tresses, coarse and strong as the tail of a warhorse, fell about her naked shoulders.

On one such night, I was coming out of a patisserie in the Rossio, where I had just bought a box of sweetmeats for my Adélia, when I met Dr Margaride who, having embraced me in fatherly fashion, announced that he was off to the Teatro São Carlos to see *The Prophet*.

'I assume, since you're in your dress coat, that you're on your way there too.'

I was dumbstruck. I was indeed wearing my dress coat and had indeed told my aunt that I was off to see *The Prophet*, an opera as virtuous, I said, as holy church music. And now I really would have to sit through it, squeezed into a seat in the gods, rubbing knees with the learned magistrate, instead of lazing on an amorous couch, watching my goddess in her nightgown, eating the sweets I had bought for her.

Defeated, I murmured:

'Yes, I was just on my way there now. They say it's a most virtuous work. My aunt was really keen for me to see it.'

Clutching my useless bag of sweets, I walked glumly up Rua Nova do Carmo at Dr Margaride's side.

We took our seats. And in the splendid auditorium, painted white with touches of gold, I was still thinking longingly of Adélia's darkened bedroom and of her rumpled petticoats, when I noticed a mature, blonde lady in one of the side boxes, a Ceres in the autumn of her years, dressed in straw-coloured silk. Every time the violins struck up, she would gaze on me with pale, serious eyes.

I immediately asked Dr Margaride if he knew the lady 'whom I had frequently seen on Fridays at the church in Graça, visiting Our Lord of the Stations of the Cross with a most exemplary fervour and devotion . . .'

'The fellow behind her, the one who's speaking now, is the Viscount of Souto Santos. She's either his wife, the Viscountess of Souto Santos, or his sister-in-law, the Viscountess of Vilar-o-Velho.'

On the way out, the viscountess (of Souto Santos or Vilar-o-Velho) paused for a moment at the exit to await her carriage. She was wearing a white cape delicately edged with downy feathers. Her head seemed rather haughty; it was impossible to imagine it rolling from side to side, dazed and pale, upon a lover's pillow. Her straw-coloured train dragged across the paving stones. She was magnificent, she was a viscountess. And once again I felt her pale, serious eyes search me out, transfix me.

It was a starry night and walking in silence down the Chiado by Dr Margaride's side, I was thinking that, when all my aunt's gold was mine to do with as I liked, I would be able to meet the Viscountess of Souto Santos or Vilar-o-Velho, not in her box at the opera, but in my bedroom, her great white cape cast aside, the straw-coloured silks discarded, and, pure white in her shining nakedness, all snuggled up in my arms. Ah when, oh when would that sweetest of moments come, when my aunt would die?

'Do you fancy having some tea at the Martinho?' Dr Margaride asked me as we reached the Rossio. 'I don't know if you've ever had their toast. It's the best in all Lisbon.'

In the Martinho, quiet by that hour, the gaslamps between the dim mirrors were sputtering out. One sad, solitary waiter was sitting before a glass of sugar water at a table near the back, his chin resting on his fists.

Dr Margaride ordered the tea and, seeing me looking anxiously at the hands of the clock, he assured me that I would still be home in time to carry out my touching devotions with my aunt. I said:

'Auntie doesn't mind now if I get in a little later. God be praised, she trusts me more than she used to.'

'And you deserve that trust. The sensible thing to do is simply to comply with her wishes. According to Father Casimiro, she's grown quite fond of you.'

Then I remembered the old bonds of affection between Dr Margaride and Father Casimiro, Aunt Patrocínio's proctor and zealous confessor. And, seizing the opportunity, I gave a little sigh and opened my heart to the magistrate, as if to a father.

'It's true, Auntie is fond of me. But you know, Dr Margaride, sometimes I worry about my future. I've even thought of applying for a job as a civil servant. I've even tried to find out what the chances are of getting a post as a clerk at the customs house because, although Auntie is rich, very rich, and I am her only nephew, her only relative, her sole heir, I . . .'

And I looked anxiously across at Dr Margaride thinking that perhaps the loquacious Father Casimiro might have revealed to him what was in my aunt's will. The heavy silence with which he received my words, his hands folded on the table, seemed to augur ill, and at that moment the waiter brought the tray of tea, smiling and saying how glad he was to see that the magistrate had recovered from his cold.

'Delicious toast!' murmured the doctor.

'Excellent!' I sighed politely.

From time to time Dr Margaride would poke about in his teeth, then wipe his face and his fingers and begin to chew again, slowly, delicately, devoutly.

I ventured another timid word.

'Auntie really is fond of me . . .'

'Oh, she is,' the magistrate broke in, his mouth full, 'and you are her only relative. But there's a problem Teodorico. You have a rival.'

'I'll kill him,' I burst out, my eyes blazing, bringing my fist down hard on the table.

The sad waiter at the back of the café looked up from his drink. And Dr Margaride severely reprimanded me for my violence.

'Such words are improper in a gentleman and a respectful young man. One does not, in general, kill anyone. And besides, Teodorico, your rival is none other than our Lord Jesus Christ!'

Our Lord Jesus Christ? I only understood what he meant when the illustrious lawyer, calmer now, revealed to me that my aunt, even in the final year of my studies, had still had every intention of leaving her fortune, her lands and her property to her favourite brotherhoods and to a few favoured priests.

'Then I'm lost,' I murmured.

By chance my eyes fell upon the sad waiter sitting in front of his glass of sugar water at the back of the café. And it occurred to me that he was as like me as a brother, that he *was* me, Teodorico the disinherited, shabbily dressed and wearing worn-out shoes, coming here every night to sit before a glass of sugar water and ponder the griefs of my life.

But Dr Margaride had finished his toast now. And, toothpick in mouth, luxuriously stretching his legs, he offered me these friendly, astute words of consolation.

'Not everything is lost, Teodorico. Not everything. Your aunt may have changed her mind. You're a good lad, cheer her up, read the newspaper to her, say your prayers with her ... That's what counts. Because, it must be said, you have a powerful rival.'

'Unbeatable!' I moaned.

'He's certainly powerful and, I should add, worthy of our respect. Jesus Christ suffered for us, he's the state religion and one can but bow before him. Look, do you want to know what I think? Well, I'll tell you, frankly and honestly, just as a guide. You will only inherit everything if Dona Patrocínio, your aunt and my employer, can be

43

persuaded that leaving her fortune to you would be the same as leaving it to our Holy Mother the Church.'

Dr Margaride generously paid for the tea. Then, out in the street again, his jacket tightly buttoned up, he said in a low voice.

'Tell me frankly, what did you think of the toast?'

'There's none better in the whole of Lisbon, Dr Margaride.'

He squeezed my hand affectionately and we parted, just as the old Carmo clock was striking midnight.

Quickening my pace along Rua Nova da Palma, I saw clearly and bitterly the error of my ways. Yes, the error! Because up until then, the complex act of devotion I put on to placate my aunt and her gold had always been adequate but never fervent. What did it matter if I primly murmured my prayers before Our Lady of the Rosary, before Our Lady in all her many incarnations. If I was to move my aunt, I must skilfully and ostentatiously reveal to her a soul consumed by the flames of holy love, a body crushed, penitent and chafed by the hairshirt. Only then would my aunt say approvingly: 'He's an example to us all.' But to inherit her wealth I would have to force her to exclaim, drooling, her hands raised in prayer: 'He is a saint!'

Yes, I would have to identify myself so closely with things ecclesiastical, immerse myself in them to such a degree that, little by little, my aunt would be unable to distinguish me from that rancid pile of crosses, images, prayerbooks, surplices, candles, scapulars, palm leaves and litters which, for her, constituted Religion and Heaven. She would mistake my voice for the saintly murmur of Latin at mass and my black overcoat would appear to her as if already spangled with stars and diaphanous as the tunic of Heavenly Bliss. Then, and only then, would she make out her will in my favour, convinced that she was making it out in favour of Jesus Christ and his sweet Mother Church!

I was now determined not to let Knight Commander G.

Godinho's delectable fortune go to Jesus, son of Mary. Certainly not! Did the Lord not have enough already with his countless treasures, the bonds and letters of credit that human piety was constantly signing in his name, the spadefuls of gold that nation states reverently placed at those feet pierced by nails, the silver plate, the chalices, the diamond studs he wore in his tunic at his church in Graça? And yet, from his wooden cross, he nonetheless had his voracious eye trained on a silver teapot and a few measly luxury items! Right then! We would fight over who should have those paltry, transient possessions – you, the Son of the Carpenter, displaying to my aunt the wounds you bore for her, one afternoon, in a barbarous city in Asia, and me, adoring those wounds so loudly and ostentatiously that my aunt will not know who is more deserving of merit, you who died because you loved us too much or me who longs to die because I cannot love you enough! Such were my thoughts as I gazed up into the heavens, in the silence of Rua de São Lázaro.

When I reached the house, I heard my aunt praying alone in the chapel. I slipped furtively into my room and took off my shoes and my dress coat. Rumpling my hair, I dropped to my knees and shuffled down the corridor, moaning, wailing, beating my breast and calling out mournfully to Jesus, my Lord.

When, in the silence of the house, she heard these lugubrious lamentations of weary penitence, my aunt was startled and came to the door of the chapel.

'What's all this, Teodorico, my boy, what's wrong with you?'

I threw myself on the floor sobbing, overcome with divine passion.

'Forgive me, Auntie. I was at the theatre with Dr Margaride and afterwards we went on to drink tea together and to talk about you. And then suddenly, on the way home, right there in Rua Nova da Palma, I was seized by the thought that I too must die, by thoughts of my soul's salvation and about all that our Lord suffered for us, and I just felt like weeping . . . So I wonder, Auntie, would you be so kind as to leave me alone for a while here in the chapel, so that I can ease my soul . . .'

Dumbstruck, awed, she reverently lit the candles on the altar, one by one. She moved the image of her favourite saint, St Joseph, a little nearer to the edge so that he would be the first to receive the ardent outburst of prayer about to flow tumultuously forth from my overflowing, grieving heart. She let me shuffle in, then silently disappeared, quietly drawing the curtains behind her. And there I stayed, sitting on my aunt's cushion, rubbing my knees, sighing loudly and thinking about the Viscountess of Souto Santos, or was it Vilar-o-Velho, and of the greedy kisses I would plant on those mature, succulent shoulders if I could have her for only an instant, right there if necessary, in the chapel, at the golden feet of Jesus, my Saviour!

Thenceforward I refined and perfected my devotions. On the grounds that the salt cod we ate on Fridays was not mortification enough, I would instead merely sip ascetically from a glass of water and chew on a crust of bread. (I would eat my salt cod cooked in an onion sauce, followed by steak à l'anglaise, later that night at Adélia's house). In my wardrobe that harsh winter I kept only an old jacket in order to show how utterly I had renounced the guilty pleasures of the flesh; on the other hand I prided myself on the presence there of the purple surplice belonging to the brotherhood of Our Lord of the Stations of the Cross and the devout grey habit of the Third Order of St Francis purifying the more profane fabrics there. The eternal flame of a nightlight burned on my bureau before a coloured lithograph of Nossa Senhora do Patrocínio – Our Lady of Grace and Favour. Every day, to perfume the air round about, I would place fresh roses in a vase beneath it and whenever my aunt came in to have a rummage in my drawers, she would stop and look proudly at her patron saint, never quite sure whether the flame and the perfume were a homage and a eulogy to the Virgin or, indirectly, to herself. On the walls, I hung images of the most eminent saints, a kind of gallery of spiritual antecedents, whose example I constantly drew upon in the difficult acquisition of virtue; but there was no saint in Heaven, however obscure, to whom I did not offer up a sweet-smelling bouquet of paternosters in full bloom. It was I who introduced my aunt to St Telesphorus, St Secundina, the pious António Estroncónio, St Restituta, St Umbelina, sister of the great St Bernard, and our beloved and gentle fellow countrywoman, St Basilissa, who is commemorated, together with St Hipácio, on that festive day in August when people float candles out to the lighthouse.

I became frenetically devout! I went to matins and to vespers. I visited every church or hermitage where they performed the adoration of the Sacred Heart of Jesus. Wherever the Sacrament was displayed I would be there, prostrate on the ground. I prayed as many novenas as there are stars in the sky. And the Septenary of Christ's Suffering became one of my sweetest duties.

Some days I spent my time running breathlessly through the streets, taking in the seven o'clock mass in Santana, the nine o'clock mass at the church of São José and midday mass at the hermitage of Oliveirinha. I would rest for a moment on a corner, my book of divine service beneath my arm, and hurriedly smoke a cigarette; then I would fly off to visit the reservation of the Sacrament in the parish of Santa Engrácia, to the service at terce in the Convento de Santa Joana, to the blessing of the Sacrament in the chapel of Nossa Senhora às Picoas, to a sung novena for Christ's Wounds in the church of that name. Then I would jump into one of Pingalho's carriages and make fleeting, random visits to the churches of the Martyrs and São Domingos, the church of the Convent of the Atonement and the church of the Visitation of the Salesians, the chapel of Montserrat in Amoreiras and the Glória in Cardal da Graça, and then on to Flamengas, Albertas, Pena, Rato *and* the Cathedral!

At night, at Adélia's house, I would sit slumped at one end of the sofa, so washed-out, grumpy and tired that she would pound on my back and scream:

'Wake up, you great pudding!'

Alas, the day came when I was so exhausted from my service to the Lord that I barely had the energy to unlace her corset and Adélia stopped calling me 'pudding' and started calling me 'creep' and pushing me away whenever my insatiable lips lingered too long upon her breast. That was in the fifth month of my new regime of perfect devotion, around the festive time of St Anthony, when the first of the basil began to appear.

Adélia often seemed pensive and distracted, and sometimes when I spoke to her, she had a way of saying 'Hmm?', and keeping her eyes firmly fixed on some other vague, shifting point, that was a torment to my heart. Then one day she suddenly stopped doing the thing I liked most, she stopped giving me kisses on the ear.

Oh, she was still very charming to me. She still folded up my jacket for me in a motherly fashion, still called me 'sweetheart', still accompanied me to the landing in her nightdress and, as she emerged from my embrace, still gave that slow sigh, which I always took as precious proof of her passion for me - but she no longer favoured me with that penetrating kiss on the ear.

On the occasions that I arrived there all aflame, I would find her not yet dressed, her hair unbrushed, looking limp and sleepy, with dark circles under her eyes. She would hold out an unfriendly hand to me, yawn and lazily pick up her guitar, whilst I sat, in one corner, smoking endless, silent cigarettes, waiting for her to open the glass door that led to her bedroom and to Heaven. But cruel Adélia, lying stretched out on the sofa, her slippers fallen on the floor, would simply pluck the bass strings of her guitar and hum strangely nostalgic ballads, interspersed with long sighs.

If, on a tender impulse, I got up and knelt down beside her, she would immediately throw that hard, cold word in my face: 'Get off me, creep!'

Now she always denied me her love. She would say: 'I can't, I've got indigestion' or 'You'll have to leave, I've got a pain in my side.'

Then I would brush down my trousers and return to Campo de Santana feeling usurped and wretched, mourning, in the darkness of my soul, for the ineffable times when she used to call me 'pudding'!

One July night, soft and black as velvet, the sky sown with stars, I arrived at her house earlier than usual and found the little door open. The oil lamp placed on the landing floor, filled the stairs with light, and there I found Adélia, wearing only a white slip, talking to a young man with a blonde moustache and rather melodramatically draped in a Spanish cloak. When I appeared, large and bearded, with my stick in my hand, Adélia turned deathly pale and he shrank back. Then she smiled, apparently untroubled, honest and pure, and introduced me to her 'nephew Adelino'. He was the son of her sister, Ricardina, the one who lived in Viseu, the brother of little Teodorico ... Taking off my hat, I clasped Senhor Adelino's fingers in my large, loyal palm.

'Delighted to meet you, sir. And how are your mother and your brother? Well, I hope.'

That night Adélia was resplendent and once again she called me 'pudding' and once again she kissed me on the ear. Indeed that whole week was like one long, delicious wedding night. The summer blazed on and the novena of St Joachim had started in Conceição Velha. Feeling happier than the birds chirruping in the trees in Campo de Santana, I would leave home at the quiet time of morning when the streets are still being hosed down. In the bright little living room, with its chairs upholstered in white fustian, I would find my Adélia in her dressing gown, fresh from her bath, smelling of eau de cologne and the pretty red carnations she wore in her hair; and, after the hot mornings, there was nothing more idyllic, nothing sweeter, than our tea-time feasts in the kitchen, eating strawberries by the open window, looking out over green fragments of garden and humble long johns hung out to dry on the line. Then on just such a blissful afternoon, she suddenly asked me to lend her eight *libras*.

Eight *libras*! As I walked down Rua da Magdalena that night, I wondered who could possibly lend me that amount without expecting any interest and without asking any questions. Good Father Casimiro was in Torres, the excellent Rinchão was in Paris ... And I was just considering approaching Father Pinheiro (whose complaints about his backache I always listened to with affectionate sympathy), when who should I see creeping, hunched and stealthy, out of one of those squalid alleyways where Venus wears slippers and a mercenary face, but José Justino, *our* José Justino, the pious secretary of the Brotherhood of St Joseph, that most virtuous of men, my aunt's notary!

I cried out: 'Why, good evening, Justino!' And I walked back to Campo de Santana feeling much calmer and already anticipating the resounding kiss Adélia would give me when I smilingly handed her the eight coins. Early the next day, I hurried to Justino's office, in Praça de São Paulo, and told him the sad tale of a fellow student of mine, tubercular and destitute, reduced to gasping for breath on a mattress in some stinking guesthouse near Largo dos Caldas.

'It's just terrible, Justino! He hasn't even got enough money to buy a bowl of broth. I do what I can, of course, but, devil take it, I'm flat broke at the moment. I just keep him company, that's all I can do, really, that and reading him prayers from *Exercises for a Christian Life*. That was where I was last night. You know, Justino, I really dislike walking those streets so late at night. Heavens, what streets, what indecency, what immorality! Especially those alleyways with the steep steps, eh? When I saw you yesterday, I could tell you were as horrified by it all as I was ... Anyway, I was in the chapel this morning with my aunt, praying for my fellow student and asking our Lord to help him and provide him with some money when, do you know what happened? I thought I heard a voice issuing forth from somewhere immediately above the cross saying: "Come to some agreement with Justino, talk to our Justino, he'll give you eight *libras* for the boy." You can't imagine how grateful I felt to our Lord. And here I am, Justino, on His orders.'

Justino was listening to me, his face as white as his shirt collar, anxiously cracking his knuckles. Then, without saying a word, he placed the eight gold coins, one by one, on the desk. Thus did I serve my Adélia.

Alas, my moment of glory was all too fleeting!

Some days later, I was sitting contentedly in the Café Montanha, sipping iced lemonade, when the waiter came to tell me that a dark young woman wearing a shawl, a Senhora Mariana, was waiting for me on the corner. Good God! Mariana was Adélia's maid. Trembling, I ran to meet her, certain that my beloved must be suffering again with that terrible pain in her side. I even considered saying the rosary of the eighteen appearances of Our Lady of Lourdes, which my aunt claimed to be so efficacious in cases of stitch or runaway bulls.

'Has anything happened, Mariana?'

She led me into an evil-smelling courtyard and there, furiously plucking at her shawl, her eyes red and her voice still hoarse from the row she had had with Adélia, she began telling me vile, abominable, disgusting things about Adélia. How she was deceiving me, how Senhor Adelino was not her nephew, but her lover, her pimp. The moment I left, he arrived. Adélia would hang excitedly about his neck and then they would talk about me and refer to me mockingly as the 'creep', the 'zealot', the 'goat', and even worse calumnies, then they would spit on my portrait. The eight *libras* had been for Adelino to buy a summer suit and they'd had enough left over for them to go to the fair in Belém, in an open carriage and with a guitarist in tow ... Adélia was madly in love with him, she even trimmed his corns, and the way she sighed impatiently whenever he was late resembled nothing so much as the bellowing of deer in the hot forests in May! If I still doubted her, if I still needed proof, then I should go there late that night, after one o'clock, and knock on Adélia's door. Pale as death,

51

leaning against the wall for support, I could not tell if the stench choking me came from some dark corner of the courtyard or from the filth bubbling up out of Mariana's mouth, as if from the pipe of a broken drain. I wiped away the sweat on my brow and murmured, close to fainting:

'That's fine, Mariana, thank you, I'll be there, you take care of yourself.'

I reached home looking so sombre, so sad that my aunt asked me, with a little laugh, if I had 'fallen off my horse'.

'My horse? Good heavens no, Auntie! I was in the Igreja da Graça.'

'It's just that you look so done in and your legs are shaking . . . But anyway, tell me, how did our Lord look today? Lovely, eh?'

'Oh yes, Auntie, he looked wonderful! But, I don't know why, he looked so sad, so very sad. I even said as much to Father Eugénio: "Eugénio," I said, "the Lord is sad today!" And he said to me: "What do you expect, my friend. He sees all the knavery that goes on in this world!" And just look what he sees, Auntie! He sees ingratitude, faithlessness, betrayal!'

I let out a furious roar and clenched my fist as if I were about to bring it smashing down, punitive and terrible, upon all of human perfidy. But I restrained myself, slowly buttoned up my jacket and choked back a sob.

'It's true, Auntie. It so upset me to see the Lord's sadness, it left me feeling quite downcast. And worse still, I had some bad news. A fellow student of mine is very ill, poor lad, on the point of death . . .'

And once again, as I had with Justino (making use of my memories of Xavier in Rua da Fé), I laid out on a putrid mattress the carcass of a fellow student. I spoke of basins full of blood, of no money, not even for a bowl of broth. Such poverty, Auntie, such poverty! And he had always shown such respect for all things holy and wrote so well of them in *The Nation!*'

'Terrible,' murmured Aunt Patrocínio, wielding her knitting needles.

'It certainly is, Auntie. And since he has no family and the people in the house don't take proper care of him, we, his fellow students, are taking it in turns to nurse him. It's my turn tonight. And I wondered if you could give me permission to stay out until about two o'clock in the morning. Another boy takes over from me then, a very learned chap, a deputy.'

Aunt Patrocínio gave me her permission and even offered to ask the patriarch St Joseph to prepare a gentle, joyful death for my fellow student.

'You would be doing him a great favour, Auntie! His name is Macieira ... the one with the squint, just in case St Joseph needs to know.'

I spent the whole night wandering the city, lulled by the soft July moonlight. And two floating, transparent figures accompanied me along every street, one in a night dress, the other in a Spanish cloak, entwined in a passionate embrace and only breaking off from their furious kisses to laugh out loud and call me a 'humbug'.

I reached Rossio just as the clock on the Carmo church was striking one. I stood under the trees there, undecided, smoking a cigarette. Then I turned and made my slow, fearful way towards Adélia's house. A drowsy, flickering light burned in her window. I grasped the heavy door-knocker but hesitated, terrified that what I would find would prove to be categorical, irreparable ... My God, what if Mariana had slandered my Adélia out of revenge! Why only the previous evening she had called me 'sweetheart' and she had said it so ardently. Would it not be more sensible and more to my advantage to believe her, to tolerate her fleeting passion for this Senhor Adelino and to continue, egotistically, to enjoy her kiss on my ear?

But then I was beset by the lacerating thought that she might also kiss Senhor Adelino on the ear and that Senhor Adelino would also moan with pleasure as I did, and I was gripped by a wild desire to batter her scornfully to death, right there on the very steps where she had so often cooed her sweet farewells to me. And then I beat ferociously on the door with my fist as if I were already beating on her frail, ungrateful breast.

I heard the bolt on the window being shot. She appeared in her nightdress, her lovely hair all dishevelled.

'Who the devil is it?'

'It's me, open up.'

She recognised my voice. The light inside went out and it was as if, with the dousing of that lamp, my heart was left in darkness too, cold and empty for ever after. I felt utterly alone, bereft, with nothing to do and nowhere to go. Standing in the middle of the street, I gazed up at the black windows and murmured: 'Ah, my heart will break!'

Adélia's white nightdress reappeared on the verandah.

'I can't let you in. I had a very late supper and I'm really tired!'

'Open up!' I shouted, raising my arms desperately in the air. 'Open up or I'll never come back here again!'

'Go to hell then, and give my regards to Auntie.'

'Drunken slut!'

And having hurled those harsh words back at her like a stone, I marched off down the street, very erect, very dignified. But when I reached the corner, I collapsed in pain and leaned sobbing in a doorway, dissolved in tears, undone.

After that, the slow melancholy of the summer days weighed heavily on my heart. Having told my aunt that I was writing two articles, which I piously intended submitting to the 1878 *Almanac of the Immaculate Conception*, I shut myself up in my bedroom all morning, watching the stone slabs outside on the balcony glittering in the sun. Dragging my slippers across the cool floor, I would brood and sigh over my memories of Adélia or, standing in front of the mirror, I would contemplate the soft part of my ear where she used to kiss me. Then I would hear again the sound of a window being flung open and her treacherous, wounding cry of: 'Go to hell!' Lost, my hair unkempt, I would pound the pillow with the blows I could not vent on Senhor Adelino's narrow chest.

Towards late afternoon, when it grew cooler, I would wander down to the Baixa. But every window open to the evening breeze, every starched muslin curtain reminded me of Adélia's cosy boudoir. A pair of stockings in a shop window was enough to fill me with nostalgic longing and I would see again the perfection of her legs; any luminous object I saw would remind me of her eyes and even the strawberry ice cream I ate in the Café Martinho brought to my lips the taste of her exquisitely sweet kisses.

At night, after taking tea, I would retreat to the chapel, as if to a fortress of sanctity, and gaze upon the golden body of Christ, nailed upon his beautiful blackwood cross. But then the brilliant gleam of precious metal would gradually dim and take on the colour of pale, warm, tender flesh; the skeletal body of the sad Messiah would fill out, become divinely transformed into beautiful curves; lascivious ringlets of black, curly hair would twine amongst the crown of thorns; on his chest, above the two wounds, two rosebud-nippled breasts would bloom, splendid, firm, erect; and I would see my Adélia there on the cross, naked, proud, smiling, victorious, profaning the altar and opening her arms to me!

I did not regard this as a temptation from the Devil; rather it seemed an act of grace from the Lord. I even began mingling my own lover's complaints with the words of my prayers. Perhaps Heaven is capable of gratitude, and all those innumerable saints on whom I had showered novenas and coins wanted to repay my generosity by restoring the caresses stolen from me by that cruel man in the Spanish cloak. I placed more flowers on the bureau before the lithograph of Our Lady of Grace and Favour and poured out to her all the sorrows of my heart. Through the clear glass, her sad eyes lowered, she became the confidante of the torments of my flesh and every night I would stand there in my long johns before going to bed and murmur ardently to her:

'Dear Senhora do Patrocínio, Our Lady of Grace and Favour, make Adélia love me again!'

Then I appealed to my aunt to use her influence amongst those saints who were her particular friends – kind, forgiving St Joseph and St Luís Gonzaga, so kind to the young. I asked her to intervene for me over a particular problem of mine, secret but utterly pure. She agreed with alacrity and I would spy on her through the curtains, relishing the sight of that rigid woman on her knees, rosary in hand, praying to the chaste patriarchs for Adélia once again to kiss me on the ear.

One night, quite early, I went to see if Heaven had heeded those worthy prayers. I got as far as Adélia's door and, trembling all over, I grasped the humble doorknocker. Senhor Adelino came to the window in his shirtsleeves.

'It's me, Senhor Adelino,' I mumbled abjectly, removing my hat. 'I'd like to speak to Adélia.'

I heard him mumble my name in the direction of the bedroom. I think he even used the word 'creep'. And from within, from amongst the curtains round the bed, where I imagined her lying all rumpled and beautiful, came my Adélia's angry voice:

'Empty the bucket of dirty water over him!'

I fled.

Towards the end of September, Rinchão arrived back from Paris and one Sunday evening, about the time of the novena in São Caetano, as I was going into the Café Martinho, I found him there, surrounded by a crowd of several other young men, loudly recounting tales of his deeds of love and feats of amorous audacity in Paris. Glumly, I pulled up a chair and sat down to listen to him. With his ruby tiepin in the shape of a horseshoe, his monocle dangling on its long ribbon, a yellow rose in his buttonhole, Rinchão cut an impressive figure as, wreathed in cigar smoke, he hinted at the high esteem in which he was held there: 'One night in the Café de La Paix, when I was dining with Cora, Valtesse and a terribly chic young man, a prince in fact ...' The things Rinchão had seen! The things Rinchão had experienced! A mad Italian countess called Popotte, who was related to the Pope, had fallen in love with him and used to take him for drives along the Champs-Elysées in her carriage emblazoned with her coat of arms: two crossed horns. He had dined in restaurants lit by golden candelabra, full of pale, serious waiters who addressed him respectfully as M. le Comte. And the Alcazar, its trees festooned with lights, and Paulina, her arms bare, singing 'Saucisson de Marseilles' had shown him the true meaning and grandeur of civilisation.

'Did you see Victor Hugo?' asked a young man in dark glasses, chewing his nails.

'Oh no, he was never in with the really chic set!'

All that week, the idea of one day visiting Paris — tempting and bursting with sweet promise — flickered incessantly in my mind. And it wasn't so much a desire to savour the twin pleasures of pride and the flesh, on which Rinchão had gorged himself, as a longing to leave Lisbon, where churches and shops, the clear river and the clear sky, all reminded me of Adélia, of the sour man in the Spanish cloak, of the kiss on the ear, lost for ever . . . Ah, if only my aunt would open her green silk purse, let me plunge in my hands, grab some gold coins and depart for Paris!

But, as far as Senhora Dona Patrocínio was concerned, Paris was a foul place, full of lies and greed, where a saintless people, their hands stained with the blood of their own archbishops, were all perpetually engaged, day and night, in some form of lax behaviour. How could I possibly tell my aunt of my immodest desire to visit that place of lewdness and moral darkness?

That Sunday, however, when her favourite friends were dining with her at Campo de Santana, Father Casimiro happened to mention, over the stew, that a wise fellow student of his had recently left the tranquillity of his cell in Varatojo, to take on, amidst great rejoicing, the difficult task of running the cathedral in Lamego. Our modest Casimiro could not understand that longing to wear a mitre frivolously studded with precious stones: for him, the pinnacle of ecclesiastical life was no more nor less than finding himself at the age of sixty, healthy and happy, with no regrets or fears, eating Senhora Dona Patrocínio das Neves' delicious baked rice.

'Because, dear lady, it really must be said, your rice is absolute perfection! And it seems to me that there could be no more legitimate, no finer ambition for a righteous soul than that of enjoying this rice in the company of a few appreciative friends.'

And thus we went on to discuss the proper ambitions that each of us, without offence to God, might nurture in his breast. That of Justino, the notary public, was to have a little country house in Minho, with rosebushes and vine trellises, where he could sit in his shirtsleeves and quietly live out his old age.

'But Justino,' said my aunt, 'surely you'd miss the mass at Conceição Velha ... When you're used to hearing one particular mass, no other will do. If I couldn't go to mass at the church at Santana, I think I'd simply pine away.'

That was the church where Father Pinheiro celebrated mass, and my aunt lovingly placed another chicken wing on his plate, whilst Father Pinheiro in turn revealed his burning ambition. It was a lofty, holy ambition. All he wanted was to see the Pope restored to that strong and fecund throne on which Leo X had sat resplendent.

'If only he were treated with a little more charity!' exclaimed my aunt. 'But the thought of the Holy Father, the sweet vicar of Our Lord, in a dungeon, in rags, lying on straw. It's the kind of treatment you'd expect from a Caiaphas!'

She took a sip of warm water and withdrew into the quiet of her soul to say the Ave Maria she always offered up for the health of the Pontiff and for an end to his captivity.

Dr Margaride said consolingly that, as far as he knew, the Pontiff did not actually have to sleep on straw. Indeed, enlightened travellers had assured him that the Holy Father could, if he wanted to, have the use of a carriage.

'I know that's not everything, and it falls far short of what behoves the man who wears the triple crown, but nevertheless, my dear lady, a carriage is a great comfort.'

Then Father Casimiro, smiling, enquired (since everyone else was revealing their ambitions) what the learned and eminent Dr Margaride would wish for.

'Yes, Dr Margaride, tell us your ambition!' we all shouted affectionately.

He smiled gravely.

'First, Dona Patrocínio, dear lady, allow me to help myself to a little of the braised tongue presently making its way towards us and which looks absolutely delicious.'

Once he had filled his plate, the venerable magistrate confessed that he would like to be a member of the Upper House. Not out of any love of titles or splendid liveries, but in order to defend the sacred principle of authority.

'And that's the only reason,' he added energetically. 'Because, before I die, I would also, if Dona Patrocínio will permit me the expression, like to deal a mortal blow to atheism and anarchy. And I would too, given the chance!'

Everyone fervently declared Dr Margaride more than worthy of such social heights and he thanked us all with due gravity. Then he turned to me, his face majestic and pale:

'And what about our Teodorico? You haven't yet told us what your ambition is.'

I blushed: Paris gleamed in the depths of my desire, with the golden candelabra, its countesses who were also cousins of the pope, its champagne bubbles – fascinating, intoxicating and guaranteed to dull all pain. But I lowered my eyes and said I aspired only to kneel at my aunt's side and say my prayers profitably and peaceably.

Dr Margaride, however, lay down his knife and fork and pressed me to say more. He did not think it would be considered an affront to God or ingratitude to my aunt, if I, a graduate and an intelligent, healthy young man, were to nurture some honest desire . . .

'And I do!' I declared roundly, like someone hurling a spear. 'I do, Dr Margaride. I would love to go to Paris.'

'Heavens!' cried Dona Patrocínio, horrified. 'Go to Paris!'

'Just to see the churches, Auntie!'

'There's no need to go all that way just to see nice churches,' she replied harshly. 'When it comes to organ music and splendidly dressed saints and fine street processions and lovely voices and respect and wonderful images, no one can beat the Portuguese!'

I fell silent, crushed. And the enlightened Dr Margaride applauded my aunt's ecclesiastical patriotism. Naturally one would not go to some godless republic in search of religious splendours.

'No, dear lady, if I had time, and wanted to savour the great artefacts of our holy religion, I wouldn't go to Paris. Do you know where I would go?'

'You'd make straight for Rome,' said Father Pinheiro.

'Come now, Father Pinheiro! Come now, dear lady!'

What did he mean? Neither the good Father Pinheiro nor my aunt could imagine what could possibly be better than pontifical Rome. Then Dr Margaride solemnly raised his eyebrows, dense and black as ebony.

'I would go to the Holy Land, Dona Patrocínio! I would go to Palestine, dear lady! I would go and see Jerusalem and the Jordan! I would like to stand for a moment on Golgotha, as Chateaubriand did, my hat in my hand, just thinking and taking it all in and be able to say: '*Salve!*' And I would make sketches, dear lady, and publish my historical impressions. That's where I would go . . . I'd go to Zion!'

The roast pork had just been served and, in response to this evocation of the holy land where our Lord had suffered, a reverent silence hovered over our plates. Far, far off, I seemed to see Arabia, reached only after days of exhausting travel on the back of a camel: a pile of ruins around a cross; a sinister river flowing beside it through olive groves; the sky arching above it, silent and sad as the vault of a tomb. That must be what Jerusalem was like.

'A wonderful journey!' murmured Father Casimiro, pensively.

'And of course,' said Father Pinheiro in a low voice, as if whispering a prayer, 'our Lord Jesus Christ looks with great appreciation and gratitude upon such visits to his Holy Sepulchre.'

Justino said: 'They say that anyone who goes there comes back shriven of all their sins. Isn't that so, Pinheiro? I read it in *Panorama*. They come back from there innocent as babes!'

Father Pinheiro (having regretfully declined the cauliflower, which he considered indigestible) clarified the point. Anyone who went on a devout pilgrimage to the Holy Land would receive a plenary indulgence from the hands of the patriarch of Jerusalem on the marble slab of the Holy Sepulchre itself, once they had paid the necessary fees of course . . .

'And not only for himself, according to what I've heard,' added the learned cleric, 'but for any beloved and devout family member who has been certified unable to make the trip themselves. Though that, of course, costs you double.'

'For example,' exclaimed Dr Margaride, inspired, clapping me hard on the back, 'for a kind aunt, an adored aunt, an aunt who has been an angel of virtue and generosity . . .'

'Yes,' said Father Pinheiro again, 'but it does cost you double.'

My aunt said nothing. Her dark glasses, looking from the priest to the magistrate and back again, seemed strangely dilated as if glinting with the inner gleam of an idea; a little blood had flushed her sallow cheeks. Vicência served the rice pudding. We all said grace.

Later on in my room, as I undressed, I felt infinitely sad. My aunt would never allow me to visit the lewd land of France and I would remain cloistered in Lisbon where everything was a torment to me; even its most bustling streets weighed upon the desert of my heart, and even the purity of its fine summer skies reminded me of the terrible perfidy of the one who had been my star, my queen of Grace . . . Later that day, at supper, my aunt seemed to me even more robust and solid, built to last, and sure to remain the keeper of her green silk purse and all of Knight

Commander G. Godinho's property and money for many years to come. Alas, how much longer would I have to kneel beside that hideous old woman and say those tedious rosaries, to kiss the feet of Our Lord of the Stations of the Cross begrimed by the lips of noblewomen, to trudge to novenas and bruise my knees before the scrawny figure of a suffering God? Oh most bitter of lives! And now I no longer had Adélia's soft arms to console me in my tiresome service of Christ.

In the morning, once my horse was harnessed and I had put on my spurs, I went to see if my aunt had any pious message for St Roch, it being his day of miracles. In the sitting room devoted to the glories of St Joseph, my aunt, perched at one end of the sofa, her Tonkin shawl fallen from about her shoulders, was examining her large accounts book, which lay open on her lap. Opposite her, not saying a word, his hands behind his back, good Father Casimiro was smiling thoughtfully at the flowers on the carpet.

'Come in, come in!' he said, as soon as I appeared, bowing low. 'Have you heard the news? You're a pearl among men, a respecter of the old and deserving of everything given you by God and by your aunt. Come here and let me embrace you!'

I smiled uneasily. My aunt was closing up her accounts book.

'Teodorico ...' she began, crossing her arms stiffly. 'Teodorico, I've been discussing matters with Father Casimiro and I've decided that someone close to me, a blood relative, should make a pilgrimage to the Holy Land on my behalf.'

'What do you say, you lucky chap?' murmured Casimiro, glowing.

'So,' continued my aunt, 'it has been decided that you are to visit Jerusalem and all the other holy places. And there's no need to thank me: you're doing this to please me and to honour the tomb of Jesus Christ because I cannot go there myself. Since, praise be to our Lord, I do not lack money, you will make this journey in the greatest comfort and, to avoid any unnecessary delays, and in my haste to gratify the Lord, you will leave this month. Now, be off with you, I have to talk to Father Casimiro. And no, thank you, I have no message for St Roch, I know where I stand with him.'

I stammered out: 'Thank you, Auntie, thank you very much, and goodbye, Father Casimiro.' In a state of shock, I walked on down the corridor. In my room I ran to my mirror to contemplate, amazed, this face and this beard that would soon be coated with the dust of Jerusalem. Then I fell back onto my bed.

'What a bore!'

Jerusalem! Where *was* Jerusalem? I ran to the trunk containing my schoolbooks and my old clothes. I pulled out an atlas and, with it open on the desk, before the image of Our Lady of Grace and Favour, I started looking for Jerusalem: where the Infidels live, where dark caravans wend their way and where a little water in a well is like a precious gift from the Lord.

I could already feel in my wandering finger the weariness of a long journey; I paused on the tortuous bank of a river which I supposed to be the holy Jordan. It was the Danube. And then suddenly the name Jerusalem leapt out at me, black in a vast white wilderness by the sea, with no names or borders, just bare sand. There was Jerusalem. My God! It looked so remote, bleak and sad!

But then I began to consider that in order to reach that penitential soil, I would have to cross friendly, feminine lands, full of fun. First came lovely Andalusia, perfumed with orange blossom, the land of María Santíssima, where, to tame the most rebellious heart, the women had only to stick two carnations in their hair and throw on a scarlet shawl, ¡bendita sea su gracia! Beyond lay Naples and her hot, dark streets, lined with altars to the Virgin and smelling of women, like the corridors of a whorehouse. Further away still was Greece. Ever since my classes in Rhetoric, I had always imagined Greece as a sacred wood of laurel trees through whose branches one would glimpse the gleaming white pediments of temples and where, in the shady places where doves coo, Venus suddenly appears, pink and luminous, offering up to all lips, be they bestial or divine, the gift of her immortal breasts. Venus no longer lived in Greece, but the women there had preserved the splendour of her form and the charm of her immodesty. God, what pleasures lay in prospect! An intense light seared my heart and I cried out, bringing my fist down hard on the atlas, making our chaste Lady of Grace and Favour and all the stars on her crown tremble.

'Oh yes, I'm really going to get my fill!'

Oh yes, full to the brim! And fearing that my aunt, out of avarice for her gold or distrust of my piety, might suddenly decide against that pilgrimage so full of pleasurable promise, I resolved to make it supernaturally binding, by divine order. I went to the chapel, rumpled my hair, as if a celestial breeze had blown through it, and then I ran to my aunt's room, eyes wide, arms trembling.

'Oh, Auntie, do you know what just happened? I was in the chapel giving a prayer of thanksgiving and suddenly I seemed to hear the voice of our Lord, coming from just above the cross, speaking in a low voice, though without moving his lips: "Teodorico, you do well to go and visit my Holy Sepulchre. And I am most contented with your aunt too. Your aunt is one of my own!"'

She clasped her hands in a fiery transport of love:

'Praised be His holy name! Did He really say that? Ah, He may well have, for our Lord knows that it is in order to honour Him that I'm sending you there. Praise be His holy name. Praise to Him on the Earth and in Heaven! Go, my boy, go and pray, pray to Him. You can never pray too much.'

And I left, murmuring an Ave Maria. Then, in a rush of kindness, she ran to the door:

'And Teodorico, see what underwear you need. You might have to get some more long johns. Order whatever you need, my child, for thanks to Our Lady of the Rosary, I have money enough and I want you to be decently clothed when you appear before the dear tomb of God!'

I ordered everything I needed and, having bought a *Guide to the Orient* and a pith helmet, I went to Benjamim Sarrosa & Co. owned by a wise Jew (who always took the precaution of wearing a turban on his annual trip to Morocco to buy oxen) to find out which would be the most enjoyable route to Jerusalem. Benjamim drew a detailed map of my great itinerary on a piece of paper. I would embark on the *Málaga*, a steamship run by Jadley & Co., which would carry me across an eternally blue sea, via Gibraltar and then Malta, to the ancient land of Egypt. There I would enjoy a sensual respite in festive Alexandria. Thence I would sail up the holy coast of Syria on the Levant steamship and disembark in Jaffa, city of verdant orchards, and from there, after a day and a night spent trotting along a macadam road on a gentle mare, I would see the walls of Jerusalem rising up black amongst the sad hills!

'Damn it, Benjamim, it seems to involve an awful lot of sea and steamships. Can't I see even a little bit of Spain? I want to have a good time, man!'

'You can have a good time in Alexandria. It has everything. Billiard halls, carriages, gambling, women . . . Only the best. That's where you can enjoy yourself!'

Meanwhile, my saintly enterprise was already the main topic of conversation in the Café Montanha and in Brito's cigar store. One morning, I read — scarlet with pride — these honorific lines in the *Jornal das Novidades*: 'Departing shortly for a visit to Jerusalem and all the holy places in which our Redeemer suffered for us, is our friend Teodorico Raposo, the nephew of the Senhora Dona Patrocínio das Neves, wealthy landowner and model of Christian virtue. We wish him *Bon voyage!*' My aunt, overcome, kept the newspaper in the chapel, underneath St Joseph's pedestal and I rejoiced to imagine Adélia's fury (she was a regular reader of the *Jornal*) when she saw me setting off without her, laden with gold, to those Muslim lands, where at every step one stumbles on a harem set amongst the sycamores, silent and smelling of roses . . .

The eve of my departure, in the damask living room, was heavy with lofty sentiment and solemnity. Justino regarded me as one would a historical figure.

'Imagine, our Teodorico ... What a journey! ... This will really give people something to talk about!'

Father Pinheiro murmured unctuously:

'It was an inspiration from our Lord! And it'll be so good for your health!'

Then I showed everyone my pith helmet. They all admired it. Casimiro, after scratching his chin thoughtfully, remarked that a top hat might lend me more gravity.

My aunt, in some distress, agreed:

'That's exactly what I said. It lacks dignity. After all, it is to be worn in the city in which our Lord died!'

'But, Auntie, I've already explained. This is just for the desert. Obviously in Jerusalem, in all those holy places, I'll wear a top hat.'

'It does always look more gentlemanly,' said Dr Margaride.

Father Pinheiro enquired solicitously if I had all the medicines I needed, in case of some intestinal contretemps whilst in one of those Biblical deserts.

'I've got everything. Benjamim made me a list. I've even got linseed oil and arnica.'

The sluggish clock in the corridor began to groan out ten o'clock: I had to get up early. And Dr Margaride was already sadly wrapping his silk scarf around his neck. Then, before we all embraced, I asked my loyal friends what little 'souvenir' they'd like me to bring back for them from those remote lands in which our Lord had once lived. Father Pinheiro wanted a bottle of water from the Jordan. Justino (who, when we were standing by the window, had already asked me for a packet of Turkish tobacco) wanted only an olive branch from the Mount of Olives. Dr Margaride would be content with a good photograph of the tomb of Jesus Christ that he could have framed ...

With my notebook open, having listed these pious commissions, I turned to my aunt, smiling, affectionate, humble.

'As for me,' she said, sitting in the middle of the sofa as if on an altar, stiff in her Sunday satins, 'all I want is for you to make the journey in a spirit of devotion, leaving no stone unkissed, no novena unsaid, no place unprayed in . . . Apart from that, I hope only that you enjoy good health.'

I was about to place a grateful kiss on her glittering, beringed hand when she stopped me, suddenly proud and cold:

'Up until now you've been sensible, you've kept the commandments, you haven't given in to temptation . . . Which is why you'll rejoice to see the olive groves where our Lord sweated blood and to drink from the river Jordan. But if I ever found out that during this journey you once entertained evil thoughts, gave in to temptation or chased after women, you can be quite sure that, despite being my only surviving blood relative and despite having visited Jerusalem and received indulgences, you'd be put out on the street, without a crust of bread, like a dog!'

I bowed my head, terrified. And my aunt, having dabbed at her thin lips with her lace handkerchief, continued in a more authoritative tone and with growing emotion, which provoked something resembling the fleeting rise and fall of a human breast beneath her silk bodice:

'And now, for your own good, I want to say just one thing!'

Everyone was standing in reverent silence, realising that my aunt was about to make some supreme utterance. At this moment of separation, surrounded by her priests, surrounded by her magistrates, Dona Patrocínio das Neves, was clearly going to reveal her real reason for sending me, nephew and pilgrim, to the city of Jerusalem. I would finally learn, as surely as if she had written it on a parchment scroll, what would be the most precious of my duties, sleeping or waking, in the land of the Gospels!

'Just this!' declared my aunt. 'If you feel that I deserve some reward for all that I have done for you since your mother died, educating you, clothing you, giving you a horse to ride, watching over your soul, then bring me some holy relic from one of those holy places, a miraculous relic that I may keep, that I can cleave to in my sufferings and that will cure me of my ills.'

And for the first time, after fifty years of drought, one brief tear ran down my aunt's face, from beneath her dark glasses.

Dr Margaride burst out rashly:

'Teodorico, you see how your aunt loves you! Search through those ruins, scrutinise those tombs! Bring back a relic for your aunt!'

Exalted, I shouted out:

'Auntie, I'll bring you back a splendid relic, on my word of honour!'

In the severe, damask-lined room, the clamorous, genuine emotions filling our hearts finally overflowed. I felt Justino's lips, still moist with buttered toast, planted on my beard.

Early on Sunday morning, the sixth of September, the day of St Libânia, I knocked cautiously at my aunt's door; she was still asleep in her chaste bed. I heard the muffled sound of her slippers approaching across the carpet. Shyly, in her nightdress, she half-opened the door and, through the crack, she poked one pale, scrawny hand that smelled of snuff. I felt like biting it, but instead I placed on it an obsequious kiss. My aunt murmured:

'Goodbye, my child. Give my love to our Lord!'

I went down the stairs, my pith helmet on already, my *Guide to the Orient* under my arm. Behind me Vicência was sobbing.

My new leather suitcase and my heavy canvas bag filled Pingalho's carriage. The last swallows were singing in the eaves; in the chapel of the church at Santana the bells were being rung for mass. And a ray of sun from the East, welcoming and cheerful, coming all the way from Palestine to greet me, bathed my face, like a caress from the Lord Himself.

I closed the door of the carriage, stretched out my legs and cried: 'Off we go, Pingalho!'

And thus, as a wealthy pilgrim, puffing the smoke from my cigar out onto the breeze, I left my aunt's house on my way to Jerusalem!

II

It was a Sunday, on St Hieronymus' day, that my Catholic feet finally stepped onto the quay at Alexandria, land of the Orient, sensual and religious. I gave thanks to Our Lord of Safe Journeys. And my travelling companion, the illustrious Topsius, a German doctor from the University of Bonn and a member of the Imperial Institute of Historical Research, unfurled his vast green sunshade and murmured, as gravely as if it were an invocation:

'Egypt, Egypt, I greet you, swarthy Egypt! And may your god Phthah, god of Literature, god of History, inspirational god of Art and Truth, prove propitious! . . .'

Above the buzz of science, I felt myself wrapped in a warm outbreath of air, like the air in a hothouse, languorously tinged with the scents of sandalwood and roses. On the glittering quay, amongst the bales of wool, sprawled the customs shed, banal and squalid. But beyond that, white doves fluttered around white minarets; the sky was dazzling. Surrounded by stately palms, a languid palace slept by the edge of the water and, far off, the sands of ancient Libya faded into nothing, a blur of hot, whirling, lion-coloured dust.

I fell immediately in love with that land of indolence, dreams and light. And leaping into the calico-upholstered caleche that would take us to the Hotel of the Pyramids, I in turn invoked the gods, as had the learned doctor from Bonn:

'Egypt, Egypt, I greet you, swarthy Egypt! And may . . .'

But, smiling and clutching my hat box to him, that most erudite of men chimed in:

'No, Dom Raposo, the deity you need to invoke is Isis, the amorous cow!'

I did not understand, but I bowed to his greater knowledge. I had met Topsius one cool morning in Malta, while

I was buying violets from a flower girl - in whose large eyes there was already a hint of oriental languor – as he was carefully measuring out, with his sunshade, the martial and monastic walls of the Grand Master's palace.

Thinking it was one's spiritual and pedagogical duty, in those lands of the Levant so steeped in history, to measure the monuments of Antiquity, I took out my handkerchief and, using its length as a measure, began laying it end on end along the austere masonry. Topsius threw me a distrustful, jealous glance over the top of his gold-rimmed spectacles. But, reassured no doubt by my plump, jocund face, by my musk-scented gloves and my frivolous little bunch of violets, he then courteously raised his black silk beret to me, revealing his long, straight corn-coloured hair. I reciprocated, raising my pith helmet in greeting, and we began to talk. I told him my name, where I came from and of the pious reasons behind my journey to Jerusalem. He told me that he was a native of glorious Germany and that he too was on his way to Judaea, thence on to Galilee, on a scientific pilgrimage to make notes for his next formidable work, *The History of the Herods*. But he was staying in Alexandria to collect the weighty material he needed for another monumental book, *The History of the Ptolemies* – for both those turbulent families were the historical property of the learned Topsius.

'Well, Dr Topsius, since we're following the same route, why don't we join forces!'

The tall, spindly, long-legged figure, wearing a short silk jacket bulging with manuscripts, bowed delightedly:

'Why not, Dom Raposo! What more charming way to save money!'

With his chin sunk in his collar, his dishevelled hair, sharp, pensive nose and thin legs, my erudite friend looked like a comical but very learned stork, wearing gold-rimmed spectacles perched on the end of its beak. But my animal nature was completely won over by his intellect and we went off to drink beer together.

This young fellow's learning was a hereditary gift. His

maternal grandfather, the naturalist Schlock, wrote a famous treatise in eight volumes on *Facial Expression in Lizards* that astonished all Germany. And at the age of seventy-seven, his uncle, old Topsius, the notable Egyptologist, dictated from his armchair, where he was laid up with gout, that most brilliant and accessible of books: *The Monotheistic Synthesis of Egyptian Theology as Illustrated in the Relationship of the Gods Phthah and Imhotep with the Nome Triads*.

Topsius' father, unfortunately, despite this lofty family tradition of learning, played the bass cornett in a small band in Munich. But my companion had taken up the tradition once more and, at only twenty-two years of age, in nineteen brilliant articles published in the *Weekly Bulletin of Historical Research*, had clarified once and for all the problem, vital to Civilisation, of a brick wall erected by King Pi-Sibkme of the twenty-first dynasty, around the temple of Ramses II in the legendary city of Tanis. Today, in Germany's scientific community, Topsius' opinion on this wall blazes forth as irrefutably as the sun.

I have only the warmest, loftiest memories of Topsius. Whether on the rough seas of Tyre, in the tawny streets of Jerusalem, sleeping side by side in our tent by the ruins of Jericho, or riding the green paths of Galilee, I always found him instructive, helpful, patient and discreet. I rarely understood his sonorous, well-turned sentences, precious as gold medallions, but I nonetheless bowed to his greater learning. It was like standing before the impenetrable door of some sanctuary, knowing that inside, in the shadows, gleamed the pure essence of Idea. But Dr Topsius was also not above snarling the occasional foul oath, and then a pleasant communion grew up between him and my simple graduate's intellect. He still owes me thirty *escudos*, but that tiny crumb of money is as nothing compared to the copious wave of historical knowledge with which he enriched my spirit. There was only one thing I disliked about him, apart from his scholarly throat-clearing: his habit of using my toothbrush.

He was also unbearably proud of his own country. He would tilt his chin and spout on endlessly in praise of Germany, spiritual mother of all the peoples of the world; then he would threaten me with the irresistible force of her weapons. Germany the omniscient! Germany the omnipotent! She ruled from a vast encampment entrenched behind manuscripts, where the armed might of Metaphysics prowls and roars! Being proud myself, I disliked such boasting. Thus, when they handed us the register at the Hotel of the Pyramids in which to write our names and our countries of origin, my learned friend signed himself Topsius, arrogantly adding in letters as stiff and disciplined as new recruits: 'of the German Empire'. I seized the pen and, recalling the bearded figure of João de Castro, Hormuz in flames, Adamastor, the Chapel of St Roch, the River Tagus and other such glories, I carefully wrote, in letters curved as the bellying sails of galleons: 'Raposo, Portuguese, Citizen of the World'. And then, from a corner of the room, a thin, shrivelled youth, sighing and apparently on the point of swooning, murmured:

'If the gentleman needs anything, just ask for Alpedrinha.'

A fellow countryman! He told me his sad story as he unbuckled my suitcase. He was a poor unfortunate from Trancoso. He had studied, written a necrology and knew by heart the most heartrending lines penned by Soares de Passos. But the moment his mama had died and he inherited her lands, he had fled to fatal Lisbon, to have fun. In Travessa da Conceição he had met and fallen deeply in love with a charming Spanish girl, blessed with the sweet name of Dulce, and had run off with her to Madrid. There, gambling ruined him, Dulce betrayed him and a pimp knifed him. Restored to health but still weak, he then moved on to Marseilles and for years he dragged himself, like some social pariah, through indescribable miseries. He worked as a sacristan in Rome and as a barber in Athens. In Morea, living in a shack by the shores of a lake, he was given the ghastly job of fishing for leeches; wearing a turban and carrying black leather bottles on his back, he had sold water along the backstreets of Smyrna. Fertile Egypt had always, irresistibly, attracted him ... And so there he was in the Hotel of the Pyramids, sadly working as a porter.

'If the gentleman happens to have brought with him any newspapers from Lisbon, I would very much like to know what the political situation is like there.'

I generously gave him all the copies of the *Jornal de Notícias* in which my boots were wrapped.

The owner of the hotel was a Greek from Lacedaemon, with ferocious moustaches, who spoke a little Spanish. Erect in his black frock coat adorned with a medal, he himself led us respectfully into the dining room – '¡la más preciosa, sin duda, de todo el Oriente, caballeros! – without a doubt the loveliest in the whole of the Orient, gentlemen!'

On the table was a huge bunch of wilting scarlet flowers; the corpses of flies floated familiarly in the oil carafe; the waiter, in slippers, kept stumbling over an old, wine-stained copy of the *Jornal dos Debates* that had been lying there since the previous night, stumbled over by other indolent slippers; on the ceiling, the fetid fumes from the brass candelabra added black clouds of smoke to the painted pink clouds aflutter with angels and swallows. Beneath the balcony, a violin and a harp were playing 'Mandolinata'. And while Topsius drowned his sorrows in beer, I, oddly enough, felt a growing affection for this land of idleness and light.

After coffee, with a pencil and notebook in his jacket pocket, my wise friend set off in search of antiquities and stones from the time of the Ptolemy dynasty. I lit a cigar, called for Alpedrinha and told him that, as a matter of urgency, I needed to find a church to pray in and a woman to love. The prayer was for the benefit of Aunt Patrocínio, for she had commissioned me to say a short prayer to St Joseph the moment I set foot on Egyptian soil, which, ever since the flight of the Holy Family on their donkey, was deemed to be as sacred as a cathedral. The love was necessary to meet the needs of my own bold and passionate heart. Without a word, Alpedrinha raised the blinds and showed me a bright square, its centre adorned by the statue of a bronze hero mounted on a bronze charger. Slow clouds of dust, whipped up by a hot wind, whirled about two dessicated pools surrounded by tall buildings that rose up into the blue, each one bearing its country's flag, like rival citadels built on conquered territory. Then the unfortunate Alpedrinha pointed out to me, on one corner of the square, where an old woman was selling sugar cane, a quiet little street, the Street of the Two Sisters. There (he murmured) I would see a heavy, roughly-carved, wooden hand, painted purple, hanging over the door of a discreet little shop, and above it, on a black plaque, these inviting words in gold: Miss Mary, Gloves and Wax Flowers. That was the refuge he recommended for my heart. At the bottom of the road, next to a weeping fountain set amongst trees, was a new chapel, where my soul would find consolation and shade.

'And tell Miss Mary that you were sent by the Hotel of the Pyramids.'

I put a rose in my buttonhole and left the hotel rejoicing. As I turned into the Street of the Two Sisters I saw the virginal hermitage sleeping chastely beneath the plane trees, lulled by the gentle murmur of the water. But, doubtless, at that hour, our beloved patriarch St Joseph would be attending to more urgent prayers uttered by far nobler lips than mine: I did not want to inconvenience that kindest of saints and so I stopped by the purple, wooden hand that seemed to be there waiting, stretched out and open, to clutch at my heart.

In a state of some excitement, I went in. Behind the polished counter, next to a vase of roses and magnolias, she was sitting reading her copy of *The Times*, a white cat on her lap. What immediately attracted me were her eyes which were pale blue – indeed china blue – candid, celestial eyes such as I had never seen in dusky Lisbon. Even more enchanting though was her hair: a fuzz of tight golden curls, so soft and fine that one longed, eternally, devotedly, to be able to run one's tremulous fingers through them. The secular halo of light that her hair formed about her plump little face, white as milk with just a touch of crimson, so tender and succulent, was irresistible. Smiling, and modestly lowering her dark eyelashes, she asked me if I wanted 'fur' or 'suede'.

Sliding impatiently along the counter, I murmured:

'Alpedrinha sent me.'

From the vase of flowers she chose one shy rosebud and held it out to me in her fingertips. I bit passionately into its petals. And the voracity of that caress seemed to please her, for her cheeks flushed more hotly and she said quietly: 'Naughty, naughty.' I forgot all about St Joseph and my prayer to him - her hands and mine were joined momentarily as she slipped a pale glove over my fingers and they remained thus indissolubly linked during all the weeks I spent in the city of the Ptolemies, as I revelled in joyous, infidel pleasures!

She was from Yorkshire, that heroic county of old England, where the women bloom strong and untrammelled as the roses that grow in their royal gardens. Because of her sweet nature and her golden peal of laughter when I tickled her, I bestowed on her the cacophonous but affectionate nickname of Maricoquinhas. Topsius, who admired her, called her 'our very own Cleopatra'. She loved my black, bushy beard and, so as not to have to leave the warmth of her skirts even for a moment, I saw nothing of Cairo, the Nile, or the eternal Sphinx waiting at the gateway to the desert, smiling at vain Humanity.

Dressed all in white, like a lily, I enjoyed ineffable mornings, leaning on Mary's balcony, respectfully stroking her cat's back. She was very quiet, but the way she crossed her arms and smiled at me or the delicate way she folded *The Times*, flooded my heart with luminous joy. She did not even have to call me 'her brave little Portuguese lover, her sweetie pie'. It was enough for me to watch the rise and fall of her breast; indeed, I would happily have made the trip to Alexandria just to see that sweet, languid undulation, knowing that its sole cause was her longing for my kisses; I would have gone even farther afield, travelled on foot, without respite, to where the waters of the Nile run white! In the evenings, ensconced in the calico-upholstered caleche with our learned friend Topsius, we would take long, delicious rides by the Mamoudieh canal. Beneath the leafy trees, close by the walls of seraglio gardens, I would smell the troubling scent of magnolias and other intense perfumes to which I could not put a name. Occasionally a soft purple or white flower would drop into my lap; with a sigh I would rub my beard against Maricoquinhas' soft cheek and she would tremble in response. In the water lay the heavy boats that travel up the sacred and beneficent Nile, anchoring alongside ruined temples, sailing past the green islands where the crocodiles sleep. Gradually, night would fall. We rolled leisurely along through the fragrant dark. Topsius would murmur verses by Goethe. And the palm trees on the opposite shore would stand silhouetted against the yellow sunset like a bronze relief set against a sheet of gold.

Maricoquinhas always dined with us at the Hotel of the Pyramids and, in her presence, Topsius would blossom into a thousand flowers of amiable erudition. He would describe to us the evening festivities in the old Alexandria of the Ptolemies, along the canal that flowed towards Canopus: both banks would be resplendent with palaces and gardens; silk-canopied boats would be rowed along to the sound of lutes; the priests of Osiris, dressed in leopard skins, would dance beneath the orange trees; and on the terraces, the ladies of Alexandria would remove their veils and drink to Venus Assyria, using lotus flowers as chalices. A diffuse sensuality softened their very souls. Even their philosophers were dissolute.

'And,' Topsius would say, rolling his eyes, 'in the whole of Alexandria there was only one chaste woman; she wrote commentaries on Horace and was Seneca's aunt. Only one, imagine!'

77

Maricoquinhas would sigh. How delightful it must have been to live in Alexandria then and to sail down to Canopus beneath an awning of silk!

'What, without me?' I would say with a jealous yelp.

And she would swear that without her brave little Portuguese lover she would not want to live even in Heaven!

Delighted, I would pay for more champagne.

And so the days passed, light, languid, delicious and interspersed with kisses, until the sombre eve of our departure for Jerusalem.

'What the gentleman should do,' said Alpedrinha that morning as he was polishing my boots, 'is to stay here in Alexandria and just enjoy yourself . . .'

Ah, if only I could! But Auntie's orders could not be disobeyed! And out of love for her gold, I was obliged to travel on to the dark city of Jerusalem, to kneel before withered olive trees, stand by cold tombs mumbling the rosary . . .

'Have you ever been to Jerusalem, Alpedrinha?' I asked, disconsolately, pulling on my underpants.

'No, sir, but I know what it's like . . . It's worse than Braga!'

'Good God!'

That night, supper in my room with Maricoquinhas was full of silences and sighs: the candles were as melancholy as funeral torches; the wine clouded our spirits like funeral wine. Topsius offered generous consolation:

'Sweet lady, Raposo is bound to come back . . . I'm certain that he will return from the ardent land of Syria, from the land of Venus and of the Beloved in the Song of Solomon, with a still brighter, more vigorous flame burning in his heart.'

I bit my lip, overcome with emotion.

'You'll see! We will ride once more along the canal of Mamoudieh in our caleche. I'm just going to say a few paternosters at Calvary. It'll do me good. I'll come back like a lion.'

After coffee we went and leaned over the balcony to gaze silently up at the sumptuous Egyptian night. The stars were like a great dusty cloud of light kicked up by the good Lord as he walked alone along the roads of Heaven. The silence had the solemnity of a shrine. On the dark terraces below, we occasionally saw something white moving, barely perceptible, showing that other people were there too, like us, letting their dumb souls drink in the sidereal splendour; and in that diffusely religious mood, like that of a crowd gaping, open-mouthed, at the candles on an altar, I felt the sweet words of the Ave Maria rise irresistibly to my lips . . .

Far off the sea was sleeping. And in the hot light of the stars, I could just make out, on a tongue of sand, almost lapped by the waters, an empty house, tiny, white and poetical, standing between two palm trees. And I set to thinking that, as soon as Auntie died and her money was mine, I could buy that sweet retreat, line its walls with lovely silks, dress like a Turk and live side by side with Maricoquinhas, cool, serene, free from all the disquiets of civilisation. Making atonement to the Sacred Heart of Jesus would be a matter of as much indifference to me then as are the wars kings wage amongst themselves. I would demand from Heaven only the indigo light that bathed my windows and from the Earth only the flowers blooming in my garden, to perfume my contentment. And I would spend my days in a soft, oriental idleness, smoking Turkish cigars, strumming a guitar, immersed for ever in that perfect happiness I felt when I watched the rise and fall of Mary's bosom and heard her call me 'her brave little Portuguese lover'.

I clasped her to me as if to drink her in. I mumbled ineffable names into her shell-white ear, I called her 'plumpling', 'my little love'. She trembled and raised her sad eyes to the cloud of golden dust.

'Just look at all those stars! I do hope the sea's calm tomorrow.'

Then, at the thought of those long waves that would

carry me off to the harsh lands of the Gospels, so far from my dear Mary, a feeling of infinite sorrow filled my breast and, irrepressibly, a tuneful wail escaped my lips, full of plangent longing . . . I sang. Out over the sleeping terraces of Muslim Alexandria, I loosed my sorrowing voice, my face turned to the stars above; and strumming my fingers on the front of my double-breasted jacket where the frets of my guitar would be, my voice trembling tearfully, I sighed out the *fado* that best expresses that most Portuguese of sentiments: *saudade*.

> My soul rests here with you, Maria,
> I take with me only my pain.
> For I feel in my heart of hearts, Maria,
> That never will I see you again.

I stopped, overwhelmed by passion. The ever erudite Topsius wanted to know if those sweet verses had been written by Luís de Camões. No, I whimpered, I had first heard the song performed in the Café Dafundo by a singer called 'Calcinhas'.

Topsius withdrew to note down the name of this great poet, 'Calcinhas'. I shut the window and after first going out into the corridor to make the sign of the cross, rapidly and furtively, I returned to my room and impatiently unlaced, for the very last time, my delicious beloved's corset.

How brief, how parsimoniously brief, was that starry Egyptian night!

Early, bitterly early, the Greek from Lacedaemon came to tell me that the steamship – that went by the ferocious name of *The Cayman* – was already in the bay, belching smoke, with a good head of steam up, the ship that was to carry me off to the sad wastes of Israel.

Señor Topsius, the earlybird, was already downstairs breakfasting in leisurely fashion on ham and eggs and a vast mug of beer. I drank only a sip of coffee in my room, leaning on one corner of the sideboard in my shirtsleeves, my eyes red and misted with tears. My heavy leather trunk was blocking the corridor, its lid fastened down, but Alpedrinha was still hurriedly cramming dirty clothes into my canvas bag. And Maricoquinhas, sitting forlornly on the edge of the bed, wearing her sweet little hat decorated with poppies and with dark shadows under her eyes, watched that bundling up of flannels, as if they were fragments of her heart being thrown into the bottom of the bag, to leave and never again return!

'You're taking an awful lot of dirty washing with you, Teodorico!'

'I'll get it washed in Jerusalem, God willing!'

I hung my scapulars around my neck. At that moment Topsius looked round the door; he was smoking a pipe and had his vast sunshade over his arm, large galoshes on his feet, in preparation for the damp promenade deck, and a copy of the Bible stuffed into the pocket of his alpaca jacket. Seeing me still without my waistcoat on, he reprimanded me for my amorous sloth.

'But I understand, lovely lady, I understand!' he said, bowing to Mary, crane-thin and pliant, his glasses perched on the end of his nose. 'It must be painful having to leave the arms of Cleopatra. Anthony lost Rome and all the world for them. I myself, absorbed as I am in my mission, with dim corners of History still to illumine, will carry away with me pleasant memories of these days in Alexandria! Those delicious drives along the Mamoudieh canal! Allow me to pick up your glove, lovely lady. And if I ever return to this land of the Ptolemies, I will not neglect to visit the Street of the Two Sisters: "Miss Mary, Gloves and Wax Flowers". Oh yes, I'll remember. I hope you'll allow me to send you a copy of my *History of the Ptolemies*, once it's finished? There are many piquant details ... When Cleopatra fell in love with Herod, the king of Judaea ...'

But a flustered Alpedrinha was shouting from the side of the bed:

'Sir, there's more dirty washing here!'

Rummaging amongst the tangled sheets, he had found a long lace nightdress, with pale silk ribbons. He shook it and it exhaled a nostalgic scent of violets and love. Ah, it was Mary's nightdress, still warm from my caresses!

'It belongs to Miss Mary! It's yours, my love!' I moaned, doing up my braces.

My little glovemaker got up, tremulous, white-faced, and made a final poetic, passionate gesture. She rolled up the nightdress and thrust it into my arms as ardently as if her very heart lay amongst its folds.

'I give it to you, Teodorico! Take it, Teodorico! It still bears the traces of our love. Take it and sleep with it by your side, as if you were sleeping with me. But wait, wait one moment, my love! I just want to write a little something, a dedication!'

She ran to the table, on which lay scraps of the sensible notepaper I used when I wrote to my aunt, retelling the edifying story of my fasts in Alexandria, of nights spent immersed in the Gospels. Clasping the perfumed nightdress in my arms, feeling two sad tears roll into my beard, I looked anxiously around for somewhere to store that precious relic of love. The trunks were all closed. The canvas bag was full to bursting.

Topsius had impatiently pulled out his silver watch from the depths of his bosom. Our Lacedaemonian, standing at the door, grunted:

'Don Teodorico, *es tarde, muy tarde* – it's late, very late.'

But my dearly beloved was already waving a piece of paper, covered in the words she had written, in a hand as generous, impetuous and frank as her love: 'To my Teodorico, my brave little Portuguese lover, in memory of all the pleasures we enjoyed!'

'But darling, where am I going to put this? I can't carry it in my arms, naked and uncovered.'

Alpedrinha was already on his knees, frantically unbuckling the bag. Then Maricoquinhas had a delicate but inspired idea, she grabbed a piece of brown paper, picked up a length of red ribbon from the floor and her skilful glovemaker's hands quickly made of the nightdress a neat, round, graceful parcel which I put under my arm, clutching it to me with jealous, fiery passion.

There followed a desperate, murmured exchange of sobs, kisses, sweet nothings . . .

'Mary, my angel!'

'Teodorico, my love.'

'Write to me in Jerusalem . . .'

'Don't forget your pretty little plumpling . . .'

Dazed, I stumbled down the stairs. And the caleche that had so often borne me along with my arms about Mary, beneath the aromatic groves of Mamoudieh, finally left, drawn by a pair of white horses, tearing me from a happiness in which my heart had put down roots, now ripped up and bleeding in the silence of my breast. Topsius, impassive, encamped beneath his green sunshade, started up his rumbling litany of learned facts. Was I aware what road we were driving along? It was the noble Road of the Seven States which the first of the Ptolemies had built in order to reach the island of Pharos, praised by Homer in his poetry! I was not even listening, leaning back in the caleche, waving a handkerchief damp with tears and sad yearnings. At the hotel entrance, next to Alpedrinha, stood my sweet Maricoquinhas, looking lovely beneath her poppy hat, waving her fond, amorous handkerchief; and for a moment, like a symbol of our ardent hearts, those two white scraps of cambric waved to each other in the hot air. Then I fell back against the calico cushions as if dead.

No sooner had *The Cayman* weighed anchor than I ran to hide my sorrow in my cabin. Topsius kept plucking me by the sleeve to show me famous sites from the glorious age of the Ptolemies: the port of Eunotos, the marble bay where Cleopatra's galleys used to be moored. I fled and, on the stairs, almost collided with a sister of charity, who was timidly climbing them, her rosary in her hands. I merely mumbled: 'Sorry, holy sister.' And lying at last on my bunk, I bawled my eyes out, still clasping the brown paper parcel, all that was left to me of that passion of incomparable splendour, a passion that had come to pass in the land of Egypt.

For two days and two nights *The Cayman* groaned and rolled on the billows of the sea of Tyre. Wrapped in a blanket, never once letting go of Mary's parcel, I tetchily refused the biscuits that kind Topsius occasionally brought me and, ignoring the erudite facts that he continued, imperturbably, to pour forth about the sea known by Egyptians as the Great Green Sea, I scrabbled vainly in my memory for the stray lines of a prayer I had heard my aunt say, in order to calm the angry waves.

But one evening, as night fell, and I had closed my eyes, I seemed to feel firm ground beneath my slippers, solid rock; the air smelled of rosemary and I found myself for some reason climbing a wild hill accompanied by Adélia and my fair Mary, who had somehow emerged from the parcel looking fresh and neat, the poppies on her hat miraculously uncrushed! Then, from behind a rock, a naked man appeared. He was built like a colossus, swarthy and horned. His eyes gleamed, red as the round glass of a lantern, and with his endless tail he made a noise on the ground like an angry snake creeping through dried leaves. Impudently, without so much as a by your leave, he fell into step with us. I realised at once that it was the Devil, but I felt no disquiet, no terror. The insatiable Adélia kept throwing sideways glances at his bulging muscles. I said to her, indignantly: 'You slut, you'd even go to bed with the Devil, wouldn't you?'

Thus, walking along, we reached the top of the hill where a ragged palm tree swayed above an abyss filled by utter silence and darkness. Before us, far off, the sky was unfolding like a vast length of yellow fabric, and against this brilliant background, egg-yolk bright, stood a black, black hill, on the top of which were three small, thin crosses, all in a line and all identical. The Devil spat and murmured, grabbing me by the sleeve: 'The one in the middle is Jesus, the son of Joseph, whom some also call

84

Christ, and we're just in time to see the Ascension.' And so it was. The middle cross, Christ's cross, uprooted itself from the hill, like a bush torn from the ground by the wind, and slowly began to rise, growing larger, until it blocked the sky. And then, to hold it up, bands of angels appeared from all directions, like pigeons flocking eagerly to grain. Some pulled from the top, having first tied long silken ropes about the middle; others pushed from below and we could see the effort in their taut, blue-tinged arms. Sometimes a great drop of blood would fall from the cross, like an over-ripe cherry, and a seraph would catch it in his hands and place it in the highest part of heaven where it would hang suspended, shining with all the splendour of a star. The enormous figure of an old man in a white tunic, whose features we could barely make out amongst the abundant, dishevelled mane of hair and the white tufts of his snowy beard, was directing these manoeuvres, as he lounged amongst the clouds, speaking a language similar to Latin and loud as the thundering wheels of a hundred chariots of war. Suddenly everything disappeared. And the Devil looked thoughtfully at me and said: '*Consumatum est*, my friend! Another god! Another religion! And this one will propagate in Heaven and Earth alike an unspeakable tedium.'

And then, leading me down the hill, the Devil launched into an animated account of the cults, festivals and religions that had flowered in his youth. At that time, along the whole coast of the Great Green, from Byblos to Carthage, from Eleusis to Memphis, the land was crowded with gods. Some dazzled by virtue of their perfect beauty, others by their complex ferocity. But all of them mingled freely with human life, rendering it divine: they would travel in triumphal chariots, breathe in the scent of flowers, drink wine, deflower sleeping virgins. That is why they were loved with a love that will never be repeated and the people, when they emigrated, might leave their flocks or forget the rivers they had drunk from, but they carried their gods affectionately in their hearts. 'Have you never been to Babylonia, my friend?' he asked. There, one day a year, all the women, matrons and maidens alike, would come to prostitute themselves in the sacred wood in honour of the goddess Millita. The richest amongst them would arrive in carriages inlaid with silver, drawn by buffalo and escorted by slaves, whilst the poorest wore a thong about their necks. Some would spread a rug on the grass and crouch down like patient beasts, others would stand, naked and white, their faces hidden by a black veil, like splendid marble statues amongst the trunks of the poplars. And they would wait like that until someone tossed them a silver coin and said to them: 'In the name of Venus!' They would then follow that man, whether he was a prince from Susa wearing a crown of pearls or a merchant sailing down the Euphrates in his leather boat and, amidst the dark foliage, the night would be full of the wild roar of that ritual debauchery. Then the Devil spoke to me of the human bonfires of Moloch, the mysteries of the good goddess during which lilies were watered with blood and of the funeral pyres of Adonis . . .

And pausing, he asked with a smile: 'Have you never been to Egypt, my friend?' I told him that I had and that it was there that I met Maricoquinhas. And the Devil courteously pointed out: 'That wasn't Maricoquinhas, that was Isis!' When the floods reached Memphis, the waters were crowded with sacred barks. A heroic joy, that rose up to the Sun, made men the equals of gods. Crowned with the horns of an ox, Osiris would mount Isis and, amidst the strident noise of bronze harps, the amorous roaring of the divine cow could be heard along the whole length of the Nile.

Then the Devil told me how brilliant were the religions of the natural world in Greece, how sweet and beautiful. There everything was white, polished, pure, luminous and serene: there was a harmony in the lines of their marble statues, in the constitution of their cities, in the eloquence of their academies and in the skill of their athletes. Floating like baskets of flowers amongst the islands of Ionia, on the languid silence of the sea, the Nereides would linger on the decks of ships to listen to the tales of travellers, the Muses would stand and sing in the valleys, and the beauty of Venus was like a distillation of Helen's beauty.

But then this carpenter from Galilee had appeared and all that was done for. The human face became for ever pale and full of suffering; a dark cross, weighing down upon the earth, withered the splendour of the roses, drained kisses of their sweetness; this new god took pleasure in ugliness.

Thinking that Lucifer had grown sad, I tried to console him: 'Don't worry, there's still plenty of pride and prostitution, plenty of blood and anger in the world! Don't bemoan the holocausts of Moloch. There will be holocausts of Jews one day.' Stunned, he replied: 'Me worry? What do I care one way or the other, Raposo? They are transient, I am not.'

Thus, chatting to Satan, I found myself, without realising it, in Campo de Santana. And having stopped, while he disentangled his horns from the branches of one of the trees, I suddenly heard a voice by my side screaming: 'Look at Teodorico with that filthy swine!' I turned round. It was my aunt, pale and terrible, ready to lay about me with her prayer book. I woke up, bathed in sweat.

Topsius was standing at the cabin door, shouting cheerily:

'Get up, Raposo! We're within sight of Palestine!'

The Cayman had stopped and in the silence I could feel the water lightly lapping the ship's side, a gently caressing murmur. Why had I had that dream about false gods, Jesus their conquerer and the Devil in rebellion against them all as I approached Jerusalem? What supreme revelation was the Lord preparing for me?

I disentangled myself from my blankets and then, dazed and bedraggled, still clutching Mary's precious parcel, I went up to the quarterdeck, bundled up in my double-breasted coat. I was met by a fine, strong breeze that bore on it the smell of mountain air and orange blossom. The sea had grown silent and blue in the cool of the morning. And before my sinful eyes lay the low-lying, desert land of Palestine and a dark city encircled by orchards, crowned by rays of sunlight that surrounded it like a halo.

'Jaffa!' shouted Topsius, waving his clay pipe. 'What used to be called Joppa, the most ancient city of all Asia, dating back to before the Flood! Off with your hat and greet this ancient city, rich in legends and history! It was here that that old drunkard Noah built his ark!'

I bowed in astonishment.

'Good grief! We've only just arrived and already we're seeing religious sights!'

And I kept my hat off, because *The Cayman*, as it anchored off the coast of the Holy Land, had taken on the contemplative quality of a chapel, full of pious deeds and thoughts. A Lazarist, wearing a long soutane, was walking along, eyes lowered, meditating on his breviary. Their faces hidden beneath black lustrine hoods, two nuns were palely fingering the beads of their rosaries. Along the damp ship's rail, pilgrims from Abyssinia, hirsute Greek priests from Alexandria, stared in amazement at the houses of Jaffa, haloed in sunlight, as if at an illumined shrine. And the bell at the stern tinkled in the salty breeze with the devout sweetness of a bell ringing for mass.

But, seeing that a small dark boat, a lighter, was approaching *The Cayman,* I hurried down to my cabin to don my pith helmet and a pair of black gloves, in order to disembark properly dressed in the land of my Saviour. I duly perfumed myself and brushed my hair and returned to find the small boat already packed. And as I was clambering hurriedly in behind a bearded Franciscan, Mary's beloved parcel slipped out of my loving arms, bounced down the steps like a ball, grazed the edge of the boat and was about to disappear into the bitter waters! I let out a yell and one of the nuns, lightly, mercifully, caught it.

'Thank you so much, Senhora!' I shouted, my face pale. 'It's just a bundle of clothes. Praise be to the holy love of Mary!'

She retreated modestly into the shadow of her hood and, since I had sat down farther off, between Topsius and the bearded Franciscan, who stank of garlic, the saintly creature kept the parcel on her virginal lap, right on top of her rosary.

The master of the boat took the helm and bawled out: 'Allah is great! To your oars!' The Arabs sang as they rowed. The sun rose behind Jaffa. And, leaning on my umbrella, I contemplated the modest nun bearing Mary's nightdress in her lap, on her way to the land of chastity.

She was young and, beneath the sad, black hood, her face was a pale oval of ivory, on which her long eyelashes cast a shadow of mournful melancholy. Her lips were drained of colour and warmth, lips that would only ever kiss the livid feet of the corpse of a god. Compared to Mary, that open, sensual rose of York who perfumed all of Alexandria, the nun drooped like a lily, withered before it has even bloomed in the dampness of a chapel. She was probably going to some hospice in the Holy Land. Life for her would be a succession of wounds to dress and sheets to pull up over dead faces. And it was doubtless fear of the Lord that made her so pale.

'Little fool!' I mumbled to myself.

Poor, sterile creature! Could she have any inkling of what that brown parcel contained? Would she feel rising up from it, penetrating the darkness of her hood, a strange, languid perfume of vanilla and soft skin? Would the warmth of the rumpled bed that must have permeated the lace seep through the paper and gently warm her knees? Who knows? For a moment, it seemed to me that a drop of new blood coloured her pallid cheeks and that beneath her habit, on which a cross gleamed, her troubled breast rose and fell. I even thought that, beneath her eyelashes, I saw a shy flicker of light as her eyes sought a glimpse of my thick, black beard ... But it was only a moment. Inside the hood, her face again took on the coldness of holy marble and the severe cross about her neck weighed down jealously upon her submissive breast. Beside her, the other nun, chubby and bespectacled, was smiling out at the green sea, at wise Topsius, with a bright smile that dimpled her chin and emanated from the peace in her heart.

No sooner had we jumped out of the boat and onto the sands of Palestine than I ran, hat in hand, to offer my elegant, courteous thanks.

'My dear sister, I'm so grateful ... I would have been most distressed to lose it! It's from my aunt, you see, something she wanted delivered in Jerusalem. I'll tell you about it one day. Auntie's a great respecter of holy things, mad about charity ...'

Silent, hidden in the folds of her hood, she held the parcel out to me with the tips of her fingers, as feeble and transparent as those of Our Lady of the Sorrows. And then the two black habits disappeared amongst the glittering newly white-washed walls, down some narrow steps where the flyblown corpse of a dog lay rotting. I murmured again: 'Little fool!'

When I turned round, Topsius, beneath his sunshade, was talking to the excellent man who was to be our guide across the lands of the Scriptures. He was a tall, dark young fellow with long moustaches that fluttered in the breeze; he was wearing a velvet jacket and white riding boots; his powerful chest was adorned by the silver butts of two pistols sticking out of the black woollen sash about his waist and on his head he sported a bright yellow silk scarf, the tips and fringes of which he wore tied back behind. His name was Paul Potte, his country of origin was Montenegro and he was known for his good humour along the whole Syrian coast. God, he was a jolly fellow! Happiness shone in his pale blue eyes, sang in his perfect teeth, beat in his restless hands, echoed in the tap of his heels as he walked. From Ascalon to the bazaars of Damascus, from Carmel to the orchards of Engaddi, he was always referred to as 'that jolly fellow Potte'. He generously offered me his pouch of perfumed tobacco. Topsius was amazed at his knowledge of the Bible. Clapping him on the back, I cried out: 'You're a man after my own heart!' And then, after firm handshakes all round, we went off to the Hotel Jehoshaphat to sign our contract, downing vast quantities of beer in the process.

Potte, that jolliest of men, had soon organised the caravan with which we would travel to the city of our Lord. A mule would carry our luggage and the Arab muledriver, swathed in a ragged blue cloak, was so slender and handsome that I could not resist trying to catch his eye, just to feel the black caress of his velvet gaze. And we took with us as escort – a very oriental luxury this – an old Bedouin with a bad cold, who wore a grey-striped camelhair burnous and carried a strong, rusty spear adorned with tassles.

I carefully stowed the precious parcel containing Mary's nightdress in one of my saddlebags, then, once we had mounted up and Potte had lengthened the lanky Topsius' stirrups, he brandished his whip and uttered the ancient cry of Richard the Lionheart and the Crusaders: 'Forward to Jerusalem, by the will of God!' And trotting along, our cigars lit, we left Jaffa by the Market Gate at the hour when the bell for vespers was gently ringing in the hospice of the Latin fathers.

In the luminous sweetness of the evening, the road stretched ahead through gardens, vegetable plots, orchards, groves of oranges and palm trees: the Promised Land, bright and pleasant. The fugitive song of flowing water melted away amongst the myrtle hedges. As if to help the chosen people of God to breathe more easily, the air, of an ineffable softness, exhaled the mingled perfumes of jasmine and lemon trees. The work of irrigation over for the day, the grave and peaceful creak of water wheels was slowly fading into silence, amongst the pomegranate trees in bloom. High up, serene against the blue sky, a great eagle flew.

Contented, we stopped by a fountain of red and black marble, shaded by sycamores full of cooing doves. Beside it a tent was pitched, with a carpet spread on the grass covered with grapes and bowls of milk, and the white-bearded, old man who occupied it greeted us in the name of Allah with all the nobility of a patriarch. The beer had made me thirsty and a smiling girl, as lovely as Rachel herself, gave me water to drink from a jug identical to those of Biblical times; her breast was bare and two long gold earrings bobbed against her dark cheek. A tame, white lamb followed her, tied to the hem of her tunic.

Evening was falling, silent and golden, when we entered the plain of Sharon, which, according to the Bible, was once filled with roses. In the silence, we heard the tinkle of bells from a herd of black goats watched over by an Arab naked as John the Baptist. In the background, even the sinister mountains of Judaea seemed beautiful, touched by the oblique rays of the sun as it sank into the Sea of Tyre; they looked blue and imbued with a distant sweetness, like the illusory pleasures of sin. Then everything grew dark. Two stars appeared, infinitely bright, and began to travel before us towards Jerusalem.

Our room in the Hotel Mediterranean in Jerusalem, with its whitewashed, vaulted ceiling and tiled floor, resembled a stark cell in some harsh monastery. Opposite the window, however, a thin wall covered in blue-flowered wallpaper separated it from another room, where we could hear a cool voice humming 'The Ballad of the King of Thule', and there, exuding comfort and civilisation, gleamed a mahogany wardrobe which I opened as if I were opening a reliquary, and placed in it my beloved parcel.

The two narrow iron bedsteads were lost beneath the virginal folds of white cambric curtains and, in the middle of the room, stood a pine table on which Topsius was studying his map of Palestine, whilst I paced up and down in my slippers, filing my nails. It was that devout Friday when Christianity fervently commemorates the Holy Martyrs of Évora. We had arrived in the city of the Lord that afternoon, beneath a sad drizzling rain, and every now and then Topsius would look up from his study of the roads of Galilee and observe me for a while, arms folded, and then murmur in a companionable fashion:

'So here you are in Jerusalem, friend Raposo.'

Pausing before the mirror, I would glance at my thick beard, my tanned face and contentedly murmur back:

'Yes, that handsome fellow Raposo is finally in Jerusalem.'

And then, dissatisfied, I would turn and gaze out through the misted windows at Zion. Beneath the fine, melancholy rain the white walls of a silent monastery rose in front of us, its green shutters closed, and with two huge zinc drainpipes at either corner, one emptying itself noisily into a deserted alleyway, the other falling onto the soft soil of a plot planted with cabbages, in which a donkey stood braying. Looking in that direction you saw a vast multitude of lugubrious, mud-coloured, flat-roofed houses, each topped with a small brick dome in the shape of an oven and long poles on which to hang clothes out to dry. Almost all of them were decrepit, ramshackle, wretched, apparently dissolving beneath the slow rain drenching them. To the other side rose a hill crammed with sordid shacks, with the occasional green garden, blurred and shivering in the damp mist. Winding amongst them was a thread-thin alleyway of steps, up and down which there was a constant traffic of friars wearing sandals on their feet and carrying umbrellas, sombre Jews with long hair, or the occasional leisurely Bedouin gathering up his burnous ... Above it all loomed the grey sky. That view from my window was my first impression of Zion, that architectural gem, blazing with light, the joy of all the Earth, loveliest of cities.

'This is ghastly, Topsius! Alpedrinha was right. It *is* worse than Braga! And there's not even anywhere to go for a stroll, no billiard hall, no theatre. Nothing! Fancy our Lord living here of all places!'

'Hmm, it was more fun in his day,' muttered my learned friend.

And then he suggested that on Sunday we set off for the banks of the Jordan, a trip he needed to make for his research into the Herods. There I could enjoy the delights of the countryside, bathe in holy waters and shoot partridges amongst the palm trees of Jericho. I agreed with alacrity. And we went down to eat, summoned by a funereal monastery bell clanging in the shadows of the corridor.

The dining room also had a vaulted ceiling with an esparto mat covering the tiled floor. The erudite historian of the Herods and I sat alone at the gloomy table adorned with paper flowers arranged in cracked vases. Stirring the macaroni in my watery soup, I muttered dejectedly:

'God, Topsius, this is boring!'

But then a glass door at the far end of the room opened quietly and I cried out in astonishment:

'Good grief, Topsius, what a huge woman!'

She *was* huge, as solid and strapping a figure as myself. She was freckled and as pale as much-washed linen, her head was crowned by a flaming mass of wavy, chestnut hair, her firm breasts almost bursting out of her close-fitting blue serge dress. She entered, giving off a fresh smell of Windsor soap and eau de cologne, and immediately lit up the whole dining room with the splendour of her young flesh. The inventive Topsius compared her to the powerful goddess Cibeles.

Cibeles sat down at the head of the table, proud and serene. She was joined by a calm, bald Hercules of a man – the chair creaking beneath the weight of his ample limbs – who, even in the way he unfolded his napkin, revealed that he was someone used to giving orders, accustomed to the omnipotence that wealth bestows. From a mumbled 'yes' on her part, I realised she was from the same land as Maricoquinhas. She also reminded me of the Baron's English lover.

By her plate she placed an open book which appeared to be poetry; the bearded man, chewing on his food with the majestic slowness of a lion, was also leafing silently through his *Guide to the Orient*. I forgot all about my stewed mutton and instead hungrily devoured each and every one of her perfections. From time to time she would lift the dense fringe of her eyelashes. I waited longingly for that pale, sweet gaze to rest on me, but it rested instead on the whitewashed walls, the paper flowers and then returned, cold and indifferent, to the pages of her poetry book.

After coffee, she kissed the bearded gentleman's hairy hand and disappeared through the glass door, taking with her all the perfume, light and joy of Jerusalem. Hercules slowly lit his pipe, asked the waiter to send Ibraim the guide to him in his room and then got heavily to his feet. At the door, he knocked over the umbrella left there by Topsius – that worthiest of men, that glory of Germany and member of the Imperial Institute of Historical Research – and simply kept walking, without bothering to pick it up, without even giving it so much as a haughty glance.

'The brute!' I snorted, boiling with rage.

My learned friend, displaying the social cowardice of the disciplined German, picked up his umbrella and wiped it down with a cloth, muttering tremulously that 'perhaps the bearded gentleman was a duke'.

'What do you mean a duke! What do I care for dukes! I'm a Raposo, one of the Alentejo Raposos. I'll teach him!'

But it was growing dark and we had to pay our reverent visit to the tomb of our God. I ran up to my room to don my top hat, as I had promised Auntie I would, and I was just going back out into the corridor when I saw Cibeles open the door, *the next door to ours*, and leave wearing a grey cape and a cap adorned by two white gull feathers. My heart beat in a delirium of wild hope. She must have been the one singing 'The Ballad of the King of Thule'! Our beds must therefore be separated by nothing more than the thin, fragile wall covered in blue foliage! I did not even put on my black gloves, but rushed downstairs, certain that I would meet her again at the tomb of Jesus, and I was already plotting to bore a hole in the wall through which my enamoured eye could sate itself on the beauties of her nakedness.

A lugubrious rain was still falling. We were just plunging

into the mire that was the Via Dolorosa, flanked on either side by mud-coloured walls, when I called to Potte to join me under my umbrella and asked him if he had yet seen the sturdy, freckled Cibeles staying at the hotel. Potte, the merry fellow, had already seen and admired her and, through Ibraim, his favourite confederate, I learned that the bearded man was Scottish and owned a tannery.

'You see, Topsius!' I shouted. 'A tanner . . . a duke indeed! He's a brute. I'd tear him off a strip or two. In matters of honour, I'm like a wild beast. I'd show him.'

The daughter, said Potte, the one with the thick plaited hair, bore the radiant name of a precious stone: she was called Ruby. She loved horses and was bold as they come; in Upper Galilee, where they had just come from, she had killed a black eagle.

'Now here, gentlemen, is Pilate's house . . .'

'Oh, shut up about Pilate's house, man! What do I care about Pilate. So what else did Ibraim say? Tell me everything, Potte.'

The Via Dolorosa grew narrower there, vaulted like a corridor in a catacomb. Two beggars covered in sores were gnawing on bits of melon peel, squatting in the mud and grunting. Somewhere a dog was howling. And with a smile, Potte told me that Ibraim had often noticed Miss Ruby quite carried away by the beauty of the men of Syria and, at night, while Daddy was drinking his beer, she would stand at the door of the tent and recite poetry in a low voice, gazing up at the pulsating stars. I thought: 'Crikey! She's my kind of woman!'

'Here, gentlemen, is the entrance to the Holy Sepulchre.'

I furled my umbrella. At the far end of a churchyard, full of uprooted gravestones, rose the façade of a church, decaying, sad, diminished, with two doors in the form of arches, one already blocked up with lime and gravel, as being unnecessary, the other left timidly, fearfully ajar. And clinging to the feeble flanks of this gloomy temple were two crumbling edifices besmirched by ruin (one for the Greek Orthodox church, the other for the Catholic), like two terrified girls whom death had caught up with and who now sought refuge in the bosom of their mother, who was cold and half-dead as they were.

Then I put on my black gloves. And immediately, a voracious band of repellent men swarmed about us, crying out, offering relics, rosaries, crosses, scapulars, bits of wood planed by St Joseph himself, medals, little bottles of water from the river Jordan, candles, *agnus Dei*, lithographs of the Passion, paper flowers made in Nazareth, consecrated rocks, olive stones from the Mount of Olives and tunics 'as worn by the Virgin Mary'! And at the entrance to Christ's tomb, which my aunt had recommended I enter on my knees, moaning and saying a prayer, I had to hit out at a fierce, scrawny rascal with a beard as long as a hermit's, who had attached himself to my coat tails, whining at me to buy cigar-holders made out of a piece of wood from Noah's ark!

'Damn it, man, leave me alone!'

And thus, cursing, I plunged, together with my dripping umbrella, into the sublime sanctuary where Christianity keeps the tomb of Christ. But I stopped short, surprised by a delicious smell, the welcome aroma of Syrian tobacco. On a large bench, made up like a divan and covered with carpets from Caramania and old silk cushions, three grave-faced, bearded Arabs reclined, smoking long pipes made out of cherry wood. They had hung their weapons on the wall. The floor was black with their spittle. And before them, a ragged servant stood waiting, with a steaming cup of coffee in the palm of each hand.

I imagined that the Catholic church had thoughtfully set up, at the entrance to the divine place, a shop selling refreshments and alcoholic drinks for the comfort of the pilgrims. I said in a low voice to Potte:

'What an excellent idea! I think I'll have a coffee too.'

But Potte blithely explained to me that those serious, pipe-smoking men were, in fact, the Muslim soldiers who guarded the Christian altars, to prevent the rival priests who perform their rival rituals there from tearing each other to pieces around Jesus' mausoleum out of superstition, fanaticism or envy of each other's vestments – Catholics like Father Pinheiro, Greek Orthodox priests for whom the cross has four arms of equal length, Abyssinians and Armenians, Copts descended from the people who, in former days, worshipped the ox Apis, Nestorians from Chaldea, Georgians from the Caspian Sea, Marronites from the Lebanon – all of them Christians, all equally intolerant and equally fierce. Then I gratefully greeted those armed soldiers of Mohammed who, in order to keep the pious peace around the dead Christ, calmly watch the door, smoking their pipes.

Right by the entrance, we stopped before a square tablet embedded in the dark flagstones. It had the soft sheen of mother-of-pearl, so polished and gleaming that it resembled the still waters of a pool in which the lights were reflected. Potte tugged at my sleeve and reminded me that it was the custom to kiss that slab of stone, holier than all others, which once, in the garden of Joseph of Arimathea . . .

'I know, I know . . . Should I kiss it, Topsius?'

'Kiss away,' said the prudent historian of the Herods. 'You won't catch anything and it'll please your aunt.'

I didn't kiss the stone. Silently, one by one, we entered a vast domed area, so dimly lit in the twilight that the circle of round windows at the top merely glowed palely like a ring of pearls on a tiara. The columns that supported the cupola, as slim and tightly packed as the bars on a grill, striped the shadows round about, each column punctuated by a patch of red – the flickering light from a bronze lamp. In the middle of the echoing flagstone floor there rose, smooth and white, a marble mausoleum decorated with carvings and rosettes. Above it, like a canopy, hung an old piece of damask thickly embroidered in faded gold, and two rows of torch-holders formed an avenue of funerary lights leading to the entrance, narrow as a crack, covered by a piece of cloth the colour of blood. An Armenian priest, hidden beneath his ample black cloak, invisible under his hood, was sleepily and silently perfuming it with incense.

Potte tugged at my sleeve again:

'It's the tomb!'

Oh, my pious soul! Oh, Auntie! There it was, within reach of my lips, the tomb of my Lord! But I was off like a sheepdog, through the noisy horde of friars and pilgrims, in search of a plump, freckled face and a cap with seagull feathers in it! For a long time I wandered about, dazed . . . First, I collided with a Franciscan friar, his esparto belt around his waist, then I had to step back before a Coptic priest, who slipped past me like a tenuous shadow, preceded by servants jingling small sacred tambourines dating from the time of Osiris. I stumbled into a pile of white clothes, fallen like a bundle on the flagstones, from which came groans of contrition; further on I bumped into a black man, completely naked, stretched out at the foot of a column, sleeping peacefully. Sometimes the sacred clamour of an organ would thunder forth, rolling around the marble walls of the nave, only to die away like the whisper of a wave on the shore, and then farther off, an Armenian song, tremulous and filled with longing, would beat against the austere walls like the frantic wings of a trapped bird anxious to escape into the light. Next to an altar, I pushed past two fat sacristans, one Greek, the other Catholic, red-faced and smelling of onions, who were angrily calling each other names; and I came across a band of Russian pilgrims with dishevelled mops of hair, who had obviously come all the way from the Caspian Sea, their painful feet bound in rags, not daring to move, under the spell of divine terror, twisting their felt caps round and round in hands hung with rosaries of heavy glass beads. Ragged children were playing in the darkness amongst the arches, whilst others begged for alms. The smell of incense was suffocating and priests from rival sects tugged at my coat tails to show me rival relics, some heroic, some divine – Gottfried's spurs, a piece of green reed.

My head spinning, I joined a procession of penitents, where I thought I had glimpsed, white and proud amongst the black veils of repentance, the two seagull feathers. At

99

Procession of the penitents to the Calvary

the head of the procession a Carmelite nun was mumbling the litany, making us stop at every step to gather in devout amazement at the entrance to cavernous chapels dedicated to the Passion: the chapel of the Flagellation, where our Lord was whipped, the chapel of the Tunic, where our Lord was stripped of his garments. Then, carrying torches, we went up a dark staircase hewn out of the rock. And suddenly, the whole devout crew fell to the ground, ululating, tearing their hair, moaning, beating their breasts, calling out to the Lord in mournful, frantic voices. We were standing on the stone of the Calvary.

Around us, the chapel that houses it blazed with a sensual, pagan splendour. The electric blue ceiling shone with silver suns, signs of the Zodiac, stars, angel's wings, purple flowers and, amongst all this sidereal pomp, suspended on strings of pearls, hung the old symbols of fertility, ostrich eggs, the sacred golden eggs of Astarte and Bacchus. Above the altar stood a red cross with a roughly carved Christ painted in gold, which seemed to vibrate, to come alive in the diffuse glow of the rush lights, the glittering decorations, the smoke from aromatic herbs burning in bronze dishes. Mirror-smooth globes poised on ebony pedestals reflected the jewels studding the retables and the gleam of walls faced with jasper, mother-of-pearl and agate. And on the floor, in the midst of this exquisite clearing of precious stones and light, emerging from amongst the white marble flagstones, was a small piece of rough, untamed rock with a long crack in it made smooth by long centuries of kisses and pious caresses. A Greek archdeacon with a grizzled beard cried out: 'In this rock the cross was fixed! The cross, the cross! Miserere! Kyrie eleison! Christus! Christus!' There was a gabbling of ever more ardent prayers, intercut with sobs. A sorrowful canticle broke out in time to the creaking of the censors. Kyrie eleison! Kyrie eleison! And the deacons passed rapidly and eagerly round the crowd, holding out huge velvet bags in which the offerings of the simple people jingled and were lost.

I fled, feeling stunned and confused. Topsius was walking about the churchyard beneath his umbrella, breathing in the damp air. We were again set upon by the starving band of vendors of relics. I repelled them roughly and left the holy place as I had entered it, sinful and cursing.

At the hotel, Topsius went straight up to our room to note down his impressions of Jesus' tomb. I remained in the courtyard drinking beer and smoking my pipe in the amusing company of Potte. When I went up to the room much later on, my enlightened friend was already snoring, with the candle still burning and a book lying open on the bed, a book of mine that I had brought from Lisbon to amuse me in the land of the Gospels: Paul de Kock's *L'Homme aux trois culottes*. Removing my boots, covered in the venerable mud of the Via Dolorosa, I thought about my Cibeles. Where had she spent that misty afternoon in Jerusalem? Amongst which sacred ruins, beneath which trees sanctified merely because they had once given shade to our Lord? Had she gone to the valley of the Kidron? Or to visit Rachel's white tomb?

I gave a sigh of sweet exhaustion and I was just yawning and pulling back the sheets, when I distinctly heard through the thin wall the sound of water filling a bath. In a state of some agitation, I listened, and then in that black, mournful silence in which Jerusalem is eternally wrapped, I clearly heard the light splash of a sponge being dropped into the water. I ran to the wall and pressed my cheek to the blue flowers on the wallpaper. I could make out the noise of soft bare feet walking over the mat covering the tiled floor and the murmur of water as if stirred by a sweet, naked arm testing the temperature. Then, my face aflame, I heard all the intimate noises of a long, slow, languid bath: the squeezing of the sponge, the gentle scrubbing of a soapy hand, the weary, contented sigh of a body stretching out beneath the caress of warm water sprinkled with a few drops of perfume ... The blood beat in my head and I desperately searched the wall for a hole, a crack. I tried drilling a hole in it with a pair of scissors but the thin blades crumpled on the thick mortar ... The water sang out again, dripping from the sponge and, trembling, I imagined I could see the slow drops slipping down the channel between those hard, white breasts that had seemed about to burst out of the serge dress.

I could resist no longer. Barefoot, in my long johns, I crept out into the sleeping corridor and clamped to the keyhole of her door one bulging, ardent eye, so ardent I was almost afraid I might scorch the door with the all-devouring fire of my eye's bloodshot beam. I could make out a circle of light and in it a towel thrown down on the mat, a red dressing gown and one corner of the curtained whiteness of her bed. And thus, crouched, beads of sweat running down the back of my neck, I sat waiting for her to cross that tiny disc of light, resplendent in her nakedness, when behind me I suddenly heard a door creak open and felt a blaze of light bathe the wall. It was the bearded gentleman, in his shirtsleeves, a candlestick in his hand! And I, poor, wretched Raposo, had no escape. On one side loomed his vast bulk, on the other the solid wall at the end of the corridor.

Slowly, silently, methodically, Hercules placed the candlestick on the floor, raised his heavy, thicksoled boot and kicked me in the ribs. I roared out: 'Brute!' He hissed: 'Be quiet!' And again, having cornered me against the wall, he slammed his cruel, iron-hard boot into hips, buttocks, shins, not sparing an inch of my precious, cherished flesh! Then he calmly picked up his candlestick again. White-faced, clad only in my underwear, I summoned up all my dignity and said to him:

'The only thing that saved you, Englishman, is the fact that we're so near the tomb of our Lord and the fact that I wouldn't want to get into any kind of fracas that might upset my aunt. But if we were in Lisbon, out of doors, in a certain place I know, I'd beat you black and blue! You don't know how lucky you are. Just remember that — black and blue.'

And then I limped proudly back to my room where I

patiently rubbed arnica on my wounds. And that is how I spent my first night in Zion.

The next morning wise Topsius set off on a pilgrimage to the Mount of Olives, by the clear spring of Siloe. Too bruised to consider mounting a horse, I stayed behind and spent the day lying on the striped sofa reading *L'Homme aux trois culottes*. And in order to avoid meeting the offensive bearded gentleman, I did not even go down to the dining room, saying I felt too depressed and weary. But once the sun had sunk into the Sea of Tyre, I felt restored and full of energy again. Potte had arranged a night of sensual revelry at the house of a most hospitable old woman, called Fatme, who lived in the Armenian quarter tending her sweet dovecote of doves, and we were going there to see that glorious dancer from Palestine, the 'Flower of Jericho', wiggle her way through the 'Dance of the Bee', a sight guaranteed to inflame the coldest of men and to deprave the purest.

Fatme's modest little door, adorned by a single vine, was set in one corner of a black wall beside the Tower of David. Fatme was waiting for us, a vast, majestic figure wrapped in white veils, with strands of coral woven into her hair, her naked arms each bearing the dark scars left by plague boils. She took my hand submissively, raised it to her oily brow, then to her sticky scarlet lips, and led me ceremoniously before a black, gold-fringed curtain, like the cloth used to cover a bier. Feeling that I had at last penetrated the dazzling secrets of a silent, rose-scented seraglio, I trembled.

It was a cool, whitewashed room with red cotton valances above the shutters and, along the walls, was a low divan upholstered in yellow silk, darned here and there in a lighter colour. On a scrap of Persian carpet, a brass brazier stood, unlit, on a pile of ashes. A solitary velvet slipper, spangled with sequins, lay forgotten there. An oil lamp, suspended on two chains adorned with tassels, hung from the dull white wooden ceiling, across which lay a spreading damp stain. In one corner, amongst the pillows, a silent mandolin slept. A sweet, indolent smell of mould and benzoin hung in the warm air. Stag beetles scuttled across the tiles to hide behind the mouldings of the shutters.

I sat down gravely by Topsius' side. A black woman from Dongola, dressed in scarlet, silver bracelets jingling on her arms, came out to serve us aromatic coffee, and almost immediately afterwards, Potte appeared, looking downhearted, saying that we would not after all be enjoying the famous 'Dance of the Bee' that night! The 'Rose of Jericho' had gone to dance before a German prince, who had arrived in Zion that morning to worship at the tomb of our Lord. And Fatme clutched humbly at her heart, invoking Allah and declaring herself our slave. It was most unfortunate, but the 'Rose of Jericho' had indeed gone to dance before the blond prince who had journeyed, accompanied by horses and plumes, all the way from the land of Germany!

Annoyed, I remarked that whilst I might not be a prince, my aunt was immensely rich: amongst the Alentejo nobility, the Raposos were of the purest blood. If it had been arranged that the 'Rose of Jericho' was to pleasure my Catholic eyes, then it was most inconsiderate of her to agree instead to perform before that armoured pilgrim from heretic Germany . . .

Sticking his nose petulantly in the air, Topsius snorted that Germany was the spiritual mother of all the peoples of the world.

'The gleam from a German helmet, Senhor Raposo, is the light that guides humanity!'

'Damn your helmet! No one guides me! I'm a Raposo, one of the Alentejo Raposos! No one guides me but Christ our Lord. Besides, Portugal has its great men too! There's Afonso Henriques, there's Herculano . . . Damn it!'

I rose to my feet in a threatening manner. Wise Topsius trembled and cringed. Potte intervened:

'Peace, Christians and friends, peace!'

Topsius and I sat down again on the divan, crossing our

legs, having first, generously and honourably, shaken hands.

Fatme, meanwhile, was still swearing that Allah was great and that she was our slave. And that if we would care to cross her palm with seven gold piastres, she, to compensate for the 'Rose of Jericho', would offer us a priceless jewel, a Circassian woman, whiter than the full moon, more graceful than the lilies that grow in Galgala.

'Bring her on!' I cried, excitedly. 'Damn it, I came to the Holy Land to enjoy myself. So bring on the Circassian woman! Give them the piastres, Potte. Come on, I want to have a good time!'

Fatme shuffled backwards out of the room. Potte reclined between us and opened his perfumed pouch of Aleppo tobacco. Then a small white door, barely noticeable in the whitewashed wall, slowly opened; it creaked slightly in one corner and a figure entered, veiled, vague and vaporous. Her loose Turkish trousers in crimson silk billowed languidly about her legs from her supple waist to her ankles where they were gathered in by a gold ribbon. Her small feet – white and winged – seemed barely to touch the yellow Morocco leather slippers and through the gauze veil that wound about her head, chest and arms shone golden embroidery, glinting jewellery and the two black stars of her eyes. I stretched and yawned, tumescent with desire.

Behind her, Fatme, slowly, slowly lifted the veil with the tips of her fingers and, from amidst the cloud of gauze, emerged a large, ugly face, white as plaster, with hollow cheeks and a huge nose, a squint and rotten teeth that blackened the witless languor of her smile. Potte leapt up from the divan, cursing Fatme. She cried out to Allah, beating her breasts that boomed limply like half-empty wineskins.

And the two of them disappeared, furious, swept out on a wave of anger. The Circassian woman waddled over to us, smiling her putrid smile, and held out a grubby hand, asking for 'a little something' in a voice hoarse with drink.

In disgust I pushed her away. She paused to scratch first one arm, then her side, and then calmly picked up her veil and shuffled out, slippers dragging.

'Oh, Topsius!' I roared. 'This is a disgrace!'

My wise friend made a few remarks about sensuality: it is always a deceiver; beneath the bright smile lurks the decaying tooth; all that remains of human kisses is bitterness; when the body falls into ecstasy, the soul grows sad . . .

'What do you mean "soul"? This has nothing to do with the soul! It's an out and out insult! In Rua do Arco do Bandeira, this Fatme woman would have been slapped roundly about the face by now . . . Damn it!'

I was in a ferocious mood, with a great desire to stamp on the mandolin. But Potte reappeared, smoothing his moustaches, saying that, for another nine gold piastres, Fatme would agree to show us her most marvellous secret, a virgin from the banks of the Nile, from Upper Nubia, as beautiful as the most beautiful Oriental night. He himself had seen her and would guarantee that she was worth the tribute from a whole fertile province.

Being weak-willed and open-handed, I agreed. One by one the nine gold piastres clinked into Fatme's plump hand.

Once more the whitewashed door creaked open and against the grubby white walls, stood a splendid woman, naked, built like a Venus, her bare skin the colour of bronze. For a moment she stopped, dumbstruck, slowly rubbing her knees together, startled by the light and by the sight of three men. A white loincloth covered her agile, powerful flanks. Her thick hair, lustrous with oil, entwined with ancient gold coins, hung down her back, like a wild mane. A loose string of blue glass beads wound around her neck and slipped down between her two firm, perfect, ebony breasts. Suddenly, flicking her tongue back and forth, she let out a convulsive howl, a desolate sound: Lu, lu, lu, lu, lu! She threw herself face down on the divan then crouched there, like a sphinx, grave-faced and motionless, her great dark eyes flashing from one to the other of us.

'What did I tell you, eh?' said Potte, digging me in the ribs with his elbow. 'Look at that body. Look at those arms! Look at the way her back arches. She's like a panther!'

And Fatme, her eyes cast heavenwards, kept blowing little twittering kisses in an attempt to convey the transcendent pleasures the Nubian girl's love would bring. Given the persistent way she looked at me, I felt convinced that my thick beard must have captivated her, and so I uncurled myself from the divan and went slowly over to her, as if approaching a prey that was already mine. Her eyes dilated and glittered restlessly. Gently, calling her 'my lovely', I stroked her cold shoulder and at the touch of my white skin she recoiled, shivering, uttering a muffled cry like a wounded gazelle. I didn't like that. But I wanted to be nice, so I said to her paternally:

'If ever you come to my country . . . and I might well take you there, Lisbon's the place to be. You can go to Dafundo's, dine at Silva's. This is a dungheap in comparison and girls like you are well-treated there, given respect, they get written up in the newspapers, they marry landowners . . .'

I murmured other equally sweet and meaningful words. She did not understand what I was saying and in her staring eyes there floated a terrible nostalgia for her village in Nubia, for the herds of buffalo sleeping in the shade of the date palms, for the great river that flows, eternal and serene, past the ruins of religions and the tombs of dynasties.

Thinking I might ignite her heart with the flame of my own, I pulled her lewdly towards me. She fled and crouched in a corner, trembling. Then, head in hands, she began to sob loudly.

'Oh really!' I cried, perplexed.

And I grabbed my hat and stormed out, almost tearing the black, gold-fringed cloth in my fury. We stood in an ill-smelling, brick-walled cell and there ensued a fierce shouting match between Potte and the old woman about payment for that splendid Oriental party. She wanted another seven gold piastres. His moustache bristling, Potte spat curses at her in Arabic, harsh words that clattered like pebbles thrown down a ravine. And we left that place of delight pursued by the furious shouts of Fatme, who was positively drooling with rage, waving her plague-scarred arms and cursing us and our parents and the bones of our grandparents and the land that had produced us and the bread that we ate and the shadows that concealed us. Outside in the black street two dogs followed us for a long time, barking lugubriously.

I entered the Hotel Mediterranean drenched in longing for my own smiling homeland. All the pleasures I was deprived of in gloomy, inimical Zion made me long even more passionately for the pleasures that easy, charming Lisbon would offer me once my aunt had died and I had inherited the clinking green silk purse. No more encounters with harsh, brutal boots in sleeping corridors. There, no barbarous body would flee in tears from the touch of my fingers. Gilded by my aunt's gold, my love would never be rejected, my concupiscence never reviled. Oh, dear God! And I would do it by captivating Auntie with my saintliness! I sat down at once and wrote this most tender of letters to that ghastliest of women:

My dearest Auntie,

I feel filled at every moment with more and more virtue. And I attribute it to the Lord's pleasure as he gazes down on this my visit to His holy tomb. I spend every moment, day and night, meditating on His divine passion and thinking about you, Auntie. I have just come from the Via Dolorosa. It was so moving! It is such a very, very holy street, I almost feared to walk it with my boots on, and the other day I could not contain myself and I bent down and kissed its precious stones! I have spent most of tonight praying to Nossa Senhora do

Patrocínio, whom everyone here in Jerusalem holds in the highest esteem. She has a very pretty altar here, although, in this respect, you were right (as you are in all things) when you said that there is no one like the Portuguese for festivals and processions. Anyway, to-night, as I was kneeling before the chapel of Our Lady, after saying six Hail Marys, I looked up at the lovely image and I said: 'How I'd love to know how my Aunt Patrocínio is!' And would you believe it, Auntie, Our Lady opened her own divine mouth and said to me – and I quote word for word, for I wrote them down on my shirt cuff so as not to forget them: 'My beloved daughter is well, Raposo, and hopes to make you happy!' And this is not in any way an extraordinary event, for the respectable families with whom I take tea here, tell me that Our Lady and her divine Son always have a few kind words to say to the people who visit them. I have already obtained some relics for you, a bit of straw from the crib and a piece of wood planed by St Joseph himself. My German travelling companion who, as I mentioned to you in my letter from Alexandria, is both deeply religious and extremely learned, consulted the books he has with him and confirmed that the piece of wood is indeed one of those which, as has been proved, St Joseph used to carve in his spare time. As for the *great relic*, the one that I want to bring back to cure all your ills and to bring salvation to your soul and to repay all that I owe you, *I have great hopes of finding it soon*. But for the moment I can say nothing more. Give my regards to all our friends, I often think about them and pray for them constantly, especially our virtuous Father Casimiro. Give your blessing to your faithful nephew who respects you greatly and misses you greatly and hopes you are well.

Teodorico

PS   Ah, Auntie, I was filled with such disgust when I visited Pilate's house today that I almost spat on the floor! And I told St Veronica here that you were most devoted to her. It seemed to me that she looked really pleased. As I say to all the clerics and patriarchs here: 'If you want to know what true virtue is, you have to meet my aunt!'

Before undressing, I again glued my ear to the flowery wallpaper and listened. The Englishwoman was sleeping serenely, indifferently: I snarled and shook my fist in her direction:

'Bitch!'

Then I opened the wardrobe, took out the beloved parcel containing Mary's nightdress and gave it a resounding kiss.

Early the next day, as dawn was breaking, we set off for the holy river of Jordan.

Our journey through the hills of Judah proved slow and tedious. The hills succeed each other, one after the other, pale and round as skulls, desiccated, all vegetation blasted from them by a wicked wind; the only thing you find clinging here and there to an occasional slope is a sparse gorsebush, which, from a distance, in the inexorable, shimmering light, resembles only the mould of old age or neglect. The earth glitters white, the colour of lime. The radiant silence is as sad as that filling the vault of a tomb. Against the hard brilliance of the sky, a vulture circled about us, slow and black. When the sun set, we pitched our tents in the ruins of Jericho.

It was delicious then, in the sweet evening, to lie back on soft carpets, slowly sipping lemonade. The coolness of the merry stream that flowed, chattering, past our campsite through wild bushes, mingled with the scent of their flowers, yellow as broom; before us lay a green field of tall grasses, enlivened by the white blooms of haughty, languid lilies; by the water, pairs of pensive storks walked up and down. Looking towards Judah, I saw the Mountain of the Quarantena rise up, stern and pale, wrapped in the sadness of eternal contrition, and looking towards Moab, I gazed

110

upon the old, sacred land of Canaan, a grey, desolate, sandy plain that stretches, like the white shroud of a forgotten race, as far as the deserts of the Dead Sea.

At dawn, with our saddlebags full, we set off to make that votive pilgrimage. It was December then. The Syrian winter was transparently sweet and, trotting through the fine sand by my side, erudite Topsius told me how this plain of Canaan was once covered with bustling cities, with white paths winding through vineyards, with irrigation channels cooling the walls of the threshing floors; the women, anemones in their hair, would sing as they trod the grapes; the perfume from the gardens was more pleasing to Heaven than incense; the caravans entering the valley from Segor found here the abundance of wealthy Egypt and said that this was truly the garden of the Lord.

'Then one day,' added Topsius, a smile of infinite sarcasm on his lips, 'the Almighty got fed up and razed it to the ground.'

'But why? Why?'

'A whim, bad temper, cruelty . . .'

The horses kept neighing, sensing the nearness of the cursed waters, and soon afterwards we saw them, stretching out as far as the mountains of Moab, utterly still and silent, glittering bleakly beneath the solitary sky. A scene of terrible sadness. And all too easy to believe that the wrath of God still weighs upon them, when you consider that there they lie, as they have for centuries now, with no seaside resort like Cascais nearby, with no bright canvas shelters lined up along the shore, with no regattas, no fishing, no ladies looking sweet in their galoshes as they poetically collect seashells on the sands, with no violins at some festive, animated gathering to enliven them when the stars come out – lying there dead and buried between two mountain ranges as if beneath the stone slabs of a tomb.

'Beyond lay the citadel of Makeros,' Topsius said gravely, standing up in his stirrups, pointing his sunshade in the direction of the blue strip of sea. 'The home of my Herod, Herod Antipas, the tetrarch of Galilee, son of

Herod the Great. That, Dom Raposo, was where John the Baptist was beheaded.'

And continuing on towards Jordan (whilst our jolly friend Potte rolled us cigarettes out of good Aleppo tobacco), Topsius told me that whole, sad story. Makeros, the proudest fortress in all Asia, was built atop terrifying basalt cliffs. Its walls were one hundred and fifty ells high; eagles could barely reach the tops of its towers. Outside it was black and sombre, but inside it glinted with ivory, jasper and alabaster and from the high cedar ceilings hung broad, golden shields that looked like the stars in the summer sky. In the heart of the mountain, in a cave, lived Herod's two hundred mares, the most beautiful on Earth, white as milk with manes as black as ebony; they were fed on honey cakes and were so lightfooted they could have run through a field of lilies without bruising a single one. Deeper still, in a prison cell, lay Iokanan, the man the Church calls John the Baptist.'

'But, Topsius, how did that misfortune come about?'

'It was like this, Dom Raposo . . . In Rome Herod had met Herodias, his niece, the wife of his brother Philip, who was living an indolent life in Italy, enjoying the luxuries of Rome, with no thought for Judaea. Herodias was splendidly, darkly beautiful. Herod Antipas seized her and sailed away in a galley to Syria. He repudiated his wife, a noble Moabite, the daughter of king Aretas who ruled over the desert and all those who travelled across it, and shut himself away with Herodias in that citadel of Makeros. Anger filled the devout land of Judaea at this outrage against the law of God! And then wily Herod Antipas ordered the Baptist to be brought to him, for at the time he was preaching in the Jordan valley . . .'

'But why, Topsius?'

'Why else, Dom Raposo? To see if the rough prophet, once caressed, spoiled and softened up with praise and good Sichem wine, would give his approval to that black passion and, with his persuasive powers, for his was the dominant voice at the time in Judaea and Galilee, make it seem, in the eyes of the faithful, as white as the snows on Carmel. But unfortunately, Dom Raposo, the Baptist had no imagination. He wasn't a bad saint, but he lacked originality. The Baptist slavishly imitated the great prophet Elijah in everything: he lived in a hole like Elijah, he wore animal skins like Elijah, he ate grasshoppers like Elijah, he echoed Elijah's classic curses and just as Elijah had spoken out against Ahab's incest, so the Baptist thundered against Herodias. Pure imitation, Dom Raposo!'

'And they silenced him by putting him in prison!'

'Silenced him! He roared even more, roared even louder and more terrifyingly. And Herodias hid her head beneath the blanket in order not to hear this clamorous cursing coming up from the depths of the mountain.'

With tears moistening my eyes, I stammered out:

'And so Herod ordered our good St John to be beheaded.'

'No! Herod Antipas was a weak man, spineless. He was lubricious in the extreme, Dom Raposo, but incapable of making decisions ... Besides, like all Galileans, he had a secret weakness, an irredeemable liking for prophets. And he feared the vengeance of Elijah, protector and friend of Iokanan. Because Elijah did not die, Dom Raposo. He lives on in Heaven, alive and well and still dressed in rags, an awesome, implacable, vociferous force.'

'Good grief!' I mumbled, shivering.

'Well, that's how it was ... Iokanan remained alive, still roaring. But women's hatred, Dom Raposo, is a sinuous, subtle thing. Herod's birthday fell in the month of Shevat. In Makeros there were huge celebrations, which were attended by Vitellius, who was travelling in Syria at the time. I'm sure you remember him, a coarse man who was later made lord of the world ... Anyway, when, according to the etiquette of the tributary provinces, the moment came to drink the health of Caesar and of Rome, a marvellous virgin suddenly entered the room to the sound of tambourines, performing a Babylonian-style dance. It was Salome, Herodias' daughter by her husband Philip, whom she had brought up secretly in Caesarea, in a wood by the Temple of Hercules. Salome dazzled everyone as she danced naked. Inflamed, dazed with desire, Herod Antipas promised to give her anything she wanted if she would kiss him on the lips. She picked up a golden plate and, with a glance at her mother, asked for the head of the Baptist. Terrified, Antipas offered her the city of Tiberias, any amount of treasure, the one hundred villages of Gennesarat. She smiled, looked at her mother, and again, hesitant this time, stammered out her request for the head of Iokanan. Then all the guests, Sadducees, scribes, rich men from Decapolis, even Vitellius and the Romans, cried out gaily: 'You promised, Tetrarch, you swore, Tetrarch!' Moments later, Dom Raposo, a black man from Idumaea entered, bearing a scimitar in one hand and, in the other, grasped by the hair, the head of the prophet. Thus died St John, for whom people still sing and light bonfires on sweet June nights . . .'

As we were riding slowly along, absorbed in these ancient events, we saw in the distance, amidst the burning sand, a bronze-coloured strip of sad vegetation. Potte shouted out: 'It's the river Jordan! The Jordan!' And we rode furiously off towards the river of the Scriptures.

Potte knew a delightful place where a Christian could enjoy a nap on the banks of the baptismal stream and we spent the hottest hours there, lying languidly on a carpet drinking beer cooled in the waters of the holy river. The river forms a pool there, a gentle backwater, a resting place from the slow, burning course it traces across the desert from Lake Galilee, before it plunges forever into the bitter waters of the Dead Sea. There it idles, lapping the fine sand, its voice quiet and crystalline, tumbling the lustrous pebbles that lie on its bed. In the coolest spots, it sleeps, still and green, in the shade of the tamarinds. The leaves of the tall Persian poplars murmured above us; amongst the grasses unfamiliar flowers swayed, flowers that once the virgins of Canaan wove into their hair on the mornings of grape harvests; and in the soft dark of the branches, where they would no longer be startled by the terrible voice of Jehovah, blackcaps trilled peacefully. The mountains of Moab rose before us, smooth and blue, as if carved from a single block of precious stone. The white sky, silent and withdrawn, seemed to be enjoying a delicious respite from the harsh tumult that shook it when the sombre people of God lived there, amidst prayers and massacres. Whereas once it was filled by the constant beating of the wings of seraphim and the fluttering of the robes of prophets swept up to Heaven by the Almighty, now one saw only a flock of wild doves flying serenely towards the orchards of Engaddi.

Following Auntie's recommendation, I undressed and bathed in the waters of the Baptist. At first, gripped by pious emotion, I trod the sand reverently as if it were a carpet spread before a high altar and, naked, with my arms folded, feeling the slow current beating against my knees, I thought about poor St John and whispered an Our Father. Then I laughed out loud and took full advantage of that bucolic bathtub amongst the trees. Potte threw me my sponge and I soaped myself in those sacred waters, humming Adélia's favourite *fado*.

As it grew cooler and we mounted our horses again, a tribe of Bedouin, coming down from the hills of Galgala, brought their herds of camel to drink from the Jordan. The young camels with their thick white fur bleated as they ran, the shepherds, their lances held high, uttered battle cries as they galloped, their ample cloaks flapping. And it was as if an idyll from the days of the Bible, when Hagar was still a young woman, had resurfaced there in that valley, in the splendour of evening! Sitting tensely in the saddle, the reins gathered in, I felt a sudden heroic tremor run through me: I longed for a sword, a law, a god to fight for . . . Slowly a rapt silence filled the sacred plain. And Moab's highest mountain took on a rare glow, pink and gold, as if the face of the Lord were once more fleetingly reflected upon it as he passed. Topsius raised a knowledgeable hand.

'Do you see that peak lit up by the sun, Dom Raposo,

that's Moriah, where Moses died.'

I shivered and, permeated by the divine emanations from both the river and the mountains, I felt strong, like the strong men in Exodus. I felt I was one of them, a kinsman of Jehovah, just back from darkest Egypt with my sandals in my hand. That sigh of relief carried on the wind came from the tribes of Israel, emerging at last from the desert. On the slopes beyond, followed by an escort of angels, the golden ark was borne along on the shoulders of linen-clad Levites who sang as they walked. Once more, in the dry sands the Promised Land grew green, Jericho gleamed white amongst the cornfields and, through the dense palmgroves, the trumpets of Joshua sounded, on the march again.

I could not contain myself, I snatched off my pith helmet, and let out this pious howl over the land of Canaan:

'Hail to Our Lord Jesus Christ! Hail to the hosts of Heaven!'

Early the next day, a Sunday, my tireless friend Topsius set out, equipped with pencils and parasol, to study the ruins of Jericho, the ancient city of palm trees, furnished by Herod with public baths, temples, gardens and statues, where he had conducted his tortuous love affair with Cleopatra. I stayed behind to drink my coffee, sitting astride a crate at the door of the tent, gazing out at the peaceful comings and goings in our encampment. The cook was plucking a chicken; the sad-faced Bedouin was sitting at the water's edge scouring his peaceable cutlass with sand; instead of giving the horses their feed, the handsome muleteer was gazing up at the sapphire-bright sky to watch the white passing of storks flying two by two towards Samaria.

Then I donned my pith helmet and wandered off into the sweet morning, my hands in my pockets, singing the words of a sad *fado* under my breath. I was thinking about Adélia and Senhor Adelino. I imagined them snuggled up

in her bedroom, exchanging furious kisses, perhaps referring to me as 'that creep', whilst I strolled amongst the
solitary places of the Scriptures. At that hour, Auntie,
wearing her black mantilla and carrying her book of divine
service, would be leaving for mass at Santana; the waiters
at the Café Montanha, their hair still uncombed, would be
whistling as they brushed the green baize of the billiard
tables; and Dr Margaride would be sitting at his window
overlooking the Praça da Figueira and putting on his
glasses to read the *Diário de Notícias*. Oh my sweet Lisbon!
But closer still, beyond the desert of Gaza, in green Egypt,
my Maricoquinhas would at that moment be filling the
vase on her balcony with magnolias and roses, her cat
would be asleep on the velvet chair and she would be
sighing for her 'brave little Portuguese lover'. I sighed too
and the song I was singing sounded even sadder on my
lips.

And suddenly, looking about me, I found that I was lost
somewhere in a place of great solitude and melancholy. I
was far from the stream and from the aromatic bushes
with their yellow flowers, I could no longer see our white
tents and before me lay an arid wilderness of palest sand,
enclosed by smooth cliffs sheer as the walls of a well, cliffs
so dark that the golden light of the warm orient morning
that fell upon them fainted away, faded and sad. The
desolate scene reminded me of engravings in which a
hermit with a long beard sat by the entrance to a cave
poring over a manuscript. But there was no hermit living
there, wasting away in an act of heroic penitence. In the
middle of that wild place, alone and proud, like a rarity, a
relic, as if the rocks had arranged themselves round about
in order to make for it a sheltered shrine, there grew a
solitary tree so repellent in appearance that the rest of the
sad song I was singing died on my lips.

It had a short, thick, squat trunk and no visible roots, so
that it looked like an enormous cudgel thrust violently into
the sand. The slippery bark had the oily lustre of black skin
and, growing out of its swollen head – the colour of burnt-

out embers – I counted eight branches, like the long legs of a spider, swarthy and flaccid, covered with a viscous down and bristling with thorns. After gazing in silence at this monster, I slowly took off my hat and murmured:

'Well, who'd have thought it!'

For I was clearly standing before a very famous tree. It was just such a branch (the ninth branch perhaps) which, shaped into a crown by a Roman centurion from the Jerusalem barracks, had cruelly adorned, on the day of his death, the head of a carpenter from Galilee, who had been condemned, yes, condemned to walk through quiet villages and the holy courtyards of the Temple announcing that he was the son of David and proclaiming himself the son of God, preaching against the old religion, against the old institutions, against the old order, against the old ways! And that branch, because it had touched the unruly hair of the rebel, becomes divine, is raised up on altars and, when placed on the head of an image paraded through the streets, it causes the compassionate crowds to prostrate themselves as it passes.

In the Colégio dos Isidoros, on Tuesdays and Saturdays, that grubby priest, Father Soares used to grind his teeth and say: 'There is a place in Judaea, boys . . .' This was the place! ' . . . a tree which, according to the Bible, would make your flesh creep . . .' This was the tree! Right before my frivolous young man's eyes stood the sacred tree of thorns!

And then an idea seared my spirit with all the brilliance of a celestial visitation. I would take one of those branches – the downiest and thorniest of them – home to Auntie as if it were a relic, rich in miracles, on which she could lavish her devout energies and to which she could confidently turn for divine favour. 'If you consider that I deserve some reward for all that I have done for you, then bring me from those holy places a holy relic.' That's what Senhora Dona Patrocínio das Neves had said to me on the eve of my pious journey as she sat enthroned amongst her red damasks before representatives of the Law and of the

Church, allowing one mournful tear to esc[ape] her austere spectacles. What more sacred, more efficacious gift could I give her tha[n] the tree of thorns, plucked in the Jordan [on a] bright Sunday morning?

I was suddenly gripped by a feeling [...]. What if some transcendent virtue really did flow [...] the fibres of that tree? And what if Auntie's liver condition did begin to get better, what if she grew young again, the moment I installed in her chapel, amongst the candles and the flowers, one of those branches bristling with thorns? What a wretched achievement! I would be the one who had foolishly brought her the miraculous gift of health and made her vigorous, indestructible and unburiable, with G. Godinho's money grasped firmly in her miserly hand! I, who was only just beginning to live, when she should be beginning to die!

Circling round the tree of thorns, I asked it in a hoarse, sombre voice: 'Come on then, you monster, tell me! Are you a divine relic with supernatural powers or are you just a grotesque bush with a Latin name as classified by Linnaeus? Come on, tell me! Do you, like the man whose head you crowned with scorn, have the gift of healing? Think about it. I'm not carrying you off with me to that charming Portuguese chapel, thereby freeing you from the torment of solitude and the melancholy of obscurity, and bestowing on you an altar, the bright incense of roses, the flattering flames of candles, the respect of praying hands, the caress of prayers, in order for you – by indulgently prolonging an irksome existence – to deprive me of an early inheritance and of all the pleasures my young flesh deserves! Think about it! If, by virtue of appearing in the Gospels, you drank in some puerile ideas about charity and mercy and you're going to Portugal with the intention of making my aunt better, then you can just stay here, amongst these rocks, whipped by the dust of the desert, covered in the excrement of birds of prey, doomed to boredom in this eternal silence! But if you promise to deaf to Auntie's prayers, to behave just like a poor, ...ered branch with absolutely no divine influence and ...u promise not to interrupt the longed-for decomposition of her flesh, then you'll find a heartfelt welcome in Lisbon in a chapel hung with soft damasks, enjoying the warmth of devout kisses and all the satisfactions of an idol, and I will surround you with so much adoration that you will never again need to envy the God whom your thorns wounded. Speak, monster!'

The monster did not speak. But I immediately felt my soul pervaded by the calm presentiment – as consolingly cool as a summer breeze – that Auntie would soon die and go and rot in her grave. In the terse language of nature, transmitted through its sap to my blood, the tree of thorns was sending me a sweet portent of Senhora Dona Patrocínio's imminent death, like a binding promise that, once transported to the chapel, not one of its branches would intervene to prevent the ghastly woman's liver from swelling up and her from dying. And, in the midst of that desert, this forged between us a kind of tacit pact, profound and mortal.

But was this really the tree of thorns? The speed with which it had agreed to my conditions made me suspicious of its divinity. I decided to consult my wise and solid friend Topsius.

I ran to the spring of Elisha, where he was rummaging about for stones, shards and rubbish – the remains of that proud city of palm trees. I spotted him at once, the illustrious historian, crouched by a well of water, his glasses glinting zealously, scraping away at a piece of blackened pillar, half-buried in the mud. By his side, a donkey, oblivious to the tender grass, was contemplating philosophically and with a certain melancholy the eagerness and passion of that wise man crawling about on the ground in search of Herod's public baths.

I told Topsius about my find and about my doubts. He immediately got to his feet, obliging as ever, eager and ready to tackle any erudite problem.

'A tree of thorns, eh?' he murmured, mopping the sweat from his brow. 'It must be the *Nabka*. It grows throughout the whole of Syria! Hasselquist, the botanist, claims that the crown of thorns was made from it. It has charming little green leaves in the shape of a heart, like ivy leaves. It doesn't? Oh well, it must be *Lycium spinosum* then. That, according to Latin tradition, is what was used for the crown of thorns. As for me, I think tradition is wrong and Hasselquist is just plain ignorant. But I'll sort it out for you, Dom Raposo. I'll clear this up once and for all!'

We set off. In the wilderness, standing before the terrible tree, Topsius gave a professorial lift of his head, withdrew for a moment into the inner depths of his knowledge and then declared that I could not take back to my devout aunt anything more precious. And the reason he gave for this pronouncement was dazzling. All the instruments used in the crucifixion (he said, flourishing his parasol), the nails, the sponge, the green reed, made momentarily divine by virtue of being part of the Divine Tragedy, gradually returned, according to the demands of civilisation, to their ordinary roles in life. Thus, the nail did not idle away eternity on an altar as a reminder to everyone of the sacred wounds: humanity, which is both Catholic and commerce-minded, eventually returned the nail to its original use, as a valuable bit of hardware; and though once it had pierced the hands of the Messiah, that hard-working, modest nail is now employed in holding down the lids of unclean coffins ... The reverend brothers of Our Lord of the Stations of the Cross use the reed for fishing, it serves as the wooden tail of rockets and even the State itself (so scrupulous in religious matters) is happy to use it in that form on festive nights to celebrate a new constitution or at wild junketings held for the weddings of princes. The sponge, once soaked in the vinegar of sarcasm and offered up on a lance, is now used in those irreligious ceremonies of washing, which the church has always heartily disapproved of. Even the cross, the supreme symbol, has lost its divine significance for men. Christianity, having used it as a standard, now uses it as an ornament: the cross as a brooch and a trinket. It hangs on necklaces, clinks on bracelets, it is engraved on signet rings, set in cuff links, indeed, in this proud century of ours, the cross has more to do with the world of jewellery than with religion.

'But, Dom Raposo, the crown of thorns was never used for anything else!'

No, for nothing else! The Church received it from the hands of a Roman proconsul and it remained alone and for all eternity in the Church, in memory of that most shameful of acts. In this whole wide universe it found only one congenial place: the darkness of chapels, its sole use being to arouse feelings of contrition. No jeweller has ever imitated it in gold, encrusted it with rubies to adorn some blond coiffure; it is purely and simply the instrument of martyrdom; and stained with blood, placed on the curling hair of the wooden images of Christ, it is an endless provocation to grief. Even the most astute industrialist, after turning it round pensively in his hands, restored it to the altars as something with no use in life, in commerce, in civilisation. It is merely an attribute of the Passion, a source of comfort for the sad, moving the weak to compassion. Of all the accessories mentioned in the Scriptures, only the crown can drive people to sincere prayer. Even the most devout would not prostrate themselves, babbling Paternosters, before a sponge dropped into a bowl of water or before a rod by the side of a stream. But before the crown of thorns there are always believing hands ready to be raised up in prayer; a sense of its cruelty pervades even the melancholy of the Miserere!

What greater marvel could I take to my aunt?

'Indeed, my dear Topsius . . . everything you say is like purest gold. But do you think the real crown of thorns, the one they actually used, would have been taken from here, from this tree? Do you really think so, my friend?'

Erudite Topsius slowly unfolded his checked handkerchief and declared that (contrary to that foolish Catholic tradition and contrary to that ignoramus Hasselquist) the crown of thorns was taken from a bramble bush, with fine, flexible branches and tiny purple flowers, sad and perfumeless, of the kind that abounds in the valleys of Jerusalem, the sort you use to light a fire or to spike a hedge . . .'

Downhearted, I mumbled:

'What a shame! Auntie would so have wanted it to come from here, Topsius! And Auntie is so rich!'

Then the wise philosopher understood that just as there are reasons of state so are there reasons of family and he reacted superbly. He stretched out one hand over the tree, thus generously covering it with the guarantee of his knowledge, and he pronounced these memorable words:

'Dom Raposo, we have been good friends. You can assure your lady aunt, on behalf of a man to whom all Germany listens when it comes to matters of archaeological criticism, that the branch you bear to her from here, made into a crown, was . . .'

'Was?' I blurted out anxiously.

' . . . was the very same that bloodied the brow of Rabbi Jeschoua Natzarieh, whom the Catholics call Jesus of Nazareth and still others call the Christ!'

German erudition had spoken! I got out my Seville knife and cut off one of the branches. And whilst Topsius went back to scrabbling amongst the damp grasses in search of the citadel of Cypron and other stones from the time of Herod, I returned in triumph to our tents, carrying my prize. Seated on a saddle, Potte was cheerily grinding coffee.

'That's a fine branch you've got there!' he shouted. 'Would you like it made into a crown? That way it could serve as a relic.'

And then, with extraordinary dexterity, the excellent man wove the rough branch into the shape of a holy crown. And it looked so touchingly like the real crown of thorns!

Moved, I murmured: 'The only thing lacking are a few drops of blood. Auntie will positively drool over this!'

But how were we to transport back to Jerusalem,

through the hills of Judah, that awkward thorny object which, even in its present form, seemed eager to tear at innocent flesh? This presented no problem to Potte. From the depths of his well-provided saddlebag he produced a fluffy cloud of cotton wool. He delicately wrapped the crown up in it, as if it were a fragile jewel, then with a sheet of brown paper and some scarlet string, he made it into a round package, light, neat and compact. And I, smiling and rolling a cigarette, thought of that other package containing lace and silk ribbons and smelling of violets and love, which had remained behind in Jerusalem, waiting for me and for my kisses.

'Potte,' I cried, overjoyed, 'you have no idea how much money that little branch inside that little packet is worth to me.'

No sooner had Topsius returned from the sacred spring of Elisha than I suggested celebrating our providential finding of the great relic with one of the golden-topped bottles of champagne Potte was carrying in his saddlebags. Topsius drank to knowledge! I drank to religion! And the Moët et Chandon flowed freely in the land of Canaan. That night, to complete our celebrations, we lit a bonfire and the Arab women from Jericho came to dance before our tents. We went to bed very late, as the moon was coming up above Moab, curved and slender, like the golden cutlass that had cut off Iokanan's ardent head.

The package containing the crown of thorns lay beside my bed. The fire had gone out and our encampment slept in the infinite silence of the valley of the Scriptures. Feeling calm and happy, I too fell asleep.

III

For what must have been about two hours, I lay in a deep sleep, stretched out on my camp bed. Then, suddenly, the whole tent seemed filled by a tremulous clarity, as if lit by the flame of a guttering torch, and I heard a mournful, plaintive voice calling out to me:

'Teodorico, Teodorico, arise and go to Jerusalem!'

Startled, I threw off my blanket and, by the unsteady light of the flickering candle that stood on a table still cluttered with last night's champagne bottles, I saw my friend, the learned Topsius, hurriedly buckling on an ancient iron spur. His was the voice I had heard fervently urging me awake:

'On your feet, Teodorico! The mares are saddled up and ready. Tomorrow is Passover and we must be at the gates of Jerusalem by dawn!'

Pushing back my hair from my forehead, I gazed in astonishment at the normally prudent, cautious doctor:

'You mean we're going now, Topsius, just like that, without any luggage, like frightened fugitives, leaving everyone else asleep in their tents?'

The learned man raised his head. His gold-rimmed spectacles glinted with a rare and irresistible intelligence. Wrapped about his spare, erudite frame, he wore a white cloak I had never seen before, which hung about him in heavy, clean folds like a Roman toga. Then, standing very erect, he slowly spread wide his arms and, from lips that seemed carved out of timeless marble, he let fall these words:

'Dom Raposo, this new day now dawning, which soon will light the peaks of Hebron, is the fifteenth day of the month of Nisan and never in the whole history of Israel, from the moment the tribes returned from Babylon until Titus comes to lay final siege to the Temple, never will there be a more interesting day! I must be in Jerusalem to see this page from the Gospels spring to life! So come, let us go and keep Passover at the house of Gamaliel. He is a friend of Hillel's and mine, a man learned in Greek letters, a great patriot and a member of the Sanhedrin. He it was who said: "To free yourself from the torment of doubt, simply open yourself to faith." So, on your feet, Dom Raposo!'

Thus spoke my friend as he stood before me. And, as if in obedience to a celestial command, I began submissively, silently, pulling on my stout riding boots and had no sooner thrown an Arab cloak about me than Topsius was hustling me impatiently out of the tent, not even allowing me time to pick up my watch or the Seville knife that I slipped beneath my pillow each night as a precautionary measure. The sputtering candle was beginning to smoke now and glow red . . .

It must have been about midnight. In the distance, as if from within the walls of some leafy villa, I could hear the muffled barking of two dogs. The soft, empty air smelled of garden roses and orange blossom. The sky of Israel glittered with rare splendour and, above Mount Nebo, a lovely star of almost divine radiance, whiter than the snows, looked down on me, pulsating anxiously, as if – a prisoner of its own silence – it were struggling to confide some secret to my soul!

The mares were waiting, utterly still, their long manes hanging down. Climbing onto my horse, while Topsius was still laboriously adjusting his stirrups, I saw, near the fountain of Elisha, a marvellous vision that sent a shiver of sublime terror through me.

For by the diamantine light of the Syrian stars, I saw what looked like the white wall of a new-built city! The bright pediments of temples gleamed amidst the dense foliage of sacred woods and the delicate arches of an aqueduct fled palely across the distant hills. Smoke from a fire rose up from a tower, whilst below it, the points of spears stirred and glinted and the long sound of a horn died slowly away in the shadows. Huddled against the city walls, amongst groves of palm trees, a village slept.

Topsius had mounted his horse by then and was ready to leave, his fingers plunged into his horse's mane. Overcome with emotion, I managed to stammer out:

'That white place . . . over there.'

'Jericho,' he answered tersely and set off at a gallop. I rode after him, that noble historian of the Herods, for how long I don't know, only that the road we followed was straight and paved with black basalt. How different from the rough path, bleached white and glistening, that had led us down into Canaan through hills whose sparse covering of gorse seared by the burning sun had seemed like a patina of mould and neglect! Indeed everything I saw about me now looked different: the shapes of the rocks, the smell of the hot earth, even the beating stars . . . What change had been wrought in me and in the Universe? Now and then a sudden brilliant spark would fly up from our horses' hooves. Topsius galloped on without pause, hanging on to his horse's mane, the two edges of his white cloak flapping behind him like the folds of a flag.

Then suddenly he stopped. We had reached a square-built house, set amongst trees. The house was utterly dark and mute. On a flagstaff on the roof perched the incongruous figure of a stork, as if cut out of sheet metal. By the entrance, a fire still smouldered; I stirred the embers and, in the light of the brief flame that leapt up, I saw that we were outside an old inn by the side of an ancient road. Beneath the stork, above the narrow door studded with nails, hung a Latin sign in gleaming black on white stone: *Ad Gruem Majorem*, and to one side, covering part of the façade, was a crudely carved inscription, decipherable only with difficulty, in which Apollo wished good health to all guests and the landlord, one Septimanus, guaranteed them a warm welcome and a restorative bath, as well as strong wine from Campania, cool, white wine from Engaddi and 'all the comforts of Rome'.

'Of Rome!' I murmured incredulously.

What strange paths were these I was treading? What other men, different from me in speech and dress, under the protection of other gods, had drunk their wine here from amphoras dating back to the time of Horace?

But the lean, shadowy figure of Topsius was off again into the night. The sonorous basalt road had ended now and we made our slow way up a steep path cut out of the rocks, where great boulders echoed as they rolled away beneath our horses' hooves, as if it were the bed of a once rushing stream parched dry by an implacable August. Jolted about in his saddle, the learned doctor muttered hoarse curses against the Sanhedrin, against the rigid Jewish law, unbendingly opposed to all the proconsul's projects, however enlightened. The Pharisee never viewed other than with rancour the Roman aqueduct that brought him water, the Roman road that carried him to other cities, the Roman baths that cured his rashes . . .

'A curse on all Pharisees!'

Bundled up in my cloak, I sleepily recalled ancient imprecations drawn from the Gospels and mumbled them to myself as I rode along:

'Pharisees, whited sepulchres . . . A curse on all your tribe!'

It was the silent hour when the mountain wolves come down to the streams to drink. I closed my eyes; the stars were growing faint.

The Lord makes brief the soft nights of the month of Nisan, when the white lamb of Passover is eaten, and soon, over the land of Moab, the sky began to clothe itself in white.

I woke up. Cattle were lowing on the hills. The cool air smelled of rosemary.

Just then, I saw a figure come wandering along the heights towards the path: a man of strange, fierce mien, dressed only in sheepskins. He reminded me of Elijah and of the divine wrath of the Scriptures; his chest and legs seemed made out of red granite; his eyes flashed wildly amidst the rough, matted hair and beard that grew like a lion's mane about his face. His gaze lighted on us and, stretching up his arms like someone about to throw two stones, he hurled at us instead all the curses under the sun! He called us 'pagans', 'dogs'. He screamed: 'Cursed be your mothers, withered be the breasts of those who suckled you!' His harsh, ominous cries rained down upon us from the lofty crags and Topsius, hindered by the slow pace of his horse, wrapped his cloak more closely about him, as if against a fierce hailstorm. I grew angry then and, turning in my saddle, I called the man a drunkard and flung obscenities back at him only to see the black, clamorous mouth twist and drool with holy rage beneath the savage flame of his eyes.

We emerged from the ravine onto the long, paved Roman road that leads to Shechem and we trotted along it, relieved at last to be entering a land that was civilised, God-fearing, humane and law-abiding. Water abounded everywhere; new forts had been built on the hills; sacred stones marked the boundaries of fields. On the white threshing-floors, oxen garlanded with anemones trod the wheat gathered in the Passover harvest, and in gardens where the figtree was already in leaf, the slave sang in his whitewashed tower and wielded a stick to frighten off the marauding pigeons. Occasionally we would see a man standing with downcast eyes beside a vineyard or an irrigation ditch, one corner of his cloak pulled up over his head as he recited the holy prayer of the Sachema. A potter, urging on a mule laden down with yellow earthenware pots, called out to us: 'A blessing on your mothers! A good Passover to you both!' And a leper, resting in the shade amongst the olive groves, moaned and pointed to his sores, asking us if we knew the name of the rabbi in Jerusalem who healed the sick and where he might find some canna root.

As we neared Bethany, we stopped to water the horses by a lovely fountain in the shade of a cedar tree. Just as the learned Topsius was once again readjusting his stirrups and expressing his surprise that we had not yet met the caravan that travelled from Galilee to Jerusalem each year in order to celebrate Passover, we heard, from up ahead, the slow rumble of armed men on the move. And, to my astonishment, a group of Roman soldiers suddenly came into view, looking just like the soldiers I had so often cursed in depictions of the Passion!

Bearded and burned by the Syrian sun, they were marching stoutly along, with measured, rhythmic strides, the iron soles of their sandals ringing out on the paved road. On their backs they carried their shields wrapped in sacking and, over one shoulder, a long pitchfork from which hung bundles tied with string, bronze plates, tools and bunches of dates. Some, their heads bare, carried their helmets like buckets, whilst others bore a short spear in one hairy hand. The plump, fair decurion, wrapped in his scarlet cloak, dozed as he trotted along on his mare, followed by a tame gazelle decked with corals. Behind him, beside the mules laden with sacks of wheat and bundles of firewood, the muleteers sang to the sound of a clay flute played by a half-naked negro with the number of the legion written in red upon his breast.

I withdrew to the shade of the cedar tree. But Topsius, of course, servile German that he was, dismounted, indeed almost knelt down in the dust, before the armed might of Rome and waved his arms and cloak, unable to contain his enthusiasm, crying:

'Long live Gaius Tiberius, august emperor and bringer of peace, thrice consul in Illyria, Pannonia and Germany!'

Some of the legionaries responded to this outburst with coarse laughter and then passed on, in closed ranks, with a clank of metal. In the distance, a shepherd called to his sheep and fled into the hills.

We galloped on. The basalt road came to an end again and we rode instead through groves of trees, amidst the scent of orchards, through scenes of cool abundance.

How different were these paths, these hills, to those I had seen only days before around the Holy City, dried bone-white by an unremitting wind. Here, everything was green and flourishing, full of murmurous shade. The light had lost the sad, anguished tone in which I had always seen

Jerusalem bathed before; the April leaves unfurled against a young, tender blue sky, as full of hope as the leaves themselves. And my eyes alighted again and again on gardens such as those described in the Scriptures, full of olive trees, fig trees and vines and in which the red lilies of the field grew wild, more splendidly arrayed than even Solomon himself!

I was humming contentedly to myself as we trotted past a hedgerow all intertwined with roses, when Topsius called to me to stop, pointing up at the brow of a hill where, against a dark backdrop of cypresses and cedars, there stood a house, its white portico turned towards the east and to the light. It belonged, he said, to a Roman, a relative of Valerius Gracus, the former imperial legate from Syria. Everything about the place seemed imbued with sweet peace and Latin grace. A lush lawn of smoothest grass sloped down to a path lined with lavender and, in the middle, the initials of Valerius Gracus were sown in flowers, scarlet on green. Nearby, amongst the beds of roses and lilies bordered with myrtles, gleamed noble urns made of Corinthian marble all wound about with acanthus leaves. A servant in a grey cowl was pruning a yew tree into the form of an urn, next to a box tree already skilfully fashioned into a lyre. Chickens pecked at the scarlet sand strewn along an avenue of plane trees festooned with ivy that trailed from trunk to trunk, forming garlands such as might adorn a temple, and where the leaves of laurel bushes discreetly veiled in shadow the nakedness of the statues. Beneath an arbour of vines, to the sound of slow water singing in a bronze basin, a serene old man in a toga, smiling and happy, was sitting next to a statue of Aesculapius and reading from a long papyrus scroll, whilst a girl, all dressed in white linen and with a golden arrow adorning her plaited hair, wove a chaplet out of the flowers that filled her lap. When she heard our horses passing by, she raised her clear eyes to us. Topsius shouted out: '*Salve, pulquerrima!*', I cried: '*¡Viva la gracia!*' and the blackbirds sang in the flowering pomegranate trees.

Further on, the learned Topsius, still in communicative mood, paused again to indicate amongst the cypresses another country house, dark and severe this time, and in a low voice he explained that its owner was Osanias, a rich Sadducee from Jerusalem, a member of the priestly family of Beothos and of the Sanhedrin. No pagan ornaments profaned these walls. Square, hermetic, rigid, the house reproduced in physical form the austerity of the Law. But the broad thatched granaries, the winepresses and the vineyards spoke of great wealth culled from heavy tributes; in the courtyards ten slaves barely sufficed to store away all the sacks of wheat, the wineskins, the sheep daubed with red dye, all collected in payment of the tithe for Passover. By the roadside, in ostentatious piety, the freshly whitewashed family tomb gleamed in the sunlight amongst the rosebushes.

Riding on, we reached the palm trees that surround Bethphage and, taking a leafy byway known to Topsius, we began to climb up the Mount of Olives to the Winepress of the Moabite, a stopping place for caravans along this endless, ancient royal road that begins in Egypt and continues on to the well-watered city of Damascus.

What we saw next seemed like a mirage, for there, over the whole hillside, amongst the olive groves covering the slopes as far as Kidron, amongst the orchards in the valley as far as Siloe, amongst the new tombs of the priests and even along the dusty Hebron road, we witnessed the noisy awakening of a whole encampment of people! Black desert tents made out of sheepskins and edged with stones; the canvas shelters of the people of Idumaea, gleaming white in the sun amidst the greenery; huts built out of branches by shepherds from Ascalon; awnings of carpets propped up on branches of cedar by pilgrims from Naphtali – the whole of Judaea was gathered there at the gates of Jerusalem to celebrate the holy feast of Passover! And around a hut guarded by legionaries thronged black merchants from Decapolis, Phoenician weavers from Tiberias and pagan people who had come all the way across Samaria from Caesarea and the sea.

We rode slowly and cautiously on, past camels freed from their heavy burdens, ruminating in the shade of the olive trees alongside horses from Peraea, legs hobbled and heads bowed beneath their long, thick manes. Through the half-raised flaps of tents we glimpsed the gleam of weapons hanging from walls or the enamel of huge plates and outside, young girls, their arms glittering with bracelets, were busy milking goats or grinding rye between two stones. Everywhere bright fires were lit and a long line of women, each with a tall waterjar balanced on one shoulder, walked down to the spring of Siloe, leading their children by the hand and singing as they went.

Our mares tripped on the taut ropes of the Idumean shelters. Then we stopped by some carpets spread out on the ground. A merchant from Caesarea, wearing a showy, flower-embroidered cloak from Carthage, was rolling out lengths of Egyptian linen, silks from Kos, bringing out gleaming damascened guns or extolling the virtues of spikenard from Assyria and the sweet oils of Parthia, holding a bottle of each in either hand. The men who were gathered around him drew back at our approach and looked at us with proud, languid eyes; the occasional curse was uttered; Topsius' glasses provoked the odd burst of scornful laughter that revealed sharp teeth amidst the rough, black beards.

Rows of beggars leaned against the walls beneath the trees, wailing and holding out to us the shard of pottery with which they chafed at their sores. Outside a hut improvised from branches of bay, an obese old man, ruddy as Silenus, was crying his wares: new wine from Shechem, beans picked that April. The dusky men of the desert crowded round the baskets of fruit. A shepherd from Ascalon, mounted on stilts in the midst of a flock of white lambs, blew on a horn and called to the faithful to come buy their pure Passover lamb. And amongst the multitude, where sticks were wielded in brief, intermittent scuffles, Roman soldiers patrolled in pairs, benign and paternal, olive twigs tucked in their helmets.

Proceeding on we reached two tall, luxuriant cedar trees so thickly covered in fluttering doves that they looked like huge apple trees in spring with the wind ruffling their blossom. Then Topsius froze in his tracks and flung wide his arms; I did the same and, for a moment, we both sat there on our horses, stunned into immobility, our hearts stopped, for below us lay Jerusalem, resplendent in the sun.

The whole city was bathed in sumptuous light. Above the steep banks of the Kidron, parched dry by the heat of Nisan, rose an austere, high wall, topped with newly-built towers, with gates made of stonework intermingled with gold. It encircled Mount Zion, curving round past Hinnon as far as the hills of Gareb. And within the wall, facing the cedar trees that shaded us, stood the Temple, proud and splendid, rising up on its eternal foundations, seeming to dominate the whole of Judaea. Walled in by polished granite, protected by ramparts of marble, it looked like the shining citadel of a god!

Leaning forward over his horse's neck, wise Topsius indicated to me the outer enclosure known as the Court of Gentiles, vast enough to contain all the multitudes of both Israel and the pagan lands; the smooth floor shone like the limpid waters of a pool and the columns of Páros marble that formed the deep, cool Porch of Solomon were thicker even than the trunks of trees in Jericho's dense groves of palms. From the centre of this light, airy space rose a graceful terrace, accessible only to those faithful to the Law, to the chosen people of God. This, the proud Court of the Israelites, was reached by stairs so lustrous they seemed carved out of alabaster and was adorned with doors inlaid with silver, with archways and turrets alive with flying doves. From there, up another gleaming flight of stairs, rose a second white terrace, the Court of Priests, filled by a diffuse light out of which loomed a vast altar made of unhewn stone, a sombre bronze horn at each corner. On either side, two long, serene plumes of smoke rose slowly up into the blue like an everlasting prayer. And beyond, higher still, its golden ornaments glittering amidst the marble – snow-white and tawny as if made of mingled snow and gold – was the Hieron, the Holy of Holies, the dwelling place of Jehovah, dappling the surrounding hills with shimmering reflections of its marvellous brilliance.

Above the door hung the mystic veil, woven in Babylon in the colours of fire and of the sea. Along the wall climbed vines with leaves and bunches of grapes made from emeralds and other precious stones; long spears of gold radiated out from the cupola, forming a halo of light like a sun. Thus, resplendent, triumphant, august and precious, the Temple stood open to the sky of that Passover feast, freely offering itself up, like the loveliest and rarest of Earth's gifts!

But to one side of the Temple, indeed rising above it, as Topsius pointed out, like a proud and domineering master, stood the Antonia Fortress, black, solid, impenetrable, the citadel of the Roman forces. Armed men moved about the battlements; on one side, a powerful figure wrapped in the red cloak of a centurion, stood with one arm outstretched; and the slow notes of a horn spoke out as if sending forth orders to the other fortresses, blue and distant in the limpid air, which lay like shackles about the Holy City. At that moment Caesar seemed to me more powerful even than Jehovah!

Then Topsius pointed beyond the fortress to the ancient city of David itself. Newly whitewashed walls bright against the blue sky, the throng of tightly packed houses looked like a flock of goats making their way down into the still shadowy valley at the bottom of which was a vast, arcaded square; then the houses climbed up again, forming a tangle of streets that spread out on the opposite hillside of wealthy Acra, full of palaces and round cisterns gleaming in the sunlight like shields of steel. Farther off still, beyond the old ruined walls, the new district of Bezetha could be seen, still under construction; there stood the rounded arches of the Circus of Herod and, stretching out over one last hill, near the tomb of Helena, lay the gardens of Antipas, a haven of sun and shade, bathed by the sweet waters of Enrogel.

'Ah, Topsius,' I murmured, 'what a city!'

'Rabbi Eliezer says that the man who has not seen Jerusalem has never seen a truly beautiful city!'

But by then joyful people were running past us along the grassy path that led up the hill from Bethany. An old man, tugging urgently at the halter of a donkey laden down with bundles of palm leaves, shouted to us that the caravan from Galilee had just been sighted and was nearly there. Curious, we trotted up to a small mound next to a clump of cactus, where a crowd of women, their children in their arms, were already waving bright scarves and shouting out words of blessing and of welcome. And there, in the slow dustcloud turned golden by the sun, we could just make out the dense column of pilgrims, who had come from far off, from Upper Galilee, from Gescala, from the mountains, and who are always the last to reach Jerusalem. A hum of chanting filled the festive road; palm leaves and branches of flowering almond fluttered around a green flag; the great bundles loaded onto the backs of camels swayed rhythmically amongst the advancing mass of white turbans.

Six horsemen from the Babylonian guard of Herod Antipas, the Tetrarch of Galilee, had escorted the caravan from Tiberias: they wore turbans made of plush velvet, their long beards hung in plaited strands and their legs were bound with strips of yellow leather. They wheeled about at the head of the crowd, cracking whips with one hand and with the other tossing their glittering scimitars into the air and catching them. Immediately behind them, a chapter of Levites came striding along, leaning on staffs entwined with flowers, clutching to them the scrolls of the Law and loudly chanting the praises of Zion. By their side, sturdy young men, their cheeks puffed out and ruddy, blew fiercely on curled brass trumpets that sang out to heaven.

A shout went up amongst the people crowding the roadside. It came from an old man who wore no turban, his hair hanging loose. He was dancing frenetically back and forth, clicking castanets in his whirling hands, kicking out first one leg and then the other. His face was bearded like king David's and burned with an inspired flame. Behind him, to the plangent music of the small harps they played, young girls skipped on the light tips of their sandals, whilst others, spinning on the spot, beat loudly on tambourines, silver anklets gleaming in the dust raised by their feet beneath the circle of their whirling skirts. Then the whole ecstatic crowd burst out singing, the ancient songs of holy days and the psalms of pilgrimage.

'My steps bend only towards thee, O Jerusalem, for thou art perfect! He who loves thee lives in plenitude!'

Transported, I bellowed out in turn:

'Thou art the palace of the Lord, O Jerusalem, and the solace of my heart!'

The caravan passed slowly and vociferously by. The heavily veiled wives of the Levites rode past on donkeys, so bundled up they looked like large, shapeless sacks; the poorer women, on foot, carried fruit and oatmeal in the gathered corners of their cloaks. The better-prepared had brought along with them their offering to the Lord, a white lamb attached by a string to their belt and dragged along behind them; the sick hung frail arms around the necks of the strongest; gaunt-faced, their dark, dilated eyes feverishly sought a glimpse of the walls of the Holy City where all ills are cured.

Loud, heartfelt blessings were exchanged amongst the pilgrims and the merry crowd welcoming them; some asked after neighbours, about the harvest or about grandparents who had stayed behind in the village in the shade of their vines. An old man standing next to me, with a beard like Abraham's, threw earth on his head, tore out his hair and rent his tunic when told that the grindstone from his mill had been stolen.

Bringing up the rear were mules with bells around their neck, laden down with firewood and leather bottles full of oil and, behind them, a group of fanatics who had joined the caravan in the outlying towns of Bethphage and Rephrain. They advanced hurling empty wine gourds to the ground, brandishing knives and crying death to Samaritans and to all pagans.

Then, following Topsius, I trotted back across the hill towards the two cedars still white with fluttering doves and, at that same moment, the pilgrims leaving the path at last set eyes on Jerusalem as it lay glittering below them, white and beautiful in the sunlight. It was a moment of holy, tumultuous, wild delirium! Falling prostrate, the crowd touched their foreheads again and again to the hard ground; amidst trumpet blasts, a babble of prayers rose up to the clear sky; women held out their children, offering them ecstatically up to the Lord! Some stood utterly still, as if stunned by the splendours of Zion, and hot tears of faith, of pious love, rolled down men's cheeks into wild, unkempt beards. The old pointed out the terraces of the Temple, the ancient streets, the sacred places of Israel's history: 'There's the Gate of Ephraim; that's where the Tower of the Furnaces stood; those white stones mark the tomb of Rachel . . .' And those who listened round about, clustered together, clapped their hands and shouted: 'Blessings be upon thee, O Zion!' Others ran wildly off, their belts unloosed, stumbling over the ropes of tents and the baskets of fruit, to change their Roman money and buy a lamb for the sacrifice. Sometimes a fine, clear, artless song rose up from amongst the trees and hung trembling in the air so that, for a moment, both earth and sky seemed to be listening; down below, Zion glowed serenely and from the Temple the two slow plumes of smoke drifted heavenwards, eternal as an unending prayer. Then, the singing died away; people raised their voices once more in blessing; the soul of all Judah lost itself in contemplation of the magnificence of the shrine, and scrawny, frantic arms reached out to embrace Jehovah.

Then Topsius suddenly caught up the reins of my mare, for right by my side, a wild-eyed man in a saffron tunic had sprung from behind an olive tree. Brandishing a sword, he leaped onto a rock and cried out in a desperate voice:

'Men of Galilee, draw near, you too, men of Naphtali!'

Pilgrims ran towards him, their staffs raised, and women came out of their tents, pale-faced and clasping their children to them. The man's sword trembled in the air and he himself was shaking; then he cried out again in the same desolate tones:

'Men of Galilee, Rabbi Jeschoua has been arrested! Rabbi Jeschoua has been taken to the house of Hannan, men of Naphtali!'

Topsius turned to me, eyes blazing, and said: 'Dom Raposo, the man has been arrested. He has already appeared before the Sanhedrin! Quick, quick, my friend, we must press on to Jerusalem, to Gamaliel's house!'

And at the hour when they were making the perfume offering in the Temple, when the sun was already high above the Hebron, Topsius and I rode through the Fishmarket Gate into a street in old Jerusalem. It was steep, winding and dusty, lined with poor, low houses made out of brick; above the doors, each one fastened with a chain, and above barred windows so narrow they seemed like crevices, hung Passover decorations of intertwined leaves and palms. On flat roofs surrounded by balustrades, diligent women were shaking carpets and winnowing wheat; others chatted as they hung up strings of clay lanterns for the ritual illuminations.

Walking wearily alongside us was an Egyptian harpist, who wore a scarlet plume stuck in his curly wig and a piece of white cloth wrapped about his thin waist; his arms were weighed down with bracelets and the harp he carried on his back was curved like a scythe and carved with lotus flowers. Topsius asked him if he had come from Alexandria and if they still sang the battle hymns of Actium in the taverns of Eunotos? The man gave a sad smile that revealed long teeth. Then he set down his harp and began to pluck the strings ... We spurred our horses on, startling two women wearing yellow veils, each of them carrying two doves wrapped in one corner of their cloaks. They were doubtless hurrying off to the Temple, their light, graceful steps making the bells on their sandals tinkle.

Here and there, in the middle of the road, a homely fire was burning complete with trivet and casseroles that gave off an acrid smell of garlic. Naked children with swollen bellies scrabbled in the dust, gnawed greedily at the skins of raw pumpkins and stared at us in amazement, their huge, bleary eyes thick with flies. Outside a forge, a band of hirsute shepherds from Moab were waiting, whilst inside, hammering away in a cloud of sparks, the black-smiths were forging new points for their lances. A negro, wearing a comb in the shape of the sun in his tightly curled hair, was crying his wares in a loud, lugubrious voice: rye bread rolls made into obscene shapes.

Silently, we crossed a broad, paved square, still in the process of being built. At the far end, stood a modern Roman-style bath house, with a granite portico leading to a long arcade that exuded luxury and indolence. In the inner courtyard, in the cool shade of plane trees, from whose branches hung awnings made out of white linen, naked slaves, shining with sweat, scurried about carrying armfuls of flowers and bottles containing essential oils; from the barred windows, on a level with the flagstones, came a blast of warm, hothouse air that smelt of roses. And beneath one of the columns in the atrium, where an onyx tablet indicated the women's entrance, stood a marvellous creature, utterly immobile, as if offering herself for worship like some idol: her round face was white as the full moon, her plump lips blood red and on her head was the tall, yellow mitre typical of Babylonian prostitutes. She wore a black dalmatic brilliantly embroidered with golden foliage, which fell in stiff, brocade folds from her strong shoulders and over her firm breasts. She was holding a cactus flower in one hand and her heavy lids with their dense eyelashes opened and closed in time to the undulating movement of a fan manipulated by a black slave girl, who crouched at her feet, singing. When her eyes closed everything about her seemed to grow dark and when she raised the black

140

curtain of her lashes again, a brilliant light flashed from those dark pupils, like some natural force, like the midday sun in the desert that both burns and saddens. Thus she stood, magnificent, lascivious and pontifical, with her great limbs pale as marble and her fiery mitre, reminiscent of the rites of Astarte and of Adonis. Ashen-faced, I touched Topsius' arm and murmured:

'Crikey, look at that! I'm off to the baths!'

Topsius, looking lofty in his white cape, span round and said to me harshly:

'Gamaliel, son of Simeon, is expecting us. And according to the wisdom of the Rabbis, woman is the road to iniquity.'

And with that, he turned sharply into a gloomy, arched alleyway. The sound of the horses' hooves on the paving stones set the dogs barking and prompted curses from the beggars huddled together in the darkness. Then we jumped through a breach in the old city wall built by Hezekiah, passed an old dried-up cistern full of sleeping lizards and then, after trotting through the swirling dust of a long road, between gleaming, whitewashed walls and doors thickly painted with pitch, we stopped at the top outside a far grander entrance with an archway and a low grille made out of wire to keep out the scorpions. It was Gamaliel's house.

In the midst of a vast, tiled courtyard, scorched by the sun, a lime tree shaded the clear water of a pool. Around the courtyard, built on pillars made out of green marble, ran a cool, silent veranda on which was draped the occasional Assyrian carpet embroidered with flowers. A clear, blue sky glittered up above us and, in the corner, beneath a porch, a black slave, roped like a beast to a wooden pole, with iron-tipped shoes on his feet, his body deeply scarred, was slowly turning the household's great, creaking millstone.

A fat, beardless man appeared in the darkness of a doorway, his skin almost as yellow as the loose tunic he was wearing. In his hand he held an ivory walking stick and he seemed barely able to keep his heavy eyelids open.

'Where's your master?' shouted Topsius, dismounting.

'Come in,' said the man in a voice as high and fleeting as a cobra's hiss.

We went up a splendid black granite stairway to a landing where two candelabra stood, like bronze replicas of the trunks of thin, leafless trees. And between them, waiting for us, stood Gamaliel, son of Simeon. He was very tall and gaunt and his long, lustrous, perfumed beard covered his chest, on which glittered a coral signet ring threaded on a scarlet ribbon. Beneath his white turban, which was sown with strings of pearls, you could see, fastened to his forehead, a strip of parchment covered in sacred texts; the cold, hard glint of his hollow eyes was in sharp contrast to that whiteness. The long, blue tunic he was wearing reached down to his sandaled feet and was edged with broad fringes that dragged along the ground. Stitched to the sleeves, which he wore rolled back at the wrists, were further strips of parchment bearing more ritual texts written in black ink.

Topsius greeted him in the Egyptian fashion, letting one hand fall slowly to the knee of his silk trousers. Gamaliel stretched out his arms and murmured, almost chanting:

'Come in, you're most welcome, eat and enjoy yourselves.'

And we followed Gamaliel across an echoing, mosaic floor into a room where we found three other men. One of them came over from the window to greet us; he was extraordinarily handsome, with long chestnut-coloured hair that hung in soft curls about his strong neck, as smooth and white as Corinthian marble. The golden, gem-encrusted hilt of a short sword glinted in the black sash he wore about the waist of his tunic. The second man – bald and fat, with a flabby face and no eyebrows, so pale he looked as if his skin were coated in flour - remained seated, crosslegged, on the divan made out of strips of leather, wrapped in his wine-red cloak, each arm resting on a purple cushion. His gesture of welcome was as distracted and disdainful as the alms one throws to a stranger. Topsius, however, almost prostrated himself before him, kissing the round-toed shoes made out of yellow leather and fastened with golden laces, for this was the venerable Osanias of the priestly family of Beothos, of the same royal blood as Aristobolus. We did not greet the third man and he did not even notice us; he was crouched in one corner, his face buried in the cloak of a linen tunic whiter than freshly fallen snow, as if immersed in prayer. He stirred only to wipe his hands slowly on a towel, as pure white as his tunic, which hung from a thick, knotted cord tied about his waist, like the ones worn by monks.

Meanwhile, as I drew off my gloves, I was examining the ceiling, which was made out of cedar wood decorated with scarlet-painted carvings. The smooth lustrous blue of the wall was like a continuation of the hot, perfect sky that burned outside the window through which you could see, clinging to the wall in the brilliant sunlight, a solitary branch of honeysuckle. Smoke from some kind of aromatic resin drifted up from a bronze incense holder that stood on a three-legged stool inlaid with mother-of-pearl.

Gamaliel came over to us and after a long, hard look at my riding boots he said slowly:

'It's a long ride from Jordan, you must be starving.' I murmured some polite excuse to which he replied, as gravely as if he were reciting a text:

'The hour of midday is the most pleasing to the Lord. Joseph said to Benjamin: "You will eat with me at midday." But the joy of a guest is also sweet to the All High, to the Almighty. You look worn out, come and eat that I may receive blessings from your soul.'

He clapped his hands and a servant, his hair caught back in a metal ring, entered bearing a jug of warm water, scented with roses, in which I washed my hands; another servant offered us honey cakes served on lush green vine leaves; another poured strong, dark Emmaus wine into gleaming china cups. In order that his guests should not eat alone, Gamaliel took a segment of pomegranate and, closing his eyes, he raised to his lips a glazed white bowl bobbing with ice cubes and orange blossom.

'This should keep me going until lunchtime,' I said, licking my fingers.

'May your soul rejoice!'

I lit a cigarette and leaned on the window sill. Gamaliel's house was built high up, doubtless behind the Temple, on the hill of Ophel: there the air was so sweet and soft that just to feel its caress filled one's heart with peace. Below ran the new wall built by Herod the Great and further off bloomed the gardens and orchards that gave shade to the Valley of the Fountain, covering the hill where the village of Siloe gleamed white and cool. Through a gap, between the Mount of Scandal and the Hill of Tombs, I could see the Dead Sea glittering like a sheet of silver; beyond that lay the soft, undulating mountains of Moab, almost as intensely blue as the sky itself; and the white shape I could see, trembling in the shimmering light, must have been the citadel of Makeros perched on its rock on the border with Idumaea. On the grass-grown flat roof of a house built at the foot of the city wall, a still figure, sheltering under a tall parasol fringed with bells, was, like me, gazing out at those distant views of Arabia. By his side a young girl, slim and slightly built, was holding out her bare arms, calling to a flock of doves that flew about her. Her open tunic revealed one small, vigorous breast and she looked so pretty, dark and golden standing there in the sun, that, in the silent air, I almost blew her a kiss ... I drew back, however, when I heard Gamaliel saying, as the man in the saffron yellow cloak on the Mount of Olives had said: 'Yes, tonight in Bethany the Rabbi Jeschoua was taken prisoner.'

Then he added, slowly, his eyes half-closed, fingering his long beard:

'But Pontius had a moment of doubt. He didn't want to judge a man from Galilee who was a subject of Herod Antipas. And since the Tetrarch is here in Jerusalem for Passover, Pontius sent the Rabbi to his home in Bezetha.'

Topsius' learned spectacles glittered with surprise.

'How very strange!' he exclaimed, opening wide his thin

arms. 'Pontius isn't usually so scrupulous, so formal. Since when has Pontius respected the jurisdiction of the Tetrarch? He didn't ask the Tetrarch's permission when he had all those poor Galileans killed at the time of the aqueduct revolt, when, on Pontius' orders, Roman swords mingled the blood of the men of Naphtali with the blood of the sacrificial oxen in the Temple courtyards!'

Gamaliel murmured sombrely:

'The Roman is indeed cruel, but he is also a slave to legality.'

Then Osanias, son of Beothos, gave a gentle, toothless smile and said, with a limp wave of one of the beringed hands reclining on the purple cushions:

'Or perhaps it's Pontius' wife protecting the Rabbi.'

Gamaliel quietly cursed the immodesty of the Roman woman. And seeing Topsius's spectacles turned questioningly towards the venerable Osanias, he expressed surprise that the doctor was unaware of something so frequently discussed in the Temple, even by the shepherds who come from Idumaea to sell lambs for the sacrifice. Whenever the Rabbi preached at the Porch of Solomon, next to the Susa Gate, Claudia would appear, a solitary figure veiled in black, to watch him from high up on the Antonia Fortress. Menahem, who was on guard duty at the Staircase of the Gentiles in the month of Tebet, had seen Pontius' wife wave to the Rabbi with her veil. Perhaps Claudia had grown bored with Capreia, with all the coachmen from the Amphitheatre, with all the clowns from Suburra and the games at Atalanta where the singer Acius had lost his voice; perhaps, coming to Syria, she was curious to know what the kisses of a prophet from Galilee tasted like.

The man dressed all in white looked up suddenly, shaking back the hood covering his dishevelled hair. His intense blue gaze flashed like lightning about the room, only to be extinguished at once beneath the grave humility of his lowered lashes. Then he murmured in a slow, stern voice:

'Osanias, the Rabbi is chaste.'

The old man gave a hollow laugh. Chaste, the Rabbi!

And what about that Galilean woman from Magdala, who lived in the Bezetha district and who used to hang around with the Greek prostitutes at the doors of the theatre of Herod during Purim? And what about Joanna, Khosna's wife, one of Antipas' cooks? And what about that other woman from Ephraim, Suzanna, who one night, in response to a gesture from the Rabbi, at the merest hint of his desire, had left her loom, left her children, and with the household savings tied up in a corner of her cloak, had followed him to Caesarea?

'Why, Osanias,' cried the handsome man with the bejewelled sword, clapping his hands in mock applause, 'I had no idea you were so familiar with the licentious acts of the Rabbi from Galilee, that son of the lowly grasses, who is even lowlier than they are! You're worse than Aelius Lamma, our imperial legate, may the Lord rain down ills upon him!'

Osanias' eyes, small as two black glass beads, glittered with cunning and malice.

'If I am, Manasses, it is merely so that you, the patriots, the pure followers of Judas of Galaunitis, cannot always accuse us, the Sadducees, of knowing only about what happens in the Court of the Priests and on the rooftop of Hannan's house . . .'

Seized by a hacking cough, he stopped speaking for a moment and drew his cloak more tightly round him. Then, his flour-white face blotched with purple, he said in a still wearier voice:

'In fact, it was in Hannan's house that I heard this from Menahem, whilst we were walking beneath the vine trellis. And he also told us that this Rabbi from Galilee was so shameless he had even touched pagan women and others as unclean as pork meat. On the road to Shechem, a Levite saw him emerge from behind a well, his face aflame, in the company of a woman from Samaria!'

The man in white leaped to his feet and stood, shoulders back, trembling, and the cry he uttered was as full of horror as that of someone stumbling upon the desecration of an altar.

146

But with abrupt authority, Gamaliel fixed him with his hard eyes:

'Gad, the Rabbi is thirty years old and still not married. What does he do? What fields does he work? Has anyone ever seen his vineyards? He wanders the roads and lives off whatever he is given by these dissolute women. Isn't that exactly what those beardless young men from Sybaris and Lesbos do, the ones who spend all day strolling up and down the Via Judiciaria, men whom you, the Essenes, hate so much that you run and wash your clothes in a pool if one of them so much as brushes past you? You heard Osanias, son of Beothos: Jehovah alone is great. And in truth I tell you that when the Rabbi Jeschoua, scorning the law, forgives the adulterous woman and thus charms the simple people, he is giving in to his weak morals and not to his abundant mercy.'

Face ablaze, gesturing wildly with his arms, Gad shouted:

'But the Rabbi performs miracles!'

And it was the worthy Manasses, with serene disdain, who responded to the Essene:

'Calm down, Gad, other people have performed miracles too. Simon of Samaria performed miracles. So did Apollonius and Gabbienus. And how do your Galilean's prodigies compare to those of the daughters of the high priest Anius and of the wise man Rabbi Chekinah?'

And Osanias in turn poured scorn on Gad's innocence:

'Besides, what do you know, you Essenes, in your oasis in Engaddi? Miracles! Even the pagans perform miracles! If you go to Alexandria, to the right of the gate of Eunotos, where the papyrus factories are, you can see magicians performing miracles for a drachma, the price of a day's work. If miracles are proof of divinity, then the fish Oannes, with his fins made out of mother-of-pearl, must also be divine, for, on nights when there's a full moon, he preaches on the banks of the Euphrates.'

Gad was smiling a gentle, arrogant smile. His indignation had waned beneath the sheer weight of his disdain. He took one slow step, then another. Then, looking pityingly at those proud, hard, scornful men, he said:

'You talk and talk but your words are as empty as the buzzing of a fly! You talk but you have never even heard him speak. When he spoke in the green and fertile land of Galilee, it was like a fountain of milk flowing in a land of famine and drought. Even the light felt like a great blessing. The waters in the Lake Tiberias fell silent in order to listen to him and the eyes of the children surrounding him were filled by the gravity of an adult faith. He would speak and we would see all kinds of noble, holy things – charity, fraternity, justice, mercy, as well as new and beautiful, divinely beautiful, forms of love – like doves spreading their wings and escaping through the door of a sanctuary, flying off to all the nations of the world.'

His shining face was lifted up to the skies, as if still following the flight of that divine news. But Gamaliel was already by his side, Gamaliel the doctor of Law, rebuking him with words of harsh authority:

'What's so original or unique about all those ideas? Do you think the Rabbi just pulled them out of the abundance of his heart? Our own doctrine is full of them. If you want to hear someone talk of love, charity, equality, then read the book of Jesus, the son of Sidrah. Hillel preached exactly that, so did Schemaia. You could find equally just things in pagan books which, beside ours, are like mud beside the pure waters of Siloe. Even you, the Essenes, have better teachings than that. The teachers of Babylonia, of Alexandria, always taught the pure law of justice and equality. So does your friend Iokanan, the one you call the Baptist, the one who ended his life so wretchedly in a dungeon in Makeros.'

'Iokanan!' exclaimed Gad, trembling, as if rudely awoken from a sweet dream.

His brilliant eyes grew wet with tears. He bowed to the ground three times, his arms wide, repeating the name of Iokanan, as if invoking someone from the dead. Then, two tears rolling down his cheeks, he murmured a secret that filled him with both terror and faith:

'I was the one who went up to Makeros to fetch the head of the Baptist. And when I was walking back down the path, the head wrapped in my own cloak, that woman, Herodias, was lying stretched out along the wall like a lascivious tigress, roaring and calling down curses upon me. For three days and three nights I walked the roads of Galilee, carrying the head of that just man by the hair. Sometimes, an angel would appear from behind a rock, all clothed in black, and he would open his wings and walk awhile by my side.'

He hung his head again, dropped to his knees on the flagstones and lay there prostrate, praying earnestly, arms outstretched.

Gamaliel went over to wise Topsius and, standing straighter than one of the Temple columns, his elbows pressed into his waist, his thin hands splayed out before him, he said:

'We have a Law and our Law is quite clear. It is the word of the Lord and the Lord said: "I am Jehovah, the eternal one, the first and the last, who does not communicate to others even his own name, nor his glory: before me there was no God. There is no other God besides me, nor will there be any God after me." This is the voice of the Lord. And the Lord said: "If a prophet appears amongst you, a visionary who performs miracles and tries to introduce another god and calls on the simple people to worship that god, then that prophet and visionary must die!" This is the Law, this is the voice of the Lord. Now this Rabbi from Nazareth proclaimed himself a god in Galilee, in the synagogues, in the streets of Jerusalem, in the holy courtyards of the Temple. The Rabbi must die.'

But Manasses, whose languid gaze grew dark as a sky presaging thunder, interposed himself between the doctor of Law and Herod's biographer and roundly denounced the cruel letter of doctrine:

'No, no! What does it matter if a lamp set on a tomb claims that it is the Sun? What does it matter if a man opens his arms and shouts out that he is a god? Our laws are gentle laws, for such a minor offence no one is going to seek out the executioner in his lair in Gareb.'

I was about to speak out in praise of Manasses' charity. But he was shouting now in a loud, fervent voice:

'However, this Rabbi from Galilee must die because he is a bad citizen and a bad Jew! Did we not hear him say that we should pay tribute to Caesar? The Rabbi holds out his hands to Rome, the Roman is not his enemy. He has been preaching for three years now and no one has ever heard him speak of the holy need to expel the foreigner. We are waiting for a Messiah who will come bearing a sword, who will liberate Israel, but this garrulous fool declares that all he brings with him is "the bread of truth"! When there is a Roman Praetor in Jerusalem, when Roman spears guard the doors to our God, why does this visionary speak of the bread of heaven and the wine of truth? The only useful truth is that there should be no Romans in Jerusalem!'

Troubled, Osanias glanced at the sunlight-filled window, out of which Manasses' threats flew, vibrant and free. Gamaliel was smiling coldly. And the ardent disciple of Judas of Gamala went on shouting, carried away by his own anger:

'In truth I say to you, to lull people's souls with hopes of a Kingdom of Heaven is to make them forget their real duty to this Kingdom of Earth, towards this land of Israel, which is in chains and weeps and will not be consoled! The Rabbi is a traitor to the fatherland! The Rabbi must die!'

Trembling, he had grasped his sword and his gaze grew distant, a glimmer of revolt in his eyes, as if eagerly invoking battles and the glory of suffering.

Then Osanias stood up, leaning on a gold-tipped walking stick. Grievous care seemed to cloud his premature old age. And he began to speak, gently and sadly, like someone who must rise above enthusiasm and doctrine and point out the ineluctable law of necessity:

'You're right, you're right, it matters little that a vision-ary should call himself Messiah or Son of God, should threaten to destroy the Law and destroy the Temple. Both the Temple and the Law can smile and forgive, certain of their eternal life. But, Manasses, our Laws are gentle laws and I do not believe that we should bother the executioner in Gareb just because a Rabbi from Galilee, who recalls the followers of Judas of Gamala nailed to the cross and counsels prudence and cunning in our relations with the Romans! Manasses, your hands are strong, but with those hands could you divert the river Jordan from the land of Canaan to the land of Trachonitis? No, you could not. Nor can you stop Caesar's legions which took the cities of Greece, from also taking the land of Judah! Judas Maccabaeus was wise and strong, and made friends with Rome because, on earth, Rome is like a great natural force; when Rome comes, the foolish man offers him his bare chest and is destroyed, but the prudent man withdraws to his house and stays there quietly. Galatia was unconquerable, Philip and Perseus filled the plains with their armies, Antioch the Great commanded one hundred and twenty elephants and innumerable chariots of war. Rome simply walked in and what has become of them now? They are slaves paying tribute . . .'

He bowed heavily, like an ox beneath the yoke. Then, fixing us with his small eyes that glinted, inexorable and cold, he went on, still in the same soft, subtle voice:

'But in truth I say to you that this Rabbi from Galilee *must* die because it is the duty of any man who has possessions on this earth, who owns cornfields, to stamp out with his sandal the spark on the threshing floor that threatens to set fire to his hay rick. With the Romans in Jerusalem, anyone who comes and proclaims himself a Messiah, as does this man from Galilee, is harmful and dangerous to Israel. The Romans do not understand about this Kingdom of Heaven that he promises; they see only that these sermons, these divine exaltations, stir up dark feelings amongst the people in the courtyards of the Temple. And then they say: "The fact is that this Temple, with all its gold, with all its people and all its zealotry, is a threat to the authority of Caesar in Judaea." And then, slowly, they will do away with the power of the Temple by diminishing its wealth and the privileges of its priesthood. We already suffer the humiliation of having our pontifical vestments kept in the treasury in the Antonia Tower: tomorrow it will be the golden candelabrum! In an attempt to impoverish us, the Praetor has already made use of money from the Temple treasury. Next it will be the tithes from the harvest, from the cattle, the money from the offerings, the alms paid for trumpets, the ritual tributes, all the priestly possessions, even the meat used in sacrifices; nothing will be ours, it will all belong to the Romans! And we will be left with only a wooden staff with which to go and beg in the streets of Samaria and await the arrival of the rich merchants from Decapolis. In truth I say to you, if we want to preserve our honour and our treasure, which, according to the ancient Law, are ours, and which constitute the splendour of Israel, we must present to the Romans' watchful eye a peaceful temple, well-policed, submissive, content, with no zealotry and no Messiah! The Rabbi must die!'

Thus spoke Osanias, son of Beothos, member of the Sanhedrin.

Then Topsius, that lean biographer of the Herods, reverently folded his arms and bowed three times to those eloquent men. Gad was standing absolutely still, praying. In the blue of the window, a golden bee buzzed about the honeysuckle. And Topsius announced grandly:

'You men who have welcomed me here, the truth is as abundant in your souls as the grape is on the vine! You are like three towers guarding Israel against other nations: one defends the unity of your religion, the other upholds love of the fatherland and the third, which is you, venerable son of Beothos, cautious and cunning as the serpent beloved by Solomon, you protect that most precious commodity – order! You are like three towers and against each and every one of you, the Rabbi from Galilee has raised his arm and thrown the first stone! But you watch over Israel and her God and her possessions and you must not allow all that to be destroyed. Indeed, now I see that Jesus and Judaism could never live side by side.'

And Gamaliel, making the gesture of someone breaking a thin stick, said, showing his white teeth:

'That's why we must crucify him!'

Those words were like a glittering steel blade that whistled through the air and plunged into my breast! Overwhelmed, I plucked at the learned historian's sleeve:

'Topsius, who is this Rabbi who preached in Galilee and performed miracles and is about to be crucified?'

The wise doctor rolled his eyes in amazement, as if I'd asked him the name of the planet that rises behind the mountains each day, bringing with it the morning light. Then he said abruptly:

'Rabbi Jeschoua bar Joseph, from Nazareth in Galilee, whom some call Jesus and others the Christ.'

'*Our* Christ!' I shouted, stunned and shaking.

My Catholic knees almost buckled beneath me in a desire to prostrate themselves, awestruck, whilst I uttered endless, desperate prayers. But then my whole being was seized by a burning desire to run to his side and to fix my own mortal eyes on the body of my Lord, on his all too human body, dressed in the same clothes that all men wear, covered with the dust of human roads! And at the same time, as furiously as a leaf caught in a harsh wind, my soul was trembling in sombre terror, the terror of the negligent servant before the just master! Was I sufficiently pure, had I fasted and prayed enough, to confront the shining face of my God? No. How base and bitterly inadequate my devotions had been! In the church in Graça, I had never kissed his pale, wounded foot with sufficient fervour. What could I do? In the carnal days when Adélia, the light of my life, would be waiting for me at her house in Travessa das Caldas, in her nightdress, smoking a cigarette, on how many Sundays had I not cursed the slowness of the masses and the monotony of the septenary feasts. And since I was, from the top of my head to the soles of my feet, encrusted in sin, how could my reprobate, sin-scorched body do anything other than fall to the ground when the Lord's eyes, like two halves of the sky, turned slowly round to gaze upon me?

But actually to see Jesus! To see what his hair was like, how his tunic fell in folds about him and what happened on Earth when he opened his lips to speak. Beyond these flat roofs where women were scattering grain for doves, along one of the roads whence came the clear, sing-song cry of people selling unleavened bread, at that precise, terrible moment, my Saviour Jesus would be walking amongst grave-faced, bearded Roman soldiers, his hands bound with rope. The slow breeze that made the honey-suckle sway at the window, intensifying its scent, had perhaps just brushed the forehead of my God, already bloody from the thorns! It was just a question of pushing open that cedarwood door, crossing the courtyard where the millstone creaked, and then, out into the road, where I would be able to see, in the flesh, my Lord Jesus, just as St John and St Matthew had seen him. I would follow his sacred shadow along the white wall where my own shadow also fell. In the very dust in which my own feet had trodden, I would kiss the still warm print of his feet. And muffling with both my hands the beating of my heart, I would hear, from his ineffable lips, a cry, a sob, a moan, a promise. I would be privy then to a new word uttered by Christ, one that had not been written down in the Gospels, and I alone would have the pontifical right to repeat it to the prostrate crowds. My authority in the Church would shine like the newest of New Testaments. I would be a previously unknown witness to the Passion. I would become St Teodorico the Evangelist!

Then, with a desperation that shocked those oriental men and their measured manners, I cried out:

'Where can I see him? Where is Jesus of Nazareth, my Lord?'

At that moment, a slave came running lightly in on the tips of his sandals and prostrated himself on the paved floor before Gamaliel. He kissed the fringes of his master's tunic, his scrawny sides heaving, and at last he murmured, exhausted:

'Master, the Rabbi is in the Praetorium.'

Gad ceased his praying and leaped wildly to his feet, tightened the knotted cord about his waist and rushed off, his hood flying, leaving behind him the blond trail of his dishevelled hair. Topsius wrapped about him the white cloak, which hung in folds like a Roman toga and lent him the solemnity of a marble statue, and, having compared Gamaliel's hospitality to that of Abraham, he shouted to me triumphantly:

'To the Praetorium!'

Lost in the tumult of my own thoughts, I followed Topsius for what seemed a long time as we rushed breathlessly through the old part of Jerusalem. We passed a rose garden, splendid and silent, dating back to the days of the prophets and guarded by two Levites bearing golden spears. Then we hurried along a cool street scented by all the perfumeries there, adorned with signs representing flowers or pestles and mortars. Awnings of fine cloth shaded the doorways, the ground was damp and scattered with aniseed and anemones. Languid young men sat idly in the shade, their curly hair hanging in ringlets, dark circles under their eyes, their hands so heavy with rings, they could barely lift the rustling silks of their tunics, cherry-red and gold. This indolent street opened out onto a square, scorched by the sun, covered with a thick white dust into which our feet plunged. In the middle stood an ancient palm tree, bowed beneath its plume of leaves, as motionless as if it were made out of bronze and in the background the granite columns of Herod's old palace glittered black in the sunlight. There lay the Praetorium.

By the archway at the entrance, where two Syrian legionaries were patrolling, black feathers in their gleaming helmets, a group of girls, each with a rose tucked behind one ear and baskets in their laps made out of esparto grass, were selling unleavened bread. Beneath a huge feather sunshade fixed in the ground, men in felt mitres were changing money, sitting before low tables with scales on them. From time to time the watersellers, with their rough leather bottles, would utter their tremulous cry. We went in and I was awestruck.

It was a bright courtyard open to the blue sky and paved with marble with an arcade along each side, raised up to form a balustraded terrace, as cool and resonant as the cloister of a monastery. The arches at the far side of the square, topped by the austere palace façade, were hung with a velarium made out of scarlet cloth fringed with gold that cast a harsh, square shadow. It was supported on two thick poles made out of sycamore, each pole crowned with a lotus flower.

A mass of people were gathered there, blue-edged Pharisee tunics jostling with ordinary workers' rough woollen smocks gathered at the waist with a leather belt, with the long grey-and-white striped burnous worn by the men of Galilee and the hooded, crimson cloaks worn by merchants from Tiberias. A few women had left the shade of the velarium and stood on tiptoe in their yellow slippers, one corner of their light cloaks pulled over their faces to protect them from the sun. The multitude gave off a warm smell of sweat and myrrh. Beyond and above the crowd of white turbans gleamed the points of spears. And right at the back, on a throne, sat a man, a magistrate, wrapped in the noble folds of a Praetorian toga, still as a statue, resting his dense, grey beard on one strong hand. He had hollow, indolent eyes and his hair was tied back with a scarlet ribbon. Behind him, on a pedestal that formed the back of his curule chair, was the bronze figure of the Roman she-wolf, its voracious jaws gaping. I asked Topsius who that melancholy magistrate was.

'A fellow called Pontius, Pontius Pilate, who used to be a prefect in Batavia.'

I walked slowly about the courtyard, doing my best to make my footsteps as light and respectful as possible, as if I were walking in a temple. A heavy silence fell from the glittering sky, broken only occasionally by the harsh, sad cry of the peacocks in the garden. Stretched out on the ground, next to the balustrade, black slaves were sleeping, their bellies to the sun. An old woman was counting copper coins, crouched before her basket of fruit. On scaffolding, arranged around a column, men were at work repairing the roof. And in one corner, children were playing with iron discs that tinkled lightly on the paving stones.

Suddenly, someone tapped Topsius on the shoulder. It was that handsome fellow Manasses, accompanied by a magnificent old man, who looked as noble as a pontiff. Topsius bestowed a filial kiss on the sleeve of old man's simarre, which was embroidered with green vine leaves. His white beard, lustrous with oil, reached as far as the belt that went about his waist and his broad shoulders disappeared beneath an abundance of fine, snow-white hair which flowed out from beneath his turban like a pure white collar of royal ermine. He rested one of his beringed hands on a stout ivory walking stick whilst the other held the hand of a pale child with eyes lovelier than stars who, next to the old man, resembled a lily growing in the shadow of a cedar.

'Go up to the gallery,' Manasses said to us. 'It's cool there and you can rest.'

We followed him and I asked Topsius who the august old gentleman was.

'Rabbi Robam,' my learned friend murmured respectfully. 'He's a leading light of the Sanhedrin, the most eloquent and subtle of all their thinkers, and a confidant of Caiaphas.'

Reverently, I bowed three times to the Rabbi, who had sat down on a marble bench, looking thoughtful and letting the child's head, more golden than the corn of Joppa, rest upon his vast, ancestral chest. Then we walked on along the bright, echoing gallery, at the far end of which gleamed a sumptuous door made out of cedarwood inlaid with silver. A Praetorian guard from Caesarea was standing sleepily by it, leaning on his tall wicker shield. Heart pounding, I made my way over to the parapet, where my mortal eyes fell immediately upon the incarnation of my God!

But my fickle soul surprised me, for I felt neither ecstasy nor terror. It was as if, suddenly, long, laborious centuries of history and religion had vanished from my memory. I did not even think of that lean, dark man as the redeemer of humanity. I found myself thrown inexplicably back in time. I was no longer Teodorico Raposo, Christian and university graduate; it was as if I had lost my individuality during that anxious rush from Gamaliel's house as easily as if my cloak had slipped from about my shoulders. I had become imbued with the antiquity of all the things about me, they had remade me into another, I too was an ancient. I was Teodoricus, a Lusitanian, who had sailed in a galley from the echoing beaches of that great promontory and was travelling, since Tiberius was the emperor, in lands that were tributaries to Rome, and that man was not Jesus or Christ or the Messiah, but merely a young man from Galilee who, inspired by a great dream, had left his green village to change the whole world and create a new heaven, only to be met on a street corner by a Temple *nethenin* who bound him and brought him before the Praetor on a morning when the latter was giving audience, together with a thief who had stolen on the Shechem road and another man who had drawn a knife in a fight at Emath.

Jesus was standing in an area with a mosaic floor, before the dais and the Praetor's curule chair that had been placed beneath the figure of the Roman she-wolf. His hands were crossed in front of him and loosely bound by a length of rope that trailed on the ground. He was wearing a long blue-fringed burnous made out of rough brown-striped wool and on his feet he wore sandals battered by the desert roads and tied on with leather thongs. His head was not bloodied by the cruel crown of thorns I had read about in the Gospels. Instead he was wearing a white turban made out of a long strip of linen, the ends of which hung down on either side of his shoulders; it was secured by a piece of thread tied beneath his pointed, curly beard. His dull hair, pushed back behind his ears, fell in ringlets down his back and in his lean, sunburnt face, beneath the dark, unbroken line of his heavy eyebrows, his eyes gleamed, black and infinitely deep. He stood unmoving before the Praetor, strong and calm. Only a slight trembling in his bound hands betrayed the tumult in his heart and sometimes he gave a long sigh, as if his lungs, used to the pure, open air of the mountains and lakes of Galilee, felt constricted by all that marble, beneath the heavy Roman velarium, within the narrow formality of the Law.

To one side, Sareias, the spokesman for the Sanhedrin, having laid his cloak and his golden staff on the ground, was reading from a dark strip of parchment, unrolling it as he read in a sleepy, singsong murmur. Seated on the stool, the Roman counsellor, suffering in the already harsh heat of the month of Nisan, was cooling his cleanshaven, chalk-white face with a fan of dried ivy leaves; a fat, old scribe, sitting at a stone table covered with official documents and metal rulers, was carefully sharpening his quill pens. Between these two men stood the interpreter – a beardless Phoenician – head erect, arms akimbo, puffing out his chest beneath his linen waistcoat, which was painted with a red parrot. And all the while doves flew in and out about the velarium. And that was how I first saw Jesus of Galilee, standing captive before the Praetor of Rome.

Meanwhile Sareias, having rolled the dark parchment up again, bowed to Pilate, kissed a signet ring he was wearing, in order to impress on his lips the seal of truth, and immediately launched into a verbose and adulatory speech in Greek, larded with quotations. He was speaking of the Tetrarch of Galilee, the noble Antipas; he praised his prudence, extolled the virtues of his father, Herod the Great, the restorer of the Temple. The glory of Herod filled the Earth; he had been powerful, always faithful to his Caesars; his son Antipas was strong and astute. However, whilst recognising his wisdom, he found it odd that the Tetrarch refused to confirm the sentence of death passed on Jesus by the Sanhedrin. Was not this sentence founded on the laws handed down by the Lord? That most just of men, Hannan, had interrogated the Rabbi, who had chosen to maintain a disrespectful silence. Was that any way to respond to a wise man, to the pure and pious Hannan? That was why a zealot, unable to contain himself, had slapped the Rabbi hard in the face. What had happened to old-fashioned respect and veneration for the priesthood?

His loud, booming voice rolled endlessly on. I felt tired and yawned. Below, two men sitting cross-legged on the flagstones were drinking from a gourd and eating dates from Bethabara, which they carried tied in a corner of their tunics. Pilate, still leaning his chin upon his fist, was gazing drowsily at his scarlet boots pricked with golden stars.

And Sareias was now proclaiming the rights of the Temple. It was the pride of the nation, the Lord's chosen dwelling! Caesar Augustus had offered up to it shields and golden vases. And how had this Rabbi shown his respect for the Temple? By threatening to destroy it. 'I will overthrow the temple of Jehovah and build it again in three days!' On hearing this crude sacrilege, pious witnesses had covered their heads with ashes in order to ward off the wrath of the Lord. Any blasphemy uttered against the sanctuary echoed even in the breast of God.

Beneath the velarium, the Pharisees, the scribes, the temple *nethenin* and even mere slaves were whispering amongst themselves, like wild trees stirred by the wind. And Jesus remained utterly still, abstracted and indifferent, with his eyes closed, keeping his beautiful and enduring dream as far removed as possible from any harsh, vain things that might stain it. Then the Roman counsellor stood up, placed his fan of leaves on the stool next to him, drew his blue-edged cloak elegantly about him, bowed three times to the Praetor and began to trace shapes in the air with his delicate hand, on which a single jewel glittered.

'What's he saying?'

'Extremely subtle things,' murmured Topsius. 'He's a bit of a peasant, but he's quite right, he says that the Praetor is not a Jew, that he knows nothing of Jehovah, nor are prophets who rise up against Jehovah of any interest to him, and that the sword of Caesar is not used to wreak vengeance on gods who do not protect Caesar. He's a cunning man this Roman.'

Out of breath, the counsellor fell back languidly on his stool. And Sareias immediately resumed his speechifying, waving his arms at the crowd of Pharisees, as if to provoke their protests, seeking comfort in their strength. Now, in a still louder voice, he was accusing Jesus, not of his rebellion against Jehovah and the Temple, but of his pretensions to being a prince of the house of David. Only four days ago, everyone in Jerusalem had seen him enter in false triumph through the Golden Gate, amidst the waving of green palm leaves, surrounded by a multitude of Galileans shouting: 'Hosanna to the son of David, Hosanna to the king of Israel!'

'He *is* the son of David, who has come to make us perfect!' cried the distant voice of Gad, a voice full of love and conviction.

But then Sareias suddenly dropped his fringed sleeves to his side and stood silent and rigid as the shaft of a spear. The Roman scribe stood up, resting his fists on the table, and reverently bowed his plump neck. The counsellor was smiling, intent. It was the Praetor's turn to interrogate the Rabbi and, trembling, I noticed that one of the legionaries gave Jesus a shove and I saw Jesus raise his head.

Leaning slightly towards the Rabbi, his hands open as if disowning all interest in that ritual trial between subtle sectarians, Pontius murmured, irritated and hesitant:

'Are you the King of the Jews? You have been brought here by your fellow countrymen. What did you do? Where is your kingdom?'

161

Rather too loudly, the arrogant interpreter, who was standing beside the marble throne, repeated these words in the ancient Hebraic tongue of the holy books and, since the Rabbi remained silent, he then shouted them out in the Chaldean tongue spoken in Galilee.

Then Jesus took a step forward. I heard his voice. It was clear, firm, masterful and calm:

'My kingdom is not of this world. If, by the will of my Father, I were king of Israel, I would not be standing before you with my hands bound by this rope. But my kingdom is not of this world.'

A desperate shout roared forth:

'Let him depart this world then!'

Like dry kindling lit by a spark, the fury of the Pharisees and the Temple servants erupted into wild, impatient cries:

'Crucify him! Crucify him!'

For the benefit of the Praetor, the interpreter solemnly translated into Greek the tumult of shouts uttered in the Syrian tongue spoken by the people of Judaea. Pontius stamped hard on the marble dais. The two lictors raised their staffs that bore the emblem of the eagle, the scribe called out the name of Caius Tiberius, and the gesturing arms were lowered, as if in awe at the majesty of the Roman people.

Pontius spoke again, slowly, vaguely:

'So you do claim to be a king. And what have you come here to do?'

Jesus took another step towards the Praetor. His sandalled foot rested firmly on the flagstones, as if taking supreme possession of the Earth. And what came forth from his tremulous lips seemed to me to shine, to glitter in the air, like the gleam in his dark eyes.

'I came into this world to bear witness to the truth. Whoever desires the truth, whoever wishes to belong to the truth, must listen to my voice.'

Pilate regarded him for a moment, thoughtfully; then, shrugging his shoulders, he asked:

'But what is the truth?'

Jesus of Nazareth said nothing and a silence spread throughout the Praetorium, as if every heart had stopped beating, suddenly gripped by uncertainty.

Then, slowly gathering up his vast toga, Pilate descended the four bronze steps and, preceded by the lictors and followed by the counsellor, he went into the palace, accompanied by the sound of the legionaries' weapons as they saluted him, beating the steel of their lances on the bronze of their shields.

A harsh, eager whispering immediately filled the whole courtyard, a sound like that of angry bees. Sareias was speaking, brandishing his staff, standing amongst the Pharisees wringing their hands in terror. Others, standing further off, were muttering sombrely to each other. A grand old man, wearing a black cloak that fluttered about him, was running anxiously about the Praetorium amongst those sleeping on the floor, amongst those selling unleavened bread, and he was shouting: 'Israel is lost!' And I saw fanatical Levites wrenching the tassles from their tunics, as if they were witnessing a public calamity.

Gad rushed up to us, waving triumphant arms:

'The Praetor is a just man and he will free the Rabbi!'

His face shining with joy, he revealed to us his sweetest hopes. The moment the Rabbi was free, he would leave Jerusalem, where the people's hearts were harder than stones. His friends, armed, were waiting for him in Bethany and they would leave at moonrise for the oasis of Engaddi. The people who loved him would be there. Was Jesus not the brother of the Essenes? Like them, the Rabbi preached scorn of earthly goods, tenderness towards the poor, the incomparable beauty of the Kingdom of God.

I believed him and was already celebrating the news when a mob invaded the gallery, which a slave was busy sprinkling with water. It was the dark band of Pharisees, heading for the stone bench where Rabbi Robam was talking to Manasses, all the while running his fingers gently through the child's hair, more golden than the corn. Topsius and I ran towards the intolerant rabble. Sareias was already there in their midst, with bowed head but speaking in a firm, familiar voice:

'Rabbi Robam, you must go and talk to the Praetor and save our Law!'

And then, from every side, came this anxious plea!

'Rabbi, speak to the Praetor. Rabbi, save Israel.'

Slowly, as majestic as Moses himself, the old man stood up. And before him a Levite, his face terribly pale, bent his knee and trembled as he murmured:

'Rabbi, you are just, wise, perfect and strong in the eyes of the Lord.'

Rabbi Robam lifted up his two hands with their palms open to the sky. And they all bowed down as if, in response to his silent invocation, the spirit of Jehovah had descended to fill that just heart. Then, with the child's hand in his, he walked off in silence. Behind him all that could be heard was the noise of sandals flapping against the marble flagstones.

Bunched together, we stopped in front of the cedar door where the Praetorian guard first held out his spear, then pounded on the door with one of the silver rings. The heavy hinges creaked, a palace tribune came out, holding in his hand a long stem from a vine. Beyond lay a cold, bleak room, badly lit, its walls lined with dark stucco. In the centre stood a pale statue of Augustus, the pedestal piled with laurel wreaths and votive flowers. In the corners, in the shadows, glittered two great gilded bronze candleholders.

Not one of the Jews went in, because to step on pagan ground on Passover day was unclean in the eyes of the Lord. Sareias announced haughtily to the tribune that 'certain people from the nation of Israel were at the gate of their fathers' palace, awaiting the Praetor'. And then a heavy silence fell, thick with anxiety.

Two lictors approached and Pilate followed immediately behind them, walking with long strides, his voluminous toga clutched to his chest.

All the turbaned heads bent before him, bowing to the

procurator of Judaea. He had paused by the statue of Augustus and, as if echoing the noble gesture of the marble figure, he stretched out one hand, in which was held a parchment scroll. He said:

'May peace be upon you and upon your words!'

Sareias, the spokesman for the Sanhedrin, came forward and declared that they did indeed come with hearts full of peace; but, since the Praetor had left the Praetorium without confirming or annulling the Sanhedrin's sentence condemning Jesus to death, they remained there like the man watching the grape hanging on the vine, which neither withered nor ripened.

Pontius struck me as a man of justice and clemency.

'I interrogated your prisoner,' he said, 'and I could find no crime for which the Procurator of Judaea should punish him. Herod Antipas, who is wise and strong, who follows your Law and prays in your Temple, also carried out an interrogation and could find no fault with him. This man's words are like the ramblings of a dreamer. But his hands are not stained with blood, nor have I heard tell that he ever climbed his neighbour's wall. Caesar is not an unforgiving master. This man is merely a visionary.'

Then, muttering, they all drew back, leaving Rabbi Robam alone on the threshhold of the Roman room. A jewel on the diadem he wore glittered and the white hair that fell over his vast shoulders crowned him with majesty as snow crowns the mountains. The blue fringes of his loose cloak dragged on the flagstones. Slowly, calmly, as if he were explaining the Law to his pupils, he raised one hand and said:

'Pontius, Caesar's officer, most just and most wise! The man you call a visionary has for years offended against our laws and blasphemed our God. But when did we arrest him, when did we bring him to you? Only when we saw him enter in triumph through the Golden Gate, acclaimed as king of Judaea. Because Judaea has only one king and that is Tiberius, and the moment a seditionary proclaims himself to be in revolt against Caesar, we are quick to punish him. That is what we did, we who have no mandate from Caesar, who are paid nothing from his exchequer. And yet you, Caesar's officer, choose not to punish this man who has rebelled against your master.'

Pontius' long face, that seemed to have grown soft with somnolence, flushed red. The tortuous arguments of these Jews – who, although they hated Rome, now preached a noisy zeal for Caesar in order, in the name of his authority, to satisfy some priestly hatred – were as repellent to the Roman's sense of rectitude as the Rabbi's bold reproof was intolerable to his pride. He exclaimed violently, with a gesture that made them tremble:

'Enough! Caesar's procurators do not come to some barbarous Asian colony to be taught where their duty towards Caesar lies!'

Manasses, who was standing impatiently at my side, tugging at his beard, walked off indignantly. I was shaking. But the proud Rabbi went on, as indifferent to Pontius' rage as he would be to the bleating of a lamb being led to the sacrificial altar.

'What would Caesar's procurator do in Alexandria if a visionary came down from Bubastes, proclaiming himself king of Egypt? Precisely what you choose not to do in this barbarous Asian land. Your master gives you a vineyard to guard and yet you allow people into that vineyard to steal the grapes! Why are you in Judaea then, why is the sixth legion in the Antonia Tower? But we are clear enough in our minds and our voices too are clear and loud enough, Pontius, for Caesar to hear us.'

Pontius took one slow step towards the door. And with his flashing eyes fixed on those Jews who were so astutely entangling him in the subtle web of their religious rancour, he murmured:

'I'm not afraid of your intrigues. Aelius Lamma is my friend. And Caesar knows me well.'

'You see something which is not in our hearts,' said Rabbi Robam, as calmly as if they were sitting chatting in the shade of his garden. 'We see quite clearly what is in your heart, Pontius. What do you care about the life or death of a vagabond from Galilee? If, as you say, you do not wish to avenge gods whose divinity you do not respect, why then do you want to save a prophet whose prophecies you do not believe in? You have another more evil intention, Roman. You want the destruction of Judah.'

A tremor of anger, of devout passion ran through the Pharisees, some of whom rummaged inside their tunics, as if looking for a weapon. And, serenely, slowly, Rabbi Robam continued his denunciation of the Praetor.

'You want to leave unpunished the man who preached insurrection, declaring himself king in a province of Caesar's, in order, by not punishing him, to tempt others with greater ambitions, another Judas of Gamala, to attack the barracks in Samaria. What you are preparing is an excuse to bring smashing down upon us the imperial sword and thus extinguish our national life in Judaea once and for all. You want a rebellion in order that you can steep your hands in blood and then present yourself afterwards to Caesar as a victorious soldier, a wise administrator, worthy of a proconsulate or a governorship in Italy. Is that what you call Roman honour? I have never been to Rome, but I know that there they call it Punic honour. Do not imagine, however, that we are as simple as some shepherd from Idumeia. We are at peace with Caesar and we are doing our duty by condemning the man who has risen up in revolt against Caesar. If you do not want to do your duty and ratify this death sentence, fine. We will send emissaries to Rome bearing news of our sentence and of your refusal to accept it, and having proved our sense of responsibility towards Caesar, we will show him just how the person who represents imperial law in Judaea carries on. And now, Praetor, you may return to the Praetorium.'

'And remember the votive shields,' shouted Sareias. 'Then perhaps you'll see who Caesar agrees with.'

Pontius lowered his head, troubled. Doubtless he was picturing, on a bright terrace by the sea of Capreia, Sejanus,

Cesonius and all his enemies whispering in Tiberius' ear and pointing to the emissaries from the Temple. Caesar, ever anxious and distrustful, would immediately suspect some pact between him and this 'King of the Jews' to incite rebellion in the wealthy imperial province. His sense of justice and his pride in maintaining it could cost him the proconsulate in Judaea. At that moment pride and justice rose like waves in his weak heart, beating one against another, rising and falling. He went slowly over to the threshold of the door, opening wide his arms, as if brought there by some magnanimous, conciliatory impulse. Then, his face whiter than his toga, he began:

'I have governed in Judaea for seven years now. Have you ever found me to be unjust, have I ever failed to keep a promise? Your threats do not move me in the least. Caesar knows me well. But it is in Caesar's interests that there should be no discord between us. I have always made concessions to you. More than any other procurator since Coponius, I have respected your laws. When those two men from Samaria came to desecrate your temple, did I not make them suffer? There should be no quarrels between us, no bitter words.'

He hesitated for a moment, then, slowly rubbing his hands together and shaking them as if they were dripping with murky water, he said:

'You want the life of this visionary? What do I care? Take it. Won't a good whipping do? You want the cross? Crucify him then. But I am not the one who spilled his blood.'

The gaunt-faced Levite cried out passionately:

'We take full responsibility and may his blood fall on our heads!'

And some trembled, believing that all words have a supernatural power and breathe life into things we only think.

Pontius had left the room. With a bow, the decurion closed the cedar door. Then Rabbi Robam turned, as calm and resplendent as one of the Just, and, walking back through the gathered Pharisees, who stooped to kiss the hem of his tunic, he murmured with grave sweetness:

'It is better that one man should suffer than that a whole people should suffer.'

Wiping away the beads of sweat pouring from my brow, provoked by the intense emotion, I slumped shaking onto a bench. And in my state of lassitude, I could vaguely make out two legionaries in the Praetorium, their belts unbuckled, drinking from a great metal bowl that a black slave was filling from a wineskin he carried slung over his shoulder; beyond them I could see a strong, beautiful woman sitting in the sun, her children suckling at her bare breasts; further off stood a shepherd clothed in animal skins who was smilingly displaying his bloodstained arm. Then I closed my eyes and, for a moment, I thought of the candle I had left burning in the tent, next to my bed, of the smoke drifting up from the red flame; at last I fell into a light sleep. When I woke, the curule chair was still empty, the purple cushion on the marble floor still bore the imprint of the Praetor's feet; and the ancient Atrium of Herod's palace was filled by the festive chatter of an even larger crowd than before. It was composed mainly of uncouth men wearing short woollen cloaks smeared with dust, as if they had been used as rugs to spread on the flagstones of a square. Some carried scales in their hands, cages containing turtle doves, and the scrawny, unkempt women who followed them were shaking their fists and calling down curses upon the Rabbi. Others, meanwhile, tiptoeing along in their sandals, discreetly cried their wares, lowly and magnificent, which they carried concealed amongst the folds of their tunics: toasted barley, jars of unguents, corals, filigree bracelets from Sidron. I asked Topsius who they were and, as he cleaned his spectacles, my learned friend explained to me that they were doubtless the merchants against whom Jesus had wielded a stout stick on the eve of Passover, demanding the strict application of the law that forbids the selling of profane goods in the Temple, outside the Porch of Solomon.

'Another of the Rabbi's imprudent acts, Dom Raposo,' Topsius murmured ironically.

Meanwhile, now that the sixth Judaic hour had struck and the working day was over, more people were beginning to arrive: workers from the neighbouring dyeworks, their clothes stained scarlet or blue; scribes fresh from the synagogue clutching bundles of documents in their arms; gardeners with their scythes over their shoulders, a branch of myrtle stuck in their turbans; tailors with one long needle dangling from behind their ear. In one corner, Phoenician musicians were tuning their harps, eliciting sweet notes from their clay flutes and, immediately in front of us, two Greek prostitutes from Tiberias in yellow wigs were walking up and down, waggling their tongues and shaking the hem of their tunics, which gave off a smell of marjoram. The legionaries, their spears across their chests, formed an iron circle around Jesus and, by then, I could barely see him through this whispering crowd, in which the harsh consonants of Moab and the desert mingled with the grave softness of Chaldean.

Underneath the gallery we could hear a small bell tinkling sadly. It was a market gardener selling ripe figs from Bethphage, arranged on vine leaves in a wicker basket. Worn out with emotion, I leaned over the parapet and asked him the price of that delicacy plucked in gardens so highly praised in the Gospels. And smiling, the man stretched out his arms, as if he had found his heart's desire:

'What are a few figs between me and you, a wealthy man from far across the sea? Jehovah says that brothers should exchange presents and blessings! I picked these fruits one by one from my orchard at the hour when day breaks over Hebron. They are succulent and satisfying, fit to be served at the table of Hannan himself. But of what value are vain words between you and me if our hearts understand each other? Take these figs, the best in Syria, and may the Lord bless the woman who gave birth to you!'

I knew that, in matters of buying and selling, this offer was but a time-honoured courtesy dating back to the days of the patriarchs. I fulfilled my part in the ceremony, declaring that I had orders from Jehovah, the All Powerful, to pay for those fruits of the earth with money minted by princes. The market gardener lowered his head and bowed to the divine commandment. Then, placing his basket on the flagstones, taking one fig in each of his dark, dirt-ingrained hands, he exclaimed:

'In truth, Jehovah is all powerful! If he so orders it, then I must put a price on these fruits of his goodness, sweeter than the sweet lips of a wife! It is meet, then, oh wealthy one, that for these two cool, perfumed figs that fill the palms of my hands you should give me one *traphik*.'

Great God of Judah! This eloquent Hebrew was demanding one *tostão* for each fig! I yelled at him: 'That's daylight robbery!' Then, greedy and tempted, I offered him one *drachma* for all the figs that would fit inside a turban. The man raised his hands to his breast, as if to rend his tunic, so great was his humiliation. And he was just about to invoke Jehovah, Elijah, and all the prophets who were his protectors when wise Topsius, irritated, abruptly intervened and, holding out to him a small metal coin stamped with an open lily, said:

'Jehovah is indeed great! And you are as clamorous and empty as a wine skin full of wind! I'll give you one *meah* for all the figs in that basket. And if you don't want it, I know my way to the gardens as well as I do to the Temple and I know exactly where to find the best orchards bathed by the sweet waters of the Enrogel . . . Now, go!'

The man climbed eagerly up to the marble parapet and, with a dignified frown on his face, piled figs into the corner of my burnous which I held out to him. Then, baring white teeth, he murmured, with a smile, that we were more beneficent than the dew from Carmel.

That lunch of figs from Bethphage, in Herod's palace, seemed to me both delicious and unique. We had barely sat down with the fruit in our laps when I noticed below us a fragile old man who had fixed on us the humble gaze of his clouded eyes, plaintive and weary. Taking pity on him, I was about to throw him some figs and a silver coin from the time of the Ptolemies when, plunging a tremulous hand into the rags barely covering his hairy chest, he gave an embarrassed smile and held out to me a glittering stone. It was an oval plaque made out of alabaster and engraved with an image of the Temple. And while Topsius learnedly examined it, the old man produced other precious stones from his bosom: marble, onyx, jasper, bearing representations of the Tabernacle in the desert, carved with the names of the tribes or with vague relief figures, simulating the battles of the Maccabees. Then he stood there with his arms crossed and his noble, care-lined face betrayed only yearning, as if he expected from us only mercy and rest.

Topsius guessed that he was one of the so-called Guebri, fire-worshippers and skilled craftsmen, who walk barefoot all the way to Egypt, carrying blazing torches, just to sprinkle the sphinx with the blood of a black cockerel. Horrified, the old man denied this roundly and told us his story in a forlorn mumble. He was a stonemason from Naim, one who had worked on the Temple and on the buildings Herod Antipas had ordered to be erected in Bezetha. The whips wielded by the overseers had torn his flesh, then illness had sapped his strength as surely as frost withers the apple tree. And now, with no paid employment and with his daughter's children to feed, he searched in the mountains for rare stones and engraved them with holy names and pictures of holy places in order to sell them in the Temple to the faithful. On the eve of the Passover, however, a wrathful Rabbi from Galilee had come, determined to take away his living!

'That man there!' he stammered, boiling with rage, shaking his fist in the direction of Jesus.

I protested. How could he possibly have suffered injustice and pain at the hands of this Rabbi, who bore a divine flame in his heart, who was the poor man's best friend?

'You were selling in the Temple, were you?' asked Topsius.

'Yes,' sighed the old man, 'On feast days I could earn enough money there to live on for a whole year. I would go up to the Temple, offer up my prayer to the Lord, and by the Gate of Suza, opposite the King's Gate, I would roll out my mat and place on it my stones, which glittered in the sunlight. Of course, I had no right to set up a stall there, but how could I afford to pay the Temple to rent a space on the flagstones in order to sell my work? The people who have plots in the shade, beneath the portico, on cedar tables, are all rich merchants who can afford to pay the licence fee – some pay a gold *siclo* for the privilege. I couldn't do that, not with children at home with no bread to eat. That's why I just stayed in my corner, outside the portico, in the worst spot. I would squat there, quiet as a mouse, never complaining, not even when rough men pushed me or beat me about the head with sticks. And there were other people like me nearby. Eboim from Joppa, who sold a special hair restoring oil, and Oseias from Ramah, who sold clay flutes. The soldiers from the Antonia Tower, who patrolled there, used to pass by and turn a blind eye to us. Even Menahem, who was almost always on guard at Passover, said to us: "It's all right, you can stay, as long as you don't cry your wares out loud." They all knew that we were poor and couldn't afford the hire of a stall, and that we had starving children at home. At Passover and during the Feasts of the Tabernacles, pilgrims come to Jerusalem from distant parts and they all used to buy an image of the Temple from me to show to people in their village, or else a moonstone to frighten away the devil. Sometimes, at the end of the day, I would have earned three *drachma*, I would fill the corner of my tunic with lentils and go off to my hut happy, singing the praises of the Lord.'

So touched was I by his tale that I forgot all about my lunch. The old man went on with his long complaint:

'But then a few days ago, this Rabbi from Galilee appeared in the Temple, full of angry words. He raised up his stick and wielded it against us, shouting that this was the house of his Father, that we were defiling it! And he sent flying all the stones I make my living from. I never found them again. He smashed Eboim's bottles of oil on the ground. Eboim was so shocked he didn't even cry out. The Temple guards arrived. Menahem was there too and he even said indignantly to the Rabbi, "You're very hard on the poor. Who gave you the right to do this?" And the Rabbi spoke again of "his Father" and reminded us of the harsh law of the Temple. Menahem bowed his head. And we had to flee, to the jeers of the rich merchants sitting cross-legged and comfortable on their carpets from Babylonia and with their stalls paid for, who all applauded the Rabbi. The Rabbi had nothing to say against them. They were rich, they'd paid for their stalls. And now here I am. My daughter's ill and a widow. She can't work, she just lies in a corner wrapped in her rags, and her children, who are still only small, are hungry, and they look at me with such sad eyes, but they never cry. And what did I do? I was always humble, I observe the Sabbath, I go to my local synagogue in Naim, and the few crumbs left over from my table I give to those who have neither crumbs nor land. What crime did I commit in selling my stones? How was I offending the Lord? Before I rolled out my mat, I always used to kiss the Temple flagstones; every stone I sold was purified with holy water. Jehovah is great and he knows all this ... but this Rabbi threw me out simply because I was poor.'

He fell silent and his thin hands, tattooed with mystical symbols, trembled as he wiped away the tears bathing his face.

I beat my chest in desperation. What wounded me most was that Jesus, in the grip of his passionate spirituality, would know nothing of the misfortune that his merciful hands had involuntarily created, just as the beneficent rain, whilst it causes a whole field of seeds to grow, may also bend and crush one isolated flower. And then, so that there should be no imperfection in his life, so that not a single complaint against him should remain on Earth, I paid

Jesus' debt (may His Father forgive mine) by tossing into the old man's lap all the change I had: *drachma*, gold Greek coins, Roman coins from the time of Augustus, even a large coin from Cyrenaica, which I valued because it bore the head of Zeus Amnon which was the very image of me. Topsius added a copper coin which, in Judaea, is worth a single grain of corn.

The old stonemason from Naim grew pale, barely able to speak, then, with the money tied in one corner of his tunic, which he clutched to his chest, he murmured timidly, earnestly, raising his shining eyes to heaven:

'Our Father, who art in heaven, remember the face of this man who has given me my bread for many a long day.'

Then, sobbing, he disappeared into the multitude, who were now crowding noisily into the atrium, clustering about the tall poles supporting the velarium. The scribe had appeared, red-faced and dabbing at his lips. Sareias was standing next to the Rabbi and the Temple guards, leaning on his staff. Then, from amidst the glitter of spears, there emerged the white fasces borne by the lictors. And once again, the pale, ponderous figure of Pontius, in the voluminous swathes of his toga, walked up the bronze steps and sat down on the curule chair.

A silence fell, so intent that you could hear the bugles being sounded far off on the Mariamne Tower. Sareias unrolled his dark parchment scroll and lay it flat on the stone table amongst the other scrolls, and I saw the scribe's plump, deliberate hands trace a rubric and place a seal on the lines written in red ink condemning to death Jesus of Galilee, my Lord. Then, with a kind of indolent dignity, barely raising one bare arm, Pontius Pilate ratified in the name of Caesar the 'sentence of the Sanhedrin, which holds sway in Jerusalem'.

Sareias immediately pulled one corner of his cloak over his head and sat there praying, his hands open to heaven. And the Pharisees were triumphant. Next to us, two ancient old men kissed each other silently on their white

175

beards, others waved their staffs in the air and shouted out in loud, sarcastic voices the legal phrase the Romans used in court: *Bene et belle! Non potest melius!*

But then, suddenly, the interpreter appeared, standing on a stool, the brilliant painted parrot swelling on his chest. Surprised, the crowd fell silent. And the Phoenician, having consulted with the scribe, smiled and cried out in Chaldean, spreading wide his arms adorned with coral bracelets.

'Listen! At the feast of the Passover, it has been the custom of the Praetor of Jerusalem, as decreed by Valerius Gracus and with the agreement of Caesar, to pardon one criminal. The Praetor proposes that you should pardon this man. But listen! You yourselves also have the right to choose from amongst the condemned men. The Praetor also has in his power, in Herod's dungeons, another man sentenced to death . . .'

He hesitated and, leaning down from the footstool, he again questioned the scribe, who was confusedly shuffling papyruses and scrolls. Shaking the corner of his cloak, Sareias abruptly ceased his prayers and, with hands palms upwards, was staring in amazement at the Praetor. But the interpreter was again shouting, smiling and holding his head higher still:

'One of the condemned men is Rabbi Jeschoua, whom you have here before you and who claims to be the son of David. He is the man the Praetor proposes. The other man, a hardened criminal, was imprisoned for the treacherous murder of a legionary in a fight near Xistus. His name is Bar-Abbas. Now it is up to you to choose!'

A harsh, abrupt cry emerged from amongst the Pharisees:

'Bar-Abbas!'

The name of Bar-Abbas echoed here and there about the atrium. And a Temple slave in a yellow tunic went bounding up the steps to the dais and shouted right in Pontius' face, furiously slapping his own thighs:

'Bar-Abbas! Do you hear? Bar-Abbas! The people want Bar-Abbas!'

A legionary's spear sent him reeling across the flagstones. But now the whole multitude, more flammable than hay in a haystack, was crying out for Bar-Abbas! Others were furiously stamping with their sandalled feet and beating their iron crooks on the ground as if to shake the whole Praetorium; others, further off, sat cross-legged in the sun and lazily raised one finger. The rancorous sellers in the Temple were rattling their metal scales and ringing bells, raining down curses upon the Rabbi and screaming out: 'Bar-Abbas is the best!' Even the prostitutes from Tiberias, daubed like idols with vermilion, pierced the air with their shrill cries:

'Bar-Abbas! Bar-Abbas!'

Hardly anyone there knew who Bar-Abbas was, nor did they hate the Rabbi, but everyone promptly joined in the tumult, sensing in the call for that prisoner who had attacked legionaries some insult against the Roman Praetor, sitting august and togaed on his throne. Pontius, meanwhile, indifferent to all this, was busily writing on a vast sheet of parchment resting on his knees. And around him the measured cries echoed rhythmically, like flails beating on a threshing floor:

'Bar-Abbas! Bar-Abbas! Bar-Abbas!'

Then Jesus turned slowly round towards that hard, rebellious world condemning him and in his brilliant eyes, damp with tears, in the fugitive tremor of his lips, there flickered, just for an instant, a look of pity and pain for Man's opaque lack of awareness that he was thus hurrying towards his death the dearest friend Man ever had. With his bound wrists he wiped away a drop of sweat, then stood before the Praetor, as untroubled and unmoving as if he were already no longer of this world.

The scribe, beating with an iron ruler on the stone table, thrice cried out the name of Caesar. The excited crowd lost heart. Pontius stood up and gravely, without betraying any impatience or anger, he uttered the final commandment, gesturing with his hand:

'Go then and crucify him!'

He stepped off the dais and the mob applauded fiercely.

Eight soldiers from the Syrian ranks appeared, carrying large flasks containing mead. They were equipped for marching, their shields covered in canvas, their implements bundled up. Sareias, the spokesman of the Sanhedrin, touched Jesus on the shoulder and delivered him to the decurion. A soldier untied Jesus' bonds, another pulled off his woollen burnous and thus I saw the sweet Rabbi from Galilee take his first steps towards death.

Rolling ourselves a cigarette each, we hurriedly left Herod's palace by a passageway known to the learned Topsius; it was damp and gloomy, lined with barred windows from which issued the sad songs of imprisoned slaves. We emerged into a square, sheltered by the wall of a garden planted with cypress trees. Two camels lay ruminating in the dust, next to a pile of cut grass. Topsius was still following the path to the Temple when, beneath the ruins of an archway covered in ivy, we saw people crowding about an Essene, whose white linen sleeves were beating the air like the wings of an angry bird.

It was Gad, hoarse with indignation, loudly denouncing a dishevelled man, with a sparse, blond beard and wearing large gold earrings, who was trembling and stammering:

'It wasn't me, it wasn't me . . .'

'It *was* you!' shouted Gad, stamping hard on the ground with his sandal. 'I know you well. Your mother is a carder in Cafarnaum, and cursed may she be for the milk she gave you!'

The man recoiled, lowering his head, like a trapped animal:

'It wasn't me! My name is Refraim, son of Eliezer from Ramah! Everyone knows me, I've always been healthy and strong as a new palm tree!'

'You are as useless and twisted as an old branch from a vine, you cur, you son of a cur!' shouted Gad. 'I saw you. It was in Cafarnaum, in that sidestreet where there's a fountain, next to the synagogue. You appeared before Jesus, the Rabbi from Nazareth! You kissed his sandals and said: "Rabbi, cure me! Rabbi, look at this hand that can no longer work!" And you showed him your hand, that one, the right one, withered and black, like a branch that has died on the tree! It was on the Sabbath and three leaders of the synagogue were there, as well as Elzear and Simeon. And they were all watching Jesus to see if he would dare to heal someone on the day of the Lord. You were weeping, lying on the ground, and did the Rabbi send you away? Did he send you to look for some canna root! You cur, you son of a cur! The Rabbi, indifferent to the accusations of the synagogue, and listening only to his sense of mercy, said to you: "Hold out your hand!" He touched it and it immediately grew green again, like a plant watered by the dew from Heaven! It was healthy, strong and firm again and you stood there, amazed and trembling, and moved first one finger, then another.'

A murmur of delight ran through the crowd, astonished at such a sweet miracle. Gad was shouting now, gesturing with his arms in the air:

'That was how charitable the Rabbi was! And did he hold out to you one corner of his cloak, as the rabbis in Jerusalem do, so that you might place a silver coin in it? No. He told his friends to give you some lentils to eat. And you raced off down the road, a new man, agile, crying out as you approached your house: "Mother, Mother, I am cured!" And it was you, you pig, you son of a pig, who just a short while ago in the praetorium called for the Rabbi to be crucified and shouted out in favour of Bar-Abbas! Don't deny it, you filthy swine, I heard you. I was right behind you and I saw the veins in your neck swell with the rage of your ingratitude!'

Some people were so scandalised, they began shouting: 'Curse him! Curse him!' With righteous gravity, an old man had picked up two large stones. And the man from Cafarnaum, shrinking and humiliated, was still muttering quietly:

'It wasn't me, it wasn't me. I'm from Ramah!'

Enraged, Gad seized him by his beard:

'When you knelt down before the Rabbi, we all saw two curved scars on your arm, as if made by two blows with a scythe! Show your arm to us now, you son of a dog!'

He ripped off the sleeve of the man's new tunic; he dragged him round, gripping him with his hands of bronze, as if the man were some terrified sacrificial goat. He showed them the two scars, livid amongst the blond hairs, and then he hurled him disdainfully into the crowd, who kicked up the dust along the road as they pursued the man from Cafarnaum with jeers and stones.

We went over to Gad, smiling and praising his faithfulness to Jesus. He had calmed down by then and was holding out his hands to a waterseller who poured a long stream of water over them to cleanse them. Then, drying his hands on the linen towel that hung from his waist, he said:

'Listen! Joseph of Arimathea has claimed the body of the Rabbi and the Praetor has approved his claim to do so. Wait for me at the ninth Roman hour in the courtyard of Gamaliel. Where are you going now?'

Topsius confessed that we were on our way to the Temple for intellectual reasons to do with art and archaeology.

'Only the futile marvel at stones!' growled the haughty idealist.

And he went off, pulling his hood over his face, receiving as he went the blessings of the people who love and believe in the Essenes.

To avoid the difficult walk to the Temple via the Tyropoeon valley road and the bridge of Xistus, we decided to take two litters which an ex-slave of Pontius was hiring out, 'in Roman style', next door to the Praetorium.

I lay down wearily, my hands behind my head, on the mattress of dried leaves that smelled of myrtle. And a strange, fearful disquiet began to fill my soul, a feeling I had already sensed brush past me in the Praetorium like the tremulous wing of a bird of ill omen. Was I to remain forever in this fortified town of the Jews? Had I lost forever my individuality as Raposo, Catholic, university graduate, a contemporary of *The Times* and of gaslamps to become a man from classical antiquity, coeval with Tiberius? And, given that I had made this marvellous journey back in time, were I to return to my own country, what would I find on the banks of that bright river?

I would doubtless find a Roman colony: a stone-built house on the coolest side of the hill, occupied by the proconsul; next to it, a small, slate-roofed temple to Apollo or Mars; on the highest hills, fields dug with trenches for the legionaries; and round about, the Lusitanian people would be scattered along rutted roads, living in huts made out of loose stones, with sheds to keep their cattle in and stakes driven into the mud to moor their rafts. That would be the state I would find my country in. And what would I do there, poor and alone? Would I be a shepherd on the hills? Would I sweep the steps of the temple, chop firewood for the army to earn a Roman wage? What utter wretchedness!

And if I stayed in Jerusalem? What career would I follow in this sombre, devout city of Asia? Would I become a Jew, saying the Sachema, observing the Sabbath, perfuming my beard with spikenard, wandering the courtyards of the Temple, following the lessons of a Rabbi and, in the evenings, with my golden walking cane, strolling in the gardens of Gareb amongst the tombs? That existence seemed to me equally horrifying! No, if I were to remain imprisoned in the ancient world with my learned friend Topsius, then we should ride to Joppa that very night, at moonrise, and from there embark on some Phoenician trireme leaving for Italy and go and live in Rome, even if it was in one of those dark sidestreets in Velabro, in one of those smoky attics, up two hundred stairs, stinking of garlic and tripe, perched at the top of one those tenements that can barely go two months without falling down or going up in flames.

Such were my disquieting thoughts as the litter stopped;

I drew back the curtains and I saw before me the vast granite slabs of the Temple wall. We plunged in beneath the vaulted roof of the Hulda Gate and were immediately held up by Temple guards who were disarming a stubborn, unruly shepherd of a club bristling with nails he had wanted to take into the sanctuary with him. Even the continuous distant hum coming from the atrium, like the sound of a great forest or a mighty sea, filled me with terror.

And when we finally emerged from beneath the narrow vault, I grasped Topsius' scrawny arm, feeling dazzled, awestruck! The soft air shimmered with the profuse, brilliant white and gold light given off by the pale marble, the polished granite, the exquisite embroidery all bathed by the divine sun of the month of Nisan. The smooth courtyards, which had been deserted that morning, glinting white like the still waters of a lake, had disappeared, filled now by hordes of people in fine and festive clothes. There was a dizzying mixture of acrid smells: dyed cloth, aromatic resins, fat sizzling on hot coals. Over the impenetrable buzz of noise could be heard the hoarse bellowing of oxen. And above it all, the smoke from the votive offerings rose endlessly into the radiant skies.

'Good grief!' I murmured, turning pale. 'I'm dumbstruck. I've never seen such magnificence.'

We continued on and passed through the Porch of Solomon which echoed with the profane tumult of the marketplace. Behind thick, barred windows, moneychangers sat cross-legged, the usual single golden coin dangling from one ear just visible amongst their greasy, dishevelled hair. They were engaged in exchanging the priestly money of the Temple for pagan coins from every region and every age, from the thick roundels of ancient Lactium, heavier than shields, to the engraved tiles that are used as 'notes' in the markets of Assyria. Further on we could see what appeared to be the cool, glittering abundance of an orchard: pomegranates, ripe and bursting, were piled in wicker baskets; market gardeners, a branch of flowering almond stuck in their caps, were selling garlands of anemones or bitter herbs for Passover; jugs of fresh milk rested on sacks of lentils; and lambs, lying down on the flagstones, tethered by their legs to the columns, were bleating forlornly for water.

But the densest mass of people was to be found, uttering envious sighs, around the stalls selling cloth and jewels. Merchants from the Phoenician colonies, from the Greek isles, from Tardis, Mesopotamia and Tadmor – some selling superb cymars in embroidered wool, others selling rough tabards in painted leather – were unrolling lengths of blue cloth from Tyre that imitated the burning brilliance of the Orient skies, wanton silks from Sheba of a transparent green that drifted on the breeze, and that solemn cloth from Babylonia which I had always loved, black with great blood-red flowers on it. In cedar coffers, spread upon carpets from Galatia, gleamed silver mirrors in the shape of the moon and its rays, the tourmaline brooches that the Hebrews wear pinned to their breast, bracelets of precious stones looped about antelope horns, diadems made out of rock salt as worn by brides and, kept under even closer guard, talismans and amulets that struck me as rather puerile, bits of root, black stones, scorched scraps of leather and bones with words written on them.

Topsius had paused amongst the shops selling perfumes to admire a splendid walking stick from Tilos, made out of a strange wood striped like a tiger skin, but then we fled the overwhelming, suffocating smells that emanated from resins, glues from Africa, bundles of ostrich feathers, myrrh from Oronte, waxes from Cyrenaica, pale pink oils from Cisico and from the great cauls made out of hippopotamus skins, full of dried violets and bacaro flowers.

Then we went into the so-called Royal gallery, devoted to Doctrine and the Law. Every day it resounded to the rancorous debates held amongst Sadducees, scribes, Sophorins, Pharisees, supporters of Schemaia and of Hillel, lawyers, grammarians and fanatics from the whole of Judaea. The teachers of the Law would sit on high stools by the marble columns, with a metal dish to one side to receive the alms of the faithful. And around them, sitting cross-legged on the floor, their sandals hanging about their necks, cured skins covered in red lettering unfolded on their knees, their disciples, some still beardless youths, others decrepit old men, would mumble the precepts, slowly swaying back and forth. Here and there, surrounded by a circle of devotees, two doctors, their faces flushed with excitement, were arguing about sticky points of doctrine: 'Can one eat a chicken's egg that was laid on the day of the Sabbath? With which bone of the spinal cord does the resurrection begin?' Topsius the philosopher was laughing at them behind his cloak, but I trembled when the doctors, hollow-cheeked and bearded, threatened each other, shouting: 'Racca! Racca!' and plunged a hand into their tunics in search of a hidden knife.

We kept coming across the kind of Pharisee, noisy and empty as drums, who come to the Temple simply to show off their piety, some with their backs bent, as if crushed by the great weight of all human sin; others, stumbling and feeling the air, their eyes closed, so as not to glimpse the impure forms of women; whilst others, their faces smeared with ash, moaned and clutched their bellies, in testimony to their long fasts! Then Topsius pointed out to me a Rabbi who was an interpreter of dreams: his deep-set eyes glittered in his pale, gaunt face, as sad as lamps set on a tomb. Sitting on woolsacks, he spread over each devout person, who came to kneel before his bare feet, the corner of a vast, black cloak painted with white symbols. I felt so curious, I was even thinking of consulting him myself, when agonised cries suddenly filled the atrium. We ran towards them. It was a group of Levites armed with ropes and sticks, who were furiously beating a leper who had entered the Court of the Israelites in a state of uncleanness. Blood splattered the flagstones. Children stood around laughing.

It was nearly the sixth Judaic hour, the hour most pleasing to the Lord, when the sun, in its progress to the sea, pauses above Jerusalem and looks lovingly down upon it. And in order to approach the Court of the Israelites, we had to push our slow way through the crowds gathered there, people from both civilised and barbarous lands. The rough animal skins worn by shepherds from Idumaea jostled the short chlamys of clean-shaven Greeks, their faces white as marble. There were solemn men from the plain of Babylonia, who wore their beards caught up in blue bags attached by a silver chain to mitres made of painted leather. And there were fair-haired Gauls with moustaches as long as the weeds that grow in their lakes, who laughed and chattered, devouring sweet Syrian lemons, peel and all. Sometimes a Roman in a toga would pass by, as grave-faced as if he had stepped down from a pedestal. People from Dacia and from Mysia, their legs swathed in felt bindings, stumbled, bedazzled, amongst the bright splendour of the marble statues. And it was just as strange that I, Teodorico Raposo, should be strolling around there in my riding boots, behind a priest of Moloch, a vast, sensual figure in his purple cymar, who was speaking disdainfully to a group of merchants from Serepta about that Temple bereft of images and trees and noisier than any Phoenician marketplace.

Thus we made our way to the gate known as the Beautiful Gate, which gives access into the sacred Court of the Israelites. It is indeed beautiful, splendid and triumphant. It stands at the top of fourteen steps made out of green Numidian marble mottled with yellow: the long door jambs, faced with silver plate, glinted like those of a reliquary and the two doorposts, like great bundles of palm leaves, each supported a tower, round and white, decorated with shields taken from the enemies of Judah, shining in the sun like a glorious necklace about the strong neck of a hero. But in front of this marvellous entrance rose a stark pillar, bearing at the top a black plaque engraved with letters of gold, on which was written the following warning in Greek, Latin, Aramaic and Chaldean: 'Let no stranger enter here, on pain of death!'

Fortunately we spotted the thin figure of Gamaliel, who was on his way to the holy courtyard, barefoot and clutching to his breast a sheaf of votive corn. He was accompanied by a plump, jolly man, his face red as a poppy, who wore a huge black woollen mitre decorated with coral beads. Bowing low to the ground, we greeted the austere doctor of the Law. Eyes closed, he muttered:

'I bid you welcome. This is the best hour to receive the blessing of the Lord. The Lord said: "Leave your rooms, come to me with your first fruits and I will bless in them the labour of your hands." Today, by some miracle, you belong to Israel. Go up unto the dwelling of the Eternal One. This man by my side is Eliezer of Silo, a kind man who knows all there is to know about the natural world.'

He gave us two ears of corn and, following behind him, our Gentile feet entered the forbidden courtyard of Judah.

Walking by my side, Eliezer of Silo, courteous and gentle, asked me if my country lay far off and if its roads were dangerous.

I mumbled something vague, evasive:

'Yes. We've just arrived from Jericho.'

'Has the balsam harvest been good there?'

'Wonderful!' I assured him ardently. 'Blessed be the Eternal One, for in this year of His grace, we're up to our eyes in balsam!'

He seemed pleased. He told me then that he was one of the doctors who live in the Temple, since the priests and those who perform the sacrifices suffer continually from 'intestinal disorders', because they're always walking about, sweating and barefoot, on the cold flagstones of the courtyards.

'That's why,' he murmured, his kind eyes glinting playfully, 'the people in Zion call us "gut doctors"!'

I bent double with laughter and pleasure at that joke whispered to me in the austere dwelling place of the Eternal One. Then, recalling my own intestinal disorders in Jericho, provoked by my passion for the divine but treacherous melons of Syria, I asked the amiable physician if in those circumstances he would prescribe bismuth.

The learned man cautiously shook his woollen mitre. Then, raising one finger in the air, he entrusted me with this incomparable remedy:

'Take glue from Alexandria, saffron from the garden, an onion from Persia and dark wine from Emmaus, mix it all up, then boil it. Leave it to cool in a silver vase and place it at a crossroads at sunrise . . .'

But then he suddenly fell silent, his arms outstretched, his head bowed. We had entered the wonderful courtyard known as the Courtyard of the Women and at that moment, the blessings spoken at the sixth hour by a priest standing above the Gate of Nicanor were just drawing to a close.

The Gate was very plain, made entirely out of bronze, and through it you could glimpse, right at the back, the serene glitter of the golds and whites and precious stones of the sanctuary. On the broad steps, more lustrous than alabaster, two groups of Levites dressed in white were kneeling, some bearing curled trumpets, some resting their fingers on the silent strings of lyres. And between these two ranks of prostrate men, a small, emaciated old man came slowly down the steps, carrying a golden censer in one hand.

His close-fitting, linen tunic was edged with clusters of emeralds alternating with tiny, tinkling bells. His bare, henna-dyed feet looked as if they were made out of coral and, in the middle of the sash that wound about his lean waist, shone a great sun, embroidered in gold. The faithful knelt down silently, without a murmur, their heads – hidden beneath cloaks and veils – almost touching the flagstones, and the festive colours, in which anemone red and fig green predominated, made it look as if the court-yard were scattered with flowers and leaves for Solomon to walk upon on a victorious morning.

With his sharp, neat beard raised to the skies, the old man wafted the incense first to the East and to the sands, then to the West and to the sea; and the silence was so intense you could hear at the far end of the sanctuary the gentle lowing of oxen. He came further down the steps, his head with its bejewelled mitre held still higher, swinging the censer that creaked and glittered in the sunlight, and the blessing of the Almighty billowed forth over Israel along with the white smoke, tenuous and perfumed. Then, in unison, the Levites plucked the strings of their lyres, a cry of bronze issued forth from the curled trumpets, and all the people got to their feet, their arms reaching up to the sky, intoning a psalm celebrating Judah the eternal. And then everything stopped abruptly. The Levites withdrew noiselessly up the marble staircase on their bare feet; Eliezer of Silo and the rigid Gamaliel had disappeared beneath the porticos and the bright courtyard around us was resplendent with sumptuous crowds of women.

The alabaster facings on the walls were so highly polished that Topsius could admire the noble folds of his cape in them as if he were standing before a mirror; all the fruits of Asia and the flowers of the gardens intertwined, in heavy silver work, on the doors of the ritual chambers where the oil is mixed with scent, the wood consecrated and leprosy cleansed. Between the columns hung heavy garlands of pearls and beads made out of onyx, like the many necklaces that adorn a bride; and on the flagstones around the bronze coffers, made in the shape of colossal trumpets of war, were placed inscriptions written on scrolls in glittering gold relief, advertising the various gifts, in verses as lovely as a canticle: 'Burn incense and spikenard, offer up doves and pigeons.'

The holy courtyard was packed with women and my eyes soon abandoned metals and marbles to fix delightedly on those daughters of Jerusalem, so full of grace and dark as the tents of Kedar! In the Temple they all had their faces uncovered, or wore only a soft veil made out of muslin, light as air, caught up in their turban, in the Roman fashion, framing their faces in whiteness as delicate as foam, which only made their dark, shining eyes – outlined in kohl to make them seem even larger – all the more captivating, their gaze languid amongst their dense eyelashes. The wild profusion of gold and precious stones wrapped them in a tremulous radiance from their full breasts to their hair more tightly curled than the wool of the goats of Galaad. Their sandals, decorated with bells and chains, made silvery music on the flagstones, so graceful were their grave, undulating movements; and the embroidered cloth, the cottons from Galatia, the fine, coloured linens that they wore, all steeped in the powerful scents of amber, mallow and bacaro flowers, filled the air with fragrance and the souls of men with tender longing. The rich women walked solemnly along shaded by parasols made out of peacock feathers borne by slaves dressed in yellow who also carried the learned scrolls on which the Law is written, bags of sweet dates and delicate silver mirrors. The only jewels adorning the poorer women, who wore simple striped cotton shifts in many colours, were perhaps rough talismans made out of coral, but they ran about, chattered, their arms bare and their necks the colour of the fruit of the strawberry tree when it is just ripe for picking. And my desire hovered and buzzed about them all, like a bee hesitating amongst flowers all of equal sweetness.

'Oh Topsius,' I groaned, 'what women! It's all too much for me, my learned friend!'

My wise friend remarked, scornfully, that they had no more intellect than the peacocks in the gardens of Antipas and that he was quite sure that not one of them had ever read Aristotle or Sophocles. I shrugged. Heavens above, were I Caesar, for which of these women, who had never read Sophocles, would I not give a city in Italy and the whole of Iberia. Some stunned me with their sad, mournful grace, like that of devout virgins living in the constant penumbra of cedar-lined rooms, their bodies bathed in perfumes, their souls crushed by the weight of prayer. Others dazzled me with the solid, succulent sumptuousness of their beauty. What large, dark, idolatrous eyes! What bright, sturdy, marble-smooth limbs! What dark languor! What magnificent bare flesh they would reveal when, sitting on the edge of a low bed, their heavy hair finally tumbled free and all the veils and linens from Galatia fell gently away!

Topsius had to grab hold of my burnous and drag me bodily away towards the Stairs of Nicanor. And even then I stopped dead on every step, gazing back with ardent eyes, snorting like a bull in the May meadows.

'Oh, daughters of Zion. You're enough to drive a man mad!'

When I turned, wrenched forwards by Topsius, I ran straight into a white lamb, its legs tied together, its head crowned with roses, which an old man was carrying on his shoulders. Ahead of us was a long balustrade of carved cedar where a gate made entirely of silver hung open and swaying on its hinges, silent and glittering.

'It is here,' said my erudite friend Topsius, 'that adulterous women are given the bitter waters to drink ... But there, Dom Raposo, is where Israel adores its God.'

We had at last reached the priestly courtyard and I trembled at the sight of that most monstrous and most dazzling of sanctuaries. In the middle of a vast open space there rose the sacrificial altar built out of great, black stones. At each corner there was a bronze horn: one was hung with garlands of lilies, another with coral necklaces, a third dripped blood. A slow, red-tinged plume of smoke rose up from the immense grill on the altar and all around it stood a crowd of sacrificers, barefoot and all in white, small bronze pitchforks or silver spits in their pale hands, knives stuck in their sky-blue belts. Amidst the grave bustle of sacrosanct ceremonial could be heard the bleating of lambs, the silvery tinkle of cymbals, the crackle of firewood, the dull blows of a mallet, the slow babble of water in marble basins, the shriek of the bugles. Despite the aromatic herbs burning in the censers and the long fans made out of palm leaves with which the slaves stirred the air, I had to hold a handkerchief to my face, sickened by the sweet smell of raw meat, blood, frying fat and saffron, which the Lord had demanded from Moses as the best gift Earth had to offer.

In the background, oxen garlanded with flowers, white heifers with their horns painted gold, bellowed and butted, tugging at the ropes by which they were tethered to heavy bronze rings; further off, great sides of meat, red and bloody, lay on marble tables amongst shards of ice, surrounded by Levites wielding feather fans to shoo away the flies. From columns topped with glittering glass globes, hung dead lambs, which the *nethenin*, their clothes protected by leather aprons covered with sacred texts, were busy flaying with silver knives, whilst, with straining arms, the sacrificers in their blue tunics carried off buckets overflowing with entrails. Idumaean slaves, wearing round, metal mitres, swabbed the flagstones with sponges, whilst others were bent beneath the weight of bundles of firewood and still others crouched by small stone stoves tending the flames.

Every few minutes, an old man, one of the sacrificers, would approach the altar barefoot, carrying in his arms a young lamb, so warm and contented in the man's bare arms it did not even bleat. He was proceeded by a man playing a lyre and followed by Levites bearing jars full of aromatic oils. Before the altar, surrounded by acolytes, the sacrificer would sprinkle a fistful of salt over the lamb, then, chanting, he would cut off a little of the wool from between its horns. The bugles would sound and the wounded animal's cry would be lost amidst the sacred tumult. Above the white headdresses two red hands would be raised, dripping with blood, and a flame of happiness and oblation leapt up from the grill on the altar. Then the slow, reddish smoke would rise serenely up into the blue, bearing with it in its curling path the smell that is so pleasing to the Eternal One.

'It's a butcher's shop!' I murmured, stunned. 'It's nothing but a butcher's shop! Topsius, why don't we go back down and join the women again?'

Topsius glanced up at the sun. Then, gravely, placing a friendly hand on my shoulder, he said:

'It is nearly the ninth hour, Dom Raposo. And we have

to leave the city by the Gate of Judgement and go out beyond Gareb, to a wild place they call the Calvary.'

I went pale. And it seemed to me that my soul would gain no spiritual advantage, that no unexpected acquisition would increase Topsius' learning, by our going up to the top of a gorse-grown hill to watch Jesus suffering, roped to a piece of wood: it would merely be a torment to our sensibilities. However, I submissively followed my learned friend down the Stairway of the Waters that led to the great square paved with basalt where the first houses of Acra can be found. As neighbours of the sanctuary, and being mainly inhabited by priests, the houses were profuse in their display of Passover devotion, with palm leaves, lamps, carpets spread over the roof terraces, and some even had their thresholds scattered with the fresh blood of a lamb.

Before entering a sordid, ragged street that wound away from us beneath old awnings woven out of esparto grass, I turned round to look back at the Temple. Now I could see only the immense granite wall, the bastions along the top, sombre and indestructible, and the sheer arrogance of its strength and durability filled my heart with anger. Meanwhile, on a hill of execution intended for slaves, the man from Galilee, an incomparable friend to all men, was growing cold on his cross and that pure voice of love and spirituality would be extinguished forever, whilst the Temple responsible for his death would remain, glistening and triumphant, along with the bleating of its sheep, its strident sophistry, the usury carried out within its gates, the blood on its altars, the iniquity of its harsh pride, its importunate, perennial incense. Then, gritting my teeth, I shook my fist at Jehovah and his citadel, and I cried out:

'May you be razed to the ground!'

I did not open my dry lips again until we reached the narrow gate in the walls of Hezekiah which the Romans called the Judiciary Gate. And then a shiver ran through me when I saw, fixed to a stone pillar, a piece of parchment with three death sentences written upon it: 'that of a thief from Battebara, that of a murderer from Emath and that of Jesus of Galilee'. The scribe from the Sanhedrin, who, in accordance with the Law, had to wait there until the condemned men had passed by, to take note of any last-minute witness to their innocence, was about to leave, his bundle of files under his arm, having ruled a thick red line through each sentence. And that final mark, the colour of blood, hurriedly drawn by a clerk returning contented to his home to eat his Passover lamb, moved me more than all the melancholy of the Holy Books.

Hedges of flowering cactus bordered the path and beyond lay green hills where low drystone walls covered in wild roses marked the boundaries of the different farms. Everything about us shone, festive and peaceful. In the shade of the fig trees, beneath the vine trellises, women sat cross-legged on carpets weaving flax or making up bundles of lavender and marjoram for people to offer up at Passover, and around them children, heavy coral amulets about their necks, were swinging on ropes, playing with bows and arrows. Along the street came a string of slow dromedaries, carrying merchandise to Joppa. Two strong men were coming home from the hunt, their high red boots covered in dust, their quivers knocking against their thighs, a net thrown over one shoulder, and their arms laden with partridges and vultures tied by their feet. Ahead of us, walking slowly along, leaning on the shoulder of the child who was leading him, was a ragged old man with a long beard; he had a five-string Greek lyre attached to his belt, like a bard, and wore a crown of laurel leaves on his head.

At the foot of a wall covered in flowering almond, before a gate painted in red, two slaves were sitting waiting on a fallen tree trunk, their eyes lowered, their hands resting on their knees. Topsius stopped and tugged at my burnous:

'This is the garden of Joseph of Arimathea, a friend of Jesus, a member of the Sanhedrin, a man of unquiet spirit, who inclines towards the Essenes. And here comes Gad himself.'

For Gad had indeed appeared at the back of the garden and now came running down along a path lined with myrtle and roses, carrying, suspended on a pole, a bundle of linen and a wicker basket. He stopped.

'What happened to the Rabbi?' Topsius shouted, going through the gate.

The Essene handed over to one of the slaves both the bundle and the basket, the latter was full of myrrh and aromatic herbs, and then stood before us for a moment, trembling, overcome with emotion, one hand pressed to his heart to calm his anxiety.

'He suffered greatly,' he murmured at last. 'He suffered when they drove the nails through his hands. Even more when they raised him up on the cross . . . and, at first, he refused the wine of mercy that would bring him unconsciousness. The Rabbi wanted to enter with a clear soul the death for which he had called. But Joseph of Arimathea and Nicodemus were watching nearby. They both reminded him of things he had promised one night in Bethany. Then the Rabbi drank from the bowl held to his lips by Rosmophin's wife.'

And the Essene, his blazing eyes fixed on Topsius, as if to imprint one supreme commandment forever on his soul, took a step back and said with grave slowness:

'Tonight, after supper, at Gamaliel's house.'

And then he disappeared back down the cool path, amongst the myrtle and the roses. Topsius immediately left the Joppa road and, striding briskly along a rough track where my long burnous kept snagging on the spines of the agave plants, he explained to me that the wine of mercy was a strong wine from Tharses, blended with poppy juice and spices, which was supplied by a company of devout women to render the suffering victims unconscious. But I was scarcely listening to what he was saying, for I had spotted at the top of that rugged hillside, all rocks and gorsebushes, a crowd of people standing absolutely still, precise against the bright blue of the smooth sky. In their midst rose three great wooden crosses and, moving amongst them, glistening in the sun, the polished helmets of legionaries. Troubled, I paused at the side of the track and leaned against a scalding white rock. But seeing Topsius marching on with the wise serenity of one who considers death to be a purificatory liberation from imperfect form, I did not want to seem either less strong or less spiritual. I tore off my burnous, which was suffocating me, and bounded intrepidly up the steep hill.

To one side, the ground dropped away down to the valley of Hinnon, scorched and pale, without even a blade of grass or a hint of shade, scattered with bones, carcasses, ashes. And ahead, the hill rose up before us, covered in leprous patches of black furze, occasionally pierced by a boulder, polished and white as bone. Lizards scattered before us as we advanced up the track which petered out amongst the ruins of an adobe hut: two almond trees, sadder than plants growing out of a crack in a tomb, stood there with bare, flowerless branches in which cicadas sang their harsh song. And in the tenuous shade, four barefoot women, their hair dishevelled, their shabby tunics rent in mourning, were weeping as though they were at a funeral.

One of them, leaning stiff and motionless against a tree trunk, was moaning dully, one corner of her black cloak pulled over her head; another woman, worn out with crying, was curled up against a rock, her head on her knees and her splendid blonde hair tangled, dragging on the ground. But the other two were hysterical, their faces scratched and bloody, desperately beating their breasts, smearing their faces with earth. Then, raising their bare arms to heaven, they shook the hill with their cries: 'Oh my delight, oh my treasure, oh my son!' And a dog, sniffing amongst the ruins, opened his mouth and howled along with them, a sinister sound.

Terrified, I tugged at the learned Topsius' cloak and we made our way through the furze up to the top to join the gawking, chattering crowd comprising men from the workshops of Gareb, Temple servants, sellers and a few of those wretched priests in rags who live off necromancy and alms.

Seeing the white cloak in which Topsius was swathed, two moneychangers, gold coins hanging from their ears, stepped back, murmuring servile words of blessing. We were brought up short by a length of rope made out of esparto grass, hung between posts fixed in the ground to cordon off the top of the hill and, where we were standing, tied round an old olive tree whose branches were festooned with a red cloak and the shields of the legionaries.

Then, anxiously, I looked up. I looked up at the tallest cross, its base wedged into a crack in the rock. The Rabbi was dying. And that body – which was made of neither ivory nor silver, but which was gasping for breath, alive, warm, roped and nailed to a piece of wood, a scrap of old cloth tied about his loins, another beam fixed between his legs – filled me with terror and fear. The blood, congealing about the nails, stained the new wood, blackened his hands; his feet, bound with a thick cord, were purple and twisted in pain, almost touching the ground. His head, one moment flushed dark with blood, the next paler than marble, rolled gently from one side to the other and beneath the tangle of hair, sticky with sweat, his eyes were sunken, dull, dead, as if, as the light in them faded, all the light and all the hope on Earth were also fading, for ever.

The grave-faced centurion, cloakless, arms folded over his chainmail breastplate, was patrolling up and down beneath the Rabbi's cross, occasionally staring into the hard eyes of the people from the Temple who were muttering and laughing. And Topsius pointed out to me, right at the front, a man whose sad, yellow face was almost hidden by the two long tresses of black hair that hung down onto his chest. He was impatiently rolling and unrolling a parchment scroll, keeping one eye on the slow sinking of the sun and speaking in a low voice to a slave at his side.

'It's Joseph of Arimathea,' Topsius whispered to me. 'Let's go over and find out what he's saying.'

But at that moment, from amongst the squalid band of Temple slaves and the wretched priests who live on the leftovers from the sacrifices, there burst forth a louder noise, like the cawing of crows up in the sky. And one of their number, a gaunt, massive figure, his breath stinking of wine, the scars from old knife wounds showing through his sparse beard, raised up his arms to the cross where the Rabbi was hanging and shouted:

'If you're so powerful, you who declared you could destroy the Temple and its walls, why can't you simply shatter the wood of your own cross?'

People laughed foolishly. And another man, spreading his hands on his chest, gave an infinitely scornful bow and greeted the Rabbi with these words:

'Heir of David, oh my prince, how do you like your throne?'

'Son of God, why don't you call on your Father and see if he'll come and save you!' came a hoarse cry at my side, uttered by a skinny old man, who was trembling and shaking his beard, leaning on his staff.

A few low fellows were picking up dry clods of earth and moulding them into balls with saliva in order to throw them at the Rabbi; then a stone flew past and hit the wood of his cross with a hollow thud. The centurion ran over, indignant. The blade of his long sword glinted in the air and a group withdrew cursing, whilst others wrapped in one corner of their tunics fingers that were dripping blood.

We went over to Joseph of Arimathea. But the sad man walked briskly away, avoiding the importunate Topsius. Offended by his rudeness, we stayed there by the trunk of a withered olive tree, opposite the other crosses.

In the cool evening breeze, the two condemned men had regained consciousness. One of them, heavily built and hairy, his eyes bulging, his chest thrust forward and his ribs tight, as if he wanted to tear himself bodily from the cross in one last, desperate effort, kept up a continual, terrifying roaring. The blood dripped in slow drops from his blackened feet, from his torn hands. Abandoned, with no affection or pity that might have eased his pain, he was like a wounded wolf, hunted and dying in some wasteland. The other man, thin and blond, hung there without so much as a moan, like the broken stem of a plant. Before him stood a scrawny woman in rags, who kept stepping over the rope, holding out to him a naked child and shouting in a cracked voice: 'Look, look!' The pale eyelids did not flicker. A black slave, who was bundling up the tools used in the crucifixion, went over and gave her a gentle shove. She fell silent, desperately clutching her child to her so that they would not take him as well. Her teeth chattered, she was trembling all over, and the baby sought her scrawny breast amongst the rags.

Soldiers sitting on the ground were sharing out the tunics of the crucifixion victims; others, their helmets over their arms, wiped the sweat from their brows or took leisurely sips from a metal bowl. And down below, on the dusty road, beneath the now declining sun, people were walking peacefully back from the fields and the orchards. An old man was herding his cows towards the gate of Genath; women sang as they carried their firewood; a horseman trotted by, wrapped in a white cloak. Sometimes, those walking along the road or returning from the apple orchards of Gareb would suddenly notice the three crosses raised up on the hill; then they would gather up their tunics and slowly climb up through the gorse. The sign on the Rabbi's cross, written in Greek and in Latin, never ceased to amaze. 'King of the Jews!' Who was he? Two young men, noble Sadducees wearing pearl earrings and with gold edging on their boots, questioned the centurion in scandalised voices, why had the Praetor written: 'King of the Jews'? Was the man nailed on the cross Caius Tiberius? For only Tiberius was king of Judaea! The Praetor wished to offend Israel. But in fact he was insulting only Caesar!

Unmoved, the centurion was engaged in conversation with a couple of legionaries who were poking about in the dust with two great iron bars. The woman accompanying the Sadducees, a small, dark Roman woman, with purple ribbons in her blue-powdered hair, was gently observing

198

the Rabbi and sniffing at her smelling salts, doubtless sorry for that young man, a conquered king, a barbarous king, dying a slave's death.

Feeling tired, I went and sat down with Topsius on a stone. It was nearly the eighth Judaic hour. The sun, serene as an ageing hero, was sinking into the sea behind the palm trees of Bethany. Before us lay Genath, green and full of gardens. By the walls, in the new part of Bezetha, large squares of red and blue cloth were drying on washing lines at the doors of the dyeworks; a reddish light glowed in the doorway of a forge; children ran and played along the edge of a pool. Ahead, on the top of the Hippicus Tower, already casting its shadow across the valley of Hinnon, soldiers stood on the battlements aiming their bows at the vultures flying in the blue sky. And beyond, amongst the trees, we could see the cool roof terraces of Herod's palace, tinged pink by the evening.

Sad and confused, my thoughts drifted back to Egypt, to our tents, to the candle I had left burning there, its flame red and smoking. Then, coming slowly up the hill, leaning on the shoulder of the child leading him, I saw the old man with the lyre whom we had passed on the road to Joppa. He stumbled as he walked, weary after a tiring day. He hung his head sadly so that his pale, flowing beard rested on his chest and, from beneath the wine-red cloak that he wore pulled over his head, there protruded a few sparse and withered leaves from his crown of laurels.

Topsius shouted to him: 'You there, poet!' And when he approached, skirting the furze bushes in his path, Topsius asked him if he had brought with him some new song from the sweet islands of the sea. The old man raised his face sadly and with great dignity murmured that undying youth smiled in even the most ancient songs of Greece. Then, placing one sandalled foot on a stone, he calmly took up his lyre. The child, still standing, his eyes lowered, put a flute to his mouth, and in the glow of the evening that was enveloping Zion in golden light, the poet sang a song that was at once hesitant and glorious, imbued with a spirit of adoration, as if he were standing before the altar of a temple, on a beach in Ionia. And I realised that he was singing to the gods, to their beauty, to their heroic acts. He spoke of the oracle at Delphi, beardless, with skin the colour of gold, adjusting all human thoughts to the rhythm of his zither; Athena, armed and industrious, guiding the hands of men at their looms; Zeus, ancestral and serene, bestowing beauty on all races, order on cities; and above them all, formless and diffuse, hung Fate, the most powerful of all.

Suddenly, from the top of the hill, a cry pierced the sky, as commanding and ecstatic as a cry of liberation. The old man's feeble fingers fell silent amongst the metal strings; his head drooping, the crown of epic laurels bare of most of its leaves, he appeared to be weeping over his Greek lyre, doomed to remain silent and useless from then onwards and for long ages to come. And by his side, the child, removing the flute from his lips, looked up at the black crosses with clear eyes that were filled with curiosity, with a longing for a new world.

Topsius asked the old man to tell us his story. What he told was a bitter tale. He had come from Samnos to Caesarea and used to play the konnor outside the temple of Hercules. But people gradually abandoned the pure cult of heroes and held only festivals and offerings to the good goddess of Syria. He had then joined company with some merchants on their way to Tiberius; people there had no respect for old age and had the self-seeking hearts of slaves. He had then continued on down the long roads, stopping at Roman outposts, where the soldiers would listen to his songs; in the villages of Samaria he would knock at the doors of houses with wine presses and to earn a little stale bread he would play the Greek zither at the funerals of heathens. His wanderings had brought him here, to this city with its great Temple and its fierce, formless god who hated all people. His one desire was to return to Miletus, his homeland, to hear the delicate murmur of the waters of the Maeander, to be able to touch the marble saints in the temple of Phoebus Didymeia, where, as a child, he had brought a basket containing the first shorn locks of his own hair and offered it up, singing.

Tears were rolling down his cheeks, as sad as rain running down a ruined wall. And I felt great pity for that rhapsodist from the isles of Greece, who was also lost in the harsh city of the Jews, under the sinister influence of a foreign god. I gave him my last silver coin. Leaning on the child's shoulder, he went slowly down the hill, his back bent, the ragged edge of his cloak flapping against his bare legs, his heroic five-stringed lyre silent and only precariously secured to his belt.

Meanwhile, around the crosses on the hill, a rebellious murmuring had begun. We found the people of the Temple pointing to the sky, indicating the sun that was sinking now like a shield of gold into the sea of Tyre, intimating to the centurion that he should take the condemned men down from their crosses, before the holy hour of Passover was rung. The most devout amongst them demanded that, if the crucified men were still alive, the Roman custom of *crurifragio* should be imposed, the breaking of their bones with iron bars before hurling them down the cliff at Hinnon. The centurion's indifference only exacerbated their pious zeal. Would he dare to stain the Sabbath by leaving a dead body out in the open air? Some gathered up their cloaks in order to run to Acra to warn the Praetor.

'The sun's going down! The sun is leaving Hebron!' shouted one Levite, standing on top of a stone, terrified.

'Finish them off, finish them off!'

And by our side, a handsome youth was shouting, rolling his languid eyes and waving his arms full of golden bracelets:

'Throw the Rabbi to the crows! Let the carrion birds have their Passover too!'

The centurion was watching the Mariamne Tower where the shields glittered as they caught the last rays of the sun, then he gave a slow signal with his sword and two legionaries, laboriously lifting the heavy iron bars onto their shoulders, followed him over to the crosses. Horrified, I gripped Topsius' arm. But when they reached the cross bearing Jesus, the centurion stopped, raising one hand.

The Rabbi's strong, white body had all the serenity of one asleep; his bound, dusty feet, which only a short time before had been twisted with pain, now hung down, as if he were about to step lightly to the ground. You could no longer see his face, for it had fallen back limply over one arm of the cross, gazing up at the same sky where he had placed his desire and his kingdom. I too looked up at the sky. It glittered, shadowless, cloudless, smooth, clear, dumb, lofty and utterly impassive.

'Who was it who was asking for this man's body?' shouted the centurion looking about him.

'I did, for I loved him when he was alive!' said Joseph of Arimathea, leaning over the rope and holding out his parchment scroll.

The slave waiting with him put down his bundle of linen and ran over to the ruined hut where the women were weeping amongst the almond trees.

And behind us, the Pharisees and Sadducees gathered there were wondering sourly why Joseph of Arimathea, a member of the Sanhedrin, should want the Rabbi's body, in order to perfume it and to arrange full funeral rites with flutes and mourners. One of them, a hunchback, whose wild, straggling hair glistened with oil, said that Joseph of Arimathea had been known to have a soft spot for innovators and seditionists. He had often seen him speaking to that Rabbi near the square where the dyeworks are. Nicodemus was with them too, a rich man who owned cattle and vineyards and all the houses on either side of the synagogue in Cyrenaica.

Another man, red-faced and flabby, moaned:

'What is to become of the nation when its most respected men join forces with those who idolise the poor and teach them that the fruits of the earth should be shared equally amongst everyone?'

'Messiah-lovers!' bellowed the youngest amongst them

furiously, hurling his stick into the gorse bushes. 'The ruin of Israel!'

But the Sadducee with the wild, greasy hair slowly raised one hand which was bound with sacred bonds:

'Keep calm: Jehovah is great and in truth everything he does is for the best. In the Temple and in the Council there will never be any lack of strong men to maintain the old order and, happily, on calvaries throughout the land, there will always be crosses!'

And everyone whispered:

'Amen.'

Meanwhile, the centurion, followed by the soldiers carrying the iron bars, marched over to the other crosses where the condemned men, still alive and in terrible agony, were begging for water, one hanging limp and moaning, the other all twisted, his hands torn, howling terribly. Topsius, who was smiling coldly, muttered: 'It's time, we must leave.'

With my eyes filled with bitter tears, stumbling over stones, I walked down the hill of sacrifice at Topsius' side. And a feeling of dense melancholy darkened my soul, when I thought about all those future crosses the Sadducee had spoken of. Thus it would come to pass. How wretched! Yes, from that day forth, through all the centuries to come, it would happen again and again, around pyres, in the cold of dungeons, by the steps of gallows – the infamous sight of priests, patricians, magistrates, soldiers, doctors and merchants gathered together on the top of some hill, in order to send to a cruel death a just man who, filled by the splendour of God, preaches the adoration of the spirit or, full of love for mankind, proclaims the kingdom of equality.

With these thoughts in my head, I returned to Jerusalem, while the birds, more fortunate than men, sang in the cedar trees of Gareb.

It had grown dark, the hour of the Passover supper, by the time we reached Gamaliel's house. In the courtyard, tethered to a ring, was the donkey with its black saddlebags on which that obliging physician, Eliezer of Silo, had arrived.

In the blue room, with its cedar ceiling, and perfumed with herbs, the stern doctor of the Law was waiting for us, reclining on the divan, his feet bare, his long sleeves rolled up to his shoulders. And beside him lay a walking stick, a gourd of water and a bundle of clothes, the ritual emblems of the flight from Egypt. A candlestick in the form of a tree, a pale blue flame at the tip of each branch, stood before him on a table encrusted with mother-of-pearl, between clay vases painted with flowers, and silver filigree baskets overflowing with fruit and glittering cubes of ice. His eyes fixed on the candles' tremulous brilliance, his hands folded on his belly, the kindly Eliezer was smiling beatifically, leaning back against the red leather cushions. Next to him were two benches, covered with Assyrian carpets, reserved for myself and my wise historian friend, Topsius.

'Welcome,' grunted Gamaliel. 'Great are the marvels of Zion. You must be starving.'

He clapped his hands lightly. Preceded majestically by an obese man in a yellow tunic, the slaves entered, moving noiselessly on their felt-soled sandals, holding aloft great steaming copper dishes.

To one side of us was a ball of white dough, fine and soft as linen, on which we were to clean our fingers; on the other was a large dish, edged in pearls, on which lay a heap of fried locusts, black amongst the sprigs of parsley; on the floor stood jars containing rose-water. We performed our ablutions and Gamaliel, having purified his mouth with a piece of ice, murmured the ritual prayer over the vast silver dish, piled so high with roast kid that the accompanying saffron and saumura sauce overflowed the edges.

Out of politeness, Topsius, who was familiar with oriental manners, belched loudly, to demonstrate his satisfaction and delight. Then, holding a piece of lamb between his fingers, he declared, smiling, to the learned men about him, that Jerusalem seem to him magnificent, of a marvellous brilliance, and blessed amongst all cities.

His eyes half-closed with pleasure, as if in response to a caress, Eliezer of Silo replied:

'Jerusalem is a jewel more precious than any diamond and the Lord set her in the centre of the Earth, so that she might send forth her brilliance all around in equal measure.'

'In the centre of the earth!' murmured the historian, in learned surprise.

Of course! And dipping a piece of bread into the saffron sauce, the wise physician explained. The Earth is flat and round like a disc; in the middle stands Jerusalem, the holy city, like a heart full of love for the All High; around it lies Judaea, rich in balsam and palm trees, surrounding Jerusalem with shade and perfume. Beyond live the pagans, who inhabit the harsh regions where neither milk nor honey abound, and beyond that lie the dark seas. Above it all is the sky, resonant and solid.

'Solid!' spluttered my learned friend, rolling his eyes in amazement.

The slaves were pouring golden yellow beer from Media into silver cups. Gamaliel solicitously advised me that biting into a fried locust would improve the beer's flavour. And Rabbi Eliezer, who knew more than any other man about the natural world, revealed to Topsius the divine construction of the sky.

The sky is made up of seven hard, marvellous, glittering layers of crystal; above them roll the great waters; above the waters, the spirit of Jehovah flows like a brilliant light. These layers of crystal, pierced like a sieve, slide over each other emitting a slow, gentle music heard occasionally by the most beloved of the prophets. One night when he was praying on the roof of his house in Silo, he was granted a rare favour by the All High for he himself heard that harmony, so penetrating, so sweet that his tears had fallen one by one into his open hands. During the months of Kislev and Tebet the holes in the layers coincide, and through them the drops of eternal water fall upon the Earth and make the harvests grow.

'You mean rain?' asked Topsius shyly.

'Yes, rain!' replied Eliezer serenely.

Suppressing a smile, his gold-rimmed spectacles glinting with knowing irony, Topsius looked across at Gamaliel: but the pious son of Simeon wore a look of impenetrable seriousness on his face, a face grown lean in the study of the Law. Fiddling with the olives in the dish, Topsius then asked the enlightened doctor why the crystals of the sky were always of that blue that so delights the soul. Eliezer of Silo explained:

'To the west there is a great blue mountain, which until now has always remained invisible to men's eyes. When the sun strikes that mountain, the reverberation of light bathes the crystals of the sky and turns them blue. It may also be the mountain on which the souls of the just live.'

Gamaliel coughed politely and murmured: 'Let us drink, praising the Lord!'

He raised a glass full of wine from Shechem, pronounced a blessing and passed the glass to me, calling down peace upon my heart. I grunted: 'The same to you and many happy returns!' And Topsius, who received the cup reverently, drank 'to the prosperity of Israel, to her strength and her learning'!

Then the servants, preceded by the obese man in the yellow tunic, who ostentatiously tapped his ivory cane on the echoing flagstones as he walked, brought in the most sacred part of the Passover meal – the bitter herbs.

This consisted of a tray piled with lettuce, watercress, chicory and camomile served with vinegar and coarse salt. Gamaliel chewed them solemnly, as if performing a ritual. They represented the bitter experiences of Israel in captivity in Egypt. And Eliezer, licking his fingers, declared them delicious, fortifying and imbued with many lofty, spiritual lessons.

But Topsius, basing himself on the Greek authors, recalled that all vegetables are said to sap a man's virility, strip him of his eloquence and diminish his courage. With torrential erudition he cited first Theophrastus, then Eubulus, Nicander (quoting from the second part of the latter's *Dictionary*), Phenias in his *Treatise on Plants*, Diphilus and Epicharmus.

Gamaliel sharply condemned the inanity of such knowledge, referring to Hecateus of Mileto's *Description of Asia*, the first volume of which alone contains fifty-three errors, fourteen blasphemies and one hundred and nine omissions. For example, the frivolous Greek stated that the date, that marvellous gift from the All High, actually enfeebles the intellect.

'But,' exclaimed Topsius ardently, 'Xenophon says just the same in the second volume of his *Anabasis*! And Xenophon . . .'

Gamaliel rejected Xenophon's opinions. Then Topsius, his face flushed, beating the edge of the table with a golden spoon, spoke warmly of Xenophon's eloquence, his great nobility of feeling, his tender reverence for Socrates . . . And whilst I tucked into a pasty from Comagenia, the two learned doctors launched into a bitter dispute over Socrates. Gamaliel stated that the 'secret voices' heard by Socrates, which had ruled his life so divinely and so purely, were in fact distant murmurs from Judaea, the miraculous echoes of the Lord's voice. Topsius bounced up and down, shrugging his shoulders with a kind of desperate sarcasm. Socrates inspired by Jehovah! What nonsense!

Nevertheless (insisted Gamaliel, who had turned deathly pale), it was true that the Gentiles were emerging from their darkness, drawn by the strong, pure light that flowed from Jerusalem: for a profound and awestruck reverence for the gods can be found in Aeschylus; in Sophocles that reverence is warm and serene, in Euripides, superficial and full of doubts. But even so, each of those tragedians was thus taking a giant step towards the true God.

'Gamaliel, son of Simeon,' murmured Eliezer of Silo, 'you, who possess the truth, why do you give houseroom in your soul to the pagans?'

Gamaliel replied:

'All the better to scorn them.'

Weary of this classical controversy, I passed Eliezer a saucer of honey from Hebron and told him how much I had enjoyed the path from Gareb through the gardens. He agreed that Jerusalem, surrounded as it was by gardens, did indeed seem as delightful to the eye as the brow of a bride garlanded with anemones. Then he expressed surprise that I should choose to pass my time on the outskirts of Gihon whose streets are full of slaughterhouses and which is situated immediately beneath the bare hills where they set the crosses. The fragrant air of Siloe would have been much more enjoyable.

'I went to see Jesus,' I said abruptly. 'I went to see Jesus, who was crucified this afternoon on the orders of the Sanhedrin.'

With Eastern courtesy, Eliezer beat his chest in a display of grief. And he asked if this man Jesus were a blood relative or someone with whom I had broken bread that I should go and see him die a slave's death.

I looked at him, astonished:

'He's the Messiah!'

And he looked at me even more astonished, a thread of honey dribbling into his beard.

It was extraordinary. Eliezer, a doctor in the Temple and physician to the Sanhedrin, did not know who Jesus of Galilee was. He had been so busy with his patients who, he explained, arrived in Jerusalem in droves during Passover, that he had not been to the Xistus, nor to Cleos the perfumer, nor to Hannan's house, places where news flocked like so many doves: that's why he had heard nothing of the appearance of a Messiah.

Besides, he added, he couldn't be the Messiah. The Messiah was supposed to be called Manahem 'the consoler', because he would bring consolation to Israel. And there would be two Messiahs: the first, from the tribe of Joseph, would be conquered by Gog; the second would be the son of David and a man of strength, who would conquer Magog. His birth would be preceded by seven years of marvels: seas would evaporate, stars would fall from the

208

sky, there would be famine and periods of such fertility that even the rocks would bear fruit; in the final year blood would flow amongst nations; then a portentous voice would ring out and the Messiah would rise over Hebron, bearing a sword of fire.

As he described these extraordinary events, he was busy peeling the skin off a fig; then he added, with a sigh:

'Now, my son, none of these marvels announcing the time of consolation has as yet come to pass.'

And he sank his teeth into the fig.

Then it fell to me, Teodorico, an Iberian from a remote Roman municipality, to recount the life of our Lord to a physician in Jerusalem, brought up amongst the marble columns of the Temple. I described the nice things and the unpleasant things: the three bright stars over his cradle; the way his words had calmed the waters of Galilee; the way he had moved the hearts of simple people; the promised kingdom of Heaven; and his bright, august face as he stood before the Praetor.

'Then the priests, the patricians and the rich crucified him!'

Doctor Eliezer, again prodding around in the basket of figs, murmured pensively:

'Very sad, very sad. But, my son, the Sanhedrin is merciful. In the seven years that I have served there, they have given out only three death sentences. Of course, the world should listen to words of love and justice, but Israel has suffered so much from innovators and prophets. Not that one can ever justify spilling the blood of a man ... You know, these Bethphage figs are not a patch on my own in Silo!'

I silently rolled a cigarette. And at that moment my learned friend Topsius, still debating with Gamaliel about Hellenism and the Socratic schools, his spectacles perched haughtily on the end of his nose, was roundly summing up:

'Socrates is the seed, Plato the flower and Aristotle the fruit. And that whole tree has nourished the human spirit.'

But Gamaliel suddenly got to his feet, as did Doctor Eliezer, belching loudly. Both picked up their staffs and cried:

'Alleluia! Praise be to the Lord who brought us forth from the land of Egypt!'

The Passover supper had ended. Topsius, wiping away the sweat provoked by the discussion, glanced at his watch and begged Gamaliel's permission to go up on to the terrace, to cool his emotions in the soft air of Ophel. The doctor of the Law led us to the verandah, palely lit by mica lanterns, and showed us the steep ebony staircase that would lead us up to the roof. Then calling down upon us the grace of the Lord, he and Eliezer went into a room closed off by curtains made out of cloth from Mesopotamia. A gust of perfume, the light noise of laughter and the slow chords of a lyre wafted out to us.

How sweet the air was on the roof and how joyful that Passover night in Jerusalem! In the sky, silent and sealed as a palace in mourning, not a single star shone; but the city of David and the hill of Acra, lit by their ritual lamps, seemed sprinkled with gold. On every rooftop, vases filled with tow burning in oil gave off a tremulous, red light. Here and there, on odd houses set higher up, the threads of light against the dark wall shone like a necklace of jewels about the neck of a negress. The air was sweetly fragmented by the sad sounds of a flute, by the mournful chords of a konnor and, in streets lit by great bonfires, we could see the short, pale tunics of Greeks fluttering as they danced the *kallabida*. Only the towers remained in darkness, the Hippicus, the Mariamne and the Pharsala, which seemed to loom larger in the night, the hoarse, rough baying of their bugles occasionally drifting over the holy, feasting city, like a threat.

Beyond the city walls, the joy of the Passover night continued. There were lights in Siloe. In the camps, on the Mount of Olives, bright fires burned and, since the gates of the city had stayed open, lines of smoking torches snaked along the roads, amidst a murmur of singing.

Only one hill, towards Gareb, remained in darkness. At that moment, at the foot of that hill, in a ravine amongst the rocks, where two broken bodies lay gleaming whitely, the vultures, their beaks making the sharp noise of metal against metal, were partaking of their Passover meal. At least one other body, the precious integument of a perfect spirit, lay safe in a new tomb, wrapped in fine linen, oiled and perfumed with cinnamon and spikenard. Thus he had been left that night, Israel's holiest night, by those who loved him and who would ever after, for ever and ever, love him even more dearly. Thus he had been left, with a smooth stone over him and now, amongst the houses of Jerusalem, full of light and singing, there would be some houses, dark and shuttered, where inconsolable tears were being shed. There the fire had grown cold, gone out, the sad lamp guttered in the field, there was no water in the pitchers, because no one had gone to the spring and those who had followed him from Galilee would be sitting on the floor, their hair loose, talking about him, about their early hopes, the words he had spoken to them amongst the cornfields, the sweet times they had spent at the lakeside.

Such were my thoughts, as I leaned against the wall, looking out over Jerusalem, when a noiseless presence suddenly appeared before us, a shape wrapped in white linen, exuding a scent of cinnamon and spikenard. It seemed to me that the figure gave off an aura and that its feet did not step upon the stones. My heart beat faster. But then, from amongst the pale cloth, there came a grave, familiar voice that spoke a blessing:

'May peace be with you both!'

What a relief! It was Gad.

'May peace be with you.'

The Essene stood before us, saying nothing, and I could feel his eyes searching the very depths of my soul, sounding out its worth and strength. Finally, standing as still as a tomb statue in his long white vestments, he murmured:

'The moon is rising. Everything we hoped for is coming to pass. Now tell me, do you have heart enough to go with Jesus, as his guards, as far as the oasis of Engaddi?'

I stood up, terrified, throwing wide my arms. Go with the Rabbi! Was he not lying dead, bound and perfumed, beneath a stone in the garden of Gareb? He was alive! And when the moon rose, he would leave with his friends for Engaddi. I grasped Topsius' shoulder anxiously, seeking shelter in his greater knowledge and authority.

My learned friend seemed enmeshed in doubt:

'Yes, possibly . . . our hearts are strong, but . . . Besides, we have no weapons.'

'Come with me,' said Gad urgently. 'We will go to the house of someone who will tell us certain things we need to know and *he* will give you weapons.'

Still trembling, still clinging on to my learned friend, I managed to stammer out:

'And what about Jesus? Where is he?'

'In the house of Joseph of Arimathea,' whispered the Essene, looking all about him like a miser speaking of his treasure. 'In order that the people from the Temple should suspect nothing, we placed the Rabbi in a new tomb in Joseph's garden, in their very presence. The women wept three times over the stone, which, as you know, according to the rites, does not seal the tomb, but left a long crack through which one could still see the face of the Rabbi. Some servants from the Temple were watching and they gave their approval. We each returned to our homes. I entered by the gate of Genath and saw nothing more. But as soon as night fell, Joseph and another utterly trustworthy man were to go and fetch Jesus' body and with the formulae given in the Book of Solomon, they were to bring him round from the fainting fit brought on by the drugged wine and the pain. Come then, you who also love and believe in him.'

Still shocked, but determined now, Topsius wrapped his long cloak about him and in wary silence we went down the stairs that led from the roof to a gravel path that followed the new wall built by Herod.

For a long time we walked in darkness, guided by the white clothes of the Essene. Sometimes, from amongst the ruined huts, a dog would leap out at us barking. On the high battlements we saw dim lanterns patrolling up and down. Then from the shadows beneath a tree, a figure emerged, coughing, as sad and limp as if it had just clambered out of its own tomb. Stroking my arm and tugging at Topsius' cloak, she begged us, amidst moans and gusts of garlic breath, to join her in her bed which she had perfumed with spikenard.

We finally stopped by a wall with a concealed entrance behind a thick esparto mat. A corridor dripping with water led us into a courtyard encircled by a verandah supported on rough wooden beams. The mud-soft floor deadened the sound of our footsteps.

Gad let out three whoops, like a jackal. We waited in the middle of the courtyard by a well covered with planks. The sky above us was still dark, hard and impenetrable as bronze. At last, beneath the veranda, the bright flash of a lantern appeared in one corner, lighting up the black beard of the man carrying it, one corner of his brown Galilean burnous pulled up over his head. But the light was blown out by a sudden gust of wind and the man walked slowly over to us in the darkness.

Gad broke the desolate silence:

'May peace be with you, brother! We are ready.'

The man carefully placed his lantern on the cover of the well:

'It is over.'

Trembling, Gad cried out:

'The Rabbi . . .'

The man put his hand over the Essene's mouth to muffle his cry. Then, having searched the shadows round about us with restless eyes that glittered like those of an animal in the desert, he said:

'These are higher things than we can understand. Everything seemed right. The drugged wine was properly prepared by Rosmophin's wife, who is skilled in these things and knows the simple people. I had spoken to the centurion, a comrade whose life I saved in Germany, on Publius' last campaign there. And when we rolled back the stone provided by Joseph of Arimathea, the body of the Rabbi was still warm.'

He fell silent and, as if the courtyard enclosed beneath the black sky were not secret and safe enough, he touched Gad's shoulder and, noiseless on his bare feet, withdrew into the denser darkness of the wall beneath the veranda. Keeping close to his side, we trembled with anxiety and I felt that some revelation, supreme and prodigious, was about to break upon us, shedding light on all life's mysteries.

'At nightfall,' the man whispered at last, in a sad murmur like water flowing in the darkness, 'we went back to the tomb. We looked through the crack. The Rabbi's face was serene and full of majesty. We lifted the stone and removed the body. He appeared to be asleep, he looked beautiful, almost divine, in the cloths in which he'd been wrapped. Joseph had a lantern and we carried him through Gareb, running through the forest. By the fountain we met a patrol of auxiliary soldiers. We said: "He's from Joppa. He fell ill, and we're taking him to his synagogue." The patrol said: "Pass." Simeon, the Essene, was already at Joseph's house. He used to live in Alexandria and knows all about the properties of plants, and everything had been prepared, even the canna root. We laid Jesus out on a mat. We gave him cordials to drink, we spoke to him, we waited, we prayed. But, alas, we felt his body cooling beneath our hands. He slowly opened his eyes, just for a moment, a word left his lips. It was unclear, we couldn't understand what it was. He seemed to be evoking his father, complaining that he had been abandoned. Then he trembled and a little blood appeared in one corner of his mouth. And with his head resting on Nicodemus' chest, the Rabbi died.'

Gad dropped heavily to his knees, sobbing and, as if there were nothing more to be said, the man went over to the well to get his lamp. Topsius stopped him and said urgently:

'Listen! I need to know the whole truth. What did you do afterwards?'

The man stopped by one of the wooden pillars. Then, stretching out his arms in the darkness, standing so close to us that I could feel his hot breath, he said:

'We had to do it for the good of the world, so that the prophecies would be fulfilled. For two hours, Joseph of Arimathea lay prostrate, praying. I don't know whether the Lord spoke to him in secret or not but, when he got up, he was all aglow and he shouted out: "Elijah came! Elijah came! The moment has arrived!" Then, on his orders, we buried the Rabbi in a cave carved out of the rock, behind the grindstone, on a piece of land he owns.'

He walked across the courtyard and picked up his lantern. And he was slowly, noiselessly withdrawing, when Gad, looking up, called to him through his sobs:

'Wait a minute! Great indeed is the Lord, but what about the other tomb, where the women of Galilee left him, bound and wrapped in cloths, perfumed with aloes and with spikenard?'

Without turning round, the man murmured as he disappeared into the darkness:

'It was left there open, empty.'

Then Topsius grabbed me by the arm, so roughly that, in the dark, we stumbled together against the pillars. A door at the far side of the courtyard opened with the sudden clank of chains falling away. And I saw a cold, gloomy square, surrounded by pale arcades, with grass growing amongst the crumbling flagstones, like an abandoned city. Topsius stopped still, his glasses glinting:

'Teodorico, the night is nearly over, we must leave Jerusalem. Our journey into the past is done. Christianity's first legend has been forged and the ancient world is about to die.'

Astonished, my skin prickling, I gazed at Topsius. His hair flew about him as if stirred by the breath of inspiration. And the words that so lightly left his thin lips echoed as they fell upon my heart like something vast and terrible:

'The day after tomorrow, when the Sabbath is over, the women from Galilee will return to the tomb of Joseph of

Arimathea where they left Jesus buried. And they will find it open, they will find it empty. "He disappeared, he isn't here!" Then, Maria Magdala, passionate and credulous, will run to Jerusalem and declare: "He has risen, he has risen!" And thus the love of a woman will change the face of the whole world and give yet one more religion to humanity.'

Waving his arms in the air, he ran across the square, where the marble pillars were beginning to fall, soundlessly, softly. Panting, we stopped at Gamaliel's doorway. A slave, the remains of his chains still hanging about his wrists, was holding our horses. We mounted. With a noise like that of stones being swept along by a stream, we rode out of the Golden Gate and galloped towards Jericho, along the Roman road from Shechem, at such vertiginous speed that we could hear our horses' hooves throwing up sparks from the black basalt flagstones. Ahead of me, Topsius' white cloak twisted about, caught up in a furious wind. The mountains rushed past us on either side, like bundles on the backs of the camels of a fleeing people. My horse's nostrils snorted reddish smoke and I clung to its mane, stunned, as if I were riding amongst clouds.

Then suddenly we spotted the vast scooped-out plain of Canaan stretching as far the mountains of Moab. Our encampment gleamed white beside the dying embers of the fire. The horses started, trembling. We ran to our tents. On the table, the candle Topsius had lit to get dressed by, one thousand eight hundred years ago, was sputtering palely out. And exhausted by our infinite journey, I threw myself down on my bed, without even bothering to take off my boots, white with dust.

Almost immediately afterwards, it seemed to me that a smoking torch had been brought into the tent, scattering golden light. I got up, frightened. Potte was coming into the tent, in his shirtsleeves, carrying my boots in his hand, and bringing with him a long ray of sunshine all the way from the mountains of Moab.

I threw off my blanket, pushed back my hair, preparing

myself to see the terrible change that had been
upon the world since last night. On the table
bottles of champagne with which we had toasted K
ledge and Religion. The package containing the crow.
thorns lay at my bedside. Topsius in his nightshirt and
with a handkerchief tied about his head, was yawning in
his bed and putting on his goldrimmed spectacles. And
Potte was smilingly scolding us for our laziness and enquir-
ing if we wanted tapioca or coffee that morning.

I gave a loud, contented sigh. And filled by the triumphant joy I felt at regaining both my individuality and my
century, I bounced up and down on my mattress, shirt-tails
in the wind, shouting:

'Tapioca, Potte! Sweet, runny tapioca, the way they
make it in my beloved Portugal!'

IV

The next day, a brilliantly sunny Sunday, we struck camp at Jericho and, travelling with the sun in the west along the valley of Cherith, we began our pilgrimage through Galilee.

However, either the consoling spring of admiration had dried up in me, or else my soul – whisked for a moment to the heights of history where it had been buffeted by cruel emotions – could now take no pleasure in the calm, desert roads of Syria: I felt nothing but indifference and weariness all the way from the land of Ephraim to the land of Zebelon.

When we camped at Bethel that night, the full moon was rising behind the black mountains of Gilead. Potte, cheerful as ever, made haste to show me the sacred place where Jacob, a shepherd from Beersheba, having fallen asleep on a rock, had seen a glittering ladder rising from his feet into the stars, linking heaven and earth, climbed by silent angels with folded wings. I gave a huge yawn and grunted:

'Hmm, fascinating!'

And thus I groaned and yawned my way across the land of miracles. I found the beauty of its valleys as tedious as the sanctity of its ruins. At Jacob's well, I sat on the very stones where Jesus, like me weary of those quiet roads and like me drinking from the jug of a Samaritan woman, had taught a new and purer way of adoring God; on the slopes of Carmel, in a monastery cell, I listened to the rustling branches of the cedars that had once sheltered Elijah and, below, to the murmur of the waves, vassals of Hiram, King of Tyre; I galloped, with my burnous flapping behind me, across the plain of Esdrelon and rowed quietly across the Lake of Gennesarat, all light and silence – and all the while boredom marched by my side like a faithful companion and, at each step, clasped me to its soft bosom, beneath its brown mantle.

Sometimes, though, a faint, delicious nostalgia for the remote past would stir my soul, like a slow breeze lifting a heavy curtain. And then, sitting smoking outside the tent, trotting along the dry bed of a stream, I would again see, with delight, occasional fragments of that antiquity that had so thrilled me: the Roman baths, where a marvellous creature wearing a yellow mitre had offered herself up, lascivious and pontifical; that handsome man Manasses placing his hand on the gem-encrusted hilt of his sword; the merchants in the Temple unfolding brocades from Babylonia; the death sentence passed on the Rabbi, with a red line drawn through it, affixed to a stone pillar at the Judiciary Gate; the brilliantly lit streets and Greeks dancing the *kallabida*. I would then immediately feel beset by a terrible desire to plunge back into that irrecoverable world. How ridiculous that I, Raposo, a university graduate, enjoying all the comforts of civilisation, should feel nostalgia for that barbarous city of Jerusalem, in which I had lived one day in the month of Nisan, when Pontius Pilate was the procurator of Judaea!

Then those memories faded, as fires do when the wood runs out. In my soul there was only ashes and, confronted by the ruins of Mount Ebal or standing amongst the orchards that perfumed the Levitical city of Shechem, I again began to yawn.

When we reached Nazareth, which, in the desolation that is Palestine, is like a bouquet of flowers placed on a tombstone, I did not even feel interested in the pretty Jewish girls who had melted the heart of St Anthony. Carrying a red water jug on one shoulder, they would walk up the hill through the sycamores to the spring where Mary, the mother of Jesus, used to go each afternoon, singing just as they did and like them dressed all in white. Potte twirled his moustaches and sang madrigals to them, and they would smile, lowering their thick, gentle eyelashes. Confronted by such sweet modesty, St Anthony, leaning on his stick and shaking his long beard, had sighed:

'Oh bright virtue, inherited from Mary full of grace!'

For my part I merely grunted:

'Bah, humbug!'

Along paths where vines and fig trees sheltered humble houses, as befits the sweet village of the man who preached humility, we climbed up to the highest point in Nazareth, buffeted all the while by the strong wind that blows in from Idumaea. When we got there, Topsius doffed his beret to greet those plains, those distant views, which doubtless Jesus also contemplated, imagining, as he gazed down on all that light and grace, the incomparable beauties of the Kingdom of God. Topsius pointed out to me all the religious sites, whose sonorous names dropped into one's soul with all the solemnity of a prophecy or the uproar of a battle: Esdrelon, Endor, Sulan, Tabor. I looked and rolled myself a cigarette. On top of Mount Carmel was a white covering of snow; the plains of Pereia glittered, wrapped in a cloud of golden dust; the Gulf of Caifa was the deepest of blues; in the distance a kind of melancholy clothed the mountains of Samaria; great eagles hovered above the valleys. I yawned and grunted:

'Hmm, nice view!'

One morning, early, we started on our way back down to Jerusalem. All the way from Samaria to Ramah we were drenched by heavy, black showers of rain from Syria which immediately sent torrents roaring down the rock faces onto the flowering oleanders; then, by the hill of Gibeah, where long ago in his garden, amongst the laurels and the cypresses, David used to play his harp as he gazed upon Zion, everything was once again serene and blue. And a feeling of disquiet flooded my heart, like a sad wind blowing through a ruined building. I was about to see Jerusalem! But which one? Would it be the same Jerusalem I had seen one day, sparkling sumptuously in the sun of the month of Nisan, with its formidable towers, its Temple the colour of gold and the colour of snow, Acra full of palaces, Bezetha irrigated by the waters of Enrogel?

'El-Kurds!' shouted the old Bedouin, waving his spear in the air, giving the city of the Lord its Muslim name.

Trembling, I galloped forward. And I saw the city below me, by the Kidron valley, sombre, packed with monasteries and crouched behind its crumbling walls, like a poor, flea-ridden woman who crawls into a corner to die, wrapped in the ragged remnants of her cloak.

Once we were through the Damascus Gate, our horses' hooves were soon thundering along the paved street known as Christian Street: right by the wall, a fat friar, his breviary and his cloth parasol under his arm, was noisily taking a pinch of snuff. We dismounted at the Hotel Mediterranean. In the narrow courtyard, beneath an advertisement for Holloway's Pills, an Englishman sat reading *The Times*, with a monocle clamped to one pale eye and his large feet up on the chintz sofa; at an open verandah, where a pair of white long johns stained with coffee were hanging out to dry, a hoarse voice could be heard bawling: 'C'est le beau Nicolas, hola!' Ah yes, Catholic Jerusalem! Then, just for a moment, when we went into our room, bright and cheery with its partition wall sprigged with blue flowers, the memory of another room flickered in my memory, a room furnished with golden candlesticks and a statue of Augustus, where a man in a toga was holding out his arm and saying: 'Caesar knows me well.'

I immediately ran to the window to breathe in the lively air of modern-day Zion. There was the monastery with its closed green shutters and its dripping eaves silent now in this afternoon of sun and sweetness. The same narrow steps twisted down past narrow strips of garden, climbed by Franciscan monks in sandals, by thin Jews with greasy, dishevelled hair. And what peace there was in the coolness of those cell-like walls after the scorching roads of Samaria. I went over and felt the soft bed. I opened the mahogany wardrobe. I gently caressed the small package containing Mary's nightshirt nestling amongst my socks, so round and charming with its red ribbon.

At that moment, Potte, his usual jolly self, came in to bring me the precious package containing the crown of thorns, neat and round and also tied with a red ribbon, and proceeded to regale me with the latest – not inconsiderable – Jerusalem news gleaned from the barber in the Via Dolorosa. An edict had arrived from Constantinople exiling the Greek patriarch, a poor old evangelist, who suffered with his liver and helped the poor. On a visit to the shop selling relics in Armenia Street, Consul Damiani had stamped his foot and declared that Italy was prepared to take up arms against Germany before January 6th, because of a terrible row that had broken out between the Protestant mission and the Franciscans. In Bethlehem, in the Church of the Nativity, a Catholic priest had become involved in a fracas while he was blessing hosts and had split open the head of a Coptic priest with a large wax candle. And finally, the most joyous news of all was that just near Herod's Gate, looking out over the Valley of Jehoshaphat, and to the great joy of Zion, *The Retreat from Sinai* – a café with a billiard table – had just opened.

Suddenly, all my painful longings for the past, all the ashes covering my soul, were swept away by a cool breeze of youth and modernity. I jumped up and down on the echoing flagstones and said:

'Long live *The Retreat*! Let's go there now and have a game of billiards. Bloody hell, I could do with a bit of fun! And then off to visit the ladies! Put the package with the crown in it there, Potte. There's a lot of money riding on that. God, Auntie's really going to love it. Put it on top of the dresser, between the candlesticks. Then, after a bit of lunch, we'll go off to *The Retreat from Sinai*.'

Just at that moment, Topsius rushed in, breathless, with a wonderful bit of historical news. During our pilgrimage to Galilee, the Commission for Biblical Excavations had discovered, buried beneath centuries-old layers of rubbish, one of the slabs of marble which, according to Joseph and Philon and the Talmuds, had once stood in the Temple, next to the Beautiful Gate, bearing an inscription forbidding entry to the Gentiles. He suggested that, once we'd had our soup, we should go over there to marvel at this extraordinary find. For a moment another gate glittered in my memory, truly beautiful, precious and triumphant, standing at the top of its fourteen steps made out of green Numidian marble.

But then I shook both my arms in the air, in a gesture of revolt:

'No, I don't want to!' I shouted. 'I've had enough! And I'll tell you this, Topsius, I tell you this most solemnly; from this day forth I'm not going to look at any more old stones or any more religious sites, ever again. I've had my fill and enough is enough!'

Topsius fled with his tail between his legs!

That week I spent documenting and wrapping up the minor relics I had collected for Aunt Patrocínio. There were plenty of them and many were valuable enough to add a certain devout lustre to the treasures of the proudest of cathedrals. Along with the articles that Zion imports from Marseilles by the crateload: rosaries, scapulars, medallions, as well as those things supplied by the vendors in the Holy Sepulchre: bottles of water from the River Jordan, pebbles from the Via Dolorosa, olives from the Mount of Olives, shells from the Lake of Gennesarat, I was also taking her other rare, marvellous and unique objects. One was a little plank of wood planed by St Joseph himself; two bits of straw from the crib where our Lord was born; a fragment of the water jug with which the Virgin used to go to the fountain; a shoe from the donkey on which the Holy Family had fled into the land of Egypt; and one twisted, rusty nail.

These precious things, wrapped in coloured paper, tied with silk ribbons and adorned with touching inscriptions, were packed into a strong crate, which I prudently reinforced with bands of iron. Then I came to the main relic, the crown of thorns, a fount of heavenly mercies for my aunt and a source of endless wealth for me, her knight and pilgrim.

I wanted the box that would contain it to be made from a wood, both fine and holy. Topsius recommended the wood from the cedar of Lebanon, so beautiful that Solomon had made an alliance with Hiram, king of Tyre because of it. Potte, however, being less archaeological, suggested a piece of honest Flanders pine blessed by the patriarch of Jerusalem. I would tell Auntie that the nails used to make the box had come from Noah's ark, that they had been found, miraculously, by a hermit on Mount Ararat, that, when dissolved in holy water, the rust left on them by the original mud was a known cure for colds. We discussed other such weighty matters while we drank our beer in *The Retreat from Sinai*.

All during this busy week, the package containing the crown of thorns had remained on the dresser between the two glass candlesticks. It was only on the eve of our departure from Jerusalem that I placed it carefully in its box. I lined the wood with blue chintz bought in the Via Dolorosa. I made the bottom of the box as soft and cosy as I could with a layer of cotton wool, whiter than the snows on Carmel and I placed upon it the charming package, without undoing it, exactly as Potte had wrapped it, in its brown paper and red ribbon: for even the way the paper had first been folded in Jericho, the way the knot in the ribbon had been tied on the banks of the River Jordan, would, for Dona Patrocínio, bear the unmistakable savour of devotion. Topsius observed these pious preparations, as he smoked his clay pipe.

'Oh, Topsius, thanks to this relic, I'll be rolling in it! But tell me, my friend, tell me, do you really think I can tell Auntie that this crown of thorns was *the* crown of thorns that . . .'

From amidst a cloud of pipe smoke, the learned man uttered a most reliable maxim:

'The value of relics, Dom Raposo, lies not in their authenticity but in the faith that they inspire. You can tell your Auntie that it was *the* crown of thorns.'

'Blessings be upon you, Doctor!'

That afternoon, the erudite Topsius had accompanied the Commission for Excavations to the tombs of the kings.

I had gone off on my own to the garden on the Mount of Olives, because, in and around Jerusalem, it was the one place where you could most pleasantly spend a quiet afternoon smoking your pipe in the shade.

I left by St Stephen's Gate, trotted across the Kidron bridge and climbed the small agave-lined path that leads to the low wall, whitewashed and rustic, that encloses the Garden of Gethsemane. I pushed open the newly painted green door with its copper door knocker and went into the orchard where Jesus had knelt and wept upon the leaves of the olive trees. Those holy trees that had rustled comfortingly above his world-weary head are still alive. There are eight of them, lethargic, black and eaten away by age, held up by wooden stakes, having long forgotten all about that night in the month of Nisan on which the angels, flying noiselessly about, had peeped through their branches to observe the human grief of the son of God. Tools and pruning hooks are hidden in holes in the trunks; at the very tips of their branches grow sparse, tenuous little leaves, of a sapless green, which tremble, barely alive, like the smiles of a dying man.

And all about them is a small garden tenderly watered and devotedly fertilized. Fresh green lettuces grow in beds surrounded by privet hedges; the small sandy paths are neat as chapels, unlittered by even a single withered leaf; by the walls, where twelve ceramic figures of the apostles glint from their niches, there are rows of onions and carrots, hedged in by sweet-smelling lavender. Why did no such gentle garden flower there in Jesus' time? Perhaps the placid orderliness of those sensible vegetables might have calmed the torment of his heart.

I sat down beneath the oldest olive tree. The friar in charge, a smiling saint with an endless beard, his habit rolled up at the sleeves, was watering pots of buttercups. The afternoon was fading in melancholy splendour.

And, filling my pipe, I smiled at my thoughts. Yes, soon I would leave this ash-grey city that crouched below me within its gloomy walls like a widow who prefers not to be consoled. One morning, cutting through the blue waves, I would see the cool hills of Sintra, the seagulls of my homeland would fly out to cry their welcome to me, fluttering about the mast of my ship; Lisbon would gradually appear with its stucco houses, the grass growing on its rooftops, indolent and sweet to my eyes. Calling: 'Auntie, auntie!', I would climb the stone steps of our house in Campo de Santana and my aunt, drooling, would tremble before the great relic which I, in all modesty, would offer her. Then, in the presence of holy witnesses, of St Peter, Our Lady of Grace and Favour, St Casimir and St Joseph, she would call me 'her son and her heir!' And then soon she would begin to grow pale and enfeebled, to moan and groan . . . Wonderful!

On the wall, amongst the honeysuckle, a bird sang out lightly and, happier even than that bird, a hope sang in my heart. Auntie in bed, her black scarf tied about her head, scrabbling anxiously at the folds of her sweated sheet, choking with terror at the thought of the Devil . . . It was an image of Auntie giving up the ghost, kicking the bucket. One soft day in May they would place her cold, putrid body in a coffin with the lid well nailed down and secure. With a cortege of carriages behind her, Dona Patrocínio would set out for her grave, for her appointment with the worms. Then the seal on her will would be broken in the damask-lined room, where I would have laid out cakes and port wine for Justino, the notary public. Dressed in heavy mourning, leaning on the marble table, I would conceal behind a crumpled handkerchief the shocking joy apparent on my face, and from amongst the sheets of official paper I could hear, rolling towards me with the tinkle of gold, with a whisper of wheatfields, every penny of G. Godinho's fortune! Pure ecstasy!

The holy friar had set down his watering can and was now strolling along a path lined with myrtle, his prayer book open. What would be my first act in my house in Campo de Santana, the moment they had taken away the hideous old woman, shrouded in the habit of our Lady? I would carry out a sentence of death: I would run to the chapel, blow out all the candles, rip the leaves off all the flowers and abandon the saints to darkness and mould! Yes, every part of myself, Raposo the liberal, cried out for revenge for having prostrated myself before those painted figures like a mere sacristan, for having bowed to the influence of their calendar like a credulous slave. I had served those saints in order to serve Auntie. But now, oh ineffable delight, she was rotting in her grave; in those eyes, which never shed a charitable tear, the worms would now be boiling greedily; beneath those lips, dissolving into the mud, her rotten, old teeth that had never smiled before would emerge at last, grinning ... All G. Godinho's gold would be mine and, liberated from that ghastly woman, I now owed her saints neither prayers nor roses. Then, having carried out this act of philosophical justice, I would flee to Paris, to the ladies of the night!

The good friar, smiling beneath his snow-white beard, clapped me on the shoulder, called me his son and reminded me that the holy garden would be closing soon and that he would gratefully receive my alms. I gave him a coin and made my slow, contented way back to Jerusalem, along the Valley of Jehoshaphat, singing a sweet song.

The next afternoon, the bell for the novena at the Chapel of the Flagellation was ringing as our caravan formed up at the door of the Hotel Mediterranean in order to leave Jerusalem. The crates containing the relics were loaded onto a donkey, along with the other bundles. Our Bedouin, who had an even worse cold now, had swathed his head in the dowdy scarf of a sacristan. Topsius mounted one of the mares, a serious, ponderous beast. And I, who out of sheer joy had placed a red rose in my buttonhole, muttered, as we set off for the last time along the Via Dolorosa: 'Good riddance to bad rubbish!'

We were almost at the Damascus Gate when a breathless voice boomed out from the other end of the street, at the corner of the convent of the Abyssinians:

'Potte, Doctor, gentlemen! A package, you left a package behind.'

It was the black servant from the hotel, hatless and brandishing a package, which I immediately recognised by the brown paper and red ribbon as Mary's nightdress! And I remembered that, when I was packing, I hadn't seen it in the wardrobe, in its nest of socks.

Panting, the servant explained that after we had left, while he was sweeping the room, he had discovered the package amongst the dust and the spiders behind the dresser. He had carefully dusted it off and as it had always been his desire to serve the Portuguese gentleman as best he could, he had rushed out without even putting his jacket on.

'Enough!' I rasped, abruptly and irritably.

I gave him the copper coins filling my pockets and I thought: 'How did it get behind the dresser?' Perhaps while he was tidying up, the servant, in his haste, had removed it from its nest of socks. It would have been better if it had stayed there amongst the dust and the spiders for good. For the truth was that this package was now extremely inconvenient.

I did love Mary. The thought that I would soon be back in the land of Egypt and be clasped again in her plump arms, still made me weak with desire. But since I carried her image faithfully in my heart, I had no need to carry her nightdress around with me too. What right then did this scrap of fine linen have to pursue me along the streets of Jerusalem, trying to worm its way into my luggage and accompany me back to my homeland?

And it was the idea of my homeland that most tortured me as we left the walls of the holy city behind us. How could I ever smuggle this lubricious package into the ecclesiastical house of my Aunt Patrocínio? Armed with duplicate keys, Auntie was forever rooting around in my room with eager malevolence, scrabbling in corners, amongst my letters and my long johns. Imagine her rage if one night, when she was searching my room, she were to find this lace nightdress besmirched by my lips, stinking of sin and bearing the inscription 'To my brave little Portuguese lover!'

'If I were ever to find out that you'd been chasing after women during this holy journey, I would banish you like a dog!' That's what Auntie had said on the eve of my pilgrimage, before the Magistrature and the Church. Was I prepared to lose the friendship of the old woman so dearly won with prayers, drops of holy water and the humbling of Liberal reason for the sentimental luxury of preserving a relic given to me by a glovemaker? Never! And if I didn't immediately drown the fatal package in the waters of some pool, as we were passing the huts of Kolonieh, it was only because I did not want to reveal to the all-seeing Topsius the base cowardice in my heart. But I decided that as soon as night fell and we entered the mountains of Judah, I would rein in my horse and, far out of sight of the historian's spectacles, far from Potte's solicitude, I would hurl Mary's dangerous nightshirt down a ravine, as being evidence of my sin and prejudicial to my fortune. And I hoped that it would soon be torn to pieces by the teeth of the jackals and soon rot beneath the rains sent by the Lord.

We had just passed the tomb of Samuel behind the great rocks of Emmaus and Jerusalem had disappeared forever from my eyes, when Topsius' mare spotted a spring in a stream bed that ran parallel with the road, and with brazen alacrity and in complete disregard of both caravan and duty, it trotted towards the water. Indignant, I stopped dead:

'Pull on the reins, Doctor! The effrontery of the animal! It's only just had a drink. Don't let it have its head! Pull harder! Whatever you do, don't kick!'

Elbows protruding, legs stiff, the philosopher tugged vainly at bridle and mane and the beast shot off regardless.

I rode over to the spring after them; I could not abandon that wonderful man to the desert. It was just a thread of turbid water, running along a narrow bed into a pool carved out of the rock. Nearby, lay the bleaching bones of a camel. There was a solitary mimosa tree, its branches scorched by a camp fire. Far off, on the bare spine of the hill, a shepherd, black against the opaline sky, was walking slowly amongst his sheep, his spear resting on his shoulder. And in the midst of all this sombre silence, the spring wept.

So desolate was it that it seemed the ideal place for me to leave Mary's nightdress to rot, like the bones of the camel. Topsius' horse was drinking greedily. And just I was looking here and there for some cliff or pool, I seemed to hear, next to the fountain, and mingling with the fountain's mournful song, the sound of human grief.

I went round the other side of a rock that rose proudly before me like the prow of a galley and found there, crouched and sheltering amongst the stones and thistles, a weeping woman with a small child clasped to her. Her curling hair fell about her shoulders and arms barely covered by the black rags she was wearing. And her tears fell upon her son, asleep in the warmth of her arms, tears sadder than those shed by the spring and seemingly never-ending.

I called to Potte to join me. When he trotted over to us, grasping the silverplated butt of his pistol, I begged him to ask the woman why she was crying. She seemed stunned by her own wretchedness; she spoke dully of a burned-out house, of Turkish knights, of the milk that had dried in her breasts. Then she clasped the child to her once more and, overcome with emotion, began to cry again into her child's tangled hair.

Potte gave her a silver coin, Topsius made a note of her misfortune for use later in his stern lecture on Muslim Judaea and I, touched, searched in my pocket for change, then remembered that I had given it all away to the black servant from the Hotel Mediterranean. But then I had a sudden inspiration. I threw down to her the dangerous package containing Mary's nightdress and, at my request, Potte explained to the unfortunate woman that any one of the women of easy virtue living next to David's Tower — fat old Fatme or Palmira, known as 'the Samaritan woman' — would give her two gold piastres for such a luxurious garment, a symbol of love and civilisation.

We trotted back to the road. Behind us, sobbing and kissing her son, the woman cried out to us all the blessings of her heart and our caravan set off on its journey again, whilst ahead of us the muleteer, straddling the baggage, was singing to the star of Venus that had just appeared, a Syrian song, harsh, protracted and mournful, in which the singer speaks of love, Allah, of a battle with lances and of the rose gardens of Damascus.

When we dismounted the following morning at the Hotel Jehoshaphat in the ancient city of Jaffa, I was astonished to see poor Alpedrinha sitting pensively in the courtyard, wearing a bulky white turban. I gave him a bone-crunching embrace and when Topsius and Potte had left, beneath Topsius' parasol, to get news of the steamship that was supposed to take us back to the land of Egypt, Alpedrinha told me his story as he brushed down my burnous.

He had left his beloved Alexandria out of sadness. The Hotel of the Pyramids, the suitcases he carried, had long since filled his soul with an endless tedium and our departure on *The Cayman* for Jerusalem had left him with a longing for the sea, for cities rich in history, for unknown multitudes. A Jew from Kesham, who was going to set up an inn in Baghdad with a billiard room, enticed him there with the promise of a job as a scorekeeper. Putting all the piastres he had saved during his bitter years in Egypt in a bag, he was all set to go off on this adventure down the slow waters of the Euphrates to the land of Babylon. However, weary of carrying other people's bags, he had first gone to Jerusalem, almost without realising it, carried there perhaps by the spirit, as the apostle had been, in order to rest quietly, hands folded, on a corner of the Via Dolorosa.

'Have you received any newspapers from Lisbon? I'd love to know how the lads are doing back there.'

While he babbled sadly on like this, his turban askew, I remembered, smiling, the hot land of Egypt, the bright Street of the Two Sisters, the little chapel amongst the plane trees, the poppies on Mary's hat. And I was again pierced by desire for my little blonde glovemaker. I imagined the sweet cry of passion that would emerge from her full lips, when one afternoon, burned by the sun of Syria and stronger than ever, I appeared before her balcony, startling her white cat. And the nightdress? Well, I'd tell her that one night, when we were encamped by a spring, some Turkish knights bearing lances had stolen it from me.

'Tell me, Alpedrinha, have you seen Maricoquinhas? How is she? As sweet as ever, eh?'

He lowered his face sadly and blushed strangely.

'She's not there any more. She went to Thebes.'

'To Thebes? Where the ruins are? But that's in upper Egypt! That's almost in Nubia . . . But how? Why has she gone there?'

'To improve the view,' murmured Alpedrinha disconsolately. To improve the view? I only understood when he explained that that ungrateful rose of York, that jewel of Alexandria, had been carried off by a long-haired Italian, who was going to photograph the ruins of the palaces where Rameses, King of Men, and Amnon, King of the Gods, lived face to face. And Maricoquinhas was going to improve the views by appearing in his photographs in the austere shadow of all that priestly granite, giving a much-needed hint of modernity in her little parasol and her hat with poppies on it.

'The nerve of the woman!' I shouted furiously. 'With an Italian, eh? And she likes him? Or is it strictly business? *Does* she like him?'

'She drooled over him,' stammered Alpedrinha.

And the Hotel Jehoshapat resounded to a sigh. Hearing that sigh, full of torment and passion, a terrible suspicion flickered in my soul.

'Alpedrinha, you sighed! There's some treachery here, Alpedrinha!'

He lowered his head so contritely that his turban unravelled onto the floor. But before he could pick it up I had already furiously grabbed his limp arm.

232

'Alpedrinha, out with it! It's Maricoquinhas, isn't it? So you've had a nibble too, have you?'

My bearded face glowed red. Alpedrinha was from the south, from our talkative land of vainglory and wine. Fear gave way to vanity and rolling his eyes he said:

'I certainly did!'

I let go of his arm, full of rage and disgust. Her as well – and with him! Oh, the world, the world, what is it but a pile of putrefying matter swaggering about the skies as if it were a star?

'But tell me, Alpedrinha, did she give you a nightdress too?'

'No, she gave me a negligee.'

So she had made him a present of her underwear too! I laughed bitterly, my arms hanging limply by my side.

'And did she call you "her brave little Portuguese lover"?'

'No, she used to call me "her sweet little Arab", because I was working with the Turks at the time.'

I was about to hurl myself onto the sofa, to tear at it with my nails and laugh out loud in desperate scorn for everything . . . But Topsius and Potte suddenly hurried in.

'What's happened?'

A steamship from Smyrna had just arrived and was leaving that afternoon for Egypt, and it was our favourite ship, *The Cayman.*

'Thank God for that!' I shouted, stamping hard on the floor. Thank God for that indeed. I'd had about all I could take of the Orient. Damn it, all I'd got there had been sunburn, treachery, terrifying dreams and kicks up the rear end. I'd had enough!

Thus I vented my rage. But that afternoon, on the beach, standing by the black boat that would carry us out to *The Cayman*, my soul was suddenly filled by a longing for Palestine, for our tents pitched beneath the splendour of the stars and our caravan of men singing as we journeyed on through ruins bearing sonorous names.

My lip quivered when Potte, equally moved, held out to me his pouch of Aleppo tobacco:

'Dom Raposo, this is the last cigarette I'll ever give you.'

And I wept openly at last when Alpedrinha, in silence, held out to me his thin arms.

From the boat, crouched on the crate containing the relics, I could still see him on the beach, waving his sad chequered handkerchief, beside Potte, who was standing in the water up to the ankles of his heavy boots, blowing us kisses. And on *The Cayman*, leaning over the ship's rail, I could still see him standing motionless on the sea wall, hanging on with both hands to his vast white turban, against the ravages of the salty wind.

Ill-fated Alpedrinha! Only I truly understood your greatness. You were the last Lusitanian, from the long line of Albuquerques, of Castros, the strong men who set out in ships for India. Like them, the same divine thirst for the unknown took you there, to that land of the Orient, from whence the light-giving stars rise into the heavens as do the gods who teach us the Law. Except that you, unlike the ancient Lusitanians, have no heroic beliefs to spawn heroic enterprises, you do not go forth like them holding a heavy rosary and a heavy sword to impose upon strange peoples your King and your God. You no longer have any God for whom to fight, Alpedrinha. Nor any King for whom to sail forth. That's why, amongst the people of the Orient, you wear yourself out in the only occupation befitting faith, idealism, the courage of the modern-day Lusitanian: hanging about on street corners or morosely carrying other people's baggage.

The wheels of *The Cayman* beat the water. Topsius raised his silk beret and gravely shouted out to Jaffa, fading into the pale evening light, amongst its sad mountains, amongst its dark green orchards:

'Farewell, farewell forever, land of Palestine!'

I too waved my hat:

'Goodbye, goodbye forever to all things religious!'

I was finally dragging myself away from the ship's rail when the long lustrine cape of a nun brushed past me, and amidst the modest shadow cast by her hood, turned slightly towards me, I saw the glint of dark eyes gazing upon my virile beard. How amazing! It was the same holy sister who had borne on her chaste knees, across those Scriptural waters, Mary's unclean nightdress.

It was the same one! Why had destiny once more placed before me, on the narrow deck of *The Cayman*, this chapel lily, as yet unopened and already withered? Who knows? Perhaps so that in the heat of my desire that flower might grow green again and not remain forever sterile and useless, fallen at the feet of the corpse of a god. And this time she wasn't watched over by that other nun, chubby and bespectacled. Fate had abandoned her to me, defenceless as a dove in the desert.

Then there flashed upon my soul the idea of a nun's love stronger even than her fear of God, her breasts scratched by her hair shirt, lying trembling and submissive in my valiant arms. I decided to whisper to her right then and there: 'Sister, I'm mad about you!' All aflame, twirling my moustaches, I walked over to the sweet nun, who was sitting on a bench, her pale fingers telling the beads of her rosary.

But suddenly, the deck of *The Cayman* shifted beneath my exultant feet. I stopped, transfixed. Oh misery! Oh humiliation! It was that sickening swell . . . I ran to the edge of the deck and vilely soiled the blue Sea of Tyre. Then I stumbled down to my cabin and only raised my deathly pale cheek from the pillow when I felt *The Cayman*'s anchors plunge into the calm waters where once, fleeing from Actium, Cleopatra's galleys had hurriedly cast their golden anchors.

And once more, stunned and dishevelled, I gazed upon the low lands of Egypt, warm and lion-coloured. Calm flocks of doves flew about its slender minarets. The languid palace slept at the water's edge amongst the palm trees. Topsius was carrying my hat box under his arm, babbling on in the most learned way about the ancient lighthouse. And the pale nun had already disembarked, a desert dove escaped from the clutches of the kite, because the kite had been forced to fold its wings in mid-flight, basely overcome by nausea.

That same evening, at the Hotel of the Pyramids, I learned with joy that a steamship carrying cattle, *El Cid Campeador*, was leaving early the next morning for the blessed lands of Portugal. In the calico-upholstered carriage, alone with the learned Topsius, I went for one last ride in the perfumed shadows of the Mamoudieh. And I spent the brief night in a street of delights. Go there, my compatriots, if you want to know the rough pleasures of the Orient. The bare gas jets whistle, twisting in the wind; the low houses, built out of wood, are closed only by a white curtain, transparent with light; everything smells of sandal-wood and garlic; and women sitting in their nightdresses on mats, with flowers in their hair, murmur sweetly: 'Eh, mossiu! Eh, milord!' I returned late to the hotel, exhausted. When I passed the Street of the Two Sisters, I spotted over the locked door of a shop the wooden hand, painted purple, that had seized my heart. I shook my stick at it. And that was the last adventure on my long journey.

In the morning, my faithful, learned friend Topsius accompanied me to the customs shed in his galoshes. I embraced him with tremulous arms:

'Goodbye, my friend, goodbye! Write to me . . . Campo de Santana, 47.'

Still clasped to my breast, he murmured:

'I'll send those thirty thousand *reis* I owe you.'

I held him closer to me in a gesture of generosity, to blot out that pecuniary explanation. Then, with one foot on the prow of the boat that was to take me to *El Cid Campeador*, I said:

'So you think I can tell Auntie that the crown of thorns is the same one that . . .'

He raised his hands, as solemn as a pope:

'You can tell her in my name that it was the very same crown, thorn for thorn.'

He stooped down to me, still looking like a bespectacled

stork, and we kissed each other on either cheek like two brothers.

The black slaves began rowing. I was carrying, resting on my knees, the package containing the supreme relic. But when my sailing boat was crossing the blue water, it passed right by another slower boat, being rowed over to the bank where the palace lay sleeping amongst the palm trees. And I caught a glimpse of a black habit, a hood pulled down low. For the very last time, one long, greedy look searched out a glimpse of my beard. Standing up, I shouted out: 'You little flirt!' But the wind had already carried me away. She, in her boat, covered her contrite face and on the delicate breast that had dared to desire, the jealous iron of the cross she wore doubtless weighed still more heavily.

I felt gloomy. Who knows? Perhaps in this whole vast earth, hers was the one heart in which mine would have found some rest, as if in some safe place of asylum. What nonsense! She was just a nun, I was just someone's nephew. She was going to her God, I was going to my aunt. And when on these waters our two hearts had crossed and, feeling some concordance, had beaten silently one for the other, my boat was sailing happily towards the west and the boat that carried her, slow and black, was rowing away towards the east: the continual divergence of compatible souls in this world of eternal struggle and eternal imperfection!

V

Two weeks later, riding along in Pingalho's carriage, across Campo de Santana, with the door half open and my foot on the running board, I saw, amongst the leafless trees, the black door of Auntie's house. And inside the old rattletrap I was riding in, I felt resplendent as a plump Caesar, crowned with leaves of gold, returning in his vast chariot from conquering peoples and gods.

This was doubtless due to my delight at seeing Lisbon again, beneath that fine, blue January sky; my Lisbon, with its quiet streets the colour of grubby clay and here and there the green shades half pulled down over the windows, like eyelids heavy with sleep and languor. But it was, above all, the certainty of the glorious change there was about to be in my domestic fortunes and my influence in the world.

What had I been in the house of Senhora Dona Patrocínio up until then? I was young Teodorico, who, despite his degree and his thick black beard, could not even give instructions for his horse to be saddled up in order to go into town and have his hair trimmed without first asking permission from Auntie. And now? I would be Dr Teodorico, who had gained, through his holy contact with the places of the Gospel, an almost pontifical authority. Who had I been up until then amongst my fellow citizens in the Chiado? Young Raposo on his horse. And now? I would be the great Raposo, who, like Chateaubriand, had made a poetic pilgrimage to the Holy Land and who, given the remote inns in which he had stayed, the plump Circassians he had kissed, could speak with equal authority at the Geographical Society and at Benta Bexigosa's bawdyhouse.

Pingalho reined in his nags. I jumped down, the box containing the relic clutched to my heart. And on the far side of the gloomy, gravelled courtyard, I saw Senhora

Dona Patrocínio das Neves, dressed all in black silk, a black lace veil covering her head, her face deathly pale behind her dark glasses, baring her buck teeth in a smile intended for me.

'Auntie!'

'My boy!'

I put down the holy box and fell upon her withered breast and the smell she exuded, of church, snuff and formic acid, was like the threadbare soul of all the domestic objects surrounding me, welcoming me back into the pious routine of home.

'How sunburnt you are, my boy!'

'Auntie, I bring you many greetings from the Lord.'

'Oh, give them all to me, all of them!'

And still holding onto me, clasping me to her hard board of a chest, she brushed her cold lips against my beard, as respectfully as if it were the wooden beard on the image of St Teodorico.

By her side, Vicência was dabbing at her eyes with one corner of her new apron. Pingalho had unloaded my leather trunk. Then, lifting up the precious box made out of blessèd Flanders pine, I murmured, with unctuous modesty:

'Here it is, Auntie, here it is! This is it, my gift to you, your holy relic, which once belonged to the Lord!'

The vile woman's pale, scrawny hands trembled as they touched the wood that contained both a miraculous cure for her health and a consolation for all her afflictions. Silent, intense, clutching the box passionately to her, she leapt up the stone steps, crossed the room of Our Lady of the Seven Sorrows and slipped into the chapel. Behind her, magnificent in my pith helmet, I mumbled hellos as I went, to the cook and to toothless Eusébia who bowed low to me in the corridor as if before the Holy of Holies.

Then, in the chapel, before the altar crammed with white camellias, I was perfection itself. I did not kneel down or cross myself; instead, I made a sign with my hand, a familiar gesture, to the golden Jesus nailed to his cross and I looked at him, smiling and polite, as one would at an old friend with whom one shares many secrets. Auntie noticed this new intimacy with the Lord and when she knelt down on the carpet (leaving me the green velvet cushion) she raised her adoring hands both to her Saviour and to her nephew.

Once the prayers of thanks for my return had been said, she remarked humbly, still prostrate on the ground:

'My boy, it would be as well for me to know what the relic is, so that I might know what candles to lay out, how much respect . . .'

I stood up, brushing off my trousers:

'You'll see. Relics should be unpacked at night. That's what the patriarch of Jerusalem told me. Just in case, though, light four more candles, for even the wooden box containing the relic is holy.'

Submissively, she lit them. She placed the box with devout care upon the altar, planted a loud kiss on it and covered it with a splendid lace cloth. Then, as if I were a Bishop, I made the sign of the cross with my two fingers over the cloth.

She was waiting, her dark glasses fixed on me, misty with tenderness:

'What shall we do now, my boy?'

'How about a bit of supper, Auntie, my stomach's rumbling.'

Senhora Dona Patrocínio immediately swept up her skirts and ran off to chivy Vicência along in the kitchen. I went to unpack my bags in my room, which Auntie had furnished with new mats. The muslin curtains puffed out, stiff with starch; a bunch of violets perfumed the dresser.

We spent a long time at the table. The dish of rice pudding bore my initials traced there in cinnamon by Auntie herself, with a heart and a cross below them. Tales about my holy journey poured unstoppably from me. I spoke of the devout days I had spent in Egypt, kissing each and every one of the footprints left there by the Holy Family in their flight; I spoke of our arrival in Jaffa with my friend, Topsius, a scholarly German, a Doctor in theology, and of the wonderful mass we had enjoyed there; I spoke of the hills of Judah, thick with shrines, before each one of which I, leading my horse by the reins, had knelt, passing on Aunt Patrocínio's best regards to the images and the monstrances there. I described Jerusalem, stone by stone. And Auntie, not even touching her food, clasping and unclasping her hands, sighed with pious passion:

'It makes one feel holy just to hear these things! It gives one a funny feeling inside!'

I smiled humbly. And each time I glanced across at her, she seemed to me a very different Patrocínio das Neves. Her dark glasses, which before had had a hard glitter to them, were now permanently misted with a damp tenderness. Her voice had lost its sibilant harshness and was softened by an errant sigh, caressing and nasal. She had grown thinner, but her dry bones seemed at last to be filled by some human warmth. I thought: 'She'll be like putty in my hands.'

And I provided more and more intemperate proofs of my intimacy with Heaven.

I said: 'One afternoon, while I was praying on the Mount of Olives, an angel suddenly passed by.' I said: 'I dragged myself away from my duties, went to the tomb of our Lord, opened the lid, and shouted inside . . .'

She hung her head, humbled before such prodigious privileges, comparable only to those of St Anthony or St Bras.

Then I enumerated my many prayers, the strict fasts I had followed. In Nazareth, by the fountain where our Lady used to fill her water jug, I had said a thousand Ave Marias, kneeling in the rain. In the desert that had been home to St John, I had lived, like him, on locusts.

And Auntie, almost drooling, said:

'How terribly, terribly touching! Imagine that, locusts! And how delighted St John would have been. He must have been thrilled. But, my boy, didn't they make you ill?'

'On the contrary, I put on weight, Auntie! As I said to my German friend: "Now we've found such a bargain, we should make the most of it and save our souls while we're about it."'

She turned to Vicência, who was standing, smiling and amazed, at her usual post between the two windows, beneath the portrait of Pius IX and Commander G. Godinho's old telescope:

'Ah, Vicência, he's returned to us positively oozing virtue. He's stuffed to the gills with it.'

'I believe our Lord Jesus Christ was not entirely displeased with me,' I murmured, reaching out my spoon for some marmalade.

And every movement I made (even sipping my soup) was watched by that odious lady as reverently as if it were a precious and holy act.

Then, with a sigh, she said:

'And another thing, my boy . . . Did you bring any prayers with you, some good ones, prayers taught to you there by the patriarchs, the friars?'

'I've got some first-class ones, Auntie!'

I had hundreds of them, copied from the notebooks of the saints, efficacious remedies for every conceivable complaint. I had prayers for coughs, for drawers that stick, for the eve of the lottery . . .

'And what about one for cramp? Because sometimes at night . . .'

'I've got one that is infallible for cramp. It was given to me by a friend of mine, a monk to whom the baby Jesus frequently appears,' I said and lit a cigarette.

I had never before dared to smoke in Auntie's presence. She had always hated tobacco, above all other manifestations of sin. But now she dragged her chair greedily over to me, as if to a miraculous coffer filled with prayers that overcome the hostility of objects, cure every illness, make old women live forever upon the Earth.

'You must tell me it, my boy. It would be an act of charity.'

'I'll tell you all of them, Auntie. But first, Auntie, tell me, how has your health been?'

She gave a sigh of infinite dejection. Bad, very bad. She felt weaker every day, as if she were about to crumble into nothing. But at least now she would die knowing that she had sent me to Jerusalem to visit the Lord and she hoped that he would bear it in mind, not to mention the expense and the pain of separation. But she was in a bad way, very bad.

I turned away in order to hide the bright, scandalous gleam of joy that lit my face. Then, generously, I did my best to cheer her up. What did she have to fear now? For did she not have that relic from our Lord to cling to, with which to prevail over the natural laws of decomposition?

'Another thing, Auntie, how are all our friends?'

She gave me some upsetting news. The best and dearest of them, the charming Father Casimiro, had taken to his bed last Sunday with his legs all swollen up. The doctors said it was oedema. She believed it was a curse a Galician had put on him.

'Whatever it is, he's stuck in bed. I've missed him terribly. Oh you can't imagine. The person who's got me through it all is his nephew, Father Negrão.'

'Negrão?' I murmured, unfamiliar with the name.

Of course, I hadn't met him. Father Negrão lived near Torres. He never came to Lisbon, the lax behaviour here disgusted him. But just for her, to help her with her affairs, the saintly man had agreed to leave his village. And he was so polite, so helpful. He was perfect!

'He's been so good to me, my boy, you can't imagine. The prayers he said that God might protect you in the land of the Arabs. And he's been such good company. He has supper here every night. He didn't want to come tonight. He said something really sweet, he said: "I wouldn't want to intrude on any scenes of family affection." He talks so well and he says such deep things. There's no one to compare with him, you can't imagine, and he's so entertaining. He's just wonderful!'

Dumbstruck, I tapped the ash from my cigarette. Why was that priest from Torres defying all our domestic habits and coming to eat here every day with Auntie? I snorted authoratively:

'In Jerusalem, the priests and the patriarchs only come to dine on Sundays. That's the virtuous thing to do.'

It had grown dark. Vicência lit the gaslamp in the corridor and, since the favoured few would soon be arriving, informed by Auntie that they must come and greet the pilgrim, I withdrew to my room to put on my black jacket.

There, looking in the mirror at my tanned face, I gave a glorious smile and thought: 'Teodorico, you've won!'

Yes, I had won! The way Auntie had greeted me with such veneration, such devotion. And she was in a bad way, very bad. Soon, my heart suffused with joy, I would hear the hammer blows nailing down her coffin lid, and there was nothing to dislodge me now from Senhora Dona Patrocínio's will! To her I was now St Teodorico. The ghastly old woman was at last convinced that leaving me all her gold was the same as giving it to Jesus and the Apostles and to the entire Holy Mother Church!

The door creaked open and my aunt came in, wearing her old Tonkin shawl. And the odd thing was that she seemed to me just like the old Dona Patricínio das Neves, erect, fierce, her skin tinged green, detesting love as if it were something dirty, and sloughing off from her for good any man who had ever had anything whatsoever to do with women. And so it was! Her glasses glittered, no longer damp with emotion, and were fixed mistrustfully on my trunk. Good God! It *was* the old Dona Patricínio. There were her pale, scrawny hands folded on her breast, gripping the fringes of her shawl, longing to inspect my underwear! There was a deep, bitter line at each corner of her thin mouth. I trembled. Then I had an inspiration from the Lord. I stood before my trunk, flung wide my arms and said candidly:

'Of course! You see before you, Auntie, a trunk that has

been all the way to Jerusalem. Here it is, wide open, so that the whole world may see that it is the trunk of a man of religion. My German friend, a man who knew just about everything, used to say: "Raposo, my dear man, when someone has sinned and indulged himself on a journey, when he has chased after women, there is always some proof of it in his trunk. However hard he tries to hide it, even if he throws the proof away, he always leaves something behind that gives off the stench of sin!" He said that to me on more than one occasion, once before the patriarch himself. And the patriarch agreed. That's why I can stand here fearlessly with my trunk wide open. You can rummage and sniff all you like and the only thing it will smell of is religion. Look, Auntie, look. Here, as is only natural, are my long johns and my socks, after all it's a sin to walk about in the nude. But the rest is entirely holy! My rosary, my prayer book, my scapulars, only the best, as holy as the Holy Sepulchre itself.'

'There are some packages there!' growled the vile woman, pointing one thin, scrawny finger.

I opened them at once, with alacrity. They contained two sealed bottles of water from the River Jordan. Gravely, with great dignity, I stood before Dona Patrocínio with a small bottle of divine liquid in the palm of each hand. Her glasses misted over again and she penitently kissed the bottle, some of her spittle running down over my nails. Then, standing at the door, sighing, overcome, she said:

'Look, my son, I'm trembling. I'm quite overcome by all these pleasures.'

She left the room. I remained there scratching my chin. Yes, there was still one thing that would get me removed from my aunt's will. And that would be if she were to see some material, tangible evidence of my misdemeanours. But how could that happen in this logical universe of ours? All my past weaknesses of the flesh were like the sparse smoke from a burned-out bonfire, which no amount of effort could bring back. And my final sin, savoured far off in old Egypt, how could my aunt ever hear of that? No human combination of events could bring to Campo de Santana its two sole witnesses: a glovemaker who would now be leaning her poppy hat against the granite slabs of Rameses in Thebes and a doctor closeted in some scholastic street, in the shadow of an ancient German university, scrabbling about in the historical detritus of the Herods. Apart from that flower of debauchery and that pillar of knowledge, not a soul on earth knew about my guilty transports of delight in the amorous city of the Ptolemies.

Besides, the terrible evidence of my union with the shameless Mary, her nightdress perfumed with violets, would now be somewhere in Zion adorning the languid waist of some Circassian or the bronze breasts of a Nubian woman from Koskoro; her compromising message 'to her brave little Portuguese lover' would have been unfolded and burned in a fire; the lace on the nightdress would already have been worn out in the energetic service of love; and torn, dirty, threadbare, the nightdress would soon join the centuries-old detritus of Jerusalem! No, nothing would come between my justifiable desire and my aunt's green bag. Nothing but the old woman's flesh itself, her creaking carcass, inhabited by a stubbornly vital flame that refused to be extinguished. What a terrible fate! What if my obstinate aunt, reluctant to die, were still alive when the carnations bloomed next year. And then I could contain myself no longer. I opened my soul to the heavens and cried out desperately, with the full fury of my desire:

'Oh holy Virgin Mary, let her die soon!'

At that moment, the great bell in the courtyard rang. And, after our long separation, it was with pleasure that I recognised my modest friend Justino's two short, timid rings and it was even more pleasant, immediately afterwards, to hear Dr Margaride's majestic peal. My aunt flung open the door of my room in a state of great perturbation:

'Teodorico, my boy, listen! I've been thinking. It seems to me that it would be best to unwrap the relic when Justino and Dr Margaride have left. I'm a great friend of theirs and they're people of great virtue, but I think that for such a ceremony it would be best if only members of the Church were present.'

She considered herself to be a member of the Church by virtue of her devoutness. And I, by virtue of my pilgrimage, was almost a member of Heaven.

'No, Auntie. The patriarch of Jerusalem recommended that it should take place before all the friends of the house, in the chapel, with the candles burning ... It's more effective like that ... By the way, could you tell Vicência to come and fetch my boots, they need cleaning.'

'I'll give them to her. Where are they? They *are* a bit dirty! They'll be back with you in an instant, my boy!'

And Dona Patrocínio das Neves seized my boots and bore them off!

She had certainly changed! And in the mirror, as I pinned a coral cross of Malta in my satin cravat, I was thinking that from that day forth I would be king there in Campo de Santana, reigning from the lofty heights of my sanctity, and that in order to hasten the slow work of death, I might even have to resort to violence.

How sweet it was to enter the living room and see all our favoured friends standing there in their serious jackets, holding out welcoming arms to me. Auntie was sitting on the sofa, stiff and pale, wearing her celebratory satin and jewels. And by her side sat a very thin priest, his spine bent, his fingers interlaced on his chest, revealing, in his gaunt face, sharp, hungry teeth. It was Father Negrão. I held out my hand to him and said dryly:

'Delighted you could come ...'

'I consider it a great honour!' he whispered, pressing my fingers to his heart. And then, his servile back even more bent, he ran to raise the shade on the lampstand, so that the light would fall more directly on me and so that everyone could see, from my new maturity, the full impact of my pilgrimage.

With the smile of an ailing man, Father Pinheiro pronounced:

'He's got thinner!'

Justino hesitated, cracking his knuckles:

'He's caught the sun!'

And Dr Margaride said affectionately:

'He's grown up!'

The unctuous Father Negrão turned round, bowing towards my aunt as if before a sacrament set amongst clusters of candles, and said:

'There's certainly something about him that inspires respect . . . as one would expect in the nephew of the most virtuous Dona Patrocínio!'

Meanwhile I was bombarded by a tumult of friendly, curious questions:

'How's your health been?' 'What was Jerusalem like?' How did you like the food?'

But Auntie tapped her fan on her knee, worried that all this familiar hubbub might upset St Teodorico. And Father Negrão added, with mellifluous zeal:

'Method, my dear sirs, method! If we all ask questions at once, none of us will be satisfied. It would be best if we simply allowed our interesting friend Teodorico to speak!'

I hated that 'our', I hated that priest. Why were his words so honeyed? Why did he enjoy that privileged position on the sofa, rubbing his squalid trouser leg against my aunt's chaste satins?

But Dr Margaride, opening his snuff box, agreed that this would indeed be the best way.

'Let's all sit down in a circle and our Teodorico can tell us all the marvels that he saw in the order that they happened!'

With rather shocking familiarity, Father Negrão ran off to get a glass of sugar water to lubricate my voice. I spread my handkerchief on one knee, cleared my throat and began to describe the wonderful journey. I spoke of the luxury on board the *Málaga*; of Gibraltar and its rock crowned with clouds; of the abundance of round tables groaning with puddings and mineral waters.

'Everything in the grand style, very French!' sighed

Father Pinheiro, with a glint of greed in his dull eye. 'But all highly indigestible, of course.'

'Well, Father Pinheiro, although it was all in the grand style and very French, they served us only healthy things, nothing that might overheat the stomach. Beautiful roast beef, beautiful lamb . . .'

'But nothing, excellent lady, that could beat your chicken cooked in its own giblets!' added Father Negrão obsequiously, by my aunt's bony shoulder.

How I detested that priest! And, stirring my sugar water, I decided in my soul that, as soon as I commenced my iron rule in Campo de Santana, the gravy from my family's chicken would never again dribble down the flattering throat of that particular servant of God.

Meanwhile, Justino, tugging at his collar, was smiling at me, delighted. And how had I spent the nights in Alexandria? Was there some group where I could enjoy myself? Had I met any respectable families with whom to take tea?

'Well, Justino, I did meet such a family, but to tell the truth, frequenting Arab households rather repelled me. After all, those people believe only in Mohammed! So, do you know what I used to do at night? After supper I would go to a little church of our own religion, where there were no foreign practices and where they held a wonderful high mass. I would complete my devotions and then I would go and meet my German friend, a teacher, in a great square which in Alexandria they claim is superior to the Rossio here in Lisbon. Well, it may be larger and cruder but it's not a patch on our Rossio, with its paved square, its trees, its statue and the theatre. Anyway, to my taste, especially in the summer, give me the Rossio any time. And that's what I told the Arabs there!'

'And you were quite right to stand up for Portugal like that!' remarked Dr Margaride contentedly, tapping on his snuff box. 'I'll go further . . . It was the act of a patriot. That was exactly how the Gamas and the Albuquerques would have behaved!'

'Absolutely. Anyway, I would go and meet my German

friend and then, to relax a little, because you do need to relax when you're travelling, we would go and have a coffee ... now that *is* something they do well. The coffee the Arabs make is absolute perfection!'

'Good coffee, eh?' asked Father Pinheiro, dragging his chair over to me with intense interest. 'Is it really strong? With a good aroma?'

'It is indeed, Father Pinheiro, as strong you can take it. So we would have our coffee and go straight back to the hotel, and there in our room, with the holy Gospels before us, we would sit and study all the holy places in Judaea where we would be going to pray. And since my German friend was a teacher and knew about everything, I just soaked it all up! Even he sometimes said: "You know, Raposo, after all these nights together, you'll be an expert by the time you go home." And as a matter of fact, I do now know everything there is to know about holy things and about Christ. And so, gentlemen, that was how we would spend our time, by the light of our candle, until it was ten or eleven o'clock. Then, we would have a cup of tea, say our prayers and go to bed.'

'Well-spent nights indeed, most fruitful,' declared the estimable Dr Margaride, smiling at my aunt.

'Oh, it certainly did him good!' sighed the ghastly woman. 'It's almost as if he'd risen up to Heaven. Even his words smell good, holy even.'

Modestly, I lowered my eyes.

But Father Negrão, with devious treachery, remarked that it would be more beneficial and of greater worth to our souls, to hear of festivals, miracles, penances ...

'I am merely following my itinerary, Father Negrão,' I replied sharply.

'Just like Chateaubriand, just like all those other famous authors!' confirmed Dr Margaride approvingly.

And it was with my eyes fixed on him, as the most learned person present, that I spoke of our departure from Alexandria one stormy afternoon; of the touching moment when a holy sister of charity (who had visited Lisbon and had heard people talk of my aunt's virtue) had saved from the salt waters a package containing Egyptian earth, earth once trodden upon by the Holy Family itself; of our arrival in Jaffa, which, by some miracle, had appeared there, crowned with rays of sunlight, the moment I went up to the poop deck wearing my top hat and thinking about my aunt.

'Magnificent!' exclaimed Dr Margaride. 'And tell me, Teodorico, did you not find some wise guide who could show you the ruins and tell you all about them?'

'Why, of course, Dr Margaride! We had an eminent Latinist with us, Father Potte!'

I licked my lips. I spoke of my feelings one glorious night when we had camped near Ramleh, with the moon in the sky illuminating the religious sites about us, the Bedouin on guard, their spears resting on their shoulders, and all about us the roaring of lions.

'What a scene!' cried Dr Margaride, getting up excitedly. 'What a wonderful scene! If only I'd been there! It sounds like one of those great scenes from the Bible, from Herculano's *Eurico*! Inspiring stuff! If I'd seen such things, I would have been unable to contain myself. I would have felt forced to pen a sublime ode!'

Father Negrão tugged at the eloquent magistrate's coat-tails and said:

'It's best to let Teodorico speak, so that we can all enjoy what he says.'

Stung, Dr Margaride frowned, wrinkling his fearsome eyebrows, blacker than ebony:

'No one in this room, Father Negrão, knows better than I how to enjoy the great and the grandiose!'

And Auntie, insatiable, tapped her fan and said:

'Now that's enough . . . Go on, my boy. Tell us about some incident involving our Lord, something moving.'

A reverent silence fell. I then spoke of our journey towards Jerusalem, with two stars above to guide us – as always happens with the more refined pilgrims, the ones from good families; I spoke of the tears I had wept when, one rainy morning, I first saw the walls of Jerusalem; and of my visit to the Holy Sepulchre in full evening dress, with Father Potte, and the words I had stammered out before the tomb, sobbing and in the midst of other acolytes: 'Oh my Jesus, oh my Lord, here I am. I am here on Auntie's behalf!'

And the frightful woman, quite overcome, said:

'How touching! And right before the tomb itself!'

Then, mopping my brow with my handkerchief, I said:

'That night I went back to my hotel to pray. And now, my friends, I must tell you something rather disagreeable.'

And, contritely, I confessed that, obliged by my religion, by the honourable name of Raposo and the dignity of Portugal, I had had a disagreement at the hotel with a large bearded Englishman.

'A brawl!' cried the vile Father Negrão mischievously, keen to dull the glow of sanctity with which I was dazzling my aunt. 'A brawl in the city of Jesus Christ! Oh really, how disgraceful!'

Gritting my teeth, I turned to this most stupid of priests:

'Yes, sir. A real humdinger! But I'll have you know that the patriarch of Jerusalem himself supported me, he even clapped me on the shoulder and said: "Congratulations, Teodorico, you bore yourself like a real man!" What have you got to say to that?'

Father Negrão bowed his head; his tonsure had the bluish pallor of the moon in time of pestilence:

'Well if his eminence approved . . .'

'He did indeed, sir. And this, Auntie, was the reason for the row! In the room next to mine there was an Englishwoman, a heretic, who, the moment I began my prayers, would start playing the piano and singing tunes and silly songs and other immoral nonsense from *Bluebeard*, theatre songs. Now you can imagine, Auntie, how I felt, kneeling there fervently praying: "Santa Maria do Patrocínio, give my dear aunt many more years of life." And then to hear the voice of some excommunicant bawling away on the other side of the wall: "Bluebeard is my name, olé, and being a widower is my game." It's enough to drive anyone mad. So one night, in desperation, I could control myself no longer and I went out into the corridor, pounded on her door and shouted: "Please be quiet, there's a Christian here trying to pray!"'

'And quite right too,' declared Dr Margaride. 'The law is on your side there!'

'That's just what the patriarch said. But as I was saying, my friends, after I had shouted those words and was gravely returning to my room, her father came out, a huge, heavily bearded man carrying a hefty stick in his hand. I was sensible, I folded my arms and explained very politely that I had no desire to cause any scandal so near to the tomb of our Lord, and that I simply wanted to be allowed to pray in peace. And do you know what he said to me? That he was ... no, I can't possibly repeat it. He made some indecent remark about our Lord's tomb ... And well, Auntie, I just saw red and so I grabbed him by the scruff of the neck.'

'Did you hurt him?'

'I demolished him, Auntie.'

They all praised my ferocity. Father Pinheiro cited canonical laws authorising the Faithful to thrash the Impious. Justino leapt up and down in celebration of this felling of John Bull by a solid Portuguese blow and, fired up by this praise as if by bugle calls to the attack, I stood up and cried out in a terrifying voice:

'I will not permit impious behaviour in my presence! I'll simply knock the perpetrator to the ground and grind him into the dust! I'm a wild beast when it comes to religion!'

And I made use of this fit of holy rage to brandish my hairy, terrifying fist before Father Negrão's meek chin, like a warning. That pale, crane-thin servant of God shrank back. But just then, Vicência brought the tea in, served on the splendid china that had once belonged to G. Godinho.

Then, toast in hand, the favoured few burst out in words of ardent praise:

'Such an educational journey! It's as good as taking a degree.'

'What a wonderful night we've had here tonight! Better than the theatre any day! This is what I call having a good time!'

'It's the way he tells it! What passion, what a memory!'

Justino, his plate piled high with cakes, had gone slowly over to the window as if to peer out at the starry sky, and from amongst the fringes of the curtains, his gleaming, greedy little eyes called to me confidentially. I went over to him humming the 'Blessing' and we both plunged into the shadows provided by the damasks. Almost brushing my beard with his lips, the virtuous notary said:

'And what about the women, my friend?'

I trusted Justino. I whispered into his ear:

'They could drive a man mad, Justino!'

His eyes glittered like the eyes of a cat in January; his cup trembled in his hand.

Thoughtful, I stared out again at the night sky:

'It's certainly a lovely night. But they are not the holy stars we used to watch from the banks of the Jordan!'

Then Father Pinheiro, sipping cautiously at his tea, came over and tapped me timidly on the shoulder. With all the many distractions in that holiest of lands, had I remembered to bring him his little bottle of Jordan water?

'Of course I did, Father Pinheiro! I brought everything! Even the olive branch for our Justino here from the Mount of Olives itself. And the photograph that Dr Margaride asked for. I brought everything!'

I ran to my room to fetch those sweet souvenirs of Palestine. And when I returned, carrying by its corners a handkerchief full of devout and precious objects, I heard my name being mentioned in the room and I stopped short behind the drapes. What sweet delight! It was the inestimable Dr Margaride assuring Auntie, with all the weight of his tremendous authority:

'Dona Patrocínio, I did not want to say anything in front of him, but this is more than having a nephew and a gentleman in the family. It's more like having an intimate friend of our Lord Jesus Christ right here in the house.'

I coughed and went in. But Dona Patrocínio was muttering jealously. It seemed ill-mannered to our Lord (and to her) to distribute these minor relics before she, as a lady and as my aunt, had received the major relic in the chapel . . .

'Because you see, my friends,' she announced, her flat chest swelling with pride, 'my Teodorico has brought me a holy relic, to which I can turn with all my afflictions and which will cure me of all my ills!'

'Excellent!' shouted the impetuous Dr Margaride. 'So, Teodorico, you followed my advice, eh, and searched those tombs? Excellent! You are a most generous pilgrim!'

'There are not many nephews like him in Portugal nowadays!' added Father Pinheiro, standing at the mirror, where he was studying his furred tongue.

'It is the act of a son, the act of a son!' proclaimed Justino, standing on tiptoe.

Then Father Negrao, showing his hungry teeth again, uttered this vile remark:

'We still do not know, gentlemen, what kind of relic it is.'

I felt a thirst, a terrible thirst for the blood of that father! I gave him a piercing look, sharper and fiercer than a red-hot skewer:

'You, sir, if you are a true priest, will throw yourself to the ground in prayer when you see the marvel!'

And I turned to Dona Patrocínio, with the impatience of a noble, offended soul demanding reparation:

'Right, Auntie, let's go to the chapel now! I want everyone to share in our amazement. That's what my German friend said: "The unveiling of that relic will be enough to strike a whole family dumb!"'

In her excitement, my aunt got up, her hands pressed together as if in prayer. I rushed off to arm myself with a hammer. When I came back, Dr Margaride, grave-faced, was pulling on his black gloves. And following Dona Patrocínio, whose satin dress rustled on the tiled floor like the vestments of a prelate, we all filed down the corridor where the tall jet of gas whistled inside its opaque glass. In the background, Vicência and the cook were watching, fingering their rosaries.

The chapel was resplendent. Behind the altar, in a glow of glory, the old silver trays glinted with the flames from the candles. Against the pure white of the newly washed lace, amongst the fresh snow of the camellias, the glossy silk of the saints' blue and red tunics looked like new, specially made in the wardrobes of Heaven for that rare night of celebration. Occasionally one ray on a halo would tremble, flash forth, as if tremors of joy were running through the very wood the images were made from. And on his blackwood cross, the splendid, solid figure of Christ gleamed, all gold, sweating gold, bleeding gold.

'So tasteful! Absolutely divine!' murmured Doctor Margaride, revelling in his passion for the grandiose.

With pious care, I placed the box on the velvet cushion and mumbled a prayer over it. Then I removed the cloth covering it and, with the cloth over one arm, I solemnly cleared my throat and said:

'Auntie, gentlemen . . . This is not the moment I would have chosen to reveal the relic contained here in this box, nor is it the moment recommended by the Patriarch of Jerusalem. But now I will tell you what . . . First, however, I feel I should explain that everything about this relic is holy, the paper, the ribbon, the box, the nails, everything. The nails, for example, were taken from Noah's ark. See for youself, Father Negrão, touch them if you like. They're from the ark itself, you can still see the rust. Only the best, most virtuous materials have been used! I would also like to declare before everyone that this relic belongs to Auntie and that I have brought it back for her as proof that during my time in Jerusalem I thought only of her and of our Lord who suffered for us, and of finding her this bargain.'

'You may count on me always, my boy!' the ghastly woman spluttered, enraptured.

I kissed her hand, sealing that pact, with the Magistrature and the Church as witnesses. Then, returning to my subject:

'And now, so that everyone is forewarned and can say the prayers that best suit him or her, I should say what the relic is.'

I coughed and closed my eyes.

'It is the Crown of Thorns!'

Overcome, letting out a hoarse cry, Auntie hurled herself upon the box, embracing it with tremulous arms. Dr Margaride, however, stood pensively rubbing his austere chin, Justino disappeared into the depths of his collar and sly Father Negrão merely gaped at me, his black mouth hanging open, amazed and indignant! Good God, both magistrates and priests alike displayed an incredulity that could prove fatal to my fortunes!

I was trembling, the sweat was pouring off me, then, very gravely and with great conviction, Father Pinheiro knelt down, clasped Auntie's hand and congratulated her on the lofty position within the Church to which the possession of this relic would elevate her. Then, accepting Father Pinheiro's strong, liturgical authority, they all lined up to offer their congratulations and dumbly shake the drooling old woman's hand.

I was saved! I quickly knelt down by the box, placed the chisel in the crack in the lid, triumphantly raised the hammer . . .

'Teodorico! My son!' yelped Auntie, trembling all over, as if I were about to hammer into the living flesh of the Lord.

'Don't be afraid, Auntie! In Jerusalem I learned all about handling these holy objects.'

The final nail was removed from the final plank to reveal the white layer of cotton wool. With tender reverence I removed it and, before their ecstatic eyes, I lifted out the sacred package wrapped in brown paper and tied with red ribbon.

'Oh, what a perfume! I feel quite faint!' sighed Auntie swooning with saintly pleasure, the whites of her eyes showing above the black lenses of her glasses.

I stood up, flushed with pride:

'Given her great virtue, it should be left to my aunt to unwrap the package.'

Rousing herself from her languor, still tremulous and pale, but with the grave demeanour of a pontiff, Auntie took up the package, bowed to the saints, placed it on the altar and devoutly untied the knot in the red ribbon. Then, with the solicitude of one who fears she might bruise a divine body, she undid the folds of brown paper one by one. A piece of white linen appeared. Auntie picked it up with the tips of her fingers, pulled it brusquely out and there on the altar amongst the saints, on the camellias, at the foot of the cross, lay the lace and ribbons of Mary's nightdress!

Yes, Mary's nightdress, in all its glory and immodesty, still creased by my embraces, with every fold redolent of sin! Mary's nightdress! And pinned to it, clearly legible by the light of the candles, the note that went with the gift, written in large letters: 'To my Teodorico, my brave little Portuguese lover, in memory of all the pleasures we enjoyed!' Signed 'M.M.' Mary's nightdress!

I can barely remember what happened next in the chapel. I found myself at the door, kneeling on the green curtain, my legs buckling under me, as if in a faint. Crackling about me, like logs thrown on to a bonfire, I heard Father Negrão's accusations screaming out to me, as he stood at Auntie's side: 'Debauchee! What a vile joke! The nightdress of a prostitute! Making a mockery of Dona Patrocínio! Profaning the chapel!' I glimpsed his boot kicking the white bundle furiously out into the corridor. One by one, I saw my friends pass me by, like long shadows carried away by a terrifying wind. The flames of the candles bent sorrowfully. And, drenched in sweat, wrapped in the folds of the curtain, I watched as Auntie came slowly over to me, pale, erect, frightening. She stopped. Her fierce, cold glasses pierced me. And through gritted teeth she spat out one word:

'Pig!'

And then she left.

I stumbled back to my bedroom and fell on the bed, devastated. A murmur of scandal had woken the stern house and Vicência appeared before me, her white apron in her hand.

'Master Teodorico! The Senhora has sent orders that you must leave the house immediately. She doesn't want you to stay in the house a moment longer. And she says you can take your underwear and all your other filthy stuff with you!'

Dismissed!

I raised my crumpled face from the lace pillow case. Vicência was standing there stunned, twisting her apron about in her hands:

'Oh sir, sir. If you don't leave the house this minute, the Senhora says that she'll call the police!'

Banished!

I placed my unsteady feet on the floor. I stuck a tooth-brush in my pocket. Bumping into the furniture, I fumbled for my slippers which I wrapped up in a copy of *The Nation*. Barely noticing what I was doing, I picked up an iron-bound trunk from amongst my luggage and crept on tiptoe, shrunken and abject, down Auntie's stairs, like a mangy dog ashamed of its scabs.

I had barely crossed the courtyard, when Vicência, carrying out my aunt's furious orders, slammed the door behind me – scornfully and for ever.

I was alone in the street and in life. By the light of the cold stars, I counted the money I had in the palm of my hand: 2 *libras*, 18 *tostões*, one Spanish *duro* and some copper. And then I discovered that the box, plucked foolishly from amongst the trunks, was the one containing the minor relics I had brought back with me. What a complex work of irony on the part of Destiny! To cover my body, I had nothing but a few planks of wood planed by St Joseph himself and some shards from the Virgin's pitcher. I put the package containing my slippers in the bag and, not allowing my sad eyes a single backwards glance at my aunt's house, I set off on foot, carrying the box on my shoulders, in the night full of silence and stars, down to the Baixa, to the Hotel da Pomba de Ouro.

The next day, sitting pale and wretched at the table in the hotel, I was stirring my spoon round a sombre plate of corn and turnip soup, when a gentleman in a black velvet waistcoat came and sat down opposite me, bringing with him a bottle of mineral water, a box of pills and a copy of *The Nation*. Two thick veins stood out on his vast forehead, which was curved like the gable of a chapel. Beneath his large nostrils, blackened with snuff, he wore a short tuft of a moustache, its greyish hairs hard as the bristles on a brush. The Galician waiter growled affectionately as he was serving him his soup:

'Good to see you, Senhor Lino!'

When the stew had been served, the gentleman lay aside his newspaper, in which he had been scouring the advertisements, fixed his dull, bilious eyes on me and remarked that we had been enjoying some glorious weather since January.

'Lovely,' I murmured shyly.

Senhor Lino tucked his serviette further into his loose collar and said:

'And you sir, if you don't mind my asking, are you from the north?'

I slowly passed a hand over my hair and said:

'No, sir. I've just come back from Jerusalem.'

Senhor Lino was so amazed that he dropped a forkful of rice. And, having mulled over his excitement in silence, he confessed that he was fascinated by all those holy places because he was, God be praised, a religious man. He also, again all praise to God, had a job on the Patriarchal Council.

'Oh, the Patriarchal Council,' I said. 'Very good. I knew a patriarch once. In fact, I knew the Patriarch of Jerusalem extremely well. A very holy man, very elegant. We were on quite intimate terms.'

Senhor Lino offered me a glass of his mineral water and we chatted about the lands of the Scriptures.

'What's Jerusalem like, I mean, as regards shops?'

'Shops? You mean clothes shops?'

'No, no!' said Senhor Lino. 'I mean shops selling holy objects, relics, ...'

'Oh, I see. Not bad. There's Damiani in the Via Dolorosa. They have everything, even the bones of martyrs. But the best thing to do is to look for yourself, dig around. I found some marvellous things that way!'

A flicker of unusual greed lit the yellow pupils of Senhor Lino of the Patriarchal Council. And suddenly, with a decision informed by inspiration, he cried:

'André, a little glass of port. Today we celebrate.'

When the Galician brought the bottle, with its date written in hand on an old label made out of ordinary writing paper, Senhor Lino offered me a full glass.

'Your health!'

'God willing. And yours!'

Out of courtesy, once we had eaten the cheese, I invited the gentleman, who, God be praised, was a religious man, to come up to my room and admire my photographs of Jerusalem. He accepted eagerly. But the moment he was through the door, he made a beeline for my bed, on which lay some of the relics I had unpacked that morning.

'How do you like this, sir?' I asked, unrolling a view of the Mount of Olives and thinking of making him a gift of a rosary.

In his fat hands with their gnawed fingernails he was silently turning over a bottle of water from the River Jordan. He sniffed it, weighed it, tapped it. Then very seriously, the veins in his vast forehead beating, he said:

'Do you have a certificate to go with this?'

I held out to him the certificate the Franciscan friar had given to me, guaranteeing it as being pure, authentic water taken from the baptismal river. He pored over the worthy piece of paper and then said enthusiastically:

'I'll give you fifteen *tostões* for this bottle!'

It was as if a window had been flung open in my graduate's mind and the sun had suddenly poured in. By its brilliant light, I unexpectedly saw the true nature of those medals, scapulars, bottles of water, shards, small stones, bits of straw, which until then I had considered as so much ecclesiastical dust left behind by the broom of philosophy! The relics were *money*! They had all the omnipotent virtues of money! You gave someone a fragment of a jug and you received a gold coin in return! Thus enlightened, I began, almost without noticing, to smile, my hands resting on the table as if on the counter of a shop:

'Fifteen *tostões* for pure water from the Jordan! That's a good one. You obviously don't hold St John the Baptist in very great esteem. Fifteen *tostões*! That verges on the sacrilegious! You surely don't imagine that water from the River Jordan is like water from the tap, do you? Really! I turned down an offer of three thousand *reis* from a priest from Santa Justa this very morning, he was standing right there at the foot of the bed.'

He weighed the bottle in his fat palm, considered, calculated and said:

'I'll give you four thousand *reis*.'

'Oh, all right then, since we're both guests in the same hotel.'

And by the time Senhor Lino had left my room with the bottle of water from the River Jordan wrapped in a copy of *The Nation*, I, Teodorico Raposo, found myself set up, fatefully, providentially, as a seller of relics.

Thanks to them I dined out, smoked and made love for two whole months, living quiet and contented at the Hotel da Pomba de Ouro. Almost every morning Senhor Lino would appear in my room, in his slippers, select a shard from the Virgin's water jar or a piece of straw from the crib, wrap it up in *The Nation*, give me the money and leave, whistling the 'De profundis'. The worthy man was obviously reselling my precious items at a fat profit, for I soon noticed that he was wearing a gleaming new gold chain on his black velvet waistcoat.

Meanwhile, very sensibly and tactfully, I had made no

attempt (no entreaties or explanations or special pleading) to calm my aunt's saintly rage or to regain her respect. I contented myself with visiting the church in Campo de Santana, all dressed in black and carrying a prayer book. I never met my aunt there, for she now heard mass every morning in her own chapel from the vile Father Negrão. But there, nonetheless, I would prostrate myself, beating my breast contritely, sighing at the shrine, certain that news of my unaltered devotion would reach the ears of the hateful woman through Melchior the sacristan.

Even more cunningly, I did not seek out my aunt's friends either, for they would, out of prudence, be obliged to share the passions of her soul in order to gain favour in her will. I thus saved those worthy men of the Magistrature and the Church any moments of anxious embarrassment. Whenever I met Father Pinheiro or Dr Margaride in the street, I would fold my hands in front of me and lower my eyes, pretending humility and compunction. And this reserve was certainly welcomed by my friends, because one night, I met Justino near Benta Bexigosa's bawdyhouse and the worthy man, having first ascertained that we were quite alone in the street, whispered in my ear:

'That's how it is my friend! It will all work out. But for the moment she's like a wild beast. Oh hell, there are some people coming!'

And he was off.

Meanwhile, I continued to sell relics through Senhor Lino. However, remembering those books I'd read on economics, I soon realised that my own profits would be much larger if I eliminated Senhor Lino and boldly approached the pious consumer myself.

So I wrote letters accompanied by a list of relics and prices to noblewomen and to servants of Our Lord of the Stations of the Cross in Graça. I sent letters to provincial churches detailing the availability of martyrs' bones. I plied sacristans with brandy in order to encourage them to mention my name to old ladies with aches and pains: 'When it comes to holy knicknacks, Dr Raposo's your man, he's just back from Jerusalem!' And Fate smiled on me. My speciality was water from the River Jordan, in zinc bottles, sealed and stamped with a heart in flames. I sold this water for baptisms, mealtimes and baths and, for a time, there was another River Jordan, much broader and cleaner than the one in Palestine, that flowed through Lisbon and had its source in a room in the Hotel da Pomba de Ouro. I used my imagination and introduced certain poetical novelties that proved most profitable: with great success I launched on the market 'a piece of the pitcher used by Our Lady when she went to the fountain'; I was the person who endowed national piety with 'one of the horseshoes from the donkey on which the Holy Family fled'. Now, when Senhor Lino came in his slippers to knock at the door of my room, where stacks of straw from the crib alternated with piles of planks planed by St Joseph himself, I would open it a miserly crack:

'It's all gone. I've sold out! I'll have some more in next week. I'm getting a new consignment from the Holy Land then.'

The veins on the forehead of this most capable of men would swell with the indignation of the despoiled intermediary.

All my relics were taken up with great fervour, because they came from 'Raposo, just back from Jerusalem'. The other sellers of relics could not give this splendid guarantee of having themselves journeyed to the Holy Land. Only I, Raposo, had travelled through that vast warehouse of sanctity. Only I could inscribe a greasy sheet of paper with the flowery signature of the Patriarch of Jerusalem authenticating the relic.

I soon realised, however, that I had saturated the market for devotion in my own country with this profusion of relics. Stuffed to the gills, the Catholic land of Portugal had no more room, not even to receive one of those little sprays of dried flowers from Nazareth which I sold at five *tostões* apiece.

Worried, I took the sad step of lowering my prices. I

splashed out on tempting advertisements in the *Diário de Notícias*: 'Treasures from the Holy land, reasonable prices, all enquiries to the Tabacaria Rego.' I frequently went out in the morning, wearing an ecclesiastical jacket and a silk scarf to cover my beard, in order to ambush devout old ladies at the doors of churches and offer them scraps of material from the Virgin Mary's tunic, the laces from St Peter's sandals, and I would mumble anxiously, brushing past the cloaks and bonnets:

'Very cheap, my lady, very cheap. An excellent cure for colds!'

By now I owed a large amount of money to the hotel; I would sneak down the stairs in order to avoid meeting the owner; I would address the Galician waiter in wheedling tones as: 'Dear André, my dear fellow.'

And I put all my hope in a renewal of national faith. I would take enormous delight in some snippet of news about a church festival, seeing it as proof of people's return to the Faith. I was fierce in my condemnation of republicans and of philosophers who attacked Catholicism thereby diminishing the value of the relics the Church had instituted. I wrote ranting articles in *The Nation* declaring:

'If we do not cleave to the bones of the martyrs, how can we expect this country to prosper?' In the Café do Montanha I would thump the table and say: 'Religion is necessary, damn it! Without religion even your beef steak loses its flavour!' At Benta Bexigosa's I would tell the girls that if they did not wear their scapulars, I would take my custom elsewhere, to Dona Adelaide's! My preoccupation with earning my daily bread became so all-consuming that I even sought the intervention of Senhor Lino, a man with a vast network of acquaintances in the ecclesiastical world, a relative of convent chaplains. Again I showed him my bed cluttered with relics. Again, I said to him, rubbing my hands: 'How about a little business, my friend? I've just got a new selection here, just arrived from Zion!'

But from the worthy man from the Patriarchal Council I received only bitter recriminations.

'I'm not falling for your smooth talk, sir!' he shouted, the veins in his red face swelling with rage. 'It was you who ruined the business! The market's overflowing, I can't even sell one of Baby Jesus' nappies, which always used to sell so well before. That horseshoe business is positively indecent. Really! Why just the other day I was saying to a chaplain, a cousin of mine: "There are simply too many horseshoes for a small country like ours!" Fourteen horseshoes, sir, it's too much! Do you know how many nails you've sold – all said to have been used to nail Christ to the cross, every one of them documented? Seventy-five, sir! Need I say more? Seventy-five!'

And he left, slamming the door, leaving me duly humbled.

Fortunately, that night at Benta Bexigosa's I met 'Rinchão' and got a large order for relics from him. 'Rinchão' was going to marry one of the Nogueira girls, the daughter of Senhora Nogueira, a rich and extremely devout woman from Beja, who was also the owner of a large number of pigs; and he 'wanted to give the fanatical old woman a really elegant present, something linked to Christian doctrine and the Holy Sepulchre'. I made him up a lovely box of relics. In it I placed my seventy-sixth nail, adorned with charming dried flowers from Galilee. With the generous sum of money Rinchão gave me, I paid my hotel bill and prudently took a room in a guesthouse in Travessa da Palha.

But my prosperity diminished. My new room was on the fifth floor, with an iron bedstead and an ancient mattress whose stuffing of malodorous cotton was bursting out from the torn fabric cover. The only ornament hung above the chest of drawers: a coloured lithograph of Christ crucified, in a frame decorated with tassels. Black storm clouds rolled beneath his feet and his wide, pale eyes followed and watched my every act, even the most intimate, even the delicate business of trimming my corns.

I had been installed there for a week, during which time I had scoured Lisbon in search of that elusive daily bread, in boots whose soles were beginning to crack. Then, one morning, André from the Hotel da Pomba de Ouro, brought me a letter that had been left there the evening before, marked urgent. The paper was edged in black and the seal was in black wax. I opened it, trembling. I saw Justino's signature.

'My dear friend, it is my sad and painful duty to inform you that your worthy aunt and my employer has unexpectedly succumbed . . .'

Good grief! The old woman had kicked the bucket!

I hastily jumped a few lines, skipping over the details:

'Congestion of the lungs. . .sacraments received. . . everyone crying. . .Father Negrão!. . .' Growing pale, drenched in sweat, I saw, at the bottom of the page, the fearful news:

'In the virtuous lady's will, it is stated that she leaves to her nephew Teodorico the telescope that always hung in the dining room . . .' Disinherited!

I grabbed my hat and, bumping into people as I went, I ran through the streets to Justino's office in Praça de São Paulo. I found him at his desk, wearing a black tie, his pen behind his ear, eating slices of veal out of an old copy of the *Diário de Notícias*.

'What do you mean, the telescope?' I said panting, leaning on a bookshelf.

'That's what it says: the telescope,' he mumbled, his mouth full.

I lay down on his leather sofa, almost in a faint. He offered me a glass of wine. I drank the whole glass. And passing a tremulous hand over my pale face, I said:

'All right, Justino, tell me everything.'

Justino sighed. The saintly lady, poor thing, had left him some stocks and shares. And for the rest, she had distributed all of G. Godinho's wealth in the most incoherent, perverse manner possible. The house in Campo de Santana and forty *contos*' worth of shares went to Our Lord of the Stations of the Cross in Graça. Her shares in the gas company, her best silver and the house in Linda-a-Pastora went to Father Casimiro, who was a dying man and no longer even stirred from his house. Father Pinheiro inherited a house in Rua do Arsenal. The public credit bonds, the furniture from Campo de Santana, the golden Christ, the delightful Quinta do Mosteiro, with its picturesque doorway, on which were carved the arms of the Counts of Lindoso, all went to Father Negrão. Three thousand *reis* and the clock went to Doctor Margaride. Vicência got the bed linen. And I got the telescope.

'Presumably so that you can view the rest of your inheritance from afar,' Justino remarked philosophically, cracking his knuckles.

I returned to Travessa da Palha. And for hours I sat there in my slippers, my eyes blazing, brooding over my desperate desire to mutilate my aunt's corpse, to spit in her pale face, bore into her rotten belly with a walking stick. I called down upon her all the wrath of Nature. I asked the trees to deny shade to her tomb. I asked the winds to sweep up all the rubbish of the world and deposit it on her grave. I invoked the devil: 'You can have my soul, if only you promise eternal torment for that old woman.' Arms outstretched, I cried to heaven: 'God, if there is a Heaven, throw her out!' I plotted to smash the stones of the mausoleum that had been built for her. I decided to write letters in the newspapers, saying how she had prostituted herself to a Galician, every evening, in the attic, wearing only her dark glasses and a petticoat.

Worn out with hatred, I fell into a profound sleep.

It was Pita who woke me, as it was growing dark, bearing a long, thin package. It was the telescope. Justino had sent it to me with these friendly words: 'Herewith your modest inheritance!'

I lit a candle. With a feeling of terrible bitterness, I took up the telescope, opened the lens and peered through it, as if from the deck of a ship that was lost at sea. Yes, Justino had been quite right, the ghastly Dona Patrocínio had left me the eyeglass as a final act of rancorous sarcasm, so that through it I might view the rest of my inheritance. And, despite the dark night, I saw, clearly saw, the image of Our Lord of the Stations of the Cross stuffing the money into his purple tunic; Father Casimiro touching with his dying hand the designs on the silver scattered about his bed; and that most vile of people, Father Negrão, in a cotton drill jacket and galoshes, strolling happily by the waterside beneath the elms at the Quinta do Mosteiro. And there I was with the telescope!

There I was for ever, in the Travessa da Palha, with just 720 *reis* in the pockets of my patched trousers with which to struggle through the city and through life. With a roar, I hurled the telescope to the floor and it rolled over towards the hatstand where I kept the pith helmet I had worn on my journey to the Holy Land. There they were, the pith helmet and the telescope, symbols of my two existences, the one in splendour and the other in penury. Wearing that hat, there had been whole months when I had been Raposo triumphant, heir to Dona Patrocínio das Neves, turning over the gold coins in my pockets and sensing about me, just waiting for me to pluck them, all the perfumed flowers of civilisation. And now, with only that telescope to my name, I was poor Raposo in worn boots, sensing all around me, black and waiting to prick me, all of life's thistles. And why? Because one day, in an inn in a city of Asia, two packets wrapped in brown paper had been switched.

Had Fate ever played such a dirty trick on anyone! To a pious aunt, to whom love was something detestable and dirty and who, in order to bequeath to me houses and silver, required only that I should scorn women and scour Jerusalem for a relic, to her I brought a nightdress belonging to a glovemaker. And in a charitable impulse, designed to captivate Heaven, I had given what I thought to be a generous gift to a poor woman in rags, with a starving child crying at her breast, but which turned out to be a crown of thorns. Oh God, tell me! Tell me, oh Devil, how that happened, how that exchange of packages, the tragedy of my whole life, came about!

They looked alike as regards shape, wrapping paper and ribbon. The package containing the nightdress lay in the dark at the back of the wardrobe and that containing the relic was displayed victoriously on the chest of drawers, between two candlesticks. And no one had touched them, not even Potte or the erudite Topsius, not even myself. No human hand, no mortal hand had dared move those two packages. Who had moved them then? It could only have been someone with invisible hands!

Yes, someone incorporeal and all-powerful, who, out of sheer hatred, had miraculously turned thorns into lace, so that my aunt would disinherit me and I would be cast forever into the social wilderness.

And when I was raving on like this, my hair dishevelled, I became aware that the pale eyes of the crucified Christ, inside his frame decorated with tassels, were fixed coldly on me and open even wider than usual, as if taking pleasure in the failure of my life.

'It was you!' I cried in a moment of sudden enlightenment and understanding. 'It was you! You!'

And shaking my two fists at him, I unburdened myself of all the complaints and sorrows in my heart:

'Yes, it was you who, before the devout eyes of my aunt, transformed the crown of suffering into Mary's grubby nightdress. But why? What did I ever do to you? Ungrateful, fickle God! Where and when did you have a more devoted follower? Did I not dress up in black every Sunday and go to hear the best masses offered up to you in Lisbon? Did I not stuff myself every Friday night with dried cod in oil, just to please you? Did I not spend whole days in Auntie's chapel, my knees hurting, mumbling your favourite prayers? I learned by heart every prayer there was to learn. There was scarcely a garden where I did not pick flowers in order to decorate your altars.'

Overcome with emotion, tearing at my hair and tugging at my beard, I cried out, standing so close to the image that the hot breath of my rage misted the glass:

'Look at me! Don't you remember seeing this face, this

270

hair, centuries ago, in a marble courtyard, beneath a velarium, where you were being judged by a Roman Praetor? Perhaps you don't remember. There's a vast difference between a victorious god being borne along on a litter and a provincial rabbi with his hands tied. Anyway, on that day in the month of Nisan, before you had any cosy places in Heaven and the Celestial City to distribute to the faithful, on that day, before you had become a source of wealth and a shortcut to power, on that day, when my aunt and all those who now prostrate themselves at your feet would have booed you along with all the sellers in the Temple, the Pharisees and the rabble from Acra, on that day, when the soldiers who now escort you with brass bands, the magistrates who now imprison anyone who speaks out against you or denies you, the landowners who now lavish gold on you and put on religious festivals for your benefit, would have given all their weapons and all their moral codes and all their moneybags in order to obtain your death as a revolutionary, an enemy of the social order, a threat to property; on that day, when you were merely a man of creative intelligence and active kindness, and therefore considered by all serious men to be a social menace, there was in Jerusalem one heart which, with no hope of reaching Heaven nor fear of Hell, spontaneously beat for you. That heart was mine. And yet now you persecute me, why?'

Suddenly, incredibly, tremulous rays, the colour of snow and the colour of gold, poured forth from the crude tasselled frame. The glass split open with the blinding crash of a door opening in Heaven. And from inside the frame, his arms still nailed to the cross, Christ slid serenely towards me, growing in size until he touched the ceiling, more beautiful in his majesty and brilliance than the sun rising behind the mountains.

I fell to my knees with a cry and, terrified, beat my forehead on the floor. And then, filling the room, like the soft murmur of a breeze amongst jasmine blossoms, I heard a calm, gentle voice:

'When you went to Alto da Graça to kiss the feet of an image, it was so that you could then obsequiously describe to your aunt the piety with which you gave that kiss; because the only reason you had a prayer on your lips and humility in your eyes was in order to impress your aunt with your holy fervour. The God you prostrated yourself before was Commander G. Godinho's wealth and the Heaven your tremulous arms reached out for was your aunt's will. To acquire the best place in that will, you pretended to be devout even though you did not believe, to be chaste though you were a libertine, to be charitable when you were mean and you feigned the tenderness of a son when all you felt was the rapacity of an heir. You were, in every way possible, a hypocrite. You led two lives: one for the benefit of your aunt's eyes, all rosaries, fasts and prayers and another life lived on the sly, far from your aunt, all greed, all Adélia and Benta Bexigosa. You lied constantly and the only time you were honest with Heaven, honest with the world, was when you prayed to Jesus and the Virgin for your aunt to die as soon as possible. Then you wrapped up this whole laborious fraud of a life in a single package in which you placed a branch as false as your heart and, with it, you hoped to ensnare for ever all the silver and all the property belonging to Dona Patrocínio. But in another package, a similar package that you brought from Palestine, full of lace and ribbons, was the irrefutable proof of your deceit. Now it happened, quite rightly, that the package you offered to your aunt and which your aunt opened, was the one that revealed your wrongdoing. And that just goes to show, Teodorico, the pointlessness of hypocrisy.'

I was lying groaning on the floorboards. The voice was whispering, more slowly now, like the evening breeze in the branches:

'I don't know who was behind that picaresque and terrible exchange of packages, perhaps no one was, perhaps you did it yourself. The sadness of your disinherited life comes not from that transformation of thorns into lace, but from having lived two lives, one that was at once true and iniquitous, and the other at once false and holy. Since you were living a contradiction, on the right side the devout Raposo and on the left the debauchee, you could not go on living with your aunt for very long, showing only one side, the one that wore dark suits on Sunday and glowed with virtue; the day would inevitably come when she would see with a shock the naked, natural side of you, bright with the black stains of vice. And that is what I meant, Teodorico, when I spoke of the pointlessness of hypocrisy.'

I dragged myself across the floor and reached out abject lips to the transparent feet of the Christ, hanging in the air, the nails in his hands and feet giving off the tremulous radiance of precious stones. And a voice passed over me, resonant and murmurous, like the gust of wind that bends the cypress trees:

'You say that I persecute you. I do not. The telescope and what you call the social wilderness are all the work of your own hand, not mine. I do not construct the episodes of your life; I witness them and judge them calmly. Without my lifting a finger, with no intervention from supernatural influences, you could descend to still murkier depths or raise yourself up to the profitable paradises of Earth and become the director of a bank. This depends entirely on you and your strength as a man. But listen! You were asking me, a little while ago, if I remembered your face. I ask you now if you remember my voice. I am not Jesus of Nazareth, nor any other God created by man. I pre-date all transitory gods; they are born in me; they live in me; they are transformed in me and they dissolve in me; and I remain eternally around and above them, conceiving them and destroying them, in an unending struggle to realise outside of myself the absolute God I can feel within me. I call myself conscience. At this precise moment I am your own conscience reflected outside yourself, in the air and in the light, and taking on in your eyes the familiar form, which you, ill-educated and unphilosophical, are used to recognising. But all you have to do is get up and look at me closely for this resplendent image to disappear completely.'

And even before I had looked up, the apparition had vanished.

Then, transported, as if I had been witness to some manifestation of the supernatural, I held out my hands to Heaven and cried:

'Oh my Lord Jesus, God and son of God, who became flesh and suffered for us.'

But then I fell silent. That ineffable voice still echoed in my soul, showing me the pointlessness of hypocrisy. I consulted my conscience, which had returned inside me, and, quite certain that I did not believe that Jesus was the son of God and of a married woman from Galilee (the way Hercules was the son of Jupiter and a married woman from Argolida), I spat out the vain remainder of that prayer, my lips thenceforward for ever honest.

The next day, quite by chance, I went into the garden of São Pedro de Alcântara, a place I had not set foot in since my years at school. I had gone only a short away amongst the flower beds when I met my old friend Crispim, the son of Teles, owner of Crispim & Co., the textile mill in Pampulha, the classmate I had not seen since I was at school. It was this same blond Crispim, who used to plant voracious kisses on my cheek in the corridor at the Colégio dos Isidoros and write notes to me at night promising me gifts of boxes of steel-nibbed pens. Crispim Sr had died; Teles, rich and fat, had become Viscount São Teles; and my friend Crispim *was* now the company.

Once we had embraced each other heartily, Crispim & Co. remarked thoughtfully that I was looking 'absolutely dreadful'. Then he spoke with envy of my journey to the Holy Land (which he had learned about through the *Jornal das Novidades*) and alluded, with friendly glee, to the 'huge amount of money that Senhora Dona Patrocínio must have left me'.

Bitterly, I showed him my worn-out boots. We sat down on a bench, next to a rose trellis, and there, in the silence and the perfume, I told him about Mary's fateful nightdress, the relic in its package, the disaster in the chapel, the telescope, my miserable room in Travessa da Palha.

'So you see, my dear Crispim, I haven't a penny to my name.'

Shocked, Crispim & Co. stroked his blonde moustaches, mumbled something about how in Portugal, thanks to the Constitutional Charter and to Religion, everyone at least had a crust of bread, although some perhaps had to do without the cheese.

'But I can provide you with the cheese, my old friend!' Crispim added happily, slapping me on the knee. 'One of the clerks in the offices at Pampulha began writing verses and getting involved with actresses. And he was terribly republican, always making fun of religion. In short, he was a complete disaster, so I got rid of him. Now you always had very nice handwriting and you were always good at sums. If you like, you can have that man's job, why not, it pays 25 *milréis*, you could at least afford to buy some cheese with that.'

With two tears trembling on my eyelashes, I embraced Crispim & Co. He again mumbled something, screwing up his face as if he had bitten into something sour:

'You really do look dreadful!'

I began working diligently at the textile mill in Pampulha and every day, sitting at my desk in my silk oversleeves, I would copy out letters in my beautiful handwriting and write out columns of figures in a vast cash-book. The company taught me the 'rule of three' and other such skills. And just as from seeds blown by some chance wind onto a neglected piece of land, there grow unexpectedly useful plants that prosper, so from the lessons taught to me by the company there bloomed, in my uncultivated law graduate's nature, a considerable aptitude for the textile business. The company itself was moved to say as much at the Assembleia do Carmo:

'Despite having studied at Coimbra and despite all the text books they tried to cram his head with, my friend Raposo has a real knack for serious business.'

Now one Saturday in August, in the afternoon, when I was closing my cash-book for the day, Crispim & Co. paused by my desk, smiling and lighting a cigar:

'I say, Raposo, where do you usually go to mass?'

I said nothing and merely pulled off my silk oversleeves.

'I only ask,' Crispim added, 'because tomorrow I'm going with my sister to the other side of the river, to a villa of ours, in Ribeira. Now unless you're very keen on a particular mass, you could come to the mass at Santos, at nine, we could have breakfast at the Hotel Central and get the boat from there to Cacilhas. I really would like you to meet my sister.'

Crispim & Co. was a religious gentleman who considered religion to be indispensable to his health, to his commercial prosperity and to the good order of the country. He was a devout visitor to Our Lord of the Stations of the Cross in Graça and he belonged to the Brotherhood of St Joseph. The clerk whose desk I now occupied had become intolerable more than anything because he had written articles for the republican magazine *Future* as well as pamphlets praising Renan and insulting the Eucharist. I was about to tell Crispim & Co. that I was so devoted to the mass at the Church of Conceição Nova that I couldn't possibly go to any other . . . but then I remembered the austere, salutary voice I had heard in my room in Travessa da Palha. I bit back the holy lie about to soil my lips and I said instead, firmly, my face very pale:

'Look, Crispim, I never go to mass. It's all a load of lies. I can't believe that the body of God is there every Sunday in a bit of host made out of flour. God doesn't have a body, he never did. It's all just idolatry and fanaticism. I tell you this straight out and you can do with me what you will. But that's how I feel.'

The Company looked at me for a moment, biting his lower lip:

'You know, Raposo, I like your frankness. I like straight-forwardness in people. The other chap who used to work at this desk would say to my face: "He's a great man, the Pope!" and then he would go to the bars and vilify the Holy Father. Well, that was that. You may not have religion but you are a gentleman. So I'll see you at ten in the Hotel Central for breakfast and then we'll get the boat across to Ribeira!'

That was how I met his sister. Her name was Dona Jesuína, she was thirty years old and had a slight squint. But after that Sunday by the river in the country, her hair, thick and red as Eve's, her firm, succulent bosom, her skin the colour of ripe apples, the healthy smile of her bright teeth, gave me much to think about when I went home to the Baixa later that evening, smoking my cigar, watching the masts of the passing barges.

She had been educated by the Salesians: she knew geography, the names of all the rivers in China, she knew history and the names of all the kings of France and she called me Teodorico the Lionheart, because I had been to Palestine. After that I dined in Pampulha every Sunday; Dona Jesuína would make a special dessert made from eggs; her squint eye would rest, with unceasing pleasure, on my bold, bearded face. One evening, as we were having coffee, Crispim & Co. was praising the royal family, their constitutional moderation and the charitable grace of the Queen. Then we went down into the garden and, while Dona Jesuína was watering the plants and I was walking by her side rolling a cigar, I sighed and murmured in her ear:

'Were I ever to be made King, then you would be my Queen, Dona Jesuína.' She blushed and handed me the last rose of summer.

On Christmas Eve, Crispim & Co. came to my desk, placed his hat playfully on the page in the cash-book that I was busy filling with figures and, folding his arms, he gave a loyal and respectful laugh and said:

'So she would be Queen would she, if Raposo were King? Now tell me, Senhor Raposo, do you harbour genuine love for my sister Jesuína in that heart of yours?'

Crispim & Co. admired passion and idealism. I was about to tell him that I adored Senhora Dona Jesuína as I would a remote star. But I remembered the pure, imposing voice I had heard in Travessa da Palha. I bit back the sentimental lie that was already languishing on my lips and I said bravely:

'Well, not exactly love, no. But I think she's a fine figure of a woman, I very much like the fact that she has a dowry and I believe I would make her a good husband.'

'Give me your hand then, for being an honest man!' shouted Crispim.

I got married. I'm a father. I have a carriage and the respect of my neighbours. I am a Knight of Christ. And Dr Margaride, who dines with me every Sunday in his dress coat, declares that, given my education, my many travels and my patriotism, the State should bestow on me the title of Baron do Mosteiro because I have since bought the villa, the Quinta do Mosteiro. One evening at table, the worthy magistrate announced that that horrible man Father Negrão had decided to get rid of some of his properties in Torres and had decided to sell the old family home of the Counts of Lindoso.

'Those trees, Teodorico,' the worthy man recalled, 'gave shade to your dear Mama. I'll go further, Teodorico, the shadows they cast also fell upon your most respectable father. If I were you and I had the honour to be a Raposo, I wouldn't hold back, I'd buy the Quinta do Mosteiro and have a castle built there with turrets.'

Putting down his glass, Crispim & Co. said:

'Buy it, it belongs to your family, it would suit you.'

And on the eve of Easter, in the office of Justino, who was acting as procurator for Father Negrão, I signed the contract that would make me, at last, after so much waiting and so many disappointments, the lord of the Quinta do Mosteiro.

'What's that scoundrel Negrão up to these days?' I asked Justino, the moment I saw the vile priest's agent.

My dear, faithful friend cracked his knuckles. Father Negrão had come into an unexpected fortune. He had inherited everything from Father Casimiro, whose body now lay in the cemetery in Alto de São João and his soul in God's bosom. And Negrão was now an intimate friend of Father Pinheiro, who had no heir and whom he had carried off to Torres, in order 'to look after him'. Poor Father Pinheiro spent his days there, looking ever gaunter, stuffing himself on the vast suppers provided by Father Negrão and sticking out his tongue in front of every mirror. And he wouldn't last, poor thing. And so it seemed that Father Negrão would finally receive (with the exception of the money that had gone to Our Lord of the Stations of the Cross, who could definitely not be expected to die again) the major part of G. Godinho's fortune.

I turned pale and snorted:

'The cad!'

'You may well call him "cad", my friend, but he has a carriage, a house in Lisbon and he's taken up with Adélia . . .'

'Which Adélia?'

'A good-looking woman, who used to be with Eleutério. Then she had a very secret affair with some booby, a graduate he was, I don't know who exactly.'

'I do.'

'Anyway, her. She's being kept by Negrão now, in great luxury, with carpet on the stairs, damask curtains, everything. And he's got fatter. I saw him yesterday, he'd just been preaching. Or rather what he said to me was: "I've just come from St Roch exhausted with saying nice things about some devil of a saint!' Because Negrão can be quite amusing sometimes. And he's got good friends, the gift of the gab, a lot of influence in Torres. He'll probably end up being made a Bishop.'

I returned to my family, thoughtful. Everything I had hoped for and loved (even Adélia!) was now legitimately owned by that vile man Negrão. A huge loss. And it wasn't the result of that exchange of packages nor of the mistakes I had made as regards my hypocrisy.

Now, as father, knight commander, landowner, I had a more positive understanding of life and I really felt that I had been plundered of G. Godinho's wealth simply because I had been found wanting when I was in Auntie's chapel — because I had not had the courage to lie!

Yes, when a sinful nightdress had appeared on the altar instead of the crown of thorns, I should have declared confidently:

'There is the relic! I wanted to give you a surprise. It's not the crown of thorns, it's better than that! It's the nightdress that belonged to Mary Magdalene. She gave it to me herself in the desert.'

The bit of paper proved it, written in perfect handwriting:

'To my brave little Portuguese lover, in memory of all the pleasures we enjoyed.'

That was the letter the saint had given me along with her nightdress. Her initials were there for all to see — M.M. So was that clear, obvious confession - in memory of all the pleasures we had enjoyed; the pleasure I had felt in sending my prayers to Heaven through the saint, the pleasure the saint had felt in Heaven when she received my prayers.

And who would doubt it? Do not the missionary saints from Braga, in their sermons, display notes sent from heaven by the Virgin Mary, without so much as a stamp on them? And does *The Nation* not guarantee the divine authenticity of these missives that bear in their folds the fragrance of Paradise? The two priests, Fathers Negrão and Pinheiro, conscious of their duty and naturally eager to procure support for a wavering faith, would immediately have acclaimed that nightdress, that letter and those initials as a miraculous triumph for the Church. Aunt Patrocínio would have fallen upon my breast, calling me 'her son and heir'. And I would be rich! I would be beatified. My portrait would be hung in the sacristy of the cathedral. The Pope would telegraph me an apostolic blessing.

Thus would all my social ambitions have been satisfied.

And who knows? Perhaps the intellectual ambitions I had caught from the learned Topsius would also have been satisfied. Because science, jealous of the triumph of faith, might well have claimed that nightdress belonging to Mary Magdalene for itself, as an archaeological document. It might well have illumined certain obscure points in the history of contemporary costume in the New Testament, the way nightdresses in Judaea were made in the first century, the industrial state of lacemaking in Syria under the Roman administration, the way the Semitic races did their hemming. In Europe I would have been considered the equal of all the Champollions, the Topsiuses, the Lepsiuses and all the other wise resuscitators of the past. The Academy would immediately have cried out: 'Raposo is mine!' Renan, that sentimental heresiarch, would have murmured: 'Charming chap that Raposo!' Soon, wise, ponderous books in German would have been written about Mary's nightdress, with maps showing the route of my pilgrimage to Galilee. And thus I would have been beloved by the Church, celebrated by the Universities, certain of my place in the Celestial City, my page reserved in History, growing peacefully fat on all the money left by G. Godinho!

And I had lost it all. Why? Because for one moment, I lacked the 'shameless heroism needed to tell a lie', which, thanks to some universal illusion, is responsible for creating all sciences and all religions, whether it loudly strides the earth or merely lifts its eyes palely to Heaven.